A DARING JOURN...

Shadows swirled in a dark towe... ankles like a ghostly cat. Yellow eyes ... monster oozed toward me with a su... ...ping sound. Long arms reached out and talons glinted, deadly sharp. I gave in to terror and ran, jumping right out the window. My back tingled from the imminent slashes of those terrible claws as I launched myself onto the wind.

THE TAROT POINTS THE WAY

"Looking forward is a very good thing," Henry said. "Sometimes we can change our direction and avoid disaster. Other times it's useless to try, and our energy is better spent preparing for trouble."

"It would be good to know when we're going with the grain, and when we're going against it," I nodded, picturing the invisible pattern that lay underneath reality, like a texture.

EMILY FACES HER DARKEST FEARS

I felt stupid, inconsequential and utterly devastated. I kept thinking that he would change his mind, he would come back. I hallucinated seeing him for years afterwards, in a crowd, in the grocery store, passing in a car on the highway. But he never returned, and I never found out what happened to him. It was a long time before I opened up to anyone again.

Until now, until Tony.

...AND OPENS HERSELF TO MAGIC

In the tender season, the very early spring when red buds swell up on the tips of branches and flocks of little birds chase clouds of little flies across the sky, I began to sprout new ideas like the seedlings that erupted from the newly thawed earth that quickened all around us.

DESTINED

A NOVEL OF THE TAROT

by

Gail Cleare

Illustrated by
The Payen Tarot of Marseille (1713)

G&G Publications
USA

Paperback edition published in the United States by

G&G Publications

PO Box 18, Whately, MA 01093 USA

ISBN-13: 978-1461007760

ISBN-10: 1461007763

Cover photographs and book design by Gail Cleare ©2011.

for the

Ladies of the Green Circle

Author's Note

The Tarot cards known as the Major Arcana describe 22 sequential steps on the path to enlightenment. They begin with number 0, The Fool, and end with number 21, The World. The chapter heads of this novel follow the same order. The process of self-discovery and transformation symbolized by this series of archetypal images is called "The Fool's Journey."

— G.C.

DESTINED

Chapter 0

The Fool

A CHOICE IS OFFERED

Description: The Fool heads off on a journey carrying a pack and staff. He is blissfully unaware of a dangerous chasm nearby. A cat with sharp claws chases him into the unknown.
Meaning: A new direction or phase. Embarking on a journey of self-discovery.

Only one thing stopped me from punching her. Knowing that the other girls would probably call the cops, I struggled for self-control. My hands were clenched into fists, my heart pounding. This time she had gone too far and I couldn't ignore it any more.

Lexi tossed her sparkling blonde hair and sneered at me with her hands on her hips. Her long manicured nails were painted vampire red. "Don't be so fussy, Emily," she scolded me like a naughty two-year-old. "We all have to pitch in. Get busy!"

"Lexi, I was hired to sell art, not to clean the bathrooms!" I didn't call her a bitch, though it nearly slipped out.

She gave me her most exasperated look. "Sometimes we all have to rally for the cause! Don't be ridiculous, Emily, there are some very big clients on the way over."

Lexi called to the other two Gladstone Gallery employees, who were standing in the doorway of the storage room with their eyes bugging out of their heads.

"Girls, quickly! Pull this list of paintings from the racks. Emily can empty the trash, too."

She handed them a slip of paper and glared at me, sending the message that the case was closed. Lexi fully expected me to roll up the sleeves of my silk blouse, which had cost the equivalent of a week's pay, and grab the toilet brush.

That's when the famous "fight or fly" instinct kicked in, and I flew. I got my bag from behind the counter and headed for the front door, saying, "Lexi, it's obvious this job isn't working out for either of us."

They all spun around in surprise.

"Oh no you don't!" Lexi screamed, running over to clutch at me as I slipped out into the fresh air of freedom. "You can't leave at a time like this!" She caught my arm with her claws, digging them into my skin.

I said firmly, "Sorry about the short notice, but I quit!"

Sheer fury shone from her flashing blue eyes. I yanked my arm away and escaped down the sidewalk, stopping at the corner to look back. She was standing in the doorway, staring at me with her mouth distorted in an ugly scowl. It looked for a minute like she was crying. I had a vivid flash of knowing that something would soon go terribly wrong for Lexi, something important and personal. Her path was leading to it. I almost felt sorry for her.

But she did look silly with her face all contorted like that. Hyper from the drama, I started to giggle. She saw me doing it and got even angrier, stamping her foot, and it was such a cartoon-character thing that I totally lost it and hooted outright. I scurried off to my car snickering madly all the way. People on the sidewalk gave me strange looks and a wide berth. When I was safely inside my little Honda I laughed until the tears rolled down my face. Enveloped by an enormous sense of relief, I sort of floated home to my apartment. I honestly don't remember driving but somehow I arrived there and parked the car.

Getting my anger under control was a very positive thing. My former therapist would approve. She had always accused me of making emotional decisions based on past traumas, rather than living in the here and now. She wanted me to give life a chance and see what happened. So I stuck with the job at Lexi's gallery for nearly a year, plenty of time to judge it realistically. Now I could leave the whole humiliating episode behind and explore my alternatives. I would choose a new direction for my future and it would be a wonderful, rewarding adventure. All I had to do was pay attention to the signs.

*   *   *

The day I answered the ad in the newspaper I awoke from a terrible nightmare with an inexplicable feeling of optimism. I'd been dreaming about a monster chasing me, one with long scary claws who looked a little bit like Lexi. Of course, the last thing I did before turning out the light was update my check-book. I definitely should have known better.

Shadows swirled in a dark tower, wisping up against my ankles like a ghostly cat. Yellow eyes smoldered as the giant monster oozed toward me with a sucking, scraping sound. Long arms reached out and talons glinted, deadly sharp.

Large windows offered escape but far below, a cliff gave way to dangerous rocks. Then there was a tiny movement against the back of my hair and I gave in to terror and ran, jumping right out the window. My back tingled from the imminent slashes of those terrible claws as I launched myself onto the wind.

Down through the soft air, drifting in a slow-motion spiral like the swollen pink petal that drops from the climbing rose on the garden gate, I fell.

It was horrifying and ecstatic at the same time. I didn't rush downwards but simply floated in a leisurely spiral, with the sun on my face and the soft air buoyant under my back. An effort-less, peaceful feeling like swimming in salt water on a balmy day.

Before I could hit the ground, I woke up.

I stroked my cat, Tree, and looked around my third floor studio apartment with relief. He blinked at me solemnly with his beautiful green eyes and purred a message of serenity and peace. Obviously I should trust in my good luck and relax, wait for the new direction to reveal itself. Sunlight was pouring in through the blue skylight overhead and it looked to be a glori-ous spring day.

Perfect weather for job hunting! Today was the day, and my life was going to change.

I dressed conservatively in a black and white checked skirt and crisp white blouse. I blow-dried my wavy brown hair until it looked straight and serious. My face in the mirror seemed pale and tense, so I painted on some blusher and lipstick. Now I felt more self-confident. Calm blue-gray eyes stared back at me with an expression of resolve.

Slinging my bag over my shoulder, I tucked a folder of resumés and newspaper clippings under my arm and headed off.

*　　*　　*

I looked up at the shabby brick building on the corner of Market Street and glanced down at the scrap of paper in my hand. This was the right address. I studied the building curiously. It had good bones, but had definitely seen better days.

Ancient ivy snaked up the exterior, parting over the closed front door to show a peek of stonework underneath. The number 33 was just visible, the second "3" missing a nail and hanging askew. Wide steps with wrought-iron railings led up to the entrance, where a small faded sign said "Books & Etc., H. Paradis."

At ten o'clock on a weekday morning the street bustled with people out and about their business. Trucks braked loudly and double-parked to unload goods. A parade of small children dodged between the pedestrians, giggling and hooting, while a stately Indian woman wearing a sari pursued them at a more sedate pace, pushing a stroller containing two fat-cheeked babies, one with dark skin and one fair.

The ad in the newspaper said, "Manager Wanted. Retail store with established customers. Library experience a blessing."

But the building looked deserted, its front door coated with grime. Suddenly there was a loud clack as the brass door handle moved and the door swung inwards. I instinctively took a step backwards as an old man with white, shaggy hair appeared.

He beckoned to me and chuckled. "No, no...sorry to startle you! We spoke on the telephone? Emily Ross?" He cocked one ragged white eyebrow at me, his gaze piercing.

I nodded and swallowed, waving the newspaper clipping in my hand. "Mister...um...Paradis?" I said hesitantly. I wasn't sure how to pronounce it, so I tried "Para-deece," and that seemed to work.

"Yes, yes, come in." He stepped back into the shadowy interior.

Peering inside, I could see very little. The heavy door slammed shut behind me when I entered, abruptly cutting off the light from outside. My eyes gradually adjusted as I looked around the large room. Cluttered with stacks of boxes and odd pieces of furniture, it stretched deep and long with a very high ceiling, like a giant shoebox. Glass cases filled with mysterious objects (the "& Etc?") lined the interior walls. At the very back of the room, a large brass samovar sat on a counter of dark wood.

On the right-hand wall were two wide windows, both covered by heavy curtains. A slit between them admitted a single bar of light that shot across the room to reveal motes of dust flying in swirls caused by our passing.

I wondered about the wording of the newspaper ad. This might be a wild goose chase. I glanced at my watch and thought about where to go for an early lunch.

"Right in here," he said, leading the way.

He went into the front hallway where a wide staircase curved up to the second floor. He crossed and entered a comfortable sitting room where bright sunlight poured in through tall casement windows.

"*Lapsang Souchong?*" He had laid out some tea things on the beautiful old mahogany table, with a shiny electric kettle on a tray. Steam was rising from the spout.

"It's my favorite kind!" I decided to stay for a quick cup of tea.

"Most people don't like the strong smoky flavor, but I love it." He filled the round white teapot with hot water.

"I do too," I said with a nostalgic twinge, thinking of my beloved Dad, who died a few years back. "It reminds me of camping as a child." I felt a little teary.

"The stronger the better, I always say. Do have a seat, won't you?" He pulled out a chair and motioned for me to do likewise. As the tea steeped he launched into a rambling tale of his travels in "tea country" as he called it, "i.e. the Orient," as a "young lad." He was a good storyteller and had obviously lived an interesting life. I realized he was trying to put me at ease. And he was also watching me like a hawk.

"My resumé, by the way," I murmured, pushing it toward him across the table.

He fumbled in various pockets, eventually coming up with a pair of tortoise shell reading glasses. I tried to be patient while he read my credentials.

"Very good." He whipped the glasses off and peered at me sharply. "You seem fully qualified for the retail aspect. But we were really hoping for someone who knows how to organize books. You see, we have rather a lot of them."

It occurred to me that he might have a thriving book business via the Internet, though I hadn't seen a computer so far. Maybe there was something to this opportunity, after all.

"Well, I worked in the library for one semester as a work-study job in college," I hesitated, thinking this would never be enough.

He brightened and sat up taller. "Excellent! Just as I suspected! And, what else? Other talents? Useful skills?"

"I am a voracious reader." Leaning toward him, I spun the tale as I went along, "Have been all my life. I go through at least four or five books every week. Well, maybe three or four." I thought of the paperback Romance and Mystery novels stacked on my bedside table with a guilty twinge, lowering my eyes.

"Yes." He regarded me with a knowing smile. "About what,

I wonder?" he mused, leaning over to pour the tea.

Taking advantage of his distraction to stretch the truth a bit more, I mumbled, "Um…I read a lot of philosophy and psychology, and…classic literature, that kind of thing. I have fairly eclectic taste."

"Very good," Mr. Paradis repeated, with a thoughtful expression that made me a little nervous. There was an air of magic about the man, he seemed to be reading my mind.

It's not often that I meet someone else who can do that.

A kindred spirit.

He served the tea in two stout white mugs. It smelled fantastic. I was immediately transported back to campfires in the Maine woods and felt like I had been trying to con my own grandfather. I hadn't exactly lied, but exaggeration is almost as bad. And he was a nice old guy. I tried to set things right.

"Actually," I sipped the tea, "I read a lot of novels as well." I hoped the confession would balance my precarious karma.

"I do love a good mystery, don't you?" he said and I nodded. We smiled like two conspirators, sipping our tea and looking at each other appraisingly.

"What kind of books do you sell?" I tried to get him talking again. "What other merchandise?"

"Many things, whatever we come across. If it's remarkable." He put his mug on the table and gestured with his lean, wrinkled hands. "Curiosities, art, antiques and rare books. Much of it is acquired and sold through private connections, more so in recent years. Not getting out as much as I used to." He appeared to make a decision and stared at me with a searching expression. "I'd like to liquidate some inventory. The showroom there, it used to be our store. I want to open it again. Turn some of these dust-catchers into cash!"

A tingle of excitement sizzled through me.

"Would you be interested in getting things up and running again?" he asked.

"As the store manager?"

He nodded, and relief shot through me. In the back of my mind I felt something click like a domino falling into place, and the pattern and fabric of my world shifted. My chest relaxed and I breathed full and deeply for the first time in months.

This was it, this was my path.

"Just you and me, to start," he said, "Someone else to help us when we know what we need. Eventually I'd want you to run the whole shebang, while I do what I do, upstairs." He pointed at the ceiling.

"You mean...the private connections?" I asked, thinking he must have an office on the second floor. I wondered about his repeated use of the word "we," since there did not seem to be anyone else around.

He nodded again, confirming his private sales activities.

"Well?" he asked and named a salary figure. Though not huge, it was enough to pay my living expenses and keep my car on the road. In fact, it was more than I had been making at my last job.

I hesitated briefly, hovering between trust and fear, but then I plunged in and accepted his offer. We shook hands and he seemed very pleased. I was too, considering my rent was due and I had saved barely enough to survive beyond then without begging my mother for another loan.

We chatted about what time I should appear in the mornings and leave at night, when I was to start (tomorrow), days off (Sunday and Monday plus holidays), and he took me on a brief tour of the first floor.

What I'd thought from a distance was a brass samovar turned out to be an elaborate espresso machine. The wooden counter was referred to as "the coffee bar." I peeked into one of the glass cases and saw the glint of sparkling crystals and an enormous geode, amethyst perhaps. A stack of framed Redouté rose prints and small oil paintings leaned against the wall. Feeling excited, I could sense potential.

And, I would be the *manager*. A step up for me. Best of all, it appeared that I would have quite a bit of autonomy, which I have always found necessary for the longevity of the arrangement. I am self-motivated, to say the least. (Lexi would call it "bossy!")

Which reminded me. I wondered if Mr. Paradis would call the previous employers I had listed and talk to her. She'd better not say anything to ruin my chances. Stop it right now Emily, I said to myself sternly. You are going to jinx it! I deliberately imagined a smooth road ahead.

At the back of the showroom a door led into a hallway at the rear of the building. Narrow stairs went up from here and the closed door next to them was secured with a heavy bolt, probably the entrance to the basement. A skinny door under the stairs revealed a tiny bathroom with a slanted ceiling and pull-chain light fixture. Across the hall was the entrance to a huge old-fashioned kitchen. There was also a back door leading outside to a covered porch that opened onto a narrow alley behind the building, occupied by a row of dumpsters and recycling bins. I thought I heard a noise and wondered if someone else might be in the building after all, but nobody appeared and my new employer led me back around to the front entrance without further comment.

Mr. Paradis opened the door for me in the manner of a host showing out an honored guest. "Knock here at ten," he said. "I will have a key made for you directly."

We shook hands again.

"Thank you so much." I was filled with emotion. "I am really looking forward to it!"

"Looking *forward* is a very good thing!" he exclaimed and waggled his shaggy eyebrows humorously.

Then he leaned closer for a moment and said something odd.

"I knew I was right about you, my dear, " he murmured.

Our eyes locked and I had a moment of *déjà vu*, with the feeling that we had known each other for a long time and he was an old family friend or relative. My vision blurred as I started to spin inside my head, then I took a deep breath and shook myself back into the present. He was staring at me with interest, as though he had somehow seen what had happened.

Mr. Paradis stepped back and waved his right arm vigorously, exclaiming in a very loud voice that could easily have been heard down the street.

"Farewell! Adieu! Until tomorrow!"

He closed the door and the latch snapped.

I stared at the door feeling almost as though I had imagined the whole interlude. Then I noticed a small man wearing a white apron who stood with a broom in front of the Italian market across the street. He was looking over at me curiously. We made eye contact and he nodded his head very slightly in acknowledgment before returning to his task.

I couldn't wait until Lexi heard I already had a new job, and a promotion at that! My angry feelings came flooding back, with a large dose of I-told-you-so satisfaction. Take that, you creep, I thought.

I sailed off down the sidewalk into the buzzing activity of the neighborhood with a fresh breeze blowing the hair back from my face, uplifted by the possibilities of my exciting new future.

Chapter 1

The Magician

CREATIVE POWER

Description: The adept stands before a table where various magical tools are arranged. Money (pentacles), the emotions (cups), communication (swords), and creativity (wands) are all in this bag of tricks. Meaning: Mastery of creative power. The creation of illusion to dazzle or manipulate others.

At nine forty-five the next morning, I entered Sorrentino's Market. Strolling through the aisles, I found it was actually a small grocery store with beautiful fruit and vegetables. There were a self-service coffee area and a glass case filled with Italian sausages and exotic cheeses. A huge pot of red sauce was simmering on the stove behind the deli counter. The man I had seen the previous day was standing behind the cash register.

He had thinning silver hair and perfect, shiny pink skin on his completely unlined face. He stood with a bit of a hunch, but it was difficult to guess his age.

"Good morning," I tried to sound friendly. He nodded at me as he had the day before, and this time a little smile glimmered. His eyes showed intense interest.

I poured myself a cup of coffee and selected a lovely ripe pear. I rubbed it with a paper napkin and took a bite. It was absolutely fabulous.

"Just this, for now," I said, putting my money on the counter.

He still did not speak and I thought perhaps his English was not so good. He did seem to understand me, though. His twinkling blue eyes spoke volumes.

He made change and passed it to me.

His lips opened.

"You came yesterday," he observed.

His voice was low and had a slight Italian accent.

"Yes."

"Over there, 'cross the street," he gestured.

"Yes," I nodded.

He wiped his already-clean hands on the clean towel that hung at his waist.

"You...are back," he observed, and squinted at me inquiringly.

"I am going to work there," I confided. "Mr. Paradis has decided to reopen his shop. I am going to manage it for him," I finished proudly, and waited for the welcome-fellow-merchant-to-the-neighborhood that was undoubtedly to follow.

"Oh," was all he said.

He stood in silence, his curiosity apparently fulfilled. Or perhaps he had just run out of steam from all that talking. I felt disappointed and a little annoyed.

"OK, well, got to go to work now!" I said, sidling toward the doorway.

He continued to stare at me.

"You tell him, good," he said, raising his hand and pointing toward the "Books & Etc." shop.

"Good luck?" I asked.

"Good…to open again!" He folded his hands together across his chest.

"Good to reopen the store? I'll tell him," I smiled, sipping my coffee as I went out the door. "I'm sure he'll be glad to hear that the neighbors approve!"

I waved cheerfully and left my taciturn new friend as two Asian women entered the store, talking loudly to each other in a language I did not understand. I crossed the street and made my way to number 33. It still appeared dark and deserted.

We will change that soon enough, I thought. My knock on the door echoed. Nothing happened, so I repeated it. This time, the latch clacked and the door sprang open.

"Here she is!" my new employer exclaimed, "Right on time! What did I tell you?"

"Good day to you both, then, Henry," said a second man, who was standing just inside. He stepped back and held the door wide as I entered. Dark and tall, probably in his late twenties, he nodded at me politely as I slipped past. I glimpsed a handsome face with a flashing smile and then he was gone, out the door and down the street.

"Farewell, my friend!" called my employer, with a wave at his visitor.

Mr. Paradis beckoned me inside and led me into the sitting room, chattering about paperwork and tax forms. We sat down and filled out various documents for the U.S. government. He seemed totally in control of all these details, I was relieved to note. I saw his full business name on one of the papers: *Henry Paradis Imports, Inc.*. Then he bundled everything into a folder and sat back in his chair.

He took off his reading glasses and fixed me with his eye. "Well, Emily, have you decided where you want to start?"

I was confounded. I had assumed I would be told. I rallied quickly, however.

"Um, I thought, maybe, to dust and vacuum, you know. Then I will know more about the, er, merchandise?"

"Very, very good. Excellent plan," he said and stood up, grabbing his pile of papers. "I'll be off then." He rapidly headed across to the front hallway. "Getting myself out of the way," he said, "Be right up here if you want me! Don't hesitate to call if you have a question." He pointed at the ceiling again, then he disappeared.

So much for interfering bosses, I thought. That will obviously not be the problem here! I was back to doing the cleaning again, but this time I was actually eager to get started. I felt a burst of optimism.

I left my jacket and bag on the coat rack in the corner and slowly entered the showroom. It looked dirty and jumbled, and for a moment I was daunted by the mountain of work ahead of me.

Then I found a brass switch plate on the wall and I slowly pushed the buttons, one at a time. Three beautiful art deco chandeliers glowed, hanging from the faraway ceiling. They were gorgeous works of art radiating golden suffused light, very elegant and flattering.

The jewel tones of the Oriental rugs looked warm and rich now. A sense of adventure and discovery began to percolate through me.

Walking around the room looking for a closet, I made my

way through the obstacle course of crates and boxes to pull
back the heavy velvet curtains that covered the two big display
windows.

A flood of bright natural light poured into the room.

The sun shone from behind the rooftops of the buildings
across the street. This street, Crescent Street, was mostly residential and it looked relatively upscale. In fact, a black BMW
was parked in front of our windows. Most of the buildings
were red brick townhouses built around a century ago, with
elegant pillars and steps leading up to three stories of prime
living space.

Eventually I found a big pantry closet in the kitchen. I
stood inside it and rotated, awestruck. Here was every tool or
broom or brush or solution anyone could ever possibly need,
plus about two year's worth of canned goods and dried foods.
My new boss was quite a shopper. A vacuum cleaner with a
long hose attachment squatted in the corner.

Lugging my cleaning apparatus across the hall, I set to
work. Inspired to make a clean slate in the space where I would
spend the majority of my hours for who-knows-how-long, I
cranked open the casement windows and propped open the
back door to let in some fresh air. By the end of the day I was
beginning to have a plan for the space. There was still a ton of
work to do, but being here was oddly soothing, peaceful. In
fact, it was actually fun.

Before I went home that night, I burned a Native American
smudge stick of dried sage that I found behind the counter.
The fragrant sacred smoke was supposed to purify the space
as I moved clockwise around the room, following the printed
instructions. The vibrations in the room felt cleansed and pure
now, ready to accept whatever I chose to create.

By the end of the week I had made serious progress.
Everything had been dusted and polished and I knew exactly
what was where. The glass cases were filled with wonders from

around the globe. There was truly a gold mine here.

Some of the merchandise was very unusual, like a wonderful carving made from a tree stump that hung over the front door. The trunk spread down from a peak like a triangular pointed wizard's hat, revealing a man's sly bearded face beneath carved out of the roots, which curled down and around in spiraled tendrils partly natural and partly contrived. It was very lifelike.

The wizard watched as I feather dusted and slid the furniture from here, to there, and back again. Bringing my portable CD player into work with me, I played my favorite music, spinning across the polished wooden floor in my stocking feet. The besom broom that I found leaning against the wall in a corner made a good dancing partner.

There was a cobra basket filled with hand bells like the ones belly dancers use, and small gourds filled with rice or beans. I shook the gourds and stomped my feet.

I reorganized the energy of the place while I cleaned and designed the physical space. I exorcised the ghosts of old thoughts and old tales to make a new spirit flow here, my creation, my hope and dream.

I was alone most of the day every day, but didn't feel lonely. I didn't think about Lexi or my unhappy past. The anger and hurt faded away as my new life came into focus. I was still nervous about making this all work but the more effort I put into it, the clearer my goals became. I was looking forward, as Mr. Paradis had recommended. I had opened my mind to change.

I polished the espresso machine and cleaned the area behind the counter, where I found twenty-four small white cups and saucers with a set of little spoons that seemed to be solid silver. I found some silver polish in the pantry and soon they sparkled.

I arranged a group of chairs and small tables with rugs to define the seating area. The faded fabric that lined the display windows was replaced with a rich purple felt. Signs made on my computer at home said, "Opening Soon!" and were propped up against wooden blocks so they could easily be seen from outside. People who walked by read them curiously and peered inside.

I worked with very little direction from my employer, who spent most of his time upstairs in his private world. He seemed distracted and quite contented to leave me on my own. At the end of the first Saturday, he handed me a check for the agreed-upon amount, which cleared through my bank swiftly. I was thrilled and immersed in my job.

The thumping noise I had heard that first day did not repeat itself, and there were no signs of anyone else living in the building. I did get the feeling that the shadows of people who had lived here in the past might still linger. In my mind's eye, I saw women wearing silk and pearls, who sipped espresso and laughed as they sat around a small round table. A little boy dressed in knickers and a cap seemed to run by when I was unpacking a box of antique toys. I felt welcomed and cozy with these spirits surrounding me. There was a history of happiness here, and my future customers would feel it too.

One afternoon I was bringing a tray of recently washed blue and white Chinese porcelain rice dishes from the kitchen. I heard my name called and thinking Mr. Paradis wanted me for something, I paused in the hallway to look up the back stairs. "Emily!" I heard it again.

Just then one of the dishes jumped off the tray and sailed across the hallway, hitting the basement door and shattering into a million pieces.

Thinking that I had somehow made this happen, I cursed my clumsiness and put the tray down on the stairs. A cold breeze blew in through back door, which was propped open. I shivered and turned to get the broom and dustpan from the pantry. There on the back porch was a young Chinese man dressed in black pants and tunic. I heard a giggle and he looked straight into my eyes, grinning. I realized then that his slippered feet hovered three or four inches above the floor. It made me feel quite uneasy as he looked very real, outlined by a faint shimmer of energy against the scene behind him, opaque and apparently three-dimensional.

"Go!" I whispered urgently, flapping the dishtowel in my hand at him. When the towel passed right through him, he instantly disappeared. I caught my breath and blinked carefully. I was alone again.

My hand shaking slightly, I closed the porch door and locked it. Then I got the broom and dustpan and swept up the broken china, feeling a little sick to my stomach. This kind of thing had happened before when I was lucid dreaming, but never in broad daylight when I was fully conscious. It made me quite uncomfortable, and I wondered who the man was and what he wanted with me. I worried that my new employer might not be too happy if he knew that his store manager was hallucinating on the job. Daydreaming about the building's past inhabitants was one thing, but a full-body apparition was something else again.

I picked up the tray and brought it into the showroom, stacking the rice bowls carefully in the china cabinet next to a matching tea set. Then I went about my business, relieved that the vision seemed to have passed. I vowed to try to stay alert and not to let my mind wander off.

Sometimes this was difficult, since during those first days of discovery in the curio shop I spent my days in a perpetual state of bedazzlement. The showroom was a jewel box of delights. To the left of the street entrance there was a long horizontal glass case. In it was a wonderful bracelet of Italian cameos carved from volcanic lava stone which featured famous Renaissance painters, their names inscribed on the backs: Leonardo, Caravaggio, Botticelli, Donatello and Raphael. It was a collector's dream. There were Egyptian scarabs carved from lapis lazuli and moonstones from India. Old canary diamonds were set in a platinum bow that held the miniature portrait of a matron long passed in its filigreed clasp.

A relatively modern cash register stood at the end of the counter, plugged into the wall and apparently functioning properly. It was empty except for an old Tarot card, the ace of pentacles, and a yellowed scrap of paper which read, "1 Tuna, 1 RB horse w on's." I decided to leave these, for old times' sake.

I imagined the register clanging as each sale rang up and started to drift off again into a dream…until a noise brought me back to earth, and I realized my employer was coming down the stairs to make one of his infrequent appearances. Standing up straighter, I tried to look efficient.

He appeared in the sitting room doorway wearing his habitual attire, a pair of baggy black sweat pants, black corduroy slippers and a long dark jacket with many pockets, worn over several layers of shirts in various shades of brown, gray and black. His shaggy white hair looked as though it had not been cut for several months, and was combed perhaps weekly.

"Coming along, are we?" he inquired, pausing in the doorway.

I smiled and nodded, proud of my accomplishment.

"Everything all right, dear?" He looked at me sharply, seeming to tune in on something in the atmosphere.

"Yes, everything is fine. Ready to finalize pricing and open the doors!" I was getting used to his mind reading and had grown to expect it. "You really have some wonderful things here, " I said, "There's nothing like it in town! And, about the Grand Opening…I'd like to send out invitations, to the neighbors that is. We could make a splash, score points with the local business community, and possibly get some newspaper coverage. What do you think?"

"A grand idea!" He nodded with approval. "Very diplomatic. And, of course, we mustn't forget to invite my loyal customers."

I wondered about this, having seen neither hide nor hair of any customers, except for the man who was leaving on that first day. I wondered when he would be back. There had been several telephone calls for Mr. Paradis, all from a man with a smooth baritone voice and a sexy foreign accent, possibly the same guy.

Another mystery was the fact that the only books I had found were two piles of used encyclopedias and hardcover novels starring Cherry Ames, the Hardy Boys and Nancy Drew—who originally drove a "blue roadster," I discovered. These were now arranged in a low bookcase in the children's corner, near a huge puffy beige leather hassock and some colorful floor pillows.

"You mean, " I asked, "We should invite the rare book people?"

He nodded, with a considering look on his face.

"I do believe it's time," he said. He turned abruptly and flapped his arm, motioning for me to follow.

"Come along upstairs," he said. "You'd better get acquainted with the rest of our stock."

Holding onto the rail, he clambered up the long, curving staircase. I followed, somewhat skeptical yet hoping for at least a few literary surprises of a caliber similar to the treasures I had discovered below. I was very intrigued to see his private rooms, and this was the first time he had invited me up to the second floor.

As we rose further up the stairs, a spacious landing appeared at its head. My employer continued down the upstairs hallway where an open door showed a glimpse of his study, located directly above the sitting room downstairs. He went past it to the closed door beyond.

Mr. Paradis flung the door open and revealed a darkened room, which popped into focus when he reached inside and turned on the overhead lights. A million rectangles of every color of the rainbow met my amazed eyes. Stacked on shelves from floor to ceiling, were thousands and thousands of books.

He stepped aside in silence and I entered the room slowly, staring.

Stretching on and on, from the front of the house to the back, fully as large as the shop room downstairs, were row after row of loaded bookshelves. The smell was musty, dusty and leathery. I filled my lungs with it, detecting a sweet hint of sandalwood or cedar.

As I walked down the main corridor, he clicked on more overhead lights. Some were long fluorescent work lights, some were elegant antique ceiling fixtures, some merely bare spiral-shaped bulbs with pull-chains hanging down. Extension cords wove a spider's web of wires overhead.

When I reached the end of the long corridor, I turned. My employer was still standing in the doorway, watching me with a little smile and the sparkle of mischief in his eyes. I was, once again, flabbergasted.

"How many?" My voice echoed down the rows.

"Ten thousand three hundred and eighty-two," he declared proudly, folding his hands. "Approximately. At the moment." He gestured vaguely. "As I mentioned, they come…and go."

I swallowed, considering that the preparations I had thought nearly completed were possibly far from that. My confidence began to ebb. But then I noticed a small sign made from a pink index card at the end of the row next to me. It was attached to the side of the bookshelf with silver duct tape. In faded brown ink, spidery handwriting had inscribed, "Art History, Ren. - Imp." Entering the row, I saw that the books seemed to be arranged alphabetically by author and then title, with all the spines neatly aligned to the front of the shelves. This was encouraging.

He had quietly shuffled to stand beside me. His eyes shone

with pride, or a touch of obsession.

"Some of the very rare titles are kept under lock-and-key in my study," he confided. "Just another hundred or so."

I nodded, still feeling overwhelmed. He looked at me anxiously, reading my mood.

"Everything here is quite in hand," he said. "No fear. You won't need to do much to make this room ready for the public. Just a bit of spit and polish, that's the ticket!"

"Okay," I agreed in a small voice.

He patted me on the back as we turned to exit the room.

"You're doing a lovely job," he said encouragingly. "Just the thing! Keep it up!"

"Thank you," I replied bashfully. "I'm enjoying it."

He closed the library door and we went into his office. When I entered the room I was glad to see that there was a computer workstation in the corner, attached to a fat cable connection.

A stone fireplace occupied the far wall with two armchairs in front of it, a low table between them. A yellow book was lying spread open on the table, with three unusual brass coins marking the place. I thought I recognized it as the *I Ching*, an ancient Chinese tool for divination. I wondered whether he had been using it for fortune telling and was consumed by curiosity.

Mr. Paradis went to the computer and leaned over it, tapping a few keys efficiently. The screen lit up and he flipped through several directories. He showed me his system for tracking inventory.

"I found a Tarot card in the cash register," I mentioned.

"The ace of pentacles?"

"Yes, did you put it there?"

"I did, long ago. It stands for money, the start of a new business enterprise. It's there for good luck, to attract lots of other pentacles!"

"Are you interested in fortune telling?" I gestured toward the yellow book.

His eyes met mine and looked inside my head, as he seemed to do so often.

"Looking forward is a very good thing." He repeated the words he had said the first day we met. "You know, forewarned is forearmed. Sometimes we can change our direction and avoid disaster. Other times it's useless to try, and our energy is better spent preparing for trouble."

"It would be good to know when we're going with the grain, and when we're going against it." I saw a mental image of an invisible pattern underneath reality, like a texture.

He reached into one of the many pockets of his jacket and pulled out a small brown bottle. "This might help make the good luck stronger. I've been meaning to give it to you." He handed me the bottle. It was labeled "Essential Oil of Basil."

I opened it and sniffed the delicious aroma, which reminded me of Italian food.

"It's lovely. What is it for?"

"A few drops on your palms every morning when you open the store will draw money into your hands, and you might sprinkle a bit on that Tarot card too! No harm in creating a positive atmosphere where our business will flourish, eh?"

I agreed, putting the bottle in my jeans pocket. In light of his obvious interest in the occult, I decided to bring up the subject of my encounter with the hovering man on the back porch.

"By the way," I searched for the right words, "Have you ever...um...noticed anything odd in the hallway by the kitchen?"

He looked at me sharply. "Odd in what way, Emily?" His eyes pulled the answer out of me before I could hesitate. When I described the Chinese man, my employer fairly buzzed with excitement.

"It sounds like my old friend from Hong Kong! It was he who sold us the porcelain, many years ago. How intriguing, my dear! We haven't seen him in ages. He died in 1942, you know, or so everyone assumed. His body was never found, unfortunately. It was wartime you know, things were in an uproar."

He reached for my hand and squeezed it comfortingly.

"You're not upset about this, are you Emily? I do hope not. Nothing to fear."

"Not if you don't mind," I said, relieved that he didn't seem to think I was mentally unstable. Quite the opposite, in fact. He beamed at me with approval and begged me to call him immediately if I ever caught sight of the Chinese man again. My parents had always cautioned me not to speak of events like this, because it frightened people and would prejudice them against me. It was wonderful to meet someone who seemed to accept my unedited self. A rush of happiness shot through me, and I thanked my stars for putting me on the path that had led here.

Heading back down the stairs, I imagined a beautifully lettered sign in the downstairs hallway with an arrow pointing the way that said, "BOOKS." I bounced a little on the steps, happily planning my next tasks.

That evening, when I closed the front door behind me and locked it with the key Mr. Paradis had faithfully given me on my first day, I saw again the Indian woman I had noticed on my first visit to the neighborhood. She passed on the sidewalk, this time carrying two string shopping bags filled with packages and groceries. Our eyes met, and hers glowed with interest.

"Hello," I said cheerfully, with a warm smile. I was very eager to meet some of the neighbors, for several reasons. She looked interesting and friendly.

She paused and turned, bowing her head slightly. She had strikingly beautiful eyes, and shining black hair hung down her back in a long thick braid.

"Good evening, Miss," she said. "I hope you have been having a very happy day!"

Her melodious voice made me think of curry and spices. A red spot was painted on her forehead in the position of the third eye. Many thin silver bracelets cascaded down her slender arms. As before, she wore the traditional Indian sari, this one made of a deep blue patterned fabric with a silver thread woven through it.

"Why, yes, thank you! Very happy indeed," I said, charmed. "And the same to you!"

She bowed again, her beautiful flyaway eyes lowered politely, yet still observing me from behind her lashes.

"We are getting ready to open the store," I confided, hoping to engage her in conversation. She looked intrigued and lingered to talk.

I'd been spending an awful lot of time alone lately and was eager for a nice girl-to-girl chat. The women I'd worked with at the gallery never called anymore. They were probably afraid Lexi would find out if they socialized with the enemy.

"Ahh," my new friend said, her eyes alight, "Very good! Everyone has been wondering what is happening here."

She smiled shyly and turned to scurry down the sidewalk with her packages.

Across the street, Mr. Sorrentino was once more sweeping in front of his store. He solemnly raised his hand toward me for a fleeting moment. Aha! He was starting to warm up! And now I had two new friends in the neighborhood.

I turned to look back at my storefront, admiring the clean, freshly painted front door with its shining brass knocker and the neatly pruned holly and evergreen bushes on either side. The tall windows had been washed inside and out, and I'd left a small table lamp lit on the counter with the cash register. The building looked warm and inviting, as I had dreamed it would.

The future was turning out just as I had imagined, so far. My visions were manifesting in reality. And this was just the beginning.

Chapter 2

The High Priestess

KNOWLEDGE OF SECRET MYSTERIES

Description: Clad in the robes of mystery, the High Priestess holds a scroll or book containing the wisdom of the ages.
Meaning: Knowledge of arcane secrets. Psychic ability, magical powers, spirituality.

I went to the town hall and got a copy of the street lists for Market and Crescent. All the residents were included. I learned that Mr. Anthony Sorrentino and his family lived upstairs in the grocery store building. His wife Josephina and several others were also listed at that address. A person named R. Sorrentino occupied the building next door to the market, apparently living upstairs over the pizzeria.

Also listed nearby on Market Street were a restaurant called Buddha and another called the Green Thumb Café. The latter was located on the far corner of Market and Crescent, diagonally across from us.

Lime green and white striped umbrellas topped round tables scattered on the patio in front of the Café. A lime green awning shaded its many windows. It looked like the original porch of the building had been enclosed. Attractive flower boxes and stonework surrounded the entrance, which was set back from the street. I had seen them serving outside in the evenings.

A flower shop called the Potting Shed was attached to this building in the rear, located in a long one-story structure that had obviously once been the carriage house. A garden contained by a low picket fence painted lime green filled most of the little yard in front. Both businesses were listed as owned by the same two people: L. Green and J. Laroche.

Most of these buildings had apartments on the second and third floors. Some contained up to a dozen apartments, with occupants whose names were Japanese, Chinese, Arab, Indian, Polish, Italian, German and Latino, mixed in with the Smiths and the Joneses. The well-kept townhouses on Crescent were occupied by people with dignified names like Winthrop, Bardwell, Dubois and Goldstein.

Mr. Paradis gave me a list of twenty or so additional names to be sent invitations. Half of the addresses were in foreign countries. "My private customers and some friends," he confided. "They may not come, but they'll enjoy being included."

I had to do something about refreshments. There was no way we could serve my current specialty, pretzels and Diet Coke. I stood in the open doorway and looked at the Green

Thumb Café. Pulling on my jacket, I went over to see if they did catering.

As I stood and waited for the walk light to come on, I admired the landscaping around the Café. The place looked closed, at the moment. At the flower shop next door, however, the huge old carriage house doors stood open. Various small shrubs and potted plants were displayed in the sunny doorway, and two women came out of the store and walked away down the sidewalk. One of them carried a bouquet of flowers wrapped in lime green tissue paper.

The light changed and I crossed diagonally. A flagstone path led through the garden to arrive at the door of the Potting Shed. The garden was filled with perennials in bloom. I recognized yarrow, echinacea and lady's mantle. Several low-growing herbs were used for edging the path, and sweet fragrances wafted up at me as I walked along.

"Morning!"

The voice came from behind the bee balm. A waving hand appeared first, followed by a man wearing a straw hat, cut-off jeans, green rubber boots, and a black T-shirt that said in small white letters, "Stop Staring at Me." He had wispy, curly blonde hair and a mustache.

"Hi!" he said, "How are you, neighbor?" He turned around briefly to pick up a bucket of freshly pulled weeds. The back of his T-shirt said, "Stop Following Me." I grinned when I read it and his pale blue eyes crinkled as he smiled back. "I'm John Laroche. I've seen you at work across the street, welcome to the crossroads!" He wiped his right hand quickly on the blue bandana hanging out of his pocket, and then stuck it out to shake mine. He had a very firm grip.

I introduced myself and admired the garden. He told me the names of a few plants I couldn't identify as we strolled toward the flower shop entrance.

"Come on in and meet Laurie," he urged, preceding me

through the carriage house doors.

It was an old country barn, right here in the middle of the city. Golden brown wood lined the walls and ceiling, with baskets and bundles of dried herbs and flowers hanging from the rafters. Grapevine wreaths, stone cherubs and ceramic faces were displayed on the walls. John strode across the floor and disappeared through a hallway that led into the Café building. I heard the rumble of his voice and he returned, followed by a woman. He mentioned my name and she reached out to take my hand.

"I'm Laurel Green, it's so nice to meet you! We've been meaning to come over and say hello. Everyone is talking about the shop reopening."

When her hand touched mine, I felt a strong connection. In my mind's eye, I saw a group of women in a wooded clearing and the flicker of flames from a campfire. Laurie had long reddish brown, curling hair, beautiful green eyes and an elfin face. I imagined her wearing a hooded cape. She was slim and looked strong, medium height, in her early thirties.

Today she wore a jeans skirt and a lime green T-shirt, covered by a chef's apron with a Green Thumb Café logo printed on it. Little silver circles with sparkling stars inside them dangled from her ear lobes. I saw she wore a flat silver wedding band that matched John's, and concluded that the two were married despite the different last names. He touched her arm in an intimate way as he excused himself to go back outside.

Laurel and I chatted. I felt very drawn to her, as though we were old friends. I found myself wanting to tell her the entire story of my life, all my secrets. Eventually I got around to mentioning the opening, and asked if she might be able to help with the food and flowers.

"Are you kidding?" she grabbed my arm. "I'd love to help you!"

Again, at her touch, I experienced a flash of seeing her in a grove by firelight, a silver pentacle dangling from her neck on a long chain as she passed a chalice of wine to the figure standing next to her. Wiccan, I thought with excitement. She is a priestess, a wise woman.

"We'll go over there right now to see what you might need," she said, taking off her apron. I waited while she asked John to watch the flower shop, then we crossed the street and went into my store.

I turned on the art deco chandeliers, and the room glowed. Laurel oohed and aahed, amazed as I had been by the assortment of exotic goods. We strolled around the showroom admiring various treasures, and she spotted the bar at the back of the room.

"Wow!" she exclaimed, "Do you realize what this is?"

She approached the espresso machine, shining brightly now thanks to several hours of my time and a bottle of Brasso.

"If this still works, it's a gold mine," she murmured, running her hand over the elaborate design etched into the gleaming metal. An eagle with spread wings adorned the domed top like a hood ornament on the front of an elegant car, and the name *Victoria Arduino* was inscribed below.

"Lets' see what you've got here!" She slipped behind the coffee bar to open cupboards and drawers, pulling out metal containers and other mysterious objects that looked like machine parts.

Snapping the pieces together expertly, she assembled a little metal basket with a handle that fit into a slot on the machine, and slid a small glass coffee pot into place underneath it. She plugged the espresso machine into the wall and cooed with satisfaction when a little red light turned on.

Laurel picked up a stainless steel pitcher and grinned at me.

"Got any coffee beans? Wanna try this baby out?"

We found some Dark French beans in the pantry and filled

the pitcher with cold water. After grinding the beans for quite a while, Laurel packed powdery coffee into the little metal basket. She poured water into an opening in the machine. Flipping a switch, she caused a deep rumble then a steamy swish, and in a few minutes a dark thick brew oozed out into the waiting glass pot. It was thick, the consistency of honey. We filled two of the espresso cups, stirred with two of the little silver spoons, and sipped.

Outrageous! We grunted with satisfaction and sipped again. The flavor exploded in my head and I saw happy stars.

"Okay," she said, "So we will definitely serve this at your party. And," she added with a sigh, "I'll be over every morning from now on for my daily fix. We don't have an espresso machine yet, though it's on my wish list."

I laughed and told her she'd be welcome.

Laurel advised setting up a buffet on folding banquet tables positioned in front of the display windows. She said she knew a *barista* we could hire to work the event, an expert at drawing the dark nectar out of the espresso machine and making the fancy coffee drinks. I vowed to learn to do this myself, eventually.

"We use only organic fruits and vegetables in our kitchen, by the way," Laurel said. "We grow our own organic herbs and salad greens in the garden behind the restaurant. And our meats and fish are either organic, free range, wild caught or all of the above. Organic whole grain pasta, rice and baked goods, plus gluten-free alternatives. We use recycled paper products, too. We're the only truly 'green' restaurant in town. We're pretty serious about nurturing the Earth."

She reached up and touched her pentacle earring, rubbing it between her fingers as though for luck. I wondered if John was a witch too, and decided to wait until I knew them better to ask about their religion.

I remarked that considering her last name and the lime

green theme across the intersection, being "green" was a great marketing niche for them. She laughed and made a joke about hidden subtexts in the menu and subliminal messages embedded in the background music.

I felt I had found a good friend, and a very useful ally. The opening party seemed less daunting now.

Laurel seemed to know a lot about healthy foods. The way she and John lived seemed noble and smart. The idea of a lifestyle with a low impact on the environment was very cool. I had a feeling I would learn a lot of useful secrets from my new friends.

✶   ✶   ✶

That night I dreamed I was floating in outer space, looking down at the Earth. I wasn't inside a space ship or wearing a special astronaut suit, it was just me, hanging in the blackness.

The planet looked beautiful, like a blue and green jewel. I noticed that there were several bands of particles circling the Earth. On closer inspection, the particles were people and animals floating along weightlessly like me. A zebra flowed past, moving his legs as though he were running. A little girl riding a tricycle followed. Everything was in slow motion.

I moved my hand and discovered I could change position by flapping it. Waving my arms like a bird, I flew over to a little cluster of creatures and watched a mother dog nurse six squirming puppies. She smiled up at me, panting a little, then reached down and washed one of the pups with her tongue. A man and woman floated by, wrapped in each other's arms, kissing and pressing their bodies together. I started to feel lonely. But the Earth was sparkling up at me, twirling me around with all of life. I got the feeling everything would be OK.

Then Mr. Paradis appeared, seated at a small table playing

chess with the dark man I had seen that first day. My employer shook his finger at me, waggled his eyebrows and said, "Emily, time to get to work!" The younger man seemed annoyed at the interruption, but then he smiled and stared at me admiringly.

I wondered how I must have looked, wearing nothing but my scandalous shortie nightgown!

Then I woke up, lying sideways across my bed under the bright blue skylight. Tree was at the head of the bed curled up on the pillow, staring at me with his gorgeous kitty eyes. It was another glorious sunny summer day, and I was finding my place in the circle.

Chapter 3

The Empress

NURTURING, COMFORT

Description: Serene and elegant, the experienced mother rests a hand on her swollen belly. Meaning: The earth mother. Nurturing, protection and soothing. Comfort food for the body and the soul.

Just after two o'clock on the day of the Grand Opening, I walked through the store tweaking the showroom for the umpteenth time. Nursing a slight headache, I suspected I had taken on more than I could handle and actually snapped at Mr. Paradis, immediately regretting it and feeling humiliated. He scurried back up the stairs to his private lair, getting out of my way, which was probably very wise.

Two banquet tables covered by pristine white cloths had been set up in front of the broad windows that looked out on Crescent. The windows contained a smashing display of unusual objects. Banners in the windows proclaimed, "*Grand Opening Party, Tonight 6-8 p.m., Open House ~ Free Refreshments.*"

Several flower arrangements had just been delivered by a young man dressed in kitchen whites and a Green Thumb apron. I snapped at him, too, when he put the vases down too close to the edge of the coffee bar. The food was scheduled to arrive at around four o'clock.

I was looking forward to seeing the place filled with people for a change. Maybe I would even meet an interesting man or two. I hadn't dated anyone for a while, and socializing could be fun as long as things didn't get too intense. I definitely wasn't going to surrender my independence to some attractive guy who probably had more than one hidden agenda up his sleeve. I had learned a lesson about that from my last relationship.

I went outside to scrutinize the storefront one more time. I had trimmed the ivy around the front door and the stonework beneath was now fully revealed. A beautiful stone angel with long curling hair and a beatific smile looked down from above the entrance, blessing all those who passed. I was thrilled to have discovered her and hoped she'd bring us luck today.

I grabbed my broom and briskly started working on the sidewalk in front of the entrance. The sound of childish shouts came rolling toward me down the street, and I looked up to see my Indian friend approaching with her baby stroller and parade of pre-schoolers. Today she wore jeans and a purple T-shirt, but somehow looked just as exotic as before.

Our eyes met and I stopped sweeping to lean on the broom.

Just the sight of her seemed to calm me down, somehow. She was very beautiful, with a voluptuous hourglass figure and full sensual lips. She wore not a spec of make-up, but glowed with natural vitality. Her shining black hair was worn loose today, hanging down to her waist. She looked gorgeous.

"Hello again!" I said. "What a lovely day for a walk!"

She paused for a chat. The children climbed up and down the front steps, peaking inside the door but not daring to enter. Their busy hopping, shoving, tussling and clamoring would have driven me crazy, and but somehow she managed to stay cool and serene.

"I hope you received an invitation to our party tonight," I said. "I sent them to everyone who lives nearby."

"Oh yes," she replied. "We did receive it. Thank you very much, we'll stop by after my husband gets home from work."

I asked if any of the children were hers, and she proudly introduced her son and daughter. He was one of the older boys, dark and slim like his mother, and she was the hazel-eyed blonde baby in the stroller.

"My name is Siri Ajala, " she told me. "We live in the large yellow building, just there," she said, pointing down the street.

"What a lovely name," I said.

"Yes, it means, 'Beautiful Earth.' Very poetic! But my married name is Rodgers."

Two of the little boys had dared to step just inside the open front door, and she called to them sharply.

"No, no," I said, eager for the chance to get to know her better. "They're welcome to look around. Won't you come in for a minute, Siri, and give me your opinion?"

Her dark eyes gleamed.

"I would very much like to see," she said with excitement, "If you are certain that the children will not be a bother."

She lifted her daughter out of the stroller and put her into my waiting arms. The little girl looked at me with a shy smile, her fingers heading toward her mouth. Then she got distracted by my earring and gently touched it, her eyes wide. Picking up the second baby, Siri deftly stepped on a lever that folded the stroller into a narrow bundle. With a call to the children, she was up the steps and standing inside the door within seconds.

The toddlers quickly found the children's play area in the corner, I was happy to see. I had gathered some second-hand toys and games to help keep the little ones busy while their parents shopped. There was a low table with four small chairs, occupied by two little girls having an imaginary tea party with their dolls. The boys seemed to be interested in a basket of rubber dinosaurs and wooden blocks. They dumped everything out onto the floor and constructed a sprawling maze.

Siri pulled a blanket out of the big pocket on the back of the stroller and spread it out on the floor. She lay the two babies down on it. Siri's daughter rolled over onto her tummy and fell asleep, while the little brown-skinned baby cooed with excitement and began to squirm his way over to where the older children played.

"Thomas," she called to her son, who looked up obediently. "You watch, eh?" Thomas nodded.

"Who are all these other children?" I asked her, watching the activity. "Do you run a daycare center in your apartment?"

"No," she answered, "Not a real daycare, it is not allowed. I just help the other mothers from time to time. We take turns, so everyone gets a little break."

I showed her around the shop. She admired everything, speaking very quickly in a light, musical voice.

Siri told me she had been born and raised in India, living there until she reached her teens. Then her family had moved to the U.S., and she had finished her education here in the public school system. She had been accepted to the state university, but was unable to attend because of her mother's sudden illness with cancer.

Staying at home after her mother's death to care for her father and younger brother, Siri married an American boy she had met in high school. Her brother now worked for the city as a policeman and their elderly father lived with Siri and her husband, Tom. I guessed that it must be getting rather crowded, with two children and three adults in one apartment.

"And, your father, is he well?" I asked.

"Oh yes," she said, "Very well. Perhaps a bit bored, I am afraid. He is retired now, with no job to keep him busy. Just his books, his beloved books. My father was a professor. He taught at a university in Delhi, when I was little. When we came to this country, his credentials were not correct to teach in the schools, so he became a substitute teacher and a private tutor." She waved her arms, using hand gestures to underscore her words.

"Siri," I said thoughtfully, thinking of my recent conversation with Mr. Paradis about hiring some part-time help. "Would you possibly be interested in taking on a little job, just a few hours a week?"

"Here?" she asked, her eyes widening.

I nodded.

"Oh yes, please! Thank you, very much!"

"Would you be able to leave the children with one of the other mothers?" I asked. "Would your father be all right by himself for a little while?"

"Most certainly!" She was obviously excited and began to speak quickly. "My father has his chess games every day. He plays with his friends down the street. And I can arrange something for the children, too, if it's not for too long."

"What exactly would you have me here to do?" She looked around with an appraising eye.

"Help with the customers when it gets busy," I said. "Dust a little, help me keep the store clean. And, I was thinking of serving tea and espresso, maybe some baked goods or something like that. What do you think?"

"I think it is a lovely idea," she replied, her eyes shining. "There is nowhere close by to sit down and have breakfast or lunch on the weekdays. Perhaps we could offer this as a way to get people interested in browsing. Do you have the permits for serving food?"

I had already asked Mr. Paradis to look into it. He had agreed to some minor renovations in the kitchen, too. I helped her gather up the children and put the toys away, carrying the still-sleeping baby out to the sidewalk for her while she reopened the stroller and tucked the other child under the seat belt. Pulling a long shawl out of the bag on the stroller, she arranged it across her chest and knotted it at the side, making a little sling for her daughter to snuggle in. Supporting the baby with one hand, she was able to steer the stroller with the other. She managed it all effortlessly, with a calm born of much experience. I found it amazing.

Siri promised to return that evening with her husband and her father. I urged her to bring her children too. She said that many of the other women who lived in her building were also planning to attend.

"It's a good arrangement," she said. "We all help each other. You'll have to meet them!"

"We can start on that tonight," I agreed, gently stroking her baby's soft little head with the back of my index finger. What a little lovey. And what a lovely woman! It made me feel more secure just to be around her.

I felt my guard slipping down as I relaxed, the feminine softness in me welling up to replace the hard shell I had developed over recent years.

It was a comfortable feeling, and I sighed happily as I watched Siri and the children make their way down the street. Being near her was like water in the desert, and I looked forward to the next soothing sip with happy anticipation.

Chapter 4

The Emperor

LEADERSHIP, POWER

Description: The Emperor is a strong, paternal man with wealth and power, dressed in flowing dark robes and carrying the orb of power.
Meaning: A powerful leader and figure of authority. Paternal influence, fatherhood. Providing materially for the family, the community.

At seven thirty that evening, the store was packed with guests and the party was peaking. It was a huge success and I was ecstatic. Winding my way from the coffee bar through the mob in front of the buffet tables was a challenge. Everyone was talking at the same time, in various languages. The background music could barely be heard any more.

Many people had obviously come straight from work. Several women wore medical uniforms, and members of a landscaping crew all had on identical logo-emblazoned T-shirts. Laurel's team was easily spotted, with their Green Thumb aprons. The *barista* she had hired for the party pulled shot after shot of espresso. He entertained the waiting customers with jokes and coffee trivia as he worked. The combination of his upbeat personality plus the caffeine kick created a dynamic energy that had spread throughout the room.

The beautiful food Laurel had prepared was very well received. There were several salads, a vegetarian lasagna cut into squares and a big pan of *spanakopita,* flakey Greek pastry stuffed with spinach and feta cheese. The second table held an assortment of desserts. Everyone helped themselves enthusiastically.

A noisy cluster of kids was building a block city in the children's corner. Siri's father, whose name was Gupta, was a dignified gray-haired gentleman with wire-framed glasses who sat in a nearby rocker and supervised the construction. He seemed to be enjoying himself. I had also met her husband Tom, earlier. He was a friendly redhead with freckles and hazel eyes like his daughter, the little love who had stolen my heart that afternoon.

Mr. Paradis had installed himself majestically behind the cash register in the front of the room, where he held forth on many subjects. The neighbors greeted him as though they had not seen him in a long time. He had dressed for the festivities in a long purple caftan decorated with embroidery that contained little mirrors, worn over his traditional black sweatpants and slippers. He looked magical and mysterious.

He was kept busy by a steady trickle of sales, as the guests explored the shop and were thrilled to discover amazing things. We were definitely getting the word out. Two local newspapers had interviewed me so far this evening, and one of the reporters had snapped some photos.

"Welcome to *Paradis*," I said as a new group entered.

"Welcome to Paradise! Welcome to Paradise!" several of the children echoed, giggling.

I smiled. Maybe they were right!

I introduced myself to the newcomers, directing them to the food and drink, then I ducked into the front hallway for a moment to catch my breath.

"Paradise lost, or Paradise found?" A sexy male voice with a slight foreign accent came out of the darkness behind me. It sounded like the person who had been phoning my employer.

I jumped.

He leaned forward into the light with one eyebrow raised. It was the same man I had glimpsed on my first day at work and now I had a chance to get a better look at him. He was tall, dark and very handsome in a dangerous, brooding kind of way. I shivered. Dressed in a dark jacket over a black shirt and slacks, he blended in with the shadows. He looked like a vampire but I was pretty sure he was just European.

"Newly found, for me," I said, trying not to stare. A little tingle started in my cheeks as my face flushed.

"And newly re-found for my friend Henry," he said, stepping forward into the light. "Thanks to you!"

"Anton Novak," the dark man said, taking my offered hand, not to shake it but to hold it in both of his, dashing European-style.

His fingers were long and elegant, his grasp warm and firm. It was an intimate gesture, and my breath caught. I couldn't help noticing that he wore no rings. A lot of married men don't, though. Sometimes they carry their wedding rings around with their pocket change, presumably to slip them back on when they head for home and wife. I've seen it several times at the cash register, when I've been making a sale.

"Hi, I'm Emily. I'm so glad you could come," I said, reclaiming my hand and pretending to adjust one of my earrings. I recognized his name from the list of special customers. "Were you already in the U.S.? Or did our invitation reach you in London?"

"I was in New York when Henry emailed me about the party. He said he had something he particularly wants me to see."

He looked at me frankly and approvingly. I mean, from head to toe.

"Well, well then, " I stammered nervously, "I'll just have to, um, relieve him from his cashier's duties and let him talk with you personally."

I smiled and nodded, cursing myself for feeling so awkward, then spun around to slip back into the showroom and behind the jewelry counter. I indicated to Mr. Paradis that he should go mingle. Anton Novak leaned in the doorway, watching.

They caught eyes and my employer headed over to take the European by the arm, clapping him on the back like an old friend. A broad genuine smile transformed the younger man's face. Mr. Paradis waved his arm in my direction as though he was discussing me. Novak looked over at me too, in a suspicious manner. He seemed gloomy, dark. I glared back at him, my guard going up like the wall around a medieval castle. The two of them turned and disappeared up the stairs.

I was kept busy with sales and conversation for the next half hour, when things started to wind down. Siri and her family found me at the front of the store and lined up to say goodnight. She also introduced me to her neighbors.

Rolando and Isabella Reyes were a beautiful young couple with shining dark eyes and hair. They had a one-year-old daughter and lived across the hallway from Siri. Isabella congratulated me on hiring her friend, complimenting my wisdom. Isabella seemed outgoing and full of fun. Her husband was more restrained, a little shy.

Tom Rodgers introduced his friend James Godard, who was a carpenter and worked with Tom at a local construction company. Wearing a brown plaid flannel shirt and jeans, James was very attractive in a huggable All American way. His large, calloused hand engulfed mine. He seemed like someone I might enjoy knowing better.

"Well, are you pleased?"

Laurel's voice came from behind me as I stood in the open front door looking out into the street. The sun was going down, and the streetlights dotted the sidewalks with bubbles of light.

"Everyone had a wonderful time, don't you think?" she asked, coming to stand beside me. We leaned in the doorway cozily, two old pals.

Laurel had been in the kitchen cleaning up, supervising her staff as they re-packed the van.

"We actually made some pretty good sales," I said.

"Most of the merchants from the neighborhood were here," Laurel said.

"Thank you so much," I said, "I could never have gotten through it without your help."

"Sure you could Emily, you're the perfect hostess," she said. "Give yourself some credit, too!"

Across the intersection, we could see that the Green Thumb was hopping with business. All the outdoor tables were occupied, and we could see John serving cocktails behind the bar on the glassed-in porch.

"I guess I'd better get back across the street," she said, and excused herself to check on her clean-up crew.

I heard voices behind me coming down the stairs, and Mr. Paradis appeared with his European friend. They shook hands formally, and Anton Novak slipped out the front door, saying "good night" to him and "*au revoir*" to me.

We locked eyes for a moment as he passed, and I couldn't help wondering when our next encounter would occur. He was definitely flirtatious but even aside from the question of his marital status, as far as I knew he traveled constantly for his business. I was not terribly interested in a one-night stand, no matter how attractive the man might be. And frankly, I didn't trust him. There was something kind of threatening about his smooth, practiced charm. He made me feel awkward and un-sophisticated.

"Ms. Green is in the back, I presume?" Mr. Paradis interrupted my thoughts, waving his checkbook in the air. I nodded and he wended his way toward the rear of the building.

I stood alone in the doorway looking out into the street for a moment longer. I thought about what the children had said, "Welcome to Paradise!"

"Paradise," I whispered aloud. I thought about what that word meant, to me.

I didn't believe in conventional religion, but didn't really consider myself an agnostic, either. I took a practical view of life and death, assuming that this is our one chance on the planet and we'd better make the most of it.

From time to time, however, I did get a sense that some kind of "higher power" might exist. Also, there did seem to be something very true in the idea of karma, the concept that your actions have an effect on your future "luck."

In my personal view, paradise is much more likely to be a state we might achieve by pursuing experiences to evolve ourselves while here on Earth, rather than a magical place to go after leaving it.

From the mouths of babes, I thought.

✶   ✶   ✶

Henry Paradis was the kind of reader who sat in one position, immersed in study, for such long hours that his knees
would get stuck and he'd have trouble walking when he finally
stood up.

He truly *concentrated* when he read. The kettle could boil,
the phone could ring, the smoke alarm could go off, the world
could end, and Henry would read on and on. A person could
even stand in front of him clearing her throat repeatedly and
not be in the room, as far as he knew.

I understood this about him now and had come to terms
with it.

When I went up to say goodbye after everyone else had
left that night, I found my employer in his office, sitting in his
reading chair. I was prepared to back out the door and sneak
off, but then I saw the three Chinese coins on the table. He was
reading the *I Ching*. Intrigued, I stepped into the room. He immediately looked up at me.

"Welcome," he said. He seemed alert and stimulated.

"We've finished downstairs now. They've all gone, I locked
up," I said, coming closer to take a seat in the chair opposite
his. I was very curious, having read about this but never having
seen it done before.

The parchment shade on the old brass floor lamp cast a
yellow glow onto the low table between the two chairs, where
he laid the open book. He had a little notebook in his lap too,
with a pen, and he had been taking notes. I saw a hexagram
inscribed there, a figure composed of a series of six stacked
solid or broken horizontal lines. The broken or solid lines are
achieved by throwing the coins and getting various combina-
tions of heads or tails. So the results are determined by the luck
of the toss. Each hexagram has a specific interpretation and
spiritual lesson to be learned, as described in the book, which

refers to itself as *The Oracle*.

"What does it say?" I asked him. "Did you ask about the success of the business?"

He smiled at me and put pen and notebook down on the table.

"It says, 'It furthers one to cross the great water,' which is very good!"

"Really!" I said. "But, do we have to go find a lake or something? Or, is that a symbol?"

"Exactly," he nodded. "'Crossing the great water' is a large, important enterprise, something big and complicated, an investment of time and resources."

"I see. Like, re-opening the store."

"Yes. It *furthers* us to do this. It will be to our benefit."

"Things are going to go well for us!" I was impressed.

"Yes. That's what it says tonight."

"Do you consult the Oracle often?"

He leaned back in his chair and pushed the tips of his fingers against each other thoughtfully.

"I discovered the wisdom of the *I Ching* many years ago, when I first traveled through Asia with my wife, Margaret."

"When did you wife pass away?" I had wondered about this, but hesitated to ask.

"It was 1992, in December. Cold, that year. She had breast cancer, you know."

"I'm so sorry, it must have been awful."

"Yes, it took her very quickly," he said, his expression solemn.

"Oh yes, I've heard that," I said.

"I suppose the speed might be a blessing, though." He stared into space.

"Yes, perhaps it is."

"You never know, do we?"

"No, no, we don't."

"After Margaret was gone, I closed the store, you know."

He looked at me briefly over the top of his glasses.

"Oh, that was what happened?" I said. "I wondered."

"Yes."

"I see."

"I just didn't have the energy any more," he said quietly.

He looked down for a moment. I reached across the table and touched his sleeve. I leaned into the pool of yellow light.

"But now we're supposed to cross the great water, right?"

He smiled at me and patted my hand.

"Yes, Emily. We shall cross it together."

With his touch, a flash of the young man he must have once been came to me. I saw in my mind a young American making his way along a crowded street by the docks in some Asian port. When my eyes cleared Mr. Paradis was gazing into them with interest. He looked a bit sly for a moment then he picked up the brass coins, rubbing them between his fingers.

"You have a lot of wonderful things ahead of you, my girl. Let me assure you of that!"

"What? Oh no, you mean my future, you asked about me?"

"Of course, you are part of the scene now," he said, perking up.

"The Scene? We have a Scene?"

"The scenario, the scenario. Part of the picture. Around here." He waved his arm in a vague circle.

"Ohhh, I see. Well?" I demanded, curious.

"Well what?"

"Well, what did it say about me?"

"Only good things. Success and great happiness," he pronounced firmly.

"Totally? Wow. OK, that sounds good," I tried to be persuasive. "Don't suppose you want to be more specific?"

"No, I don't think so. Not tonight. Not yet."

"I thought not. OK. Well, I'd better be off then," I said, getting up to go.

"See you in the morning!"

"Yes, see you tomorrow," I replied, feeling very glad of the fact.

He picked up his book again and started to read. As I left the room I glanced back, just to confirm that he was deeply entranced already, caught in the spell of the magical words. No real need to tiptoe quietly away, but I did anyhow.

Chapter 5

The Hierophant

THE CONVENTIONS OF SOCIETY

Description: The Heirophant card symbolizes conventional religious authority.
Meaning: The conventions of society, traditional religion, the preacher. Criticism of those who are different.

In the days and weeks that followed, things started to settle into a pattern. I still spent most of my time off alone, but working at the store all day distracted me from my boring personal life. At home, I was depressed and lonely. I couldn't wait to get back into the shop to talk to my employer and Siri, who was working there part-time now. When I arrived at work I fell on them like a ravenous beast, pumping my employer for esoteric trivia and making Siri tell me all the latest neighborhood news. Business was good, steady and growing. Our ads in the paper were starting to pay off. We sent out a postcard to the list of collectors, and they began to respond.

I came in at nine and had coffee at the kitchen table with Mr. Paradis while we discussed business and esoterica. He was teaching me how to recognize the ebb and flow of life, the seasonality of it. The metaphor of the *I Ching* is based on farming and politics, both of which involve assets and liabilities that rotate in a cyclical manner. He said that this model, though it was conceived over three thousand years ago, remains viable today. I was trying to be more aware of the weave of the universe, the patterns underlying reality. My anxiety level was diminishing as I began to see that things do not really happen at random.

Henry, as he urged me to call him, said that "magic" is all about using the invisible grid behind reality to strengthen the energy pathways toward various preferred results. He approached the whole idea in a scientific or mathematical manner. It was rather a lot for me to take in, but I was starting to get the point.

When I thought about my weird dreams, which had always forecast the future using the language of symbols, I could see that at any given point in my life it had certainly been possible to intuit the trends. If I did *this*, and then *this happened*, ultimately *that* was likely to result. The logic had a distinctly algebraic feeling to it. Therefore, making something happen "as if by magic" was a matter of putting together the right formula of circumstances and actions to inevitably lead to a certain goal.

"Very heady stuff!" Henry patted my hand as I scrunched up my face in skeptical bewilderment. "Tomorrow let's discuss

physics, my dear. You'll get the connection. All the great magicians in history were scientists, you know. Take the alchemists,
for example. And what is astrology, really? Not a fairy tale, as
many believe, but an attempt to blend scientific observation of
the natural world with intuitive analyses of the patterns of life.
You'll see, you'll see..." He chuckled and flapped his hand at
me as he shuffled out of the room to head up the back stairs to
his lair.

The shop opened at ten and I puttered around there by
myself during the mornings. When Siri came in at about twelve-
thirty, I talked her ear off for half an hour or so before taking
my lunch break. Then I usually headed over to Sorrentino's to
get something to eat and sometimes walked to the little park
down the street to sit in the sun and relax.

Other days I ended up spending my lunch break socializing.
The second time I went into Sorrentino's, a tiny woman with
curly white hair stood behind the deli counter. Mr. Sorrentino
introduced me to his wife. As I returned day after day, she and I
grew better acquainted and I realized what a hub the place was
for local information.

Josephina Sorrentino, or "Josie" as her husband called her,
was the secret power behind their business. Her traditional
southern Italian cooking was renowned, not just in the neighborhood but across the state. Her "Mama Sorrentino's" brand
of packaged dinners and tomato sauce was a raving success,
sold out by noon on the weekends. On holidays, her special
sausages were so popular they had to be ordered in advance.
Many people stockpiled her food in their freezers.

Early every morning, Anthony Sorrentino (who she called
"T") started a huge pot of onions, green peppers, garlic, herbs,
spices and canned Italian tomatoes. It sat simmering on the
back burner. He mashed up a few anchovies and stirred them
in, for extra flavor. The sauce cooked all day at a very low tem-
perature, uncovered, until it had reduced down to a thick,

luscious consistency that clung to the pasta with no need for added tomato paste. One day's sauce went into the dishes Josie made for the next day's sale.

In the small kitchen at the back of the store was a work-scarred wooden table where Josephina dispensed wisdom and philosophy while she cooked. I knew I had reached a certain level of acceptance in the neighborhood the day she beckoned to me and brought me back behind the deli counter.

"Sit," she commanded, clearing a spot at the table. I obeyed, looking around curiously.

Her brown eyes sparkled behind thick black-framed glasses. She was so small that the big white chef's apron wrapped all the way around her twice. A little step stool next to the stove raised her up high enough to reach inside the tall stainless steel cooking pots.

Taking a small bowl from a cabinet, she opened the oven and fished inside with a long-handled spoon. Amazing scents wafted out of the oven. Scooping out a dripping spoonful of something covered with melted cheese, she deposited it into the bowl. She set the bowl in front of me on the table, and pointed to a glass jar of spoons and forks.

"Eat," she commanded, crossing her arms and waiting. I chose a fork, and dug in.

It was a green pepper stuffed with spicy sausage and mushrooms, oozing with tomato sauce and covered with a thick coating of melted mozzarella.

I chewed, swallowed and sighed blissfully. Josie smiled and nodded in satisfaction.

"It's good," she agreed. I thanked her and took another heavenly bite.

She poured two cups of coffee and put them on the table, then settled herself into the chair opposite me. The sleeves of her black cardigan sweater were pushed up above the elbows. She regarded me steadily as I ate, accepting my praise for her cooking in a placid manner, as one who has heard it many times before.

When I finished the stuffed pepper and raised my coffee cup, the real conversation began. Over the next half hour, she skillfully extracted my entire life story, from birthplace and family history to my most recent romance, to the saga of my previous job and its ignominious finale.

Being quizzed by Josie was like floating on your back in the ocean on a breezy day. By the time you sit up and take notice, you're in very deep water.

But she gave as good as she got. In answer to my questions about her family and how she had met her husband, she dished up a tale full of evocative details, with humor as spicy as her meat sauce.

Anthony Sorrentino had come over from Italy when just a boy of twelve, sent by his parents to live with an aunt and uncle to take advantage of the economic opportunities he could access here. He had lived in an apartment building right around the corner, one block up Market Street. Josie was younger than he, and was literally the girl next door. Their families were friends.

"Much younger," she stressed. "When he was a man of twenty, I was just fourteen, a young girl. He used to go around with my older brothers."

"All the girls were in love with him," she added, rolling her eyes dramatically. "They used to follow him down the street."

"But he liked you, eh?" I smiled.

"Oh no," she protested, "I was just the pesty little sister."

"I didn't think nothin' of him," Josie said, snapping her fingers. "But I liked to have fun with my brothers, go to shows, go hear some music, like that. They let me hang around with them, sometimes. My mother would make them take me along."

"So, you started to grow up and things changed?" I asked.

"Not me," she said scornfully, "I didn't change. I'm still

paying no attention to him. But all the sudden he starts looking at me, and then he wants to go on a date!"

She grinned and nodded her head, affirming the unbelievable.

"I'm the only one, of all the girls, who doesn't care—and guess who is the one he wants to chase!"

She chuckled, crinkling up her eyes.

"So, you went out with him then?"

"Oh no," she shook her head, "I thought he was an old man! Way too old for me! By then he was, oh, at least twenty-two. I pretended he was joking."

That really cracked me up, as I pictured her pretending not to know he was really asking her out. What a hot ticket she was, as my Dad used to say. I wished I could have known her back then, in the old days. I resolved to call my mother that evening and repeat the whole story to her.

Josie told me Anthony had pursued her for two more years before she took his suit seriously and agreed to a real date. Six months later, they were married. A year after that, their first son was born. Joseph was a lawyer now and lived across town. Their second son, Robert, was a high school teacher. He lived upstairs with his wife and two children. Josie explained that over their business, the house had been divided into two separate apartments.

The third Sorrentino son, Rocco, ran the pizzeria next door. He had bought the building, and lived in an apartment over his restaurant. He had been married and divorced, and with no children.

"Rocco is single now," she said, looking over at me and obviously considering my likewise status. "He works so hard, he never has time to get out. That's why he didn't come to meet you at the opening night." She seemed anxious for me to not be offended at his absence.

"Well, if he learned from you he must be a great cook," I

said.

"Oh yes," she replied seriously. "All my boys have been cooking since they were very young. It's in the blood."

She showed me some newspaper clippings that proclaimed Sorrentino's Pizza the BEST in the Valley, several years running, and an article about Rocco's efforts to obtain block grant money for improving the neighborhood's historic properties. A photo showed him standing in front of his restaurant, leaning against the lamppost. He was a burly, good-looking man in his late thirties, with dark thick hair and his shirt sleeves worn rolled up like his mama's.

Once I had been admitted to Josie's kitchen, I tried to stop in and say hello whenever I passed. I picked up all kinds of information there about people in the neighborhood, heard wonderful stories and met several new acquaintances while seated at her table.

Not to mention, the stuffed peppers. The *lasagne*. The *spaghetti bolognese*. The *osso bucco*, a stewed veal shank dish that Siri's husband referred to as "Awesome Bucco." It was served on *orzo* pasta with steamed broccoli raab, which Josie called "bitter greens." She showed me how to make it and I wrote down the recipe, but somehow mine never tasted quite as good.

When I would enter the grocery and Mr. Sorrentino spotted me, he would smile and wave me towards the back, saying, "You go see her now. She wants to talk to you." He always seemed very certain of this.

The only thing that Josie and I did not seem to agree on was religion. Born and raised a staunch Catholic, she fretted about her son Rocco's divorce, and still referred to his ex-wife as his "wife." She told me when she was a girl, nobody would ever have considered getting divorced, even if your husband abused you.

"Oh yes," she said, shaking her head sadly, "There were women who would have a black eye sometimes, " she gestured,

"Or a mark on the neck, the arms. We didn't say nothing about it, though."

"Not that I'm saying it's OK, that kind of thing," she added. She sniffed disapprovingly. "But still, I just don't like all the divorce."

"It just doesn't seem right," Josie said. "I know you kids think it's OK. And sometimes even the Pope says it's OK. It just seems like, once you make the promise in front of God and everybody, you should stick to it."

"Sometimes things can get better, if you stick to it," she said wisely.

Apparently Rocco's wife had not felt the same way. She was living in Seattle now, with her new husband and baby.

*   *   *

One day I felt like having pizza for dinner, so I stopped in across the street on my way home. I'll admit I was curious about Rocco Sorrentino. His mother talked about him quite a bit. It obviously worried her that he wasn't settled and happy like her other boys.

The pizzeria was full of people. It was noisy and crowded. There were a dozen or so tables and booths in the back, all occupied, and customers were lined up waiting for their take-out. I inspected the menu options and prices that were posted on a large sign behind the counter. Not bad. Some good choices. They had eggplant and mushrooms, my favorite. I got into line to place an order.

"Order for Bellino! Right here, Bellino!" A man's voice rang out, above the din. It was Rocco, I recognized him from his pictures.

Rocco located Mr. Bellino and passed him a large pizza

box.

"What?" he asked, and leaned forward to listen to the man. I couldn't hear what he said. Rocco burst into laughter, grabbing the man by the shoulder in a warm, friendly way. He seemed to get along well with all his waiting customers, who called him by his name and joked with him.

"OK, next" he said, when it was finally my turn. "What can I get for you tonight?"

He stood waiting with his order pad and pen in his hands. He smiled, looking at me curiously. He was a big, strong, hearty man with thick dark hair that stuck out here and there as though he'd been pulling it in frustration. It was touched with gray at the temples. He was dressed in kitchen whites that had obviously been on duty for quite a few hours. He was full of vitality. When he smiled he looked like his mother, I noticed.

He took my order and accepted my offered twenty-dollar bill, then handed me my change and a receipt. I gave him my last name and he passed my order along down the line. I stepped aside to wait for my pizza. He was still regarding me curiously.

"Are you my new neighbor across the street, I think?" he ventured, "The one my mother keeps telling me so much about?"

I nodded and he grinned, reaching out to grab my hand. He pumped it up and down, smiling broadly. A warm cozy feeling came over me, like basking in sunlight. His energy was intense.

"Hey, how are you, Emily, right?" He kept on shaking my hand.

"Hi, yes, how are you? Rocco. It's great to meet you," I said, my head bobbling.

"You too!"

"So," I said, finally regaining my hand.

"So. Your first time, right?" he asked.

"Yes, yes. Hmm. What?"

"First time I saw you in here."

"Ohhh, yes! My first time. You certainly are busy, aren't you? That's wonderful."

"Yeah, it's busy tonight. Like every night!"

He looked around proudly. Two cooks, a dishwasher and a couple of waitresses were hustling around with precision. Every square inch of space was being utilized. We were packed in like sardines. The brick oven was interesting and I had high hopes for the pizza itself, which looked good. A waitress with a loaded tray of food headed out from behind the counter toward the table area, and I had a chance at a closer visual inspection. Thin crust, which I love. I wondered if his tomato sauce was as good as what they made every day next door. Rocco stepped aside to let the waitress go through the opening in the counter, then motioned for one of the cooks to step in and continuing taking orders. There were only two parties behind me at that point. The activity had started to ebb.

Rocco stood next to me leaning on the counter and we chatted, while he kept one eye on the action in the kitchen.

"Do you make your own sauce?"

"Sure we do, of course. Every day, just like my Pop."

"I love your parents, they're wonderful. And your mother is great."

"Yeah? Well she sure does like you," he said, glancing at me, then surveying the crowd again. "It's real nice of you to take time with her. She loves to talk!"

"So do I. It's been a great way to find out about the neighborhood."

He raised one eyebrow at me.

"Yeah? She tells you what's going on, eh?"

"Sure," I nodded. "She has really made me feel welcome here."

"Mom likes to know everything about everybody, if she can find out."

"Yes, she seems very interested in people."

"She has a spy network on the street, you know. All the people who come in and tell her the news, blah-blah-blah," he said, opening and closing his hand like a mouth talking.

"She's easy to talk to," I said defensively. "She's very supportive!"

Rocco shot me another of his raised-eyebrow, skeptical looks.

"Easy for her to pry personal information out of people, you mean," he commented dryly. "You sit down for a nice bowl of pasta and the next thing you know, she is giving advice about your sex life!"

Since that was roughly what had happened with me, I didn't have much of a comeback. So I asked him a few more questions about the restaurant. He had bought the building ten years ago and spent several years fixing it up, while he kept on working at the grocery next door.

"It was a real trash pile," he said. "We had to rip out all the walls downstairs here, the floors, the ceiling, everything. They were full of rat shit. Pretty disgusting."

I must have appeared dismayed, because he laughed and patted my shoulder reassuringly.

"Don't worry, honey, we got it all out!" He burst out in his big hearty laugh.

"Oh, good." I rolled my eyes and grinned.

I wondered if the "we" he referred to included his ex-wife. According to Josie, the young couple had bought the pizzeria building as newlyweds, planning to raise a family there. She still regretted the loss of their unborn children, never to be bounced on her knee.

My pizza came out of the oven and was boxed, appearing on the counter in front us when Rocco motioned to one of the cooks. The buzz of business was building up again, as a group of diners left the restaurant and a party of six entered and found seats.

"I'll let you get back to work now," I said, taking the warm pizza box into my hands. "I'm so glad to finally meet you, Rocco."

He patted me on the shoulder again and his warm aura enveloped me like a hug.

"You too, Emily! You come back again some time! Enjoy the pie!"

"Thank you! I will!"

I wormed my way through the maze of people standing in the front of the restaurant and made it out the door. The smell of the pizza was enticing, so I opened the box and took a slice as soon as I got into my car. It was superb. Just right. Nothing less than what I had expected, considering. Josie was right, I thought. Cooking *was* in the blood, with her clan.

A few days later on a rainy Sunday afternoon I decided to eat popcorn for lunch and headed to the Mall movie theaters in the next town. As I stood in front of the sign trying to decide which matinee to enter, I heard that hearty laugh again. Looking up, I saw Rocco emerging from the morning show that was just letting out. He had his arm around a petite Asian woman. She wore jeans and a black raincoat, with her long shining dark hair pulled back into a ponytail. He leaned over attentively as she spoke, then they both laughed. They were walking directly toward me. As they approached, he looked up and recognized me. He pulled back the arm that had been encircling the woman.

"Well, well," he said in a friendly voice, though his eyes showed an odd wariness. "If it isn't our new friend! How are you, Emily?" He smiled and nodded at me.

"Fine! Great! How are you Rocco? Did you see the Sci Fi, or the Sandra Bullock?"

I looked curiously at the woman, who seemed uncomfortable, so I gave her my most friendly smile. She looked startled, and then she smiled back. Rocco watched this little exchange with some apparent anxiety, stuffing his hands into the pockets of his brown leather jacket. He hovered over her protectively.

"We saw the Sci Fi, and it was good," she spoke up. Her voice was light and girlish. I kept grinning at her, and she finally gave me back a full-on, gorgeous smile. She was absolutely adorable. Flawless skin, beautiful greenish eyes, a slim athletic build. Probably over thirty, though she could have easily passed for sixteen in the right clothes. Very sweet expression, very graceful. I was totally enchanted by her.

Rocco was obviously in full appreciation of her assets as well. He appeared delighted when she spoke, as though she had said something amazing. It was either cute, or excessive, I couldn't decide which. He was definitely obsessed, but in a good way, I hoped. Something was clearly going on between them.

"Emily, this is my friend Mei, " Rocco said. He pronounced it, "My."

We greeted each other, shaking hands. Hers was tiny and frail as a bird's wing.

"Emily! I heard about you! My family has a restaurant on Market Street. It's called Buddha," she announced. "It is Asian Fusion cuisine. My father is the chef. He's brilliant."

Rocco looked slightly dismayed. It came across that he did not want me to know who she was. I assumed that he didn't want his mother to find out what he was up to. This was very interesting. Otherwise, I never would have agreed to butt in on their date when Mei politely invited me to come with them to get some lunch in the mall coffee shop.

Also I was starved, as usual. While we waited for our burgers, we talked. Or rather, Rocco leaned back with his arm stretched out along the top of the seat and watched the two of us talk. Mei and I chattered away like old friends. She told me all about her family, about their cooperative effort to start a successful new restaurant. Everyone had a financial investment in it, including her parents, her sister and her two brothers. It had taken over a year to do the construction work on the space they were leasing. They had hired a special crew from New York City to do the work, a Chinese company. It included someone expert at *feng shui*, the art of arranging objects within a space so that energy flows through it in a beneficial way.

"My family is very traditional, though we've been living here for a long time now," Mei said. "My father still does not speak English. But he understands more than he lets on."

She and her siblings were raised in the U.S., while her parents worked at a relative's Chinese restaurant. The kids all went to high school and graduated with honors, then all four children went to college and trained for high-paying jobs. One was now a lawyer, one was an accountant, a third was in medical school and Mei herself worked full-time as a project manager in the Information Technology department at a large corporation nearby. All four of them also worked at the restaurant, whenever they could. Sometimes the brother in medical school would even fly in for the weekend, if they were in a pinch.

"Your family must be very close," I remarked approvingly.

"Yes, very close. Sometimes, too close," she said, looking pointedly at Rocco.

"Yep, yep," he said, "'Close' is one word for it."

"My family is very traditional," she repeated. "They have very strict rules for how everyone must live." An angry expression fluttered across her face, and was gone.

Rocco leaned forward to join in. He lowered his voice confidentially.

"They don't approve of me."

"No!"

"Yes."

"Of you? What's not to love?" I demanded indignantly, and

we all laughed.

"It's not *you*, not you personally, though," Mei protested.

"Yeah, they love me as the pizza-head from down the street, right?"

"Right, it's just that they don't want me going out with someone who is not Chinese," she explained to me. "They have always been very definite about that." She glanced at him. "My brothers and sister have all followed the rules, they have always dated only the 'approved' kind of person. But I guess I am the rebel!"

She sat up, straightened her shoulders and grinned proudly.

"Yeah, she's a rebel all right," Rocco teased, "Four years we've been going out, and she still doesn't tell her parents."

"No! Four years! They still don't know?"

He nodded, shrugging.

"My father would be very angry if he knew we were serious about each other," she explained. "He would not want me to be a part of the restaurant anymore. He would shun me. My entire life savings is invested. They cannot afford to buy me out. It's complicated."

"So your relationship is a secret," I concluded.

"My parents don't know, either." Rocco looked at me meaningfully.

"Ohhh. OK. I get it."

"No, it's not what you think. I'm not afraid to tell them about her. I do what I want. I own my own place. It's nobody's business what I do."

"Yes, of course."

"But, you can't tell my mother."

"OK, OK, I won't. Don't worry about it."

"It would be all over the neighborhood by noon."

"Yes, yes."

"I would say, by no later than ten o'clock," Mei quipped,

grinning.

We all laughed.

"Seriously," Mei said, "We'd really appreciate it if you don't tell anyone you saw us today. That's why we always come to the Sunday morning movie. There's never anybody here. I don't want my family to find out right now. It is not a good time for us to be mad at each other."

I assured them I would keep their secret. I was sorry that Josie couldn't find out that her son was involved in a happy, loving relationship. She would have been delighted to know he was no longer alone. I thought she would probably approve despite what I assumed was a major difference in religion. I didn't think Mei could possibly be Catholic. She was probably a Buddhist. Or whatever. In any case, I was sorry for everyone that her family was not more flexible in their attitude. It seemed like they all lost something as a result.

And, it couldn't go on like this forever. What if the couple wanted to get married and have children? They couldn't keep that a secret. It seemed like eventually, things would have to change, one way or another. As things always do change, one way or another. It's one of the few things in life we can definitely count on.

Chapter 6

The Lovers

ROMANCE

Description: A man and woman stand before an angel or cupid, aiming at them with the arrow of love. A third woman, somewhat older, stands on the other side of the man, representing his past relationships.
Meaning: Romance, marriage. Choice between the old and the new. Sexual attraction.

At lunchtime one day a couple of weeks after the store opened,

I decided to enjoy the fine weather and walk down to the park. It was a perfect summer day. The birds sang, and the sky was bright blue with those little puffy white clouds that look like sheep.

I was feeling quite chipper, having sold an obscenely expensive antique grandfather clock that morning to a fashionably dressed woman who was thrilled to find it for her lawyer husband's birthday. I agreed to arrange delivery to his office at an upscale address downtown. She paid in full with her American Express card.

When you're in retail, this is what it's all about. It doesn't get much better!

So I savored the moment while strolling along in the dazzling sunshine, with the sound of kids at play echoing in the distance. I entered the gates to the park and followed the main path toward a circular pond surrounded by curving stone benches, all empty at the moment. A greenish bronze fish, a giant carp, appeared to leap up out of the pond's center. Its scales were fully articulated and they sparkled in the light. Water sprayed out of its mouth in several glistening rainbow arcs, falling back into the basin.

This was my favorite place to sit. I loved the sound of the falling water, it was very serene. I sat down and immediately relaxed. I ate my sandwich slowly, staring at the fountain and letting my vision go out of focus, my mind wandering.

In a minute or two, my eyes drifted shut. The sun on my face was warm and hypnotic. I fell into a sort of meditative state. My mind floated in the here and now. It was a Zen moment.

I let go and sank deeper into my thought body, losing more and more awareness of the physical. Then I distinctly felt my consciousness rise up along my spine and flow out through the top of my head as I left my body through the seventh chakra.

I saw myself sitting on the bench from overhead, looking

down from a bird's eye view. The bronze fish was spitting water up towards the new disembodied me as I hovered above it. Something like a shining filament of spider's silk gleamed in the sunshine, hanging down from where I floated effortlessly right above the treetops. It was leading to the top of my physical head, where my body sat on the bench, eyes closed and not moving. I looked like I was sleeping, sitting up. Then I saw a person coming toward my body across the grass. He was not scary or threatening. The figure bent over me solicitously.

Something brushed my nose. With a slightly nauseating rush, I was suddenly inside my body again.

A fly. I heard it buzz. Relaxed, I kept my eyes shut, one with the fly.

A foot crunched stones in the path. Then, only the sound of water falling. Warm sun on my forehead, my eyelids, my cheeks.

Something brushed my nose again.

I opened my eyes and looked directly into those of Anton Novak. They were amber brown with little flecks of gold in the irises. The lashes were impossibly long and lush, the kind that women struggle to achieve with expensive cosmetics. One lock of his straight dark brown hair fell casually across his forehead. He squatted in the path directly in front of me, regarding me with curiosity.

"Hello," I said.

"Hello." His voice had a serious tone. He reached out and gently tucked a little strand of hair behind my left ear. His expression was unguarded, concerned.

"Are you OK?" he asked gently, obviously ready to catch me if I fell over.

"Fine, I'm fine, just fine," I stammered, snapping out of it. "Thank you, really, I'll be just fine."

I stood up and grabbed clumsily for my lunch bag and purse, my face flushed with embarrassment. He stood up gracefully and took me by the elbow, holding on despite my ridiculous attempts to gather my belongings, which kept falling out of my fumbling hands.

"You're sure? All right, you're sure now?" he said, not letting go. His warm hand embraced my arm, helping me up.

"Yes! Oh yes, very sure!" I staggered and grabbed onto him, shocked by a buzzing tingle that started in my core then swelled into a rush of pure pleasure that swept over me, leaving behind a rash of dizzy goosebumps. "I was just, um, really, I am perfectly, perfectly…fine. I'm OK." I was more than OK, I was swelling open like a ripe red rosebud in the afternoon sun. I let go of him but I couldn't stop staring, and he looked back at me with a little smile behind his eyes, like he knew what I was feeling.

He released my elbow and allowed me to stand on my own. "What were you doing?" he demanded, "Sleeping?"

I finally got a grip on my things, and we started to walk down the path.

"No, not sleeping. Not exactly, that is." I said, "More like, kind of…meditating."

He seemed relieved to hear it.

"Ahhh…" he commented, nodding his head, "Meditating! I see."

He was wearing gray slacks and a white shirt with short sleeves, opened at the throat. Some very nice black curly hairs showed on his upper chest. He thrust his hands into his pants pockets and strode along next to me.

He smiled approvingly. He had extremely white teeth. I wondered if he had used the bleaching strips. That would make him a bit vain. I wondered if he was. Or maybe his teeth were natural. Maybe they just *looked* so white because of his tan. He did have a great tan. I wondered whether he had been at the beach. Probably some fabulous resort somewhere. Probably cruising on someone's yacht. In the blue-blue-blue

Mediterranean. Probably with some incredibly wealthy woman with huge breasts who looked like the young Elizabeth Taylor in "Cleopatra," wearing white flowing clothes made out of gauze...I sighed, and frowned.

"Do you meditate often?" he asked politely.

"Well yes, every day when I have the time," I replied. "It helps to clear my head. Makes me feel centered, focused."

"I agree," he said. "I too meditate. I learned how at the Buddhist Temple on Martha's Vineyard, of all places." He raised his eyebrows and nodded as if to confirm an amazing fact.

I chuckled, and he grinned delightedly.

He launched into a long, rambling story about Buddhist monks on the island off the coast of Massachusetts, meditating inside the Great Pyramid in Egypt at midnight on the Winter Solstice, having a vision of his grandfather that tapped him on the shoulder during a ceremony in a Lakota Sioux sweat lodge, and spending the night in a haunted chateau while doing a wine tour of the Loire Valley.

By then, we were all the way back at the store.

And most of the way toward becoming friends, surprisingly. He was a wonderful storyteller. I was completely charmed by him. I stopped feeling self-conscious and laughed out loud at his jokes. He treated me with a flattering gentlemanly courtesy that made me feel like a cherished and beautiful creature. I liked it very much. I actually envisioned myself touring those vineyards with him. His descriptions were vivid, enchanting.

It was my day for being hypnotized. First by the sun god, and next by this god of a man! I realized that today he was completely different from how I had perceived him when we first met, at the party. Then, he seemed like a slick European playboy on the make. Now he seemed like the nicest guy on earth. A little too good to be true, maybe. I reminded myself that caution was the safest path with handsome men, for sure.

I asked him why he had happened to be in the park.

"Actually, I came to look for you," he said, smoothing back his straight, dark hair with a quick nervous gesture. "I was here to see Henry, then Siri told me where you probably went."

"Why were you looking for me?"

"Well, to ask you out."

"Out?"

"Yes, out, to ask you out."

"You mean like, out to dinner?"

"Yes, out to dinner."

"Well?"

"Well what?"

"Well, are you going to ask me now?"

"Yes, yes, I *am* asking you now."

"Oh, good."

"And, will you? Have dinner with me?"

"Dinner? Hmm…When?"

"Well, I have to leave town tomorrow, for a couple of weeks."

"So, like, tonight, do you mean?"

"Yes, certainly. Dinner tonight. You and me."

He reached down and gently tucked that wandering piece of hair back behind my ear again.

"What do you say?" He looked into my eyes.

"Sure," I said, breathlessly. "What time? When I get off work?"

"Sure," he said, "When you get off work. I'll drive you home first if you want to…feed your cat or something."

"Why do you think I have a cat?"

"Because, you just seem like the kind of girl who has a cat."

"How do you know what kind of girl I am?" I demanded indignantly.

"Maybe you just seem like a nice, friendly, kind of beautiful girl who would like little soft furry animals, I don't know!"

He threw his hands up in the air helplessly, then he grinned at
me.

I frowned and walked slowly past him, starting up the steps
towards the front door.

"What's your cat's name?" he asked as I passed.

"Tree," I admitted.

"*Tree*? You have a *cat* named *Tree*?"

"Uh huh."

"Why is he named Tree?"

"He likes to climb them. He likes to sit in them. He likes
to rub up against them and scratch his back."

"OK, we will go and feed the Tree. All right?"

"OK," I said, over my shoulder.

I turned around and looked back. He was still standing
there watching me. He was showing me those pretty white
teeth again. I showed him mine back. The tingling was starting
again, and we weren't even touching.

"See you soon," he said cheerily, with a brief wave.

"See you," I replied, opening the door and stepping inside.

I waved back and shut the door, resisting the temptation to
pop it back open again and see if he was still out there.

So, my good fortune of recent times was going to continue.
I was really on a roll of good luck. New job, new friends, and
now even my love life was looking up! Or, looking down from
up, I thought, remembering my out-of-body experience in the
park. Now I just had to try not to ruin everything by getting
too deeply involved.

If I believed what Henry had taught me, this wasn't really
good luck at all but rather a predictable series of logical events.
It was the right season for me to find a new life and attract a
new man. The time of endings, loss, devastation and mourn-
ing was over and spring was finally here. The seed of my new
life was planted when I picked this fertile moment to make a

change. The instant I turned onto the path that took me away from my old, unhappy life, a whole new configuration of people and events had appeared on my future horizon. It was like pushing the first tile in a line of dominoes, I saw that, the steps were all connected. But, could I work magic, as Henry had suggested? Could I steer the direction of change and actually shape my destiny?

My mother always said that if I really wanted something, all I had to do was concentrate on it. Just visualize what I wanted to have happen, keep thinking about it, and eventually the path toward making it come true would appear.

"Thoughts are things," Henry said.

Fine with me! Perfectly, perfectly fine.

*   *   *

That afternoon I ventured down into the cellar while Siri watched the shop. Henry had briefly described his subterranean storeroom, but this was the first time I had felt brave enough to tackle the task of dealing with the contents. Ever since the incident of the ghostly Chinese man floating on the back porch I had been a little afraid to descend the stairs. It was spooky and dark, and there was a weird energy down here.

Many years' accumulation of cobwebs festooned the shadowy space, hanging down from the asbestos-covered pipes that traversed the ceiling. An ancient pile of coal occupied the rear next to the hulking corpse of the old heating system, now defunct. A rusted electric hot water heater was still in residence as well, though the shiny new system nearby was obviously what we were now using. It hummed with internal activity.

I gradually made my way around the room, examining the

forest of shipping containers and metal shelves filled with merchandise. I vacuumed, then dusted, and then vacuumed again. After the first few minutes, I had to come upstairs and find a dishtowel to tie around my face like a mask so I could breathe. Right at the foot of the stairs, an open carton was blocking the way. It was filled with framed photographs. They looked personal, so I brought the box upstairs when I finished cleaning to give it to my employer.

I found him in the book room pulling various volumes off the shelves and packing them into a large Fed Ex box. A printout in his left hand contained the shipping list. When he saw what I carried, a bemused expression crossed his face and he sat down on the wooden chair in the middle of the aisle.

"Oh my," Henry said, "Haven't thought of these in years. I must have forgotten they were down there." He flipped through the photos. He pulled one out and showed it to me.

The black and white print showed a man and a woman standing on the tarmac in front of an airplane with "Pan Am" written on the tail. They had either just arrived, or were about to take off. A staircase on wheels was pulled up to the open door of the plane. The man wore a business suit, overcoat and hat. He was portly, clean-shaven and looked successful. He carried a large briefcase and wore sunglasses with heavy black frames. The woman had neatly coiffed short dark hair, and wore a black coat with large white buttons over a plaid suit. She wore sunglasses with thick, white rectangular frames. They were both smiling, but in a stiff formal way. It looked like the shot had been taken in the 1950's. It reminded me of the old Doris Day movies I used to watch with my mother on late-night TV.

"There she is," he said, "My Margaret."

I realized the man in the picture was Mr. Paradis, forty or fifty years ago. I looked at the woman again. She was very chic and looked carefully coordinated with matching shiny patent leather purse and heels.

"That was in 1959, in Japan," he commented, flipping to the next photo.

"Here it is, this is the best one," he said.

It was a portrait done in a photographer's studio. She was posed against a plain background, turned slightly for a three-quarters view. Her dark hair was shoulder length in this shot, turned under on the ends, with bangs across her forehead. She wore a plain white blouse with pearl buttons, and a gardenia was pinned at her throat. She was very beautiful, with dramatic arching eyebrows.

"She's gorgeous!" I said.

"Yes, isn't she? This was taken when we first planned to be married."

"Her engagement picture?"

"Yes, they put it in all the newspapers. Her mother was big on that kind of thing."

"She was proud of her daughter."

"Yes, and rightly so. Margaret was an amazing woman."

"Oh?"

"She graduated from Vassar, you know. One of the few women I knew back then who finished college. Margaret was a true scholar."

"Did she like books?" I looked around the room.

"Oh yes, we shared that passion. And many others," he mused. "She was the great love of my life."

He flipped past a few more photos in the box and pulled out another one. It was a color shot and showed him, recognizable now with very long hair, a goatee and mustache, and Margaret, with two long braids and a Native-American-style leather headband across her forehead. They both wore Indian print shirts and bell-bottomed blue jeans. They were standing on a beach in front of a large palm tree. She was holding a green coconut and he held a machete.

"Hawaii, 1971," he identified the scene. He flipped again.

"Aha, you'll be interested in this one," he said, showing it to me. "1999, Hong Kong."

This one was an unframed color snapshot, faded to a greenish hue with the edges curling. It showed three people standing in front of a giant statue of Buddha. I recognized Henry and Margaret, but not the younger man, who had long dark hair pulled back in a ponytail and a very full beard.

"Who is it?" I asked.

"That's our friend Mr. Novak, don't you recognize him?"

"Ohmigosh."

"Pretty scruffy, eh?"

"He looks so…different."

"Well, it was a long time ago."

"Was this taken when you first met?"

"Yes, I think it was from that trip. He was still in college then, studying languages."

"You've been friends a long time, haven't you?"

"Oh yes. Margaret adored him. Most women do, you know." He looked at me over the top of his reading glasses. "That was taken after we opened the shop here. Business was booming, of course. Margaret had a real flair for that kind of thing! We were on a tour of Asia looking for unusual merchandise. She fell ill soon after we returned."

"I'm surprised you never had children. Was it because of all the traveling?"

"No, not because of that. Margaret wanted children very much. I was more ambivalent, though willing to do whatever would make her happy."

"What was it then?"

"Ironically, we could not conceive," he stated the fact as though still it still amazed him. "We tried everything within reason, to no avail. She miscarried a dozen times. It was very difficult, physically and emotionally.

"That must have been so hard for her."

"Margaret was a trooper," he corrected me proudly, shaking his head. "She was stalwart through even the darkest moments. She never complained. She always wanted to *seize the day*. And she was great fun. Fun to be with. Fun just to have her around."

"She sounds like a wonderful woman. I wish I had met her."

"She would have liked you, Emily."

"Oh, I hope so."

"You and she are a lot alike, in many ways."

"Really? I think I'm flattered. How are we alike?"

"Your passion for business, for one thing. Your flair for marketing," he said. "She was like that too, always dreaming up some new promotion. We did very well, financially. It was all Margaret's doing!"

"Well, I'm sure you had *something* to do with it. At least, I certainly hope so!" I said, raising one eyebrow. He just smiled and shook his head.

"You and Margaret also share an interest in our friend Mr. Novak, " he said with a grin, teasing me. "She always said he had great depth of character."

"And how do you know that I have any interest in him whatsoever?"

He looked over his glasses at me again.

"My dear, one does have one's ways of knowing things," he said. "You women aren't the only people with intuition!"

"Oh I see. So you have intuited this?"

He simply smiled.

He flipped through the photos again and stopped at a very old black and white print, brown with age and quite blurry. "Ah ha. You'll be interested in this one, Emily. Do you recognize this fellow?"

He handed me the print and I squinted to see the young version of Henry I had glimpsed in my vision of him at the docks in Asia. He stood in a warehouse with two Chinese gentlemen, one quite old and white haired, the other younger and with a mischievous expression. The memory of his giggle echoed in my ears.

"It's him! It's the floating man!"

Henry nodded. "I thought so. You're sure?"

"Absolutely. He's even wearing the same clothes. Who is he?"

"His name was Wo Tan Chung, but he changed it to Walter when he studied at UCLA. That is his father standing with him. His family owned a famous pottery based in Hong Kong in the last century. I believe it still exists, run by current generations of the same clan. Many of them were educated in Great Britain and the U.S., and they shipped merchandise all over the world. The high quality blue and white porcelain, you know. We still have a few unbroken cartons from that era in the cellar, I believe. Probably worth quite a bit more than we paid for it by now, I should think."

"What happened to Walter?" I was more interested in the man than his merchandise, even though one of his rice bowls had levitated and flown across the hallway in front of my eyes.

"They said he was a spy, and then he disappeared. Never seen again."

"The Communists took him?"

"Yes. That's what we heard. Margaret and I had left for home by then. Times were very tense in that part of the world in those days. Korea was happening, the Dalai Lama was chased out of Tibet. We were lucky to get out when we did."

"How sad for his family. Was he married?"

"Yes, yes. Passel of kids, too. Several strong sons to carry on the business."

"Why do you think he was here? I mean, when I saw him?"

"Perhaps he wanted to tell you to sell a lot of his tea sets and order more from his grandsons!"

"I suppose! Guess I'll see what I can do about that!"

"Thank you for bringing me my photographs, Emily. I've enjoyed remembering."

Mr. Paradis stood up and moved the carton of photos aside, preparing to return to his work.

"Thank you for telling me your stories," I said, turning to go.

"Just remember what Margaret would have said," he said.

I stopped in the doorway and waited.

"*Carpe Diem*, my dear. 'Seize the day!'"

"I'll remember that," I replied.

And I always have, from that day forward.

Chapter 7

The Chariot

PROGRESS, TRAVEL IN COMFORT

Description: A triumphal charioteer driving two strong horses, lions or sphinxes, usually one black and one white to symbolize duality.
Meaning: Travel in comfort, literally or figuratively. Making swift progress with a lack of impediments. Cars and other vehicles.

When I closed the store that night, Anton Novak was waiting at the curb outside. He was leaning casually against a navy blue

Mercedes sedan. He had changed into a long-sleeved silk shirt the color of dark chocolate.

I stared at the car and cautiously approached. It was very beautiful, the same way a piece of finely crafted jewelry is beautiful. It was perfectly polished. It had posh leather seats and a burled wood dashboard.

"This is your car," I said, confirming the fact. My unconscious estimation of his net worth expanded by at least one zero. It made me nervous.

He nodded. He uncrossed his arms and opened the passenger door with a flourish.

"*Mademoiselle?*" he said and raised one eyebrow. "*Vous voulez?*"

I silently slipped into the golden brown soft warm buttery leather-smelling interior of the vehicle. The wood of the dashboard was filled with swirls and circles of contrasting shades of brown and tan, polished to a high gloss super-shine. The instrument panels were outlined in shiny chrome.

He opened the driver's side door and got into the car. We were suddenly close together, nearly touching. He sat and looked at me. I looked back.

"It's beautiful," I said.

"Yes, it is," he agreed. "But I'm getting rid of it."

I felt a totally inappropriate pang of dismay.

"Oh no!"

He started the car and it hummed gently.

"Yes, I'm going to get a Prius, a hybrid. I ordered one."

He pulled out smoothly into the traffic.

"Why?" I pouted, rubbing the side of my luscious leather seat.

"I saw Al Gore's movie, that's why," he said.

"Oh, right." I said, remembering that we're all supposed to support alternative energy technology.

"Where to?" he inquired.

I told him my address, and on the way there we talked about how we had both made lifestyle changes since we'd seen *An Inconvenient Truth*, the movie about global warming. Like trying to take public transportation more, and driving around alone in our cars less. I had actually started to take the bus to work on days when I didn't really need my car. It wasn't bad, and it solved the parking problem.

"That said," I concluded, inhaling deeply the spicy leather scent, "This is one lovely machine."

"Well, I'm glad you like it," he said. He told me he kept it garaged in Manhattan, so he could use it whenever he was here on the East Coast. I gathered that was quite often, if it warranted keeping a car like this in an expensive New York City garage.

We pulled up outside the sprawling Victorian residence where I lived on the third floor.

"Shall I come in?" he asked.

I quickly tried to remember what kind of condition my studio apartment was in.

"Um...OK, sure, you can come in."

I opened my own car door before he could move, and got out of the car.

"I'll feed the cat while you change, if you like," he offered.

I did want to slip into something nicer (and sexier?). I'd worn jeans to work, and spent a long time collecting dust bunnies in the basement. I started thinking about having a champagne cocktail, possibly two. Sitting across from *him* at an intimate table. Eating salmon, perfectly broiled, with lemon butter sauce...yum.

We climbed up the twisting, turning staircase and I unlocked the door at the top. The attic of the house was all mine, one large room with four dormer windows, a skylight, a tiny galley kitchen behind a partition, and an even tinier bathroom.

Tree greeted us at the door with a polite "Mmrrrh?" He is a brown and gray striped tiger with white bib and paws. Very stylish. He goes in and out through one of the windows, getting down to the ground via a series of precarious rooftop acrobatics. He is very proud of this, and values his independence as much as I do. He sulks all winter long when I have to keep the windows closed, much preferring to come and go whenever he pleases.

Anton Novak let Tree sniff his fingers and then stroked him on the back. Tree loved it, arching up into the man's hand. Novak's touch seemed to affect the cat the same way it had me, earlier today in the park. I was impressed. Tree is a very good judge of character.

"What do people actually call you?" I asked. I couldn't imagine calling anyone "Anton" with a straight face. "I mean, like, when they *speak* to you?"

"Tony," he replied.

"Aha," I said, relieved. "I can do that."

"Can you?" he inquired, seriously.

"Yes," I said.

"Let's hear it?"

"Tony."

"Try it again," he said, closing his eyes, waiting.

"Tony," I sighed, in a sultry voice.

He shivered with mock delight. We both laughed.

"And do they call you Em? Emmie?"

"Yes," I admitted.

"And where do we keep the cat food, Em?" he asked, as Tree began to rub up against the doorway to the kitchen, leading the way.

I showed Tony where, and went to shower and change. Everything had to come into the bathroom with me, since a studio floor plan allows for very little privacy. When I emerged, dressed in black slacks and a yellow silk shirt worn open over a black lace camisole, he looked at me admiringly.

"I must say I like the idea of going out to dinner with James Bond's boss," Tony said, "Em. You look very nice."

He arose from the sofa, where he had been flipping through *National Geographic*. He smiled and came closer.

"And I have always had a crush on Mafia bosses from New Jersey, Tony," I said teasingly, hoping he had been watching *The Sopranos* and batting my eyelashes.

He laughed, thank goodness. "Well, I've spent a lot of time in New Jersey, but I am not in the Mafia, I am sorry to disappoint you!"

We went out the door and started down the stairs.

"New Jersey? Somehow I can't imagine you there," I remarked.

"Oh yes," he said, "I went to Princeton University. I spent four years in New Jersey."

This was surprising. Somehow I had pictured him at Oxford, or the Sorbonne, or some school in the Ukraine. It was hard to imagine him as an Ivy Leaguer.

When we got outside he did the one most perfect wonderful thing he could possibly have done to win my heart forever. We walked up to the Mercedes and he tossed me the keys.

"Want to drive?" he suggested, knowing the answer.

"Oh yes," I replied. "Thank you!"

I jumped into the driver's seat, slid it forward, adjusted the mirrors and fastened my seat belt. He handed me a pair of Ray Bans. I felt like a movie star.

"Where are we going?" I asked, shifting into gear and pulling out into the street. The car moved like an animal, lithe and graceful.

He leaned back in his seat and waved his hand casually.

"Just keep driving," he said. "I'll tell you where to turn."

He directed me onto the Interstate and we headed north. I stepped on the gas and pulled into the stream of traffic. The

Mercedes flew down the road so smoothly and quietly I barely
noticed when we hit seventy-five. He was playing a Putamayo
World Music CD called "Latin Lounge" on the surround sound
stereo system, singing along with the Spanish lyrics. I came up
fast behind a truck and dodged over into the passing lane to go
around it. The Mercedes responded to my every command like
a purebred horse schooled in dressage. I thought, *right*, and it
flowed gently back into the cruising lane.

We had dinner on top of a mountain in Vermont. The wide
glass sliding doors of the restaurant opened onto a flagstone
patio that perched high above the long view. We could see New
York State to the west, where a glimmer of tangerine sunset
still gilded the undersides of dark purple clouds. The Interstate
stretched out below us to the south, a thin string of twinkling
headlights that lead back toward Massachusetts. Overhead, a
million stars were sparkling. It was spectacular.

The night was warm, so we sat on the patio. Tony ordered
a bottle of champagne, specifying *Veuve Cliquot*, which I had
never tasted before. They had the salmon I'd been craving and
served it with an Asian plum sauce that was delicious. Tony
ordered the duck and offered me a bite, which I refused. When
eating something delicious, I don't like to confuse my taste
buds by mixing in other flavors. I am a purist.

We ate and we talked. He told me about growing up in
Rome with his Czech parents, who were both teachers. His
full name was Antonin Novak, but he had dropped the extra
syllable to make it easier for Americans to pronounce. His family had summered at Lake Como, on the Swiss border, before
the American movie stars discovered it and it became so fashionable. He loved boating, and had been on the crew team in
college. He had one sister, who was now living in Montreal.
After college he went to graduate school in international business and was recruited by a large multi-national firm to work
in their offices in Hong Kong. In addition to his native tongue,

he spoke fluent Mandarin Chinese as well as Russian, Spanish, French, Italian and English.

"A friend of mine and I were hired to create the standardized distribution routes for Coca Cola in Hong Kong, " he said. "Before we did it, nobody had ever formalized or kept track of this information. We wrote a software program to make it easy to update and track changes. Then we sold it back to Coca Cola, and to four other American firms who were developing the area."

His eyes shone. "That is how I won my freedom," he said. "Now I can dabble in this and that, and indulge in my obsession for collecting beautiful *objets d'art*."

"Like Mr. Paradis," I commented.

"Yes," he nodded, "Like my friend Henry. He and I first met under very unusual circumstances, you know, in a bazaar in Hong Kong. But, that is another story. Now, I want to hear about you."

I reflected that my own origins were not nearly so fascinating.

"Well, I'm originally from Iowa," I said, "Known as the Tall Corn State. My father's family owns several farms out there. They grow corn and hogs. Most of the corn is made into that new fuel people are using in the Midwest to run their cars and trucks, have you heard about it?"

"Yes," he said, very seriously, "I have heard a lot about it. This is what we want the U.S. government to start encouraging with tax breaks, instead of making more and more high fructose corn syrup, right?"

"Exactly. You can buy it all over the Corn Belt, at most gas stations. But you never see it here in the East."

"No, but I have seen something on the local news about a car that runs on vegetable oil. Do you know what that is about?"

"I saw that too. I guess some inventor figured out how to

rig his diesel engine to burn cooking oil that he gets free from the fast food places, after they've used it to make french fries and onion rings! I've seen him driving around town. It says 'This car runs on Mazola' on the trunk."

He laughed, and shook his head in amazement.

"Fantastic! I love it. Human beings are incredibly resourceful, aren't they?"

"Yes, maybe we can save the planet, after all."

We talked a bit more about our common interest in alternative energy, then he steered the conversation back to my personal history. I told him about my family, one brother and one sister, both living happily in the Chicago area. Our father died of a stroke when I was still in school. My mother lived in Florida now, near her sister. I told him about my college years here in the East, when I discovered I had an interest in art and a facility for remembering historical details. When I got to the part where I took a job at Lexi's gallery across town, I told the story with surprising calm. I hadn't actually thought about it in a while, and my intense feelings seemed to have faded.

"I'm not surprised you had trouble working for someone so domineering," he said with insight. "You are a very independent woman."

"A very powerful woman," he added, and flashed his pretty white smile at me. His hand reached across the table to barely touch my fingertips. Electricity sparked in the air between us.

I was flattered, and smiled shyly. I didn't really think of myself that way. But, it was true that I stood up for myself whenever necessary. And, I did like to run things my way. Maybe he was right! On the other hand, I warned myself not to forget he was probably just trying to manipulate me. No sense in losing my head over his compliments.

We lingered on after our meal, laughing and talking on the patio under the stars until long after all the other customers had left. I think the waiter was glad to finally see us go, though he did wait patiently.

Tony let me drive home and I sped down the deserted highway, keeping an eye out for wandering deer or moose. He leaned back in his seat, turned sideways a little so he could watch me.

"You know," he mused, "I kind of like this. I think James Bond must have the right idea."

"What?"

"I like having a powerful woman in the driver's seat," he said in a satisfied tone.

I have to admit I loved it. Corny but cute. And I always wanted to be one of Charlie's Angels, so he hit my fantasy right on target.

We traveled on down the road sitting side-by-side in the dark. I turned on the blinker and we exited the highway. Streetlights made little pools of brightness here and there on the sidewalks. Inside the car it felt cozy and secure, very intimate, lit by the hot magical glow of the instrument panels. The soft leather padded seat held my body in its warm embrace like a gloved hand. He leaned forward to turn off the radio, and I briefly caught a trace of some warm, sweet scent like cinnamon, or cloves. Suddenly I realized, it was *him*.

There was a burst of intense pleasure inside my head. I wondered if he would kiss me goodnight at the door. I pictured it. I thought about inviting him to come inside for a "nightcap." I didn't want to give him the wrong impression. Or, would it actually be the right impression? My head was spinning, and it wasn't from the *Veuve Cliquot*.

What I'm saying is, I didn't mind driving him around one bit. No, sir, not one bit. In fact, I could probably have done it all night long.

Chapter 8

Strength

LOVE OVERPOWERS FEAR

Description: A maiden sits quietly holding a lion's head in her lap. His lips are curled in a snarl, but she remains unafraid.
Meaning: Love overpowers fear. Courage. Our mental powers harness the beast in us all.

As soon as Mr. Paradis told us that the updates we'd made in the kitchen had been approved and we were now allowed to serve food, Siri and I began to put an A-frame sign out every day on the sidewalk in front of the store that said:

Welcome to Paradise
Gifts, Collectibles & Rare Books
Espresso Bar ~ Imported Teas
Scones, Soups & Sandwiches
Wonders from Around the World
Now Open for Lunch!

Laurel helped us set up accounts with several wholesale organic food suppliers. I took lessons from her on how to work the espresso machine, and got out my grandmother's recipe book. She showed me how to adapt the classic recipes to utilize the kind of clean ingredients they used in her restaurant: all natural everything, fresh whenever possible, whole grains and unrefined sugars, reduced salt, no bad fats. She was very patient and it was easier than I had expected.

Every morning first thing, I baked a batch of whole wheat scones, sometimes with organic raisins or cranberries. I kept four or five teapots at the ready on the coffee bar, with a large electric kettle filled with water, ready to boil. Several canisters of tea sat nearby, an assortment of black, green and herbal varieties.

We rearranged the furniture in the back of the room, creating seating around four of the small tables. The bar had six leather-covered stools pulled up to it, too. It was the perfect spot for weary shoppers to rest their feet for a moment, while enjoying a refreshing shot of caffeine and chocolate.

People started to stop into the store in two's and three's, some in the late mornings, some for lunch, and more in the afternoons. Most of them were well-dressed women out for fun, but some of the people who worked in the neighborhood came in for a quick lunch, too.

They ate my scones and sipped *lapsang souchong*. Some chose *cappuccino* and one of my grandmother's (updated) brownies. Last but not least, they shopped. Oh did they shop!

Merchandise seemed to fly off the shelves, and sales grew to nearly double what we had done originally. Mr. Paradis was very pleased, and told me so repeatedly.

One day he brought me down the basement stairs to show me where to find replacements for some of the items that had sold. I was glad to have his company since the atmosphere down there had always felt a little funny to me and I really didn't like going down there alone. The storeroom was stacked full of cartons, boxes, and big wooden packing crates with excelsior spilling out. The tea sets and Swedish crystal, imported stainless steel flatware, sterling silver candlesticks and wine coasters were carried in stock and occupied tall shelving units.

I thought I heard something, and turned to squint into the shadows. It was the faint echo of a giggle, like that day when I saw the floating man.

Mr. Paradis peered at me sharply. "Everything all right, Emily?"

I nodded slowly. "I just thought, for a minute...."

"Is our Chinese friend back for another visit?" he said, looking around the cavernous room. We both held our breath, peering into the maze of shipping containers. A small noise drew my attention to a wooden crate tucked away under the stairs. It was labeled with red and blue stickers inscribed with Chinese characters. As I watched, a tiny pebble rolled out from behind the crate and stopped a few inches in front of it.

"Did you see that?" my employer asked, clutching my shoulder excitedly.

I nodded, swallowing. "What do you think it means?"

"He wants us to unpack the last of the blue and white teapots, I suppose," he said, shuffling casually toward the stairs. "See to it when you can, would you?" He turned to grin at me. "There must be something very special in there that I've forgotten!" He went off whistling, elated at what he regarded as a communication from the spirit world.

I agreed to come back soon despite my uneasy feeling and followed him upstairs. I dreaded the thought of inventorying the basement and had managed to put it off indefinitely. Mr. Paradis claimed he had a fairly comprehensive list in hand, which he used for tax purposes. I decided to simply keep track of what we brought upstairs, and leave the accounting up to him.

Every few days a package or two would arrive for Mr. Paradis. It was usually books, but sometimes I would open a Fed Ex box to find antique jewelry, or hand-carved ivory fans, or a brass statue of a Chinese goddess. It seemed that eBay was a terrible temptation for a collector like my employer, especially now that his cash flow was restored.

Some days Siri came in early to make her curried chicken for lunch, or fragrant lentil soup served with pita bread. I made tuna salad with fresh dill and capers, served on soft sourdough rolls, or little delicate open-faced grilled cheese and tomato sandwiches. Carrot and ginger soup was popular, as was my newly invented version of Vichyssoise, made with potatoes, leeks and chives. We didn't offer a full menu, just one or two items every day, so between me and Siri the work was manageable.

One afternoon after lunch, I was bringing a bag of trash out to the dumpster in the alley, when I heard a clinking noise. I peered underneath the back porch cautiously. Raccoons? Rats? Ghosts? Muggers? A pale, thin face stared out at me with a fierce expression. I took a step back.

"Don't worry," the scruffy teenager said, "I won't bite you."

Dark eyes in a dirty face, surrounded by short dark hair that looked like she had cut it herself with manicure scissors. She was sitting on the ground in the shelter of the back steps.

"And I ain't stealing either. Nothin' anybody cares about, anyhow."

She wiped her nose on her sleeve. There was a big black plastic trash bag next to her. Just like the one I carried, as a matter of fact. I realized she had been going through the garbage. I saw a plastic shopping bag at her feet, with half-eaten and moldy food spilling out of it.

We regarded each other in silence for a moment. She shifted uneasily, waiting to see what I would do. I made a decision.

"Come with me," I commanded abruptly, with a firm tone.

I tossed my trash bag into the dumpster and beckoned to her.

"Wha...what?" she stammered nervously.

"Follow me," I repeated, and pointed at the back door. "Inside. It's OK, really."

She slowly emerged from her sanctuary, leaving the plastic bags under the stairs. Wearing dirty jeans, torn sneakers and a black T-shirt, she looked about fifteen or sixteen. She was anorexically thin, but I had a feeling it wasn't caused by an eating disorder.

I went up the stairs and opened the back door.

"Kitchen," I said, pointing the way. "Coming?"

Her eyes widened and something lightened in her facial expression.

"Um...OK," she said, with a studied casual air.

She slowly climbed the stairs and slipped into the back hallway. I walked ahead of her into the kitchen and went to the fridge, where I had put the leftovers from today's chicken salad. I lifted out the Tupperware container and opened it.

She drifted into the middle of the room with her eyes locked on the food, standing there awkwardly. I nodded in the direction of the kitchen table.

"Have a seat," I smiled. I took a plate out of the cabinet and filled it, then added two whole wheat rolls.

"But, I can't pay," she said, wringing her hands nervously.

Her eyes burned with intensity.

"I know," I said. I turned and put the food on the table. "We'd only get rid of it, after a while. This is just the leftovers.
"

I smiled at her reassuringly and waved her toward the table.

"Might as well enjoy it before it's spoiled," I said as she grabbed one of the rolls and stuffed it into her mouth. "Just gets stinky out there in the dumpster, right?"

She nodded enthusiastically, sitting down to devour half of the chicken salad in about thirty seconds. I poured her a glass of milk and she downed it in three gulps. She looked intensely at the remaining food on her plate, obviously still hungry but holding back for some reason.

"Do you mind if I...um...save some for later?" she asked. "I kind of promised to get back home soon. Thank you very much, and all," she added anxiously. "It's the best we've had in, I mean, it was very good. Thank you, ma'am."

"We?" I asked, "Someone at home?"

"My mother," she confirmed. "She's not been feeling too well. So she sent me out...shopping." She meant, scrounging for food in my dumpster.

I scraped her chicken salad into a plastic bag, and then I added a big dollop more. I thought again, then upended the Tupperware container and emptied it into the baggie.

"Well, I hope your mother is feeling better soon," I said, handing her the sealed bag of food.

She nodded vigorously, her eyes shining. I walked her to the back door.

"By the way," I said as she headed down the back steps. "What's your name? I'm Emily."

She turned and looked up at me, hesitating, then apparently deciding it was safe to tell me. She was clutching the bag of food to her chest like a life preserver.

"It's Amy," she answered.

"Do you live nearby, Amy?"

She gave me the wary look again.

"Um, yeah, sort of nearby."

"Because, I was thinking. Maybe you could help us out again some day. You know, with the leftovers. It's such a waste, we aren't allowed to sell them."

She stared up at me in unbelieving silence.

"Really?"

I nodded.

"You want to *give* me the leftovers, for no money?"

"Sure. Helps us to clear out the fridge. We need the space. I have to make something new every day, for the customers," I said slyly.

"Well, sure, I could help you out with that, I guess," she agreed seriously. "And, maybe I could, you know, take out the trash for you or something." She looked around the alley and spotted our large recycling bins. "I could rinse out the cans and bottles, too, if you want. There's a hose right over there," she pointed at the side of the building.

I nodded slowly in a considering way. "That would be very helpful, Amy, thanks for offering."

She smiled brightly, and ducked back under the stairs to grab the garbage bags she'd left there, tossing them into the dumpster and closing the lid neatly.

"OK then, I'd better go now!" she said, and headed down the alley toward where a little footpath cut through to Market Street. "Bye!" she called.

"See you tomorrow!" I answered.

I hoped she would return. I actually like teenagers, contrary to the feelings of many retailers, who worry about shoplifting and the large gangs of kids who hang around on the sidewalks after school, getting in the way of the paying customers and making lots of noise and litter. It didn't bother me if they wore

Goth piercings, black nail polish and green hair coloring. I looked a little strange when I was sixteen, too. It's just a way of being different from their parents, something every generation attempts to do. Until they grow up and realize how much alike we all are, that is.

I thought about Amy's mother. I wondered whether she was really sick, and where they lived. There was a house down the street where some known drug addicts lived, according to Laurel. She told me that one of the tenants had come into the restaurant in a panic one evening and asked her to call 911. I hoped this was not where Amy and her mother lived. I decided to ask around and see if the neighbors knew anything about the girl.

No time like the present! I called Laurel and invited her over for a quick espresso before the evening rush hit at her restaurant. Siri was planning to stay for a while too, taking advantage of the quiet late afternoon time to do some feather dusting of our more delicate bric-a-brac. I called Isabella Reyes too, on her cell phone. She volunteered part time at an after-school childcare center and would be getting off about now.

Bella and Laurie showed up nearly simultaneously, just as the electric kettle came to a boil. Nobody else was in the store, nor were they likely to appear at this time of day, mid-week. Siri dropped her duster, and we all gathered at the coffee bar to chat while I served up hot drinks and snacks.

Everyone talked simultaneously, but we could all still hear and understand each other perfectly well. This may seem impossible to men, but women do it all the time. It is actually a very efficient way of communicating in a group setting. Girlfriends talk partly with their words and even more with their emotions, which communicate in a psychic, unstated way. When we all talk at the same time it is not rude or like interrupting, it's our way of broadcasting our emotional states to each other. It's like touching minds. It helps create a feeling of group intimacy, which is a really good thing.

I told them about meeting the girl Amy in the alley today. They clucked with dismay at the story of her garbage picking, and approved of my decision to feed the child. None of them recognized her description or had any idea where she might live. They offered to ask around.

"And, we could ask the cards about her," Laurie offered, "If you'd like. I have them in my bag."

"You mean, Tarot cards?"

"Yes!"

"Get them, for sure."

Everyone chimed in enthusiastically.

"Let's move over here," I said, leading them to a small round table with four chairs.

We all sat down in a circle around the table. A kind of cosmic bubble started to form from our combined energies, enclosing us from the rest of the world. I could see it faintly shimmering in the air. Laurie took a dark red velvet pouch from her large handbag. She loosened the strings and pulled out a rectangular box covered with colorful pictures and lettering. Inside was her Tarot deck, fortune-telling cards that can answer questions about the past, the present and the future. Her deck was beautiful, with graceful Art Nouveau illustrations of the symbols and archetypal characters.

"Let's see what the Tarot knows about this girl. Now, everyone focus and think of our question," Laurel said, and shuffled the cards gently, over and over again. She stopped for a moment and tapped them together neatly, then inhaled and blew a long, slow breath into the cards, closing her eyes. We all stared at the deck, pushing our thoughts into the cards. Then she cut the deck in two and turned one half upside down, beginning to shuffle them again repeatedly, this time slower and with deliberation, concentrating.

With her left hand she cut the cards into three piles. She

picked them up in reverse order, so the last one was now on top.

"That's it," she said. "Here we go."

Bella clapped her hands and we all leaned forward for a better view.

Laurie laid out the cards on the table one by one, making a pattern she called the Celtic Cross. She explained the meanings of the cards as they appeared. The center of the spread showed me, the Queen of Wands, and the girl Amy, the Page of Swords. The card in the past was the five of pentacles. Laurie said it showed Amy and her mother cast out of their home, desolate and crying outside a lighted window.

The card in the present was the nine of swords, which showed a woman suffering and crying in despair, alone in bed with nine double-edged swords like vertical bars hanging above her. Laurie said it might mean Amy's mother was indeed sick, or even dying. She had definitely been struck by a disaster of some kind.

The card in the near future was somewhat puzzling. It was the eight of swords, which shows a bound blindfolded woman surrounded by a circle of eight swords, stuck into the ground to form a fence around her. Laurie said the card meant someone was a prisoner, and too weak to fight for his or her rights. The card was upside down though, which meant the interpretation was reversed. This meant the prisoner might be released soon.

The card in the far future looked better, however. It was the six of wands, which meant good news, victory and helpful friends.

The next three cards were more vague in meaning, and seemed to be talking about various other people involved in the situation. There were a powerful merchant, and a reclusive scholar, and someone who might be a priest or minister.

The final outcome card was excellent. It was the Sun, which Laurie said means success and happiness.

Siri wondered whether the prisoner was Amy's mother, sick in bed and housebound, or someone else. Where was Amy's father, we all wanted to know? Could he be the prisoner? What if he was actually in jail? If so, he might be a dangerous guy. And according to the cards, he would be getting out soon! Laurie gathered up the deck and put it away.

We ended our social hour with a quick hug all around. I liked these women, and it was such fun to see them nearly every day. I hadn't had a group of girlfriends like this since high school. In my recent past, it had always seemed like women who were friendly wanted something from me, and didn't want to give anything back in exchange. They were jealous and competitive, ready to stab me in the back if I seemed to be getting too successful or landed a desirable man. Lexi and the other women who worked at the gallery were like this. Lexi wanted to keep me under her thumb, firmly inferior to her in talent and position. She made certain to comment if I ever looked less than perfect, or stumbled over a customer's unpronounceable last name. The others gossiped about me behind my back, shushing each other slyly when I came into the room. They were jealous of my sales success. They made the old cliché about "catty" women seem quite accurate.

So far, my new friends were different. They were self-confident, happy with their lives and mates, and nurturing toward each other. I kept waiting for their flaws to be revealed and was holding back my complete trust. My own secrets were safely locked up inside. But I had started to relax and truly enjoy their company. We were talking about starting a Pilates or Yoga class at the store once a week, early some morning before we opened. If we moved the lunch tables aside, there was tons of space at the back to put down yoga mats on the floor. I was looking forward to it, even more for the fun than for the exercise.

I was also looking forward to Tony Novak's return from his trip to London. Our one date had been so great, I hadn't been able to stop thinking about it since. Of course, I still didn't really trust him either. I wondered if he was seeing someone over there, too, and decided he probably was. After all, he had been living there for years and owned a house there. He probably had a woman in New York, too, for that matter. His goodnight kiss at the door had landed politely on my cheek, perfect manners for a first date, yet somehow a little disappointing.

I received a postcard with a picture of a Rolls Royce on the front, about a week after he left town. The intriguing message was written in bold slanting letters. It said:

Dear M,
Travel is no fun without my favorite driver to
deliver me safely.
Time to come home soon!

       —A.N.

Chapter 9

The Hermit

WISE COUNSEL OFFERED

Description: An elderly pilgrim or monk stands in an isolated landscape, holding a staff and the shining lamp of knowledge.
Meaning: Wisdom. A sage offers expert advice and insight gained from a long period of contemplation and solitude. A lesson with a master.

As the third week came and began to pass, with no further sign of the elusive Mr. Novak, I sank into a mildly depressed state. I told myself it came as much from boredom as anything.

Setting up the store had been a huge task, tons of work, and now that it was over I felt a lot less productive.

Every night I went home alone and spent the evenings watching TV or reading, with Tree curled up on my lap. I called my mother and told her the whole story, touching base with her comforting optimism and love. Once a week the girls and I were getting together for what we now called "Ladies' Night," which was wonderful and so much fun, but they all went home to their families afterwards and I felt abandoned.

I tried to re-immerse myself in work, and started dreaming up a cooperative marketing campaign for the merchants in the immediate area. The ad rep from our local paper was excited about it, and offered to put together a special section for anything we might agree to do. Laurel loved the idea, and helped me distribute a flyer to the stores on Market Street, inviting the owners to attend an early morning meeting at the Green Thumb to discuss the possibilities.

Siri was sensitive to my state of mind, and kindly invited me to come home with her for dinner one night.

"It's just pot luck, no big deal," she said, shrugging with her hands tipped out. "Just us, and a couple of friends."

I modified my grandmother's recipe for chocolate cake and made two, one for the shop and one for Siri's dinner party. I used dark chocolate for the cakes and the frosting. In an inspired moment, I toasted some sliced almonds in the oven, let them cool, and sprinkled them on top of the cakes.

Siri left a little early that day to get things ready at home. I had never been to visit her before, and was curious to see her apartment. She lived in a large yellow brick three-story building that housed twelve rental units, two blocks down Market Street on the same side as our store. Isabella Reyes lived in the same building. They jokingly called it "The Palace."

"It's basically a dump, OK?" laughed Bella, when I asked her about it. "But it's got a great feeling from all the tenants, who are really pretty cool."

"The building is in disrepair," Siri added seriously. "Our landlord is not very energetic. At least the rooms are fairly large."

Bella and her husband were both coming to the dinner party, Siri told me. As were a couple of Tom's friends. It sounded like fun, and I was glad to be going out for a change. I closed the shop at six and stopped in at Sorrentino's for some vanilla ice cream, using a cake carrier I'd borrowed from Laurie and a big tote bag to carry my offerings.

I re-crossed the road and headed down the sidewalk past our corner. Next to us was a used clothing store, then a sprawling antique store, then a little tiny building set back from the sidewalk that was occupied by a seamstress who did custom-designed clothing and alterations. She was next to a hairdresser, and then came the Asian-fusion restaurant called Buddha, which smelled great. I had still not yet eaten there. My mouth watered. I glanced in the front window and saw Mei and another pretty Asian girl (her sister?) waiting on tables.

In the next block, I passed an optician, a professional building filled with lawyers' and accountants' offices, a shoe store, and a small jewelry store. Then I started closing in on my goal. I could see the big yellow brick face of it looming at the end of the block.

Two teenaged boys stood talking on the sidewalk outside the front door, one of them with a bike. A woman with a baby in a stroller sat in a folding lawn chair nearby. A small dog was leashed to the stroller, and stood alert with his tail up and wagging. They all looked at me and smiled in a friendly way as I slowly approached. The cake carrier was getting kind of heavy. It bumped against my legs.

The woman in the chair, who had glossy dark brown skin and wore a colorful African shirt and turban, observed my distress.

"Hey there, you, Superboy!" she called loudly. "Can't you see that a lady needs some help?" She winked and smiled at me. The baby grinned and hooted, waving his hands in the air. I realized it was the same little boy I had seen many times in the stroller next to Siri's daughter.

The teenagers jerked as if startled, then turned to focus on me in a dazed, distracted fashion.

"My son, Mr. Rashid the Oblivious, will now help the lady with her package," she announced, staring meaningfully at one of the boys.

Rashid seemed to snap out of it.

"Yes, Ma'am," he said politely, "Can I help you Ma'am?" He shuffled forward to take the carrier carefully out of my hands.

"Thank you, I don't want to drop it! Now I'll have to give you a piece. Do you like chocolate cake?"

He shot a shy smile over to his mother, who watched with approval as she jiggled the baby stroller with one hand.

"Yes Ma'am I sure do!"

"See," his mother observed as we entered the building, "Being polite is not such a bad thing, is it?"

"No Ma'am."

"Just like I told you, right?"

"Yes Ma'am!"

Rashid said he knew where the Rodgers family's apartment was, and led the way up to the third floor. At the head of the stairs, two apartment doors directly across the hallway from each other were standing open. Music played in both apartments, and several small children were scooting back and forth on toy vehicles. The boy carrying my cake headed straight into the door on the right, then back to Siri's kitchen, obviously familiar with the territory.

I followed at a slower pace, dodging a child riding a giant snail on wheels, and entered the living room. At the moment, no one else was there. It was extremely tidy. The furnishings were done in earth tones, and looked to be a mix of old and new items acquired over the years. Several tall, engraved brass lamps, a woven wall hanging and a hand-carved pierced wooden folding screen spoke of India. A dining table and chairs occupied one end of the room, the table set for dinner.

Siri came running out of the kitchen wiping her hands on a towel, crying, "Welcome! Welcome! Welcome to our home!" and suddenly the room was filled with people as Isabella and Rolando Reyes, Tom Rodgers, and Siri's father, Gupta, all appeared and crowded around to hug me or shake my hand. The kids crowded around too, sensing a competitor for the adults' attention, and the Reyes' little girl started to whine. She was scooped up by her daddy, who took her back across the hall to her playpen.

We three girls headed for the kitchen. Siri was roasting a leg of lamb with rosemary, to serve with curried rice. Bella had made a gorgeous salad. My cake awaited, having survived the trip with only a little superficial damage. I cut a hunk for Rashid, and put it on a paper napkin. He thanked me politely and sped off, wolfing it down as he went.

Bella poured three glasses of Chardonnay. We raised our glasses and clinked, standing together under the spotlight in front of the sink.

"To friends," I said.

"To friends," they repeated. We drank, smiling.

"Speaking of friends, I hope you're not going to kill me." Siri had turned her back to me, stirring the pot on the stove.

"What do you mean, kill you?" I asked her.

"She's matchmaking again!" Bella announced, shaking her finger.

"Matchmaking! Who? For me?" I said, indignantly.

Siri turned and grinned at me.

"No, no, not for you, not exactly that is," she said. "It's for Jim, he's the one who needs a little help, that's all."

"You mean, Jim-your-husband's-friend, that Jim?" I asked, remembering him from the opening party at the store. He was cute, as I recalled.

"Yes, Tom is very concerned about him. He just moved here, and he doesn't know anyone, and he's so lonely. "

"Oh I see. The poor boy."

"The only thing is, we kind of think there is a slight possibility that he might be, well...gay. Possibly."

"Possibly?"

"Well, maybe, he might be. He didn't actually say so. But, he never really talks about girls, you know, the way most of the tradesmen do. Tom says he seems a little embarrassed when they all start telling dirty jokes."

"So, maybe he is just more refined than they are. More polite. Or maybe he's...gay," I agreed with her logic.

"And tonight we might find out," she said cheerfully, turning back to the stove. "I invited Jim, and I invited you, the perfect temptation for any *heterosexual* single man, and, I invited my friend Larson."

"Larson?" I inquired, never having heard the name before.

Bella smiled knowingly and nodded her head.

"Larson Moss. The perfect temptation for any *gay* single man," she finished Siri's confession.

"So, you mean to dangle both of us in front of him and see which one he goes for, is that it?" I asked, incredulous.

"Yes," Siri said, picking up her wine. "That's it exactly."

"Oh, really!"

"Yes really," she said earnestly. "Whichever of you he wants to pursue a friendship with, if he does, so much the better. Isn't that true? You are all three fine, lovely people, and everyone deserves to find their happiness."

She regarded me solemnly.

"Anyhow, how are people ever going to meet each other if their friends don't introduce them?" Bella added, logical as always.

"I see," I replied. "OK. I'm in. I think Jim is cute, and I'm certainly not seeing anyone, not at the moment. I've got nothing to lose." I rolled my eyes.

We lifted our glasses and clinked them together once again.

"Let the games begin," said Bella.

"No no, no games!" I protested.

"How about, 'Gentlemen, start your engines?'" Siri suggested.

"That's better!"

We heard voices in the living room, the sound of a welcoming. Heading in to see who had arrived, we discovered Tom shaking hands vigorously with Jim, who stood in the doorway carrying a bottle of red wine. They were laughing at something we had missed. Both men looked over as we women entered the room. Jim spotted Siri and greeted her, coming over to kiss her on the cheek and hand her the wine. He shook hands with Isabella, whom he apparently knew as well.

"You remember my friend Emily, don't you Jim?"

"Yes, of course. From the wonderful shop down the street," he said, shaking my hand. He was very tall, and built solidly. His eyes crinkled up when he smiled, and his cheeks were rosy. I decided he reminded me of a young Santa Claus. Lumberjack-style. He was very friendly and seemed delighted to see me, and everyone else for that matter.

Tom opened the red wine and poured some for Jim, and for himself. We all settled down in the living room to talk. Siri had put out some cheese and crackers on the coffee table, and a little bowl of Calamata olives. It was nice. I felt like an adult. I realized I had not been out in ages.

The conversation flowed along as Tom got Jim to tell a funny story about one of their customers at work, and everyone else chimed in with laughter and comments. Jim was definitely attractive. A great guy. He looked each of us in the eyes as he spoke, including everyone and talking with big, expressive gestures. He was well spoken, and funny too. Bella and I caught eyes, and I nodded, showing my interest. I gave Jim my best, brightest smile, trying to appear responsive and attentive. He smiled back at me, obviously pleased.

Then a voice came from the door to the hall, which still stood open.

"Well, is anybody going to invite me in, or do I have to trespass?"

Larson Moss had definitely arrived, and stood posed in the doorway.

"Forgive us our trespasses, darling Siri, don't you know?" he vamped, as she sprang up and ran to greet her friend.

He was short, balding and dapper, wearing a well-cut gray suit with a black T-shirt and a tasteful gold chain. He had gold studs in his pierced ears. They hugged and she pulled him into the room to make introductions. He giggled at something she said under her breath.

"Larson," she said, "This is Emily, and Tom's friend Jim-from-work, and of course everyone else, you know. Everybody, this is Larson, my friend from the food coop." She finished and we all greeted him.

Then I glanced back at Jim again, and the mystery of his sexuality was immediately, utterly revealed. He stared at Larson with his eyes aglow. His mouth had literally dropped open. Oh, he had liked me, fine and dandy, but he was fascinated by this new guy. As in, *guy*. And Larson seemed quite taken with Jim, too. He stared up at the big man with a look of delight on his face. The sparks between them practically lit up the room.

I smiled over at Bella, who was noticing the same thing. She shrugged her shoulders, *oh well!* We caught Siri's eye too. She was grinning from ear to ear. The men all talked on and Rolando Reyes came back from across the hall with a beer in hand, to join in.

We three women excused ourselves and escaped back to the kitchen. We burst into laughter. Bella threw herself down into one of the kitchen chairs, clutching at her sides as she guffawed. Siri and I clutched at each other.

"Well, I don't think we have to worry about Jim being lonely any more!" she gasped.

"Nope!"

"And may they live happily ever after," I added. "Anyhow, I'm kind of relieved."

"You're not still pining after that handsome art dealer, are you?" Bella scolded, shaking her finger.

"I am not pining."

"Yes, you are."

"No, I'm not, I'm just—oh, nothing at all. I am feeling nothing. I'm just…bored."

I pouted and frowned. I didn't really like them getting so close to the truth.

"Don't worry," said Siri. "You are much too beautiful a person to be single for long." She put her arms all the way around me and hugged me once, hard, then let me go again.

"I know," I protested, pretending to brush her away. "OK, don't get all sappy on me. I've got a lot of good things going on for me right now, anyhow. I'm too busy to get depressed. Anyhow, I like spending time alone. I get a lot done."

The girls just smiled at me knowingly and we all pitched in to get dinner onto the table. We all gathered round, including the kids, except for the Reyes baby who was now asleep in her port-a-crib despite all the noise. Tom carved the lamb and served it like an old-fashioned host, sitting at the head of the table. Siri sat at the other end across from him and passed around the steaming bowl of curried rice. Bella dressed and tossed the salad, standing up to serve as people held out their plates. I went around with a pitcher of ice water and poured some into every waiting glass. Jim poured more wine. It was a happy, busy, noisy group as everyone filled their plates and then their mouths, and we all enjoyed each other's company.

After dessert was over and everything had been cleared away into the kitchen, where Tom and Jim were doing the dishes while Larson sat at the table and supervised, I sat on the sofa with Siri's father, Gupta, drinking tea. He preferred a green jasmine tea called "Dragon Pearls," which was light and flavorful. This was the first time I had spoken with him alone, and I enjoyed his intelligent conversation.

I was telling him about the girl Amy, who showed up every few days to do some small chores and stuff herself at my kitchen table, always holding back to save something for her mother, whom she said was still sick and unable to work. She refused to tell me where they lived, or her last name, or her mother's name, or the whereabouts of her father. I'd actually gotten pretty cagey about trying to trick the information out of her, but to no avail. I was wondering if it was a mistake not to call the police and get her some help, perhaps from the Department of Social Services.

Gupta listened carefully to what I said. He sipped his tea.

"Do you have any reason to suppose the child is being abused?" he asked.

"No, not really. She is never bruised or anything like that."

"And, the mother? Is she someone in need of protection?"

"Maybe, I don't know. Amy just tells me she is sick. Perhaps she needs a doctor, or some medicine."

He sipped the tea again and wiped his gray mustache on a napkin. He looked thoughtful, putting down his cup.

"Do you know what I think?" he said with certainty. "I think perhaps if you tell the police, they might take Amy away to a foster home, and then what will become of the mother? Who will feed her then, who will take care of her? And, how will the family ever be reunited?" He grew animated, and waved his hands in the air just the way Siri did when she got excited.

"But what should I do?"

"I think maybe it is not so hard to find these people after all," he said convincingly. "There are two places you haven't looked, that I can think of. There are probably more."

"What do you mean?"

"First, the laundromat across the street," he said, pointing. "Everyone who lives in an apartment around here goes there, at some time during the week, to wash their clothes." He smiled at me as I nodded in agreement, realizing the truth of what he said.

"Second, the church on the next corner," he continued. "They have AA meetings there with free coffee and doughnuts, and sometimes soup or a potluck dinner. People who are hungry would know this, and come there. Anyone is allowed to enter the meetings, anyone who is accepting of help."

He was right, of course. I told him so, and thanked him profusely. Why hadn't I thought of this?

"I have a good idea how we might keep an eye on the laundromat," he added. "Remember our young friend from downstairs who likes chocolate cake?"

"Rashid?"

"Yes, of course. He is the perfect investigator!"

I realized this was true, as well. Gupta was a very wise man, and full of useful suggestions tonight.

"Leave it to me," he said, rubbing his hands together with a twinkle in his eye. I got the feeling that the old fellow was actually going to enjoy this project.

"I will speak to the boy, and a few others I know. We will soon locate Miss Amy, and find out the rest of her name, too," he said.

I decided to take his sage advice, and to leave the matter in his hands for now.

Chapter 10
The Wheel of Fortune

THE UPS AND DOWNS OF FATE

Description: A clock-like wheel is adorned with symbols of the Universe. At the four corners are the fixed signs of the Zodiac: the bull (Taurus), the lion (Leo), the scorpion (Scorpio) and the man or angel (Aquarius).

Meaning: The ups and downs of fate. Destiny, fortune, luck. A risky situation. Unexpected occurrences, synchronicity, things falling into place.

The next morning I took the early bus, arrived at work around eight o'clock, and headed straight for the kitchen. Normally, I found signs of my employer's earlier presence in the room. He favored several cups of Dark French coffee in the mornings, ground his own beans, and drank it black and bitter. He was not an early morning breakfast eater. Usually he waited until the first batch of scones came out of the oven.

Today, something was different. A recently used cereal bowl was in the sink, with a spoon. I opened the fridge. Six new containers of low fat yoghurt occupied one of the shelves. I poured a cup of coffee for myself, thoughtfully, and took a sip. That was the clincher. It was a light or medium roast, maybe Moca Java. Somebody I did not know was here, probably having arrived last night, and they had brought their own food.

This could have meant any number of things, except for the final clue, which I spotted when I looked out the window into the alley. Parked next to the back porch was a brand new shiny silver Toyota Prius.

Suppressing an involuntary pang of regret for the Mercedes, I focused on the fact that Tony Novak was here, now, in this very building. At this actual present moment! It had to be his car. I ran into the little bathroom under the stairs and put lipstick on, brushed my hair, breathed deeply, and went back to the kitchen in a more grounded state of mind. I emptied the dishwasher and put the cereal bowl and spoon into it, smiling and thinking, what luck that Siri's matchmaking had worked out the way it did, or I might have ended up with Jim last night! Wow. That would have complicated things immensely. All from a lack of patience on my part. I vowed to maintain a cooler, calmer attitude from now on.

I had put two cookie sheets of scones into the oven and was well into assembling a double batch of dark chocolate brownies when I heard their voices coming down the back stairs. My pulse accelerated at the sound.

"I can tell by that delectable odor that she is here, she is at

work, and we are soon to be rewarded with a taste of Heaven,"
came Henry's voice from the back hallway.

Tony laughed and said, "Aha!" in an approving tone.

They sounded a bit giddy. I wondered if they had been up
late last night talking. The two men entered the kitchen. Mr.
Paradis looked frowsy and uncombed, and still wore his brown
plaid flannel bathrobe and slippers. Tony had obviously showered and shaved, and was dressed simply in jeans and a clean
white T-shirt. I couldn't help noticing that it clung to his body
and showed off his nicely muscled chest and arms. His straight
dark hair had grown since I last saw him, and it was still wet.
He was barefoot and looked relaxed and at home. He smiled as
soon as he saw me, his eyes smiling too.

"Hello Emily," he said quietly, intimately. "Good morning
to you."

"More coffee?" Henry asked, bustling over to the counter. "Good morning, Emily! Look what the cat dragged in last
night, at two in the morning!"

"How are you, Tony?" I asked, trying to seem casual. "It's
good to see you!"

The timer went off and I opened the oven door, mitt in
hand, to pull out the scones. I suddenly realized I was showing
him a perfect view of my backside, which has received compliments in the past, but might be sending a slightly inappropriate
message at the moment. I felt a momentary pang of embarrassment. My cheeks tingled as I flushed.

"I'm very well, thank you," he replied politely, in a distracted tone.

I turned around and saw that he was actually looking out
the window, peering at something in the alley. So was Mr.
Paradis. They gazed as they spoke, both standing with their
hands on their hips.

"What is that...person...doing with the hose, Henry?"

"She's just rinsing out the recyclables, don't worry."

"A new service provided by the city?"

"Our little protégé, a child of the streets. Emily feeds her."

"She'd better not splash my new car."

"She won't. She'll be in here in a jiffy, anyhow. Wants her breakfast."

"I see," Tony said, turning back to smile at me again. "So now you're adopting waifs, Emily?"

"I found her eating garbage in the alley," I said, transferring the hot scones off the cookie sheets onto a cooling rack. "She has a sick mother somewhere nearby, she says. She won't tell me where they live."

"You know, most people wouldn't do anything about it," Tony said reflectively. "It's admirable that you have taken the time to help."

"Yes, yes, Emily takes care of us all, don't you know?" said my employer fondly.

The two men settled into chairs at the kitchen table. They drank coffee and talked while they watched me work. I finished mixing the brownies and put them in the oven, then I took four warm scones off the rack and served them on a platter, placing it in the middle of the table. I added a crock of butter and two knives, with two small plates and a couple of napkins.

Mr. Paradis jumped up to rummage in a cupboard, coming back to the table with a jar of raspberry preserves. His guest grunted an affirmation, his mouth already full. They dug in, and I helped myself as well. Tony and I regarded each other somewhat warily as we chewed, as though many unspoken questions stood between us. There was a knock at the back door.

"I'll let her in," I said, and went to open it.

Today Amy was dressed fairly conservatively, for Amy. She wore baggy green camouflage-print pants, hacked off below the knee, with black ankle socks and black sneakers, and a ripped black T-shirt. Her ragged hair was black with Crayola red stripes, and her fingernails matched. She held a plastic shopping bag containing several cans and bottles.

"Returnables. You want 'em?" she said, knowing the answer but scrupulously honest, as always. The girl had values, regardless of her circumstances. She rinsed the recyclables every day and emptied all the trash for me. I never asked or reminded her, not once.

"No thanks, can you get rid of them for us?"

"Sure," she said, strolling into the kitchen. When she saw Tony, she stopped in her tracks and stared at him suspiciously.

"Mr. Paradis has a guest today Amy," I said, coming back into the room behind her. Tony smiled and nodded at the girl in a friendly way, his mouth still full of scone and raspberry jelly.

"A house guest, actually," Henry confirmed. "Tony will be staying with me for a while, in the rooms upstairs."

This was news to me, and Amy and I exchanged doubtful looks.

"Upstairs?" I asked, not understanding.

"On the third floor. I suppose I never took you up there? Don't use it much."

He had not. For some reason, I had assumed the third floor was an attic. I wasn't really sure how to get up there. I had never snooped further than my employer's study and the book room, not wanting to intrude on his domain.

"It's really a little apartment," Tony said. "Henry and Margaret used to rent it out sometimes."

Amy lingered in the doorway, obviously uncomfortable about entering with a newcomer in the kitchen. I noticed her looking at the fresh-baked scones and wrapped one in a paper towel, handing it to her. She silently mouthed the word "Later!" and backed out of the room, closing the back door carefully with a quiet click.

"So. Now you're back, and you're, like, moving in here?" I

asked, trying to wrap my brain around the idea. Tony seemed quite happy with my perturbation. Just then the telephone on the countertop began to ring and Mr. Paradis got up to answer it, turning his back toward us.

"Henry offered to let me stay here while I look for a new place," Tony said, sipping his coffee and waggling his bare feet.

"You're getting a new place?"

"Yes," he said, "That's why it took me so long."

"Took you so long for what?"

"Why it took me so long to get back from England," he said. "I had to deal with the agents, and sign a lot of papers, supervise the packing, and all that."

"What are you talking about?" I demanded impatiently.

He looked abashed, and spoke in a placating tone, "Don't be short, now, Emily, after all, I am homeless! You should be more *simpatico!* I have nowhere to go!"

"You are *not* homeless!" I said.

"I am," he protested. He shrugged his shoulders. "I sold my house. I literally have no home, currently."

"You sold your house in England?"

"Yes. Last week. The house in London and the Mercedes, all at once. It is almost too much to bear," he said in mock distress, one hand to his chest.

I couldn't believe it. I had no idea he was on the verge of such a major change.

"What made you decide to do this?" I asked.

"I've been thinking about it for a while," he said, seriously. "I actually put the house on the market last year. It didn't sell, so I took it off again. Then a couple of weeks ago I heard from a friend who is a real estate agent. Her client was looking for a Georgian townhouse just like mine. They made me a good offer. I decided it was the right time."

"So you just, sold it," I said, amazed, thinking that most

people agonize over major decisions of this type. "Just like that."

"Yes, Emily, just like that," he confirmed. He looked me straight in the eye, and for a moment I felt we were together in a long dark tunnel, just the two of us, with the rest of the world closed off and far away.

"I can live anywhere I like, you know," he said, rising to walk toward me.

"Yes, I know," I said, taking a step backwards.

"It was lucky she called when she did. I tell you, I was sitting there wishing I could just get rid of all my old baggage and start over again, and the phone rang. It was synchronicity. It was meant to be."

There was a tiny white patch of shaving cream on the jaw line just below his left ear. I absentmindedly reached out with my dish towel and wiped it off. He took another step toward me. We stared at one another.

My employer hung up the telephone with a melodious "Farewell!" and turned back to face us where we stood silently in the middle of the room.

"All right now, children," he said, breaking the spell and taking Tony by the arm to steer him toward the back hallway. "It's time to get to work. You mustn't distract Emily from the paying customers, Tony, it's bad for business!"

"Oh now, Henry, I would never do that!" Tony exclaimed with a quick backward look in my direction. The men started up the back stairs and I heard Tony say, "I've brought some interesting things to show you, my friend. Somewhere in my luggage…" Their voices faded as they continued up the stairs and were gone.

I danced silently around the empty kitchen for a minute or two, shaking off the nervous energy. I couldn't stop grinning. I saw a long beautiful flash of something wonderful and magical coming into my life, at last. It was like looking into a telescoping tunnel into the future, a glimpse of happiness and love. It wasn't my imagination or wishful thinking this time, it something that really could happen. I could tell the difference, now. I was late opening the store, but nobody was waiting so it didn't really matter. At least I didn't burn the brownies. And that was a minor miracle, considering my distracted state of mind.

*   *   *

When Siri came to work that day she had a message for me from her father, Gupta. It seemed the "Market Street Irregulars," as the old man called the teenagers he had rallied to watch the neighborhood, had come up with some information. A girl who met Amy's description had been seen doing laundry and Rashid had struck up a conversation with her, confirming her first name. One of the other boys had tried to follow her when she left, but had lost her somehow. She had disappeared again, for the moment. But Gupta felt he was "closing in on her," as Siri put it.

"My father is really enjoying this Sherlock Holmes fantasy, you know," she laughed. "He is the perfect armchair detective!"

"Well, he is having success where nobody did before," I said.

"Yes, but it's too bad the boys lost her again. Bad luck," Siri said regretfully.

"Well, maybe she's not ready to be found. Maybe it's not the right time," I replied.

So much has to do with luck. Luck and timing. Or is it really luck? If we influence reality simply by being observers of it, as the science of quantum physics says, by simply *thinking* about it, then is there such a thing as luck? Perhaps we actually make our own destinies in a much more pro-active way than merely by being the passive recipients of luck. What if we actually create destiny, not just from our life choices and the way one thing leads to another, but what if we *dream* our destinies? As in, "dream them up." Conjure them. Perhaps not with deliberate intention, but certainly with desire, wishes and thoughts. Thoughts can build a bridge to the future of one's choice. That has nothing to do with luck, and everything to do with the power of the human mind.

This might be where the timing comes in. When the dreamer creates his or her destiny, it's by imagining the future. This action automatically defines a path towards that future, which is like a line of dominos standing on end. The path to the dreamed future is a circuitous route, and may take many forks or turns along the way. The dominos are events, people, ideas, etc., the basic components of everyday life. When a domino on the path falls, it needs to hit the next one in the sequence. You can't jump over one or two and move on. You may feel impatient and want to, but there are probably lessons to be learned, events to occur, or people you need to meet, before you get to the step you yearn for. It's just not the right time, yet.

Had I conjured up the ad in the paper that led me to this job? I had certainly dreamed of something similar coming along. Had Tony Novak conjured up the buyer who suddenly appeared to purchase his house, just when he was wishing he could get rid of it? He seemed very sure that the timing was not merely fortuitous.

Was it just "bad luck" that Amy had disappeared before the boys could find out where she was going? Or did she have such a solid willpower investment in remaining hidden that nobody could possibly break through? If so, when she decided to let down her guard and accept help, we would find her. Maybe Amy had conjured me up. Maybe her self-created destiny was to find a safe haven about now, a place for her to go and seek nourishment emotionally and physically, to make her stronger for the tasks she had set for herself.

Luck, or destiny. Either way, sometimes the tide of life seems to be with us, and sometimes we have to fight against it to get where we want to go. I decided to stop worrying and float along with the current for now, to see where it would take us.

Chapter 11

Justice

THE CONSEQUENCES OF OUR ACTIONS

*Description: The lady Justice holds the scales held
in one hand, a double-edged sword in the other.
She deals out inescapable consequences.
Meaning: For everything we do, there is eventually a reaction. Whether bad or good, it is what
we earned and what we ourselves set in motion.*

Alexandra Gladstone was a *summa cum laude* graduate of Smith
College, an art history major. She was smart as a whip, blonde
and beautiful. Her parents lived in a mansion in Westport,

Connecticut, and they summered on Nantucket Island. Every winter she went skiing in Colorado or Switzerland, and early every spring she went to the latest fashionable Caribbean island where handsome guys wearing skimpy swimsuits deliver drinks in coconuts on the beach. I could have easily lived on what Lexi spent on cosmetics and bath products. We participated in two totally different realities.

After college, Lexi's Mummy and Daddy got a job for her at a chic New York City art gallery, where she rose rapidly through the ranks to become the manager. Lexi credited two things for her speedy success. One, she was absolutely ruthless about business and brooked no dissent from her underlings. Two, Mummy and Daddy had a lot of rich friends who bought expensive original art from her for their vacation homes in Boca Raton, Aspen or Tuscany, and for their primary residences in Washington, Boston or Manhattan.

Mummy and Daddy's friends lunched with Lexi and listened to her talk about the artists she represented and how brilliant they were. She spoke very well, and knew an impressive array of art history trivia that seasoned her conversation like fresh-ground pepper. She looked perfect, always. The women thought Lexi was darling, and the men thought she was extremely hot. She convinced them that art was a marvelous financial investment and said they would be considered trendsetters by all of their friends. She hinted that their homes might be featured in a magazine like *Architectural Digest*, or even, on a television show like the ones on the H&G Network.

Some of her customers brought their interior designers to the lunches. Lexi didn't like that much, because she wasn't good at sharing control of a client. But then she learned to manipulate the designers, too. They were even more vulnerable, in a way. She discovered that they wanted something from her. They considered her a valuable contact. They wanted her client list. And she wanted theirs, so that worked out nicely.

They all had lunch and champagne together at the most popular new restaurants in Manhattan, toasting each other in celebration of their perspicacity and wonderfulness. Afterwards everyone would get into a couple of cabs and go over to the art gallery.

This is when Lexi moved in for the big close. She walked her clients around with their espresso or brandy, looking and talking, and let them pick out a few pieces that went with the décor under consideration. Then Lexi snapped her fingers and gave a few short commands to the staff. They scurried to quickly pull out a few more pieces from the back room. These were generally similar to the client's original choices, but at least twice as expensive. She was very good at matching people with pictures, and the clients nearly always loved her suggestions. Rarely did any of them leave without purchasing at least five works of art. Many of them returned for more, bringing along their friends. Lexi's network of art buyers grew geometrically, like algae in a pond.

They bought so much art that eventually Lexi decided she really ought to be a partner in the business, rather than an employee. Her boss felt differently. So Lexi took her rich art buyers out of the big city and back to the small town environment where she had been so successful earlier in her life. She moved back to New England. She used investment money obtained from her parents to open her own art gallery in our vital downtown area, and hired two bright, pretty girls to run it for her while she went to the day spa and had those long, lucrative lunches.

I was the lowest bump on the totem pole when I worked for Lexi. I was the dirt beneath her diamond-studded heel. In her sparkling blonde presence I felt drab, dull and ugly. When she corrected me in front of a client, making a joke at my expense, I felt stupid. After a few months, I felt angry, too. I had originally thought the job would be an opportunity for me to

increase my knowledge of art retailing and make some connections of my own. Eventually I realized that I was there to
be a reasonably presentable shoplifting deterrent and cleaning
person.

Pretty much everything I did was either wrong or insuf-
ficient, in Lexi's view. And she did not hesitate to say so, in
scathing terms. It was not a job that was good for my self-image.
It didn't pay very well, either. And she protected her connections and her information so well that I didn't really have a
chance to learn from her. The day she insisted that I clean the
bathroom and I quit on the spot, I really hadn't planned it. But
it was obviously the right thing to do. I didn't struggle, I didn't
argue with her. I just walked out.

I figured I was leaving a bad time behind me, and moving
forward into what I hoped would be a more productive, positive era. It was a learning experience in terms of emotions and
people skills. I meditated for weeks on dissipating my anger,
trying to let it go. I realized how destructive anger could be to
the person who indulges in it. It actually made me feel kind
of sick and achy, nauseated. Emotionally, I felt weak and out
of control. It made me think like a victim, which was the last
straw as far as I am concerned. I had to get this anger out of my
system, out of my life.

When I answered Mr. Paradis' help wanted ad, I was still
in the process of working the anger out of my heart. I wished
for the self-control to will it away, and keep it away. As time
passed, and the magic of lots of good, hard, creative, productive work soothed my spirit, I started to feel better about what
had happened. I moved on.

Now I didn't even think about Lexi or the gallery very
often. We still lived in the same town, but obviously we did
not frequent the same places because I never ran into her. This
wasn't too surprising. I read about the openings at her gallery
in the newspaper. I assumed she was still making tons of money

and living the lifestyle of the rich and fabulous. I assumed she couldn't have cared less what had happened to me when I quit, and immediately replaced me with another reasonably attractive live body.

After lunchtime on the day of Tony Novak's return, I left Siri in charge of the shop and went over to the Green Thumb to attend a meeting of the Market Street merchants. We had been talking about organizing a kind of street fair as a promotional event, something timed to coordinate with the downtown sidewalk sales that took place at the end of every summer. We wanted to rope off the intersection of Crescent and Market to admit only walking traffic for that day and evening. We were planning to use the space to put up a tent with a big stage and have free entertainment including live bands, street magicians, clowns, jugglers, story-telling for kids and strolling musicians. We thought it would help to draw new people to our business district during the sidewalk sales, since we were only a short walk from Main Street.

Our ad rep from the newspaper loved the idea and talked to her publisher, who offered to sponsor the event. He wanted to print up a special advertising insert for that weekend's edition, listing the events and profiling the performers and the stores who were hosting. He was giving us a discounted rate for ads in the insert. He had put us in touch with a representative from the state arts council, who was trying to get us some grant money. The most popular local radio station wanted to sponsor it too, now, and volunteered their DJ's to act as announcers for the musical performances. The whole plan was falling together beautifully.

I was in charge of the budget, and could happily see that while it wasn't going to be cheap to put this event together, the bottom line investment for each neighborhood business would be pretty reasonable, considering the amount of advertising and marketing value we could derive from it.

I was on my way to present the latest figures to our group, who had gathered in the closed restaurant. I could see them milling around through the glass front of the enclosed porch. I hurried across the street and opened the lime green swinging doors, rushing into the room. And there she was, big as life, looking absolutely stunning, as usual.

Lexi had chosen to sit at the very center of the bar, with her elegant legs crossed at the knee. If the long, shining, streaked blonde hair didn't get your attention, then those amazing slim, tanned legs were sure to do it. A cherry red high-heeled sandal dangled from her extended foot with its matching cherry-red toenails. She was sitting directly in front of the doors where she couldn't be missed by anyone who came into the room, or vice versa. She wore a fluttery white sleeveless sundress, and looked like she had just come off the ferry from Nantucket. She slowly turned to see who had entered.

When she saw me, her cornflower blue eyes narrowed subtly. But she greeted me with a wide smile and unexpected enthusiasm, like an old pal, jumping down off the bar stool with her arms spread for a big Hollywood hug and two cherry-red air kisses. She smelled like lilies of the valley.

"Emily! Darling, how *are* you?" she said with a theatrical tone sure to be heard all over the room full of people. She grabbed me by the upper arms and held me with her perfectly manicured cherry-red claws. They sank into me a little, though it must have looked like a friendly gesture to everyone else. And everyone was definitely watching.

"Don't you look just *darling!*" Lexi gushed sweetly. "I love that denim skirt! Blue was always such a great color on you, Em."

"Um…thanks, you look wonderful too, Lexi. Have you been at the beach? You're so tan," I replied politely, trying to gather my wits.

She laughed dramatically, shook her hair, and twirled

around like a model showing a new gown.

"Yes, I'm living the good life this summer! Back and forth to the Island."

She threw back her head, shook her streaked blonde mane again and laughed, making sure that anyone who had not been watching before was definitely watching us now. She gracefully hopped back up on the barstool, showing off those long legs again.

I was trying to figure out what she was doing here. Her gallery was on Main Street in the prime retail district, so she was not a member of our neighborhood merchants group. She was sitting next to our ad rep from the paper, Lisa Gordon, who was deep in conversation with Rocco Sorrentino. I noticed that he looked worried. He shot me a meaningful look of dismay as he asked Lisa a question. Before I could do anything, I heard the café doors open behind me and everyone looked towards the entrance.

"Sarah!" Lexi announced, jumping down off the stool to give the air-kiss treatment to the newest arrival.

It was Sarah Bennet, president of the Downtown Business Association. The DBA was city-wide, so we were all members. Sarah was a retail marketing expert, hired to run the organization. Most of the marketing efforts made by the DBA seemed to benefit the central retail district much more than outlying neighborhoods like ours. We are mixed residential and commercial, and literally on the other side of the railroad tracks. That's why I had dreamed up this idea for how to pull people off the main drag and around the corner to visit us while they were in town. We were doing this on our own, not through Sarah's organization. In fact, she had not been invited to attend the meeting, as far as I knew. But then, neither had Lexi.

Rocco stood up and raised his hands.

"OK now everybody," he said loudly, "We're all here! Time to start! Everybody take a seat. Here, Mom, you sit here," he pulled out a chair in the front of room and gently seated Josie. Everyone settled down, and I sank into a chair at the table where Laurie and John sat. I gave Laurie an amazed look. She looked at Lexi, then back at me, and discretely mimed gagging behind her hand. I leaned closer to John, who sat next to me.

"What's going on?" I whispered.

He shrugged his shoulders and shook his head silently with a concerned look on his face, crossing his arms. Rocco raised his voice again, stating that the DBA had heard about our plans and had asked Sarah Bennet to drop in today and speak with us.

"I'll let her tell you the rest," Rocco said, sitting down. He looked grim.

Sarah took over the meeting smoothly, obviously a practiced hand. She managed to give us the bad news without appearing negative or disagreeable. She was a true politician. Lexi watched her talk with a little ecstatic smile playing across her lips, as though she were hearing beautiful music or having her feet massaged. This did not bode well for the rest of us, I suspected.

The DBA's members had learned about our promotion from the newspaper and radio advertising reps, Sarah told us. The DBA was concerned about the fact that we had not come to them with this idea, not for their *permission* of course, since that obviously wasn't necessary, but for their advice and collaboration. Sarah was very diplomatic. She congratulated us on our imagination and our marketing acumen. She called the idea, "fantastic!" Then she started to steer things a different way. Some of the DBA members on Main Street had a few concerns, she said, that needed to be addressed. We had to understand that they counted on the income from the sidewalk sales to weather the slow summer vacation season. The Main Street merchants were worried that our free entertainment would detract from their sidewalk sales, pulling traffic away from the center of town. She looked pointedly at Lexi, a prominent Main Street merchant. Lexi smiled at her calmly, not looking worried at all. Why should she? The gallery certainly didn't count on the income from selling a few prints and picture frames on the sidewalk to fill its coffers. Whoever Sarah was talking about, it obviously did not apply to Lexi. She had to be here for another reason. I wondered what it was.

"Sarah?" I said, raising my hand. She nodded at me. "What exactly do the Main Street merchants want us to do about this, er…problem?"

"Well, there have been several suggestions. But the simplest idea was proposed by Alexandra Gladstone here from the Gladstone Gallery," Sarah replied, waving her hand toward Lexi, who sat up straighter and tossed back her hair.

"The obvious thing to do, to keep everyone happy, is for you people to have your little event on another weekend," Lexi said, with a charming smile. She spoke as though delighted to have discovered such a fair, simple solution. "That way, everyone will get more attention, with no competition for the spotlight!"

Silence in the room followed her statement. Rocco and Josie looked over at me.

"But," I said slowly, "The whole idea was to piggyback the two events. So we can all make the most of each other's advertising money, and have more of a draw to pull people into town. The timing is essential to make the budget for our event work."

Lexi turned to focus on me, with a nasty glint in her eye.

"Why, Emily, you can't possibly be saying that you want to take advantage of all the effort and money spent over the past ten years to make our sidewalk sales a success! Steal our customers away, and give us nothing in return!" She regarded me triumphantly. "Anyone with a bit more, well, *experience*, must see that it just isn't fair to the rest of us after all our hard work."

I wondered how much hard work exactly she had put in, and decided it was probably zip.

Rocco stood up and took the floor.

"I think we all agree that we certainly don't want to piss off the Main Streeters," he said with a grin, lightening the mood and drawing a few chuckles out of the crowd. "Sarah, what if we think about coming up with some kind of compromise on this?"

Sarah nodded her head in agreement, as compromise was her business.

"I think we can give it a try," she said. "Do you have anything specific in mind?"

Rocco looked over at me, hoping for a contribution.

"Well, maybe there is a way," I said, thinking very fast. Everyone looked at me expectantly. Lexi frowned, but nobody saw her except me.

"For example, what if some of the entertainment isn't just down here? What if we had the street performers cover Main Street too?" I started to get excited about the idea. This could actually benefit us, in the end.

"Street performers?" Lexi asked, with a dubious tone.

"Clowns, jugglers, magicians and buskers — strolling musicians, that is," I answered. I already knew she was going to react negatively, but everyone else was nodding their heads and making sounds of approval.

"We could still rope off the intersection here and have the stage events under a tent, so there's something special to pull people down this way," Rocco observed. "The police would never let that happen in a high traffic area anyhow, so it isn't an option for Main Street."

"Yes, and the street performers would actually add some new interest to the sidewalk sales on Main," Sarah added. "I think it would be fun, festive!"

"Yes," I agreed, "And you could mention it in your adver-

tising, which would be a great added feature!" Plus, I thought
silently, we could put posters up along Main Street advertising
the events in the tent, so all the shoppers would be sure to see
them.

"Yes, yes," Sarah said, picturing it and nodding her head.
She looked at our ad rep, who nodded enthusiastically.

"We were planning to run profiles of the Market Street
merchants in the special insert," Lisa said, "But we could cover
selected businesses from all over downtown." She spoke to Lexi
anxiously. "We could do a little article on your gallery, Lexi!
How would that be?"

Lexi was still frowning, but nobody paid much attention
to her as they all discussed the new development. She did not
reply to Lisa's suggestion and sat silently, radiating displeasure.
She looked at me with an expression of extreme distaste, as
though she had encountered a nasty smell. I ignored it, and
went up to Sarah so she could hear me over the noisy conversation.

"Do you think the rest of the DBA will agree to the idea?"
I asked.

"I think so," she replied. "I'll bring it up at the next meeting of the sidewalk sales committee." She looked at me. "This
actually might be a shot in the arm for our tired old event.
Sometimes people get sick of the same old thing, you know? I
like your creativity, Emily!"

She and Lisa, who had been listening, both smiled at me
approvingly.

"We should get you to join the committee!" Lisa suggested.

"Yes, that's a great idea! Why don't you come to the next
meeting with me?" Sarah said. "You can make this suggestion
yourself. You'll represent this neighborhood, and we'll work
something out that is to everyone's benefit!"

"Of course we'll want to contribute to the expense of the

street performers, you understand," she added quietly, turning her back to Lexi slightly. "We know how much these things cost."

"Sure," I answered. "That can be arranged!" I looked past Sarah at Lexi, who was glaring at me. But she knew when she had been defeated. She picked up her purse off the bar and slung the strap over her tanned shoulder.

"Well, I must fly!" she proclaimed with a bright, false smile. "A client is waiting."

She hugged and air-kissed Sarah and Lisa, in that order. When she came toward me I almost stepped away. I didn't like the look in her eye.

"*Bitch!*" she hissed privately in my ear as she hugged me, grabbing me with her talons when I stiffened in response. "I'll never forget what you did! You'll get what you deserve."

That's when I finally realized what all of this was about. She was still mad at me for defying her. She was willing to hurt the whole neighborhood just to get back at me! I remembered being worried that she would do something to scare off any prospective new employers, if they called for employment verification. I didn't think Mr. Paradis had ever spoken with her. If he had, it didn't seem to have made any difference.

"I'll be sure to remember," I said, pulling away from her. She let go of me reluctantly, but Rocco came over just then and threw his arms around both of us, a wide grin on his face.

"So, you see what can happen when we all cooperate, Ladies?" he said happily. "This will be the biggest sidewalk sales event ever!" He stood between us, shielding me from her. He turned his head toward me and winked.

"Yes," I said, "And how lucky for us that the DBA might pay for part of the entertainment expense! We're so grateful for the community support, Lexi!"

I turned towards her and raised one eyebrow, daring to pull the tiger's tail. She looked furious, but said nothing and gave

Rocco one of her brilliant smiles. Without another word, Lexi swept out through the front doors and was gone. Rocco and I stood and watched her exit. He shook his head in disbelief and gently held my upper arm, pointing to the crescent shaped indentations she had left there with her fingernails.

"So what did you do to the Countess Vampira in a former life?" he asked. "She wanted to rip you apart!"

"It's a long story," I said, rubbing the red marks. "I didn't realize she took it so personally."

"I'm glad she didn't screw things up for us today," he said seriously. "But I get the feeling she's not done trying."

"Don't worry about Lexi," I reassured him. "She carries around a lot of bad karma for all the nasty things she does."

"Yeah, I guess what goes around, comes around, right?" Rocco said. His mother had come up behind us and was listening.

"You talkin' about that skinny woman with the bleached hair?" Josie asked, to the point as always. "Grouchy, isn't she?"

"She just needs more fiber in her diet," said Laurel, coming up to join us. She smiled innocently, and we all laughed.

"I guess we should schedule our next meeting for after I talk to the DBA," I said. "What they say will probably affect the budget, so my numbers aren't accurate anymore."

Everyone agreed, so Rocco made the announcement and the merchants started to file out the door and back to their places of business. Sarah Bennett promised to call me soon with the date and time of my presentation to the DBA. Rocco and Josie said goodbye and headed across the street, the big man bending over to listen as she chattered away. John had vanished into the kitchen. Soon, Laurie and I were the only ones left in the room.

"So, what's new?" she asked, with a speculating look at the big smile on my face.

"Guess who just moved in upstairs across the street?"

"Moved in? I can't imagine."

"It's *him*," I said, "He's back!"

"Aha! Our wandering hero returns! Well, well, well!"

"Yes, I found him there when I got in this morning. And guess what else?"

Wisely, she waited for me to tell her. I did, explaining the whole situation. When I described his sudden decision to sell his house and move back to the U.S., she looked at me with a serious expression.

"Now you be careful, Em! Maybe there's more to the story."

"You mean, like, maybe he's a spy or running from the law or something?"

I pretended to be serious, but she wasn't pretending.

"I mean, like, maybe he wanted to leave something behind in London, or some*one*."

Now, that was a thought. I had figured he was probably dating somebody over there, back when I hadn't heard from him for so long.

"He did say something about getting rid of old baggage," I mused.

"See?" Laurie said warningly. "Be careful! You don't want to get too involved if he just split up with somebody. Rebound love doesn't last long."

I agreed to proceed with caution. I wondered how I could find out more about Tony Novak's personal life, without seeming to intrude. I suspected that Mr. Paradis might know, if they were as close as it appeared. My employer had definitely encouraged my interest in his friend. He had said that Margaret would approve. That meant as far as the old man knew, there was nothing to hold us back from developing a relationship. But there might be things, or people, of which he was not aware. I tossed these ideas back and forth in my mind.

I waited for the walk light and crossed the intersection

diagonally, thinking about what had happened with Lexi. It was clear to me that she felt totally justified in trying to ruin my plans. The action that I had taken in self-defense all those months ago, she regarded as an unwarranted attack. Even though I had behaved in a passive way, not engaging her in debate or putting up a fight. In her world, anything that inconvenienced or diminished her in any way was wrong, evil. She thought I had deliberately tried to hurt her business by leaving them in the lurch when some new clients were on the way over. I wondered who had finally cleaned the toilet that day. I could guarantee it wasn't Lexi. But in any case, I doubted she sacrificed any art sales because of my unexpected absence.

It was ironic how things had turned out today. Lexi had tried to make us change the date of our event so we wouldn't get any benefit from the DBA's planned promotion, hoping our plans would fail and I would look stupid. But instead, now it looked like they were going to end up paying part of the tab and giving us some additional advertising power. Well, it served her right!

I realized that was only true from my point of view. In addition to the scales, Lady Justice holds a double-edged sword and it cuts with both sides. We all need to think very carefully before we decide that our views are perfectly justified, and our opponents are totally in the wrong. In fact, that is probably a very rare occurrence. Because every action has a reaction. You can never really be sure where people are coming from when they act negative or unpleasant. Sometimes they think they're defending themselves. I hoped that I hadn't inadvertently set something in motion that we would all regret when it came time to weigh the final outcome.

Chapter 12

The Hanged Man

SURRENDER TO SPIRITUAL GROWTH

> *Description: A man hangs upside down by one foot, and appears quite comfortable. Rays surround his head, where amazing realizations are taking place.*
> *Meaning: Deliberately attempting to achieve a higher consciousness, contemplation of universal truths, meditation.*

When I returned to the shop, I found Siri serving tea to two elderly matrons dressed in floral print dresses who sat at one of the little tables in the back of the showroom. They were discussing birds and looking at a couple of framed Audubon prints, obviously under consideration for purchase, which Siri had displayed nearby on an easel.

"Yes it was, dear, it was a Great Blue Heron!" one of the ladies insisted triumphantly, speaking in a small quavering voice.

"No, dear, we saw the Great Blue when we went birding in North Carolina. You've forgotten!" the other piped up emphatically, trembling with vehemence.

The two frail, gray-haired women sipped their tea and bickered affectionately. They seemed to be having a wonderful time. Siri looked over at me and smiled, the picture of graceful self-control. She was always patient, always considerate, always polite, and she always seemed to be truly happy. She was a paragon. I yearned to be as composed and balanced as Siri. Today she was dressed in one of her saris, various shades of purple and blue. She looked like a water goddess, cool and deep.

"Hi Em!" she said in a bright voice. "Cup of jasmine tea?"

I accepted gratefully. The two bird ladies had fallen silent and were looking at me attentively. I drank tea and chatted with them for a few minutes. They were very talkative. We considered the Audubons, which were very nicely framed in gold. I mentioned the prices I had seen on the Internet for similar pieces. Looking at each other and nodding, the ladies both said, "We'll take them!" We clinked teacups all around.

"Oh I do think Father would have approved of the expenditure, don't you dear?"

"Oh yes, dear! He would have adored these prints."

"They'll look lovely in the breakfast nook, don't you think?"

"Lovely, yes, or in the hall by the mirror, perhaps?"

"Well as long as Father would approve, it is his money after all."

"Oh yes, it is. I think he would feel it is a good investment, you know. After all, you can't go wrong with these collectible prints."

"That is true, dear, very true."

Each of the ladies was carrying a little black pocketbook, nearly identical, and they both pulled out reading glasses and wrote checks for exactly half the total due. They had different last names, but we learned that they were sisters. They had both been married and were now widows with grown children. The sisters lived together in the house where they had grown up. When their father died, he left it to them.

"We didn't want to move in with any of the kids," said Irene, the little one.

Her sister Rose nodded.

"Young families need their space, especially when the babies are growing," she said.

"Anyhow, " said Irene, "We like our independence!"

They looked at each other and chuckled mischievously. In their eighties, they still had plenty of *joie de vivre*. And they obviously adored one another. It was inspiring. After the upsetting scene across the street, I started to feel less anxious. Being near Siri was like a balm in itself. After saying goodbye to our new customers, we cleared off the tea table and brought the dirty dishes into the kitchen. I told Siri what had happened at the meeting. She looked at me with concern.

"Emily! This is the time for you to finally deal with your feelings about this woman! You see what happens when you allow things like this to drag on?"

"What do you mean by that?" I asked. "How can I deal with it? We just hate each other, apparently."

"That is a *terrible* thing to say!" she cried, getting excited and waving her hands.

"Why is it so terrible?"

"Because if you accept this reality, if you allow this terrible negative emotional state to exist, then you bind it to you. It becomes a part of your existence. It attracts more negativity. You've got to abandon the hate, not embrace it."

"How do I *do* that, though?"

Siri put her arms around me and held me.

"You will find the way, Em. You just need to think about it."

"I don't like the way I feel about her. And she…she attacked me!"

"She probably doesn't like the way she feels about you, either."

"I don't know, she's hard to understand. We're so different, we would never react to things the same way."

"Perhaps that is the key to understanding," Siri suggested. I stared at her, thinking about what she had said.

"I'll work on that," I agreed. "I think you're right!"

What if I could use my knowledge of Lexi's character to somehow convince her that she didn't really want to destroy me, after all? That would be an improvement. I was more than ready to let go of my side of it, now. I realized that until today, I hadn't had an angry moment since I came to work on Market Street. My life had been filled with creativity, friendship and happiness. I had been feeling terrific—empowered, productive and successful. Siri was right, there wasn't room or time in my life for this kind of trouble.

*   *   *

That evening, Mr. Paradis decided to celebrate the arrival of his new housemate by taking Tony and me out to dinner. I found out about this at closing time, when the two of them came down the front stairs and appeared in the doorway to the showroom, obviously dressed for an excursion. Tony had added a black leather jacket and running shoes to his jeans and T-shirt, and Henry wore a colorful Moroccan cap and vest over his habitual black sweats and slippers. It seemed we had reservations at Buddha, the restaurant owned by Mei's family. The men stood side by side and looked at me appealingly.

"We will be honored if you would join us, Emily?" Henry said, on his best behavior.

"If you're not busy tonight?" Tony added. "I hear the food is very good!"

I liked the fact that he didn't assume I would automatically drop everything to go out with him on his first night back in town. I would probably have done so in a flash, if I had plans, which I did not, so it wasn't an issue.

"I heard the same thing," I said. "I met one of the owners recently. I'd love to, thank you!" My two dates looked pleased, and we all went outside together.

I locked up the shop and the three of us strolled down the sidewalk enjoying the balmy summer evening. Mr. Paradis walked along slowly with his hands clasped behind his back, surveying the neighborhood. I realized that I had no idea what he normally did in the evenings, though I suspected he didn't get out much. There were usually signs to be found in the morning that he had cooked a meal and eaten it at the table in the sitting room. Tony walked along next to me, letting his hand bump lightly against mine every few steps.

"How was your day, Emily?" he asked.

"Eventful. Not very good, I guess. Challenging."

"What happened?"

"I ran into my arch enemy at the meeting about our big neighborhood promotion. She tried to ruin the whole thing."

"The art gallery woman?" Henry had been listening.

"Yes, how did you know that?" I asked him, surprised.

"Oh, believe me, I could tell she was no friend of yours, when she called."

"She called? When?"

"She called me back, after I called her. Checking your references."

"What did she say about me?" I was curious.

"Oh, not much," my employer said, "I gathered she was not happy with your abrupt departure."

He seemed unconcerned, while I was nonplussed to discover he had known all about it. It was embarrassing to me for some reason. I felt guilty.

"Don't worry, my dear," he said, patting my shoulder. "I could immediately tell from the way she spoke why you decided to leave!"

We arrived in front of the restaurant and I looked into the big windows as we approached the entrance. The interior was decorated in a warm red with black accents. A screen of live bamboo grew nearly to the ceiling and a long black-and-gray speckled granite sushi bar stretched along one side of the room. A young man wearing a neat white shirt and black pants met us at the door smiling, a stack of menus in his hands.

A moment later I saw Mei coming from the back of the restaurant, saying, "Hello! Emily! It's so good to see you again!" She took the menus from the young man and he turned to seat another party as she led us inside. Mei brought us to a table near the open window where we settled down to sniff the delicious aromas that were emerging from the kitchen. I introduced Mei to my employer, who greeted her with compliments for the handsome décor. Then I introduced her to Tony Novak, who said something totally unintelligible that caused her to react with delight. I suddenly remembered that he spoke Chinese.

She uttered a cascade of melodious syllables in response, and said to me, "Your friend speaks very well! He's nice!" She took our drink orders and headed back to the bar. We all perused the menu, enjoying a little breeze and watching the passersby on the sidewalk as we sat and talked.

Mei came back with the drinks and her sister, who was very happy to meet us. Then she brought her mother over to the table, a graceful elegant woman in her fifties who said hello to us in English, then quite a lot more to Tony in Chinese. He spoke with her at length. She seemed quite taken with him. Henry gave me an I-told-you-so look over the top of his menu. Apparently Henry spoke some Chinese too, presumably from his travels. He chimed in with a few words here and there.

Then Mei ducked into the kitchen and came out with her father, who greeted us enthusiastically. Tony stood up to shake his hand, so Henry did also. I just waved from the back of the table. I couldn't understand a word any of them were saying, but it was a lively conversation. Eventually our hosts bowed and went back to their work, leaving us to study our menus again. About five minutes later, Mei appeared with plate of something that looked delicious.

"My father sends this appetizer to you," she said, giving us each a small white plate. "We call it the Caterpillar. It is eel, rice and avocado. Very good!"

It looked like a caterpillar, too, covered with fuzzy hair made from toasted shredded coconut, with two slim carrot sticks for antennae. We thanked her and gave our orders, then shared the dish. It was delicious, mild and not fishy at all. The two men were adept at using their chopsticks to pick up chunks of food and dip it into the little bowls of sauce. I usually drop more on the table than I can get into my mouth, so I opted for a fork.

Mei and her family showered us with treats throughout our meal, ending with a warm banana dessert that was the perfect sweet finale. They were all very kind, and obviously thrilled to entertain someone who spoke their language. Tony and Henry had a marvelous time, remembering their travels together and the unusual dinners they had shared. I enjoyed watching them and listening, but held back somewhat, distracted by a slight headache.

As the three of us walked back up the sidewalk towards the shop, Tony repeated some of what Mei's parents had been saying to him.

"Mr. Sun learned to cook in Peking, making the famous Peking Duck. That is the only place in the world where it is made. You know how it's done? The ducks hang from hooks over a large cauldron of hot broth and secret herbs, which is scooped up and poured into the body cavity of the ducks, over and over again, for hours, to cook them from the inside out."

"That seems like a lot of trouble," I remarked.

Tony looked at me with shocked disapproval.

"But it tastes like nothing else, " he said firmly. "It is the most tender, delicious duck in the world!"

"Oh I see!"

"A lot of trouble is worth it sometimes, Emily."

"I suppose so."

"Take now, for example." He looked at me pointedly, and grinned.

"Oh? You're suggesting that I am a lot of trouble?"

"Yes, but you're worth it, aren't you?"

"Ha! And wouldn't you like to find out!"

"Yes, please," he said simply. "That is my plan."

"Oh? You have a plan, do you?" I asked, not sure whether to be annoyed, or flattered.

We had reached our destination, and Mr. Paradis began to climb up the stairs to the front door. He stopped and turned around to interrupt with a wave of his hand.

"Does the plan include delivering Emily safely home tonight, Tony, or should I call her a cab?" He peered down at us from the top step, a twinkle in his eye.

"Want to try out the Prius?" Tony dug the keys out of his pants pocket and dangled them in front of me invitingly. I reached out quickly and plucked them from his hand.

I thanked Mr. Paradis for the dinner, which had been magnificent and entertaining. Henry observed happily that we had received more food for free than what we had purchased. We all agreed that Mei's family was charming and her father was an inspired chef. With a fond "Farewell!" and a wave, Mr. Paradis went inside the front door and closed it with a snap of the latch.

Tony and I turned and followed the footpath that ran along the north side of the building, heading for the alley in back where he was still parked next to the porch. It was dark and quiet. The motion-activated light on the back porch turned on when we came out into the back yard.

"Hey, why don't you drive this time, OK?" I said, handing him back the keys.

"What's up, Em?" He looked at me, alert and concerned.

"I'm a little tired, that's all."

"Of course you are. Emily," he said, "Come here."

He stopped walking and turned around to put his arms around me, enveloping me in a long, warm hug. With my face gently pressed against his bare throat as we stood together, I fit perfectly under his chin. I slipped my hands inside his leather jacket and wrapped my arms around his firm body. I noticed he was giving off the same delicious, spicy scent that had made me swoon on our first date. Inhaling deeply, I closed my eyes and let all the air out again in a big sigh. It was bliss.

"It's not easy to save the world and fight evil all day long, is it?" he said, rubbing my back with one hand while continuing to hug me with the other arm. I moaned a little, first inadvertently then in an exaggerated, joking way. It was a great hug. He made me feel safe and grounded. We disengaged naturally in a few minutes, comfortable with each other.

"OK, hop in," he said, unlocking the passenger door for me. I obediently sat. The Prius was beautiful too, I noticed grudgingly. Very luxurious and comfortable. I vowed to try to appreciate it, for the sake of our planet.

Tony drove to my apartment building while I daydreamed about ways to make Lexi change her attitude towards me. They all seemed to involve kidnapping, explosives or weapons of some kind. I realized I was still holding in a lot of anger.

"What would you do?" I asked Tony.

"About Lexi?" He looked over at me.

I nodded.

"I would probably go to see her. Try to talk my way out of it. See what it was she seemed to want, and try to give it to her."

"That's very direct."

"Yes," he said, pulling up to park in front of my building. "But then, I took a seminar in negotiation. I didn't make it up! I'm not that smart."

"Oh really! I would have said you are quite smart."

"Perhaps 'diabolically clever,' some would say." He raised one eyebrow and grinned.

"Some who?"

"Some of my friends, who appreciate my finer qualities."

"I'm beginning to appreciate your finer qualities too, you know?"

"You are? Emily! I was hoping you would realize what a wonderful person I am!"

We both laughed.

"I know what you need," Tony said, leaning closer.

"You do?"

"Yes," he said quietly, and kissed me on the lips. My mouth tingled and a hot electric charge shot through me like a bolt of lightning, all the way down to my toes.

"What makes you think so?" I said, kissing him back. His lips were soft, warm, and he tasted like ginger. My logical mind started to melt into a golden mist.

Tony kissed me again, and again, putting his arms around

me and pulling me toward him. The scent of his leather jacket and his delicious natural chemistry wafted over me. It was completely intoxicating, and with every breath I spun a little more out of control.

Those piercing, dark eyes were very close now, looking intensely into mine. I felt like the earth had suddenly opened beneath me, and I was falling into a deep chasm. Drawn by his mind, mesmerized, I closed my eyes and opened my mouth, letting the kiss go deeper. Dizzying waves of sensation raced through me and fireworks glittered inside my eyelids. All the hard edges began to dissolve, and the soft vulnerable me inside the shell was exposed, pink and trembling. I'm sure my face was bright red as I pulled back and gazed at him adoringly.

His voice changed and got a little husky, like he needed to swallow.

"I know what a woman needs at a time like this, Emily, I was not born yesterday," he said.

My hypersensitive self-protective instinct immediately kicked in again. Tony seemed sincere and caring, but he was very, very smooth. He was even admitting his expertise with women, right up front, almost like a warning or a challenge. But he was so incredibly sexy, it really didn't matter.

I lowered my eyes with a coy smile.

"OK, tell me…what do I need?"

I waited breathlessly for him to tell me, or show me. Or hopefully, both.

"Hot water," he said, kissing me once more, gently, in the middle of the forehead. "Very hot water. Rosemary and sea salt. A candle. Maybe several?"

"A bath? I must admit, it sounds good." I pictured myself naked in the tub, in the flickering candlelight, perhaps not alone? I wondered if he was imagining the same thing.

"You need to soak in very hot water and let your thoughts drift. You absorb the ions from the agitated water molecules.

It's good for the body and the spirit. The famous holistic doctor Andrew Weil says so."

"Does he?"

"Yes. I read it in his newsletter," Tony said, and that seemed to settle it.

He followed me inside and actually started to run the bath for me, pausing to speak to Tree, who rubbed up against his leg. I kind of wanted to do the same thing.

"So, now are you going to put me into the tub?" I asked hopefully, as he came over and wrapped his arms around me again. He had not taken off his jacket, a bad sign.

He held me close and looked at me with an odd, kind of *overflowing* expression, his face flushed as he looked into my eyes.

"No, Emily, not tonight," he said slowly. "But I am very much looking forward to it when the time comes!" He kissed me tenderly, and departed. I was sorry to see him go, but suddenly felt too exhausted to worry about it.

I locked the door behind him and walked toward the big claw-footed bathtub, dropping my clothes on the floor as I went. I was so tired, I couldn't even stop to pick them up. I pinned my hair up on top of my head and stepped into the steaming, fragrant water. Tony had thrown in some sea salt and fresh herbs from my kitchen windowsill, rosemary and lavender. There was just one lamp lit in the main room, and two candles flickered on the shelf at the foot of the tub. I folded up a hand towel and used it for a pillow as I lay down, relaxing and letting my eyes go out of focus as the steam glowed in the fluttering, strobe light of the wavering candle flames. My eyes fell shut and I still saw a muted flashing through my semi-transparent eyelids.

I lay under the steaming water with my hands crossed over my chest like a mummy. The tub is deep and long, so most of me was submerged in liquid heat. I crossed my left leg over the right at the knee, loosening the kinks in my lower back with a stretch. An enormous yawn suddenly overtook me, and as I let it out, I sank down slowly, slowly, centimeter by centimeter, lower, looser and more relaxed, until every muscle in my body that would obey a request was limp.

But my mind wouldn't stop racing. Pictures flashed across the movie screen inside my eyelids. Lexi, furious. Tony, smiling. Siri, in her water goddess colors. The crescent moon claw marks on my arms. Lexi's gallery, where she reigned happily as the Queen and welcomed customers with pride, as though she had painted the works of art herself. She really seemed to feel that way. When we all worked together and sold several pieces to a big client, she was proud as a parent. We were a team, then. She had actually seemed to *like* me, on those occasions.

I focused on the memory of Lexi being friendly to me, when she was excited and happy. Sometimes she could be kind of fun. I remembered one day after we sold two very large paintings when she had pulled out a bottle of champagne from the fridge and we closed the gallery early, getting a little smashed while we talked about silly things from our college days. I saw her face again, laughing at me. She had hiccupped and inadvertently snorted some champagne up her nose. For some reason it was utterly hysterical. I started to giggle again in the tub, remembering.

I opened my eyes and stared up at the ceiling, turning on a trickle of hot water with my big toe to re-warm the bath. I realized I had started to feel a little better and the headache was gone. I also realized that I had somehow managed to stop thinking about Lexi's negative side, and was concentrating on the fun times. Siri was right, it was much more pleasant! I took in a deep breath and let my head slip all the way under the water, a little stream of bubbles slowly slipping out of my nose. I opened my eyes under the water and watched the bubbles rising up to the surface.

What if I could let all the bad feelings float away from me just as easily? I pushed against the anger with my mind, finding where it dwelled inside me, somewhere near my solar plexus. It felt like a balled fist, a cramped knot of muscle. I touched it with my hand. It was literally a sore spot. I pushed it with my fingers, and pushed it with my mind, massaging the knot in my imagination and starting to break it up into smaller and smaller pieces. I saw them as little shards of broken glass, sharp and glittering, dangerous.

I came up to the surface of the water to take in another deep breath, and then I submerged again. I deliberately pictured the little jagged pieces of anger each enclosed in a smooth bubble of air, then one by one slowly let them escape from between my lips. I let all of the air out of my lungs, one bubble at a time. Then I rose back to the surface and shook the water out of my eyes, my heavy wet hair coming out of the pins and streaming down my back. I inhaled a full breath of moist herb-scented, healing air. I put my hand to my midsection and realized that the painful knot was gone! A slightly tender spot remained, but not like before. My shoulders were not so tense, either.

If Lexi had thought of me as a friend, whatever that meant in Lexi Land, then maybe she felt personally upset when I quit. I knew she was totally unaware of how she sounded sometimes. She was a great salesperson and knew a lot about how to ma-nipulate people, but she was a klutz at real relationships. She told me once that she didn't have any close girlfriends at col-lege, that she had never trusted other women. She had always seemed kind of lonely and pathetic to me. Her self-centered-ness might have something to do with this, as both a cause and an effect. Maybe she thought I just freaked out for my own selfish reasons and deserted her for a better job. Maybe she had no clue about how I had felt that day, or why I had felt that way. Maybe there was something I could do now to change things, if I went to see her. I could remind her of our good times together. Charm her. It might work if I could get past my innate disapproval of her egocentricity. If I acted as if we could be friends again, then maybe it would happen.

What was it Tony said he would do? Go see her, find out what she wanted, and try to give it to her. That sounded like a pretty good plan, now that I had thought about it. I decided to follow up as soon as I could. Tomorrow! Immediately, I felt lighter and happier.

I slept very soundly that night. I lay totally relaxed in my bed under the skylight and the waxing quarter moon shone down on me from overhead. I dreamed about flying, one of my favorite dreams. I flew effortlessly through the air and steered by *yearning* towards a certain direction. In my dream I flew over to Market Street, where I hovered outside an upstairs window. Tony was inside, lying asleep in bed. I flew through the wall and hovered over him. He looked beautiful and peaceful. I wanted to lie down next to him, so I did, being careful not to disturb him. I felt his warmth all along one side of me as I snuggled into the curve of his body. It was very pleasant, and I closed my dream eyes and drifted off to dream sleep.

When I woke up, for real, it was morning. I still felt the warmth of his body next to me in the sheets. It was uncanny. I reached out with my hand and felt something furry beside me.

"Mmrrrr?" said Tree, poking his head up out of the covers.

I burst out laughing and pulled him out to tickle him under the chin. He purred ecstatically. The sun was shining, the birds were singing. It was a new day. And I'd started it with laughter and happiness, which is a good thing. I decided to try and stick with the same attitude for as long as possible.

Chapter 13

Death

CHANGE, METAMORPHOSIS

Description: A skeleton rides a black horse or rows a boat across the river Styx, sometimes flying a banner that displays a rose, the symbol of Life. Meaning: Change, death, rebirth. Reincarnation, metamorphosis. Getting rid of antiquated ideas to move forward in a new, liberated state.

When I got into work at around nine, I looked out the back window and noticed that the Prius was not in residence. There was only a little coffee left in the still-warm pot, and a neatly rinsed bowl and spoon occupied the dishwasher, which someone (joy!) had emptied. Probably someone tall, dark and handsome. Who had consumed three of the low-fat yogurts by now, I saw as I leaned into the fridge to pull out the ingredients for today's lunch special, vegetarian *moussaka*.

I had already made the thick tomato-based sauce yesterday, using lentils and mushrooms instead of ground lamb, with lots of fresh parsley and cinnamon. This morning I only had to roast the eggplant slices in the oven on cookie sheets, make a quick ricotta egg custard sauce for the top, and then assemble everything in a couple of big rectangular baking dishes. I wanted to get the eggplant sliced into disks, drizzled with olive oil and into the oven first thing, so it was ready to work with while my breakfast scones were baking.

The eggplant was nearly done and the first batch of scones was sitting ready to take its place when I heard someone coming down the back stairs. My employer shuffled into the kitchen, dressed and combed, carrying an empty white mug.

"Too early?" he inquired with a forelorn expression, looking at the tray of unbaked scones sitting on the counter.

"Sorry!" I said, "It'll just be a few minutes, they're going in right now."

He poured the last of the coffee into his mug and collapsed into one of the chairs at the table. He rubbed his eyes wearily.

"Are you feeling OK?" I asked. I pulled the three hot cookie sheets of roasted eggplant circles out of the oven and put them on the granite countertop to cool.

"Oh yes," he said. "It's just Tony, you know. Up with the birds. Full of energy. Every day. It's driving me crazy."

I smiled. Tony was driving me crazy, too. Not that there's anything wrong with that! I slid the scones into the oven and closed the door, remembering last night.

"So, where's the car?" I asked, nodding toward the alley.

"He was off at dawn today. Made me drink green tea when

I'm usually still lost in slumber. Says it will be good for me. Have you ever heard such drivel?"

"Why, yes, I think I heard some drivel just like that last night. It seems Tony has been reading the holistic health news."

"That's what comes from all this traveling around on airplanes. One is exposed to all sorts of unsuitable reading matter." He sniffed.

"Not his typical fare?"

Henry looked shocked and shook his head.

"Definitely not. But let's not be too concerned. When he starts listening to *A Prairie Home Companion* instead of salsa music, then we'll worry."

"He does seem to be making a lot of changes in his life lately, " I commented, interested in Henry's thoughts on the matter. I hoped to tempt him into revealing some significant details about Tony's precipitous move to the U.S..

The old man looked at me sharply over the edge of his coffee mug, leaning back in his chair. I started to measure out the flour and milk for the white sauce that would be the base for my custard. I didn't want to appear overly concerned with his answer.

"What do you really think of Tony?" Mr. Paradis asked bluntly.

"What do you mean?"

"Just what I asked."

"I like him very much. He seems to be a person of conscience. I admire that. And, " I said, starting to whisk flour into the melting butter in my heaviest pot, "He's very attractive, of course. That doesn't hurt."

Henry regarded me thoughtfully. He did not seem satisfied with my response.

"Tony Novak is a man of great imagination and vision, Emily. Do you believe in vision?"

"I'm not sure, I don't know what you mean."

"The power of visualization, following your vision of the future."

"You mean, deliberately? Or coincidentally?"

"Deliberately, of course. I'm not talking about mere observation. I'm talking about the actual creation of one's reality, one's future reality."

The timer dinged, and I took the scones out of the oven while the *roux* cooked on low. I was still not sure what he was trying to say.

"What does that have to do with Tony?" I asked. "You're suggesting he uses this…technique?"

He smiled, nodding an affirmation. I put two scones on a plate for him and he took it from my hand. Then I turned back to the stove and poured hot milk into the heavy-bottomed pan, whisking madly. The sauce blended and started to thicken. I turned up the heat slightly and kept on whisking, slower now.

"Tony believes in taking the bull by the horns," Henry was saying, "and I must say I approve. When he visualizes a goal, he heads straight for it. He does not falter. He takes full advantage of every opportunity that destiny puts in his path. He believes that his visualization actually creates the opportunities. It's a very interesting idea."

"Did he attend a seminar on this somewhere?" I asked.

"Yes, I believe he did."

"He took a seminar on negotiation, he told me," I said.

"Yes."

"He seems very interested in his continuing education."

"He is a natural scholar. Omnivorous. Full scholarship at Princeton, you know!"

"Why did he really leave England, Henry? What new vision of his life is he creating now?" I asked, turning off the burner and leaning back against the counter with my arms folded protectively in front of my chest.

My friend regarded me with a little smile.

"I believe you already know the answer to the second question, Emily. Is the answer to the first what you are really worried about?"

I nodded. No point in hiding it, since the old boy could read my mind anyhow.

"When Tony was a young boy," he launched into storytelling mode, "His parents had some dear friends who lived in England and came to Italy on vacation every year. They had a house near the summer home of Tony's family, at Lake Como. There were three pretty daughters, playmates for Tony and his sister every summer when they were children. It was always the dream of both sets of parents that he would end up marrying one of the three girls."

He paused for a breath then went on, waving his hand in the air for emphasis.

"The eldest daughter married young, a British military officer, I believe. The second daughter declared herself at age twenty-one to be a Lesbian, and moved into an apartment with her female lover. The youngest daughter, who was five years Tony's junior and whom he had always regarded as an infant, grew up into a beautiful young woman and fell madly in love with him. There was a fling at Como the summer after he finished graduate school. She told her sister, who told her mother, who told Tony's mother, who told his father. Everyone agreed that it was a perfect match, and the two fathers offered to buy the couple a house in Italy near their family homes."

I can't say I liked where this story seemed to be heading, but it was definitely fascinating. I made a fresh pot of coffee while we talked.

"What did he do then? Was he in love with her too?"

"Tony did the only honorable thing he could think of, as you might have predicted, my dear," Henry said. "He offered to marry her. He did not fall in love with her, though. Slight problem. He was very *fond* of her, of course. And he didn't want to upset anyone."

"Oh," I nodded, relieved. "Were they ever actually married? Did he break it off?"

I started to crack eggs and separate the yolks from the whites, whisking the egg yolks into the sauce one at a time. Then I stirred in a big dollop of ricotta cheese.

"They became engaged, " Henry continued, "And Tony ingeniously insisted that she must complete her university education before thinking of a wedding. She was very young, after all. As she was in England and he was traveling the Orient most of the time, they did not see much of each other for the next few years. She led the carefree life of a bright young student of considerable means, and he led the life of an adventurer. These were the years when our friend made his fortune, and he was constantly on the move. The remote presence of an invisible fiancé can be quite useful to a young woman at times, I hear," he said, peering at me.

"At any rate," he continued, "They managed to postpone the marriage for several years and when the time came to do something about it, neither one of them was really interested."

"Oh, that's good!"

"You might say so, but it was quite upsetting for our boy at the time."

"Why, did he mind? I thought he didn't care about her?"

"It seemed that the girl had fallen in love with someone else, someone quite inferior but Johnny-on-the-spot as it were, and she had become, well, *enceinte*."

"Oh! You mean, pregnant?"

"Yes, alas. Or, happily, depending on one's point of view."

"Very true."

"While all that time, traveling the wide world to its most exotic ports where legendary beauties reside, Tony had considered himself to be an engaged man. And being *honorable*, he conducted himself accordingly! I can bear witness."

"You mean, he was faithful to her while she was back in England having a sleazy affair with some guy?"

Mr. Paradis nodded, a twinkle in his eye.

It was hard for me to imagine. The girl must have been totally out of her mind. Lucky for me! I had no doubt from what Henry said that Tony would have gone ahead and married her, if she had expected it. Maybe she was just too young, or she thought of him as a brother. Maybe she had grown up in such a wealthy, privileged world that she never learned to appreciate real loyalty. She sounded frivolous to me.

Tony must have been crushed, even if secretly relieved. Not so much because of what he had deprived himself of over the years, as Henry indicated, but for the end of his dream of a loving wife and family. He had worked hard at school and achieved financial success, but suddenly he was heading down that road alone. Not that he had remained alone for more than a few weeks, I suspected. No longer protected by an official engagement, rich and handsome, he must have been chased around the globe by more than one enterprising husband-hunter.

I poured us both some fresh-brewed coffee. Henry's scones sat untouched on the plate, but I was too curious to stop asking questions.

"So, how did the two families react to all this?" I inquired.

"They were not a problem. They were sorry the husband was not to be Tony, but glad about the baby coming, and her parents threw the happy couple a big wedding. Tony was one of the groomsmen."

"Very civilized! I approve."

"Yes." He sipped his coffee and slowly took a bite of scone. I started to put together the layers of tomato sauce and eggplant in my two casseroles.

"When was this?" I asked.

"A few years ago. I think the child is two or three now."

"So that doesn't really explain why he decided to move so suddenly. Does it?"

"Emily," he said deliberately, "When a man like Tony suddenly sees a clear path to the future he desires, he does not waste time. Especially if he has been searching for this path for many, many years. That's why he sold his house."

"What path?"

"Ahhh, now we are getting back to your second question of the morning, the one to which you already know the answer." he said, rising out of his chair slowly, holding his back and cringing a little as he straightened. He shuffled toward the door to the hall.

"I suggest you ask him yourself, my dear, if you dare!" he called over his shoulder, heading up the stairs.

*   *   *

That afternoon when the lunch customers had tapered off I left the shop in the competent hands of Henry and Siri, gritted my teeth, and walked the eight blocks to my previous place of employment. I walked slowly, trying to decide what to say. I forced a smile onto my face and attempted to look friendly. People on the sidewalk smiled back, so it must have looked fairly natural. My upper lip stuck to my front teeth. I ried to get back to the forgiving, peaceful state of mind I had achieved the night before. By the time I reached the Gladstone Gallery, I was feeling calm and relatively optimistic. I pushed open the door with its elegant gold lettering and went inside before I could change my mind.

The first thing I noticed was the amazing new art show that the Gallery was displaying. It was obviously all the work of a single artist. Very large canvases and framed monotypes were hung on every wall, stunning abstract figures done in a bright palette, predominantly flaming red and orange but a few in bright blues. A series mounted on the long side wall had a musical theme. I saw mysterious figures playing guitars, black and white keyboards, horns, drums. The work was brilliant, and I was so transported by the images that I didn't even notice when she first entered the room.

"Good afternoon, can I help you with anything?" came Lexi's voice from behind me. She sounded stuffy, like she had a cold.

I turned around and faced her silently, trying to radiate good intentions and not knowing how to start. When she recognized me, a strange look came over her face. I realized that Lexi looked like she had been crying. Her eye makeup was smeared and her nose was red. She looked at me first in disbelief, and then with an intense emotional gush she threw her arms around me and burst into tears on my shoulder.

"Oh my god," she sobbed, "I can't believe you're here! How did you know?"

I nearly fell over when she collapsed on me, I was so surprised. I rallied, and patted her back consolingly as she wept. Obviously something had gone very wrong in Lexi Land!

"Lex? How are you doing, sweetie?" I ventured, mining for clues. I hugged her and kept on patting. She was a complete mess.

"Oh my god," she said, distraught, "I'm still in total denial. I can't believe it. I can't believe she's just, gone! Gone!" She burst into fresh paroxysms of grief. In a minute or two she straightened up again slowly and pulled back, sniffling.

I offered her a kleenex from my bag and probed cautiously, "When did you find out?"

"This morning," she sniffed, blowing her nose. "Daddy called here, just as I was opening up."

"I am so sorry, Lexi, " I said, meaning it in every way, even though I still didn't know what she was talking about,

"Thank you," she answered, trying to blot the running mascara from under her eyes.

"What exactly did he, er…say?"

"There was a tree down across the road. Nobody knows why. It must have just fallen. It was pitch dark out there, and she drove right into it. She never had a chance."

"Oh, no!"

"Yes, she died instantly. Mummy says they're planning the funeral for day after tomorrow. Will you come with me? Please, Em? I don't think I can do it alone."

"Where, Lexi?"

"The Island, that's where they're going to bury her. I just can't believe my sister is gone. I feel like when we get off the ferry, she'll be standing right there!" Tears welled up and rolled down her cheeks. She blotted them away with the kleenex.

I thought quickly, and realized that this was surely the perfect chance to transform our relationship back to into an amicable one. I wasn't terribly eager to drive her out to the Cape and take the long ferry ride to Nantucket, nor to go to a sad family funeral attended by a bunch of rich people I had never even met. However, opportunity was knocking at my door. As I had requested and right on schedule, too. *Carpe diem*, and all that. I took a deep breath and committed myself.

"Sure, I'll go to the Island with you Lexi," I said, "I'd be glad to. I'm so sorry for your loss. And, I'm also sorry that things haven't been, well, very good between us lately. I'm sorry for whatever I may have done to contribute to that. I want to be friends."

She regarded me solemnly, twisting the tissue in her hands.

"I forgive you, Emily. Do you forgive me?" she said, her lip trembling.

I nodded mutely and we hugged again. When we pulled apart we were smiling at each other. I kept one arm draped around her shoulders comfortingly as I steered her toward the seating area at the back of the gallery. Two couches and several big easy chairs were clustered around a glass-topped coffee table. We sat down together on one of the sofas.

"You know," she confided, "I feel so weird about this. I never thought I even liked Suzi very much, but now I'm just... *devastated!*"

"That's totally understandable," I said. "You always love your family, even when you're mad at them, or whatever."

"No," she protested, "It's more than that! I really didn't like her. In fact, she's the whole reason I never had many girlfriends, you know. She tortured me when we were little. I never could trust her. She made fun of me all the time."

"Was she older than you?" I asked, vaguely remembering this fact.

"Four years," Lexi answered. "She was always so pretty, so slender and graceful. And I was a pudgy little child. She used to call me The Toad."

"Oh no, that's awful!"

"Yes," she nodded seriously, "One time she locked me in the attic of the Westport house for a whole day. Nobody could find me. They thought I had run away, and Daddy called the police!"

"And nobody heard you calling?"

She regarded me with a hint of the old Lexi peeking out, giving me that "Are you stupid or crazy?" raised eyebrow. I figured she must have felt a little better.

"Are you kidding?" she asked, "In a 20,000 square foot house you don't hear a small child calling from behind a closed door on the third floor, Emily!"

"OK, well, that must have been scary for you, Lexi."

"Yes, it was!" she nodded. "I had to pee in a little bowl. There was nothing to eat or drink. I cried all day."

"You poor thing! You must have been dehydrated!"

"Yes, I suppose so! And Suzi thought the whole thing was just hysterical. She laughed and laughed."

I made sympathetic noises as Lexi related a series of incidents from their childhood, some bad and others good, gradually growing more and more calm as her crying jag receded. I received the impression that Suzi had been a mischievous bully, not a dangerous devil, but someone who had made a major impact on the growing insecurity of her little sister. I wondered if Suzi had been jealous of Lexi, who must have been just as bright and aggressive for attention then as she was now as an adult. I was willing to bet that Lexi was never pudgy at all, either. I doubted there was a single day in her life when she didn't wake up pretty first thing in the morning.

"When do you want to leave? I should make plans to be away," I said, thinking of the shop, and Tony, whom I had hoped to see again tonight.

"Oh, I'm too blown away to get organized today," she said, rubbing her temples. "I think I'll just lock up and walk over to the spa for a massage. We can go tomorrow. I'll call Mummy and tell her when to expect us."

"OK, I'll pick you up at your place in the morning, then."

She nodded, placing her hand over mine.

"Thanks for being here, Emily."

I smiled at her, genuinely glad of the same thing.

"I'll call you later to confirm after I reorganize my schedule," I said, " I'm sure it will be OK, I just need to check."

We stood up and hugged again, then I left and walked back to my shop. When I told Siri what had happened, she was ecstatic. Her beautiful eyes lit up and she gave an excited whoop.

"You did it!" she cried, "You have transformed the negative into the positive!"

"She totally adores me now! Can you believe it?" I said, grinning.

"And how do you feel about her?"

"Actually," I said thoughtfully, "I kind of like her too. I just have to remember how things are in Lexi Land, and be patient. Understanding where she is coming from really helps. Though I'll keep my guard up, too, just in case."

"That's right," Siri said approvingly, as though satisfied with me, her pupil. "If you concentrate on her good side, she will show it to you more often!"

"I've got to make plans to be out of town for a few days," I said, thinking about it.

Siri offered to bring Isabella Reyes in to help in the shop while I was gone. She felt the two of them could handle it, with Mr. Paradis' help. Siri offered to call Bella right away, and soon reported to me that she had agreed to the plan. I went upstairs to find my employer and give him the news. I wondered whether Tony had returned during my absence, but there was no sign of him on the second floor, where I found Henry in his study. He was sitting at the computer, and I saw the eBay logo at the top of the screen.

Henry listened to my story with attention, and agreed that he and the girls would mind the store while I was away. He told me that Tony had called earlier, saying that he had gone to Boston for the day and would return in time to drive me home after work. Everything seemed to be falling into place, so I dialed Lexi's cell phone and left voice mail saying that we were all set for going to Nantucket in the morning.

I was concerned about what we would find when we got there. As the afternoon passed, I imagined how the rest of Lexi's family must have been feeling right now. I had no idea how many relatives would be gathered there, but it was sure to be an emotional family event. I would feel a little out of place, never having met any of them and not exactly coming from the same social strata. I was curious to see the Gladstone summer cottage, which was sure to be fabulous. I had never been to Nantucket before. I started thinking about what clothes to bring with me, and how long we might be gone. I made a list of what to pack, and another list for Siri and Bella of things I knew had to be done later in the week.

At almost closing time, I was sitting behind the cash register doodling on my notes. I heard the back door open, and someone came into the hallway by the kitchen. Tony Novak poked his head around the corner and spotted me.

"Hey," he called, walking across the showroom, "How's it going?"

He looked happy and relaxed, as though his business had gone well today. He was dressed somewhat formally in a white shirt and tie, with a sport coat and khaki slacks. He smiled as he came towards me, flashing those gorgeous white teeth. I was struck afresh by how incredibly good-looking he was, to me anyhow. Square jaw, flashing brown eyes, and a lock of straight dark hair falling across his forehead. When he smiled at me like that, I drifted off into absentminded euphoria, and had a little trouble remembering to breathe.

"Good, it's going…good!" I stammered, remembering not to fall too hard, too fast. "How about you? I hear you went all the way to Boston today."

He stood across the jewelry case from me and reached over to take my hand, lacing his fingers through mine. Leaning closer, he kissed me on the cheek. He examined my facial expression carefully, as though reading me in some way. Then he smiled, and kissed my other cheek. He kept holding on to my hand. I started to feel lightheaded again.

"All the way to Boston and back again, like a homing pigeon," he said.

I smiled at the image. He smiled back. We floated blissfully in the air together for a moment. Then I came back down to earth and said sadly, "I have to go away for a few days, Tony. Lexi's sister died."

He considered the news. "And you found this out when you went to see her today?" he asked.

I nodded.

"Good girl, Emily. You did a brave thing," Tony said. "And you're going to the funeral?"

"Yes, I'm bringing Lexi there."

"Can I help you in some way?"

"I guess you could feed Tree for me."

"No problem," he said, stroking my arm. "And can I cook for you tonight? While you...pack?"

I looked at him dubiously. "You, cook? Are you sure of that?"

"You shouldn't underestimate me," he laughed, shaking his head.

"I'm beginning to get that message!"

"I told you before what a wonderful person I am, Emily!" he said. "And, I am a pretty good cook, too. I have taken care of myself in some relatively rustic situations, you know," he finished, more seriously.

"Well, I do have a stove, so we won't be needing you to cook over an open fire or anything," I teased, batting my eyelashes at him.

"Leave it to me," he said happily. "I'll be right back."

He sprang up the front stairs and disappeared from view. Curious, I hurried over to peak around the corner just in time to see a door on the left side of the upstairs landing swing shut. I caught a quick glimpse of stairs leading up to the third floor, which I had still never visited. I was intrigued to see the rooms, but this was obviously not the time. I went up to tell Henry that I was leaving and give him my notes. He still sat at the computer, and I came to stand behind him.

"Very efficient," he complimented me, scanning the lined yellow pages with his reading glasses perched on the end of his nose. "I believe you've covered everything. And don't you worry, we won't forget to feed Amy. If she'll dare to come inside while you aren't here, that is."

"I'm sure Siri can tempt her," I said. "She has a way with children, you know."

I put my hand on his shoulder.

"Thank you for letting me go so unexpectedly. I know this is a lot of trouble for all of you, and I appreciate it."

The old man beamed at me, patting my hand. "Always glad to help, Emily. You've been a stalwart ally, my dear, happy to return the favor!"

"Are we the three Musketeers then, Henry?" came Tony's voice as he entered the room, dressed now in his jeans and leather jacket.

Mr. Paradis looked startled for a moment, but then he smiled nostalgically, with a fond glance at Tony. "Remember when we were the three Musketeers once before?"

Tony nodded. "I do remember, Henry. It was an adventure, wasn't it?"

The old man nodded. He looked up at me. "You would have enjoyed it, my dear. And so did Margaret. I do think she would have approved of Emily, don't you Tony?"

"Most definitely," the younger man agreed. "Cut from the same piece of cloth."

"That's a compliment, dear," Henry whispered to me.

"Can you get along OK by yourself for dinner tonight?" Tony asked him. "I'm going to help Emily pack."

Henry squinted a skeptical glance his way, but told us he'd be glad to have a chance for a nice long nap. He did look tired. I offered to get him a pizza from across the street before I left for the day, but he declined, saying he preferred to rummage around downstairs and see what was in the fridge.

We locked up on our way out the back and Tony drove me home. He dropped me off and immediately left again to go and buy groceries, refusing to tell me what was on the menu and apparently quite excited to be cooking. I got out my suit-case, put it on the bed and opened the closet door to stare inside, thanking the gods of fashion for the current popularity of black, even in the summer. It goes with everything, looks formal even when it isn't, and doesn't show dirt. The perfect color for someone who can't afford a different outfit for every occasion, like me. I had several black skirts, pants and even a linen jacket. I decided to bring one of each, with a few silk shirts to go under the jacket. I had a decent navy blue sundress to wear on the way over tomorrow, too. I got out my ironing board and plugged in the steam iron.

Half an hour or so later, Tony was back with a bag of gro-ceries and a bottle of wine. My freshly ironed clothes were hanging all around the apartment on hangers, as I stood bare-foot in front of the ironing board working on one last extra pair of black capris. He put a CD on my stereo and started banging pots and pans around in the kitchen. I recognized the same music he'd been playing in the car the night we drove to Vermont. He brought me a glass of wine and we toasted.

"To our first dinner at home together," he said.

"I can't afford to get food poisoning tonight, Tony," I cau-tioned.

He pouted and we clinked glasses.

"To the three Musketeers?" I suggested.

"*Salut!*" he agreed, and we drank.

While I carefully folded and packed my clothes, he chopped and pounded and clanked and sizzled and flipped things in the kitchen, until a wonderful aroma of garlic and onions and something else delicious wafted around the partition and told me that he just might know what he was doing in there, after all. I heard the oven door screech open and shut, and a few minutes later I smelled something baking. The noises subsided, and eventually he came back around the corner into the main room.

I was just finishing up, so we sat down together on the couch.

"So," I said, leaning back against the cushions. "What were you doing in Boston? Importing and exporting?"

Tony reached down and pulled my legs up, swinging me around so I was turned sideways on the couch, my head on the pillows and my bare feet resting in his lap. He started to massage my foot, immediately finding the sore spot at the base of my second toe and rubbing it in little circles. Flashes of sensation jolted up my leg.

"I was in Boston for a job interview."

"You? You're getting a job? In Boston?" I was dismayed.

"No, the interview was in Boston. The job is here. And they haven't offered it to me yet, so don't get so excited!" He laughed at me and bore down, working his thumbs toward my heel. I squirmed, but didn't pull away. It was exquisite agony.

"What's the job?" I asked, wondering why he would want to give up his independence, since he obviously didn't need the money.

"Teaching, at the University," he said. "Something I've thought about before."

"International business?" I asked.

He nodded. "What do you think?" he asked.

He started to massage my other foot. His hands were very warm.

"I think you'd be great at it." I knew immediately this was true. "The kids would love to hear about your adventures. You would be their hero, a kind of Johnny Depp of the global economy."

"Emily, I am not a pirate, I am a legitimate businessman!"

"Yes, I know, but you are rather…swashbuckling."

He considered that word for a minute, and seemed to like it. The foot massage started to creep up my ankle.

"Be that as it may," he said, "The Powers That Be want to

consider my professional credentials and take a look at some other candidates. I had a very good recommendation, though, from an old friend of mine who teaches there."

"If they offer it, what will you say?"

He stopped rubbing my leg and looked at me appraisingly. "I believe I would say yes, I'll sign on for a two-year contract and we'll all see how it goes. How does that sound?"

We stared at each other. I couldn't think what to say. I loved the idea of him being settled around here for a while, but I hesitated to be so bold as to advise him what to do.

"It sounds adventurous, yet sensible," I replied.

"Well, that's me in a nutshell," he replied, "Don't you think?"

He grinned at me, teasingly.

"Sensible?" I challenged him.

"About most things. When it's not one of my obsessions. Like, you, for example."

Suddenly he was lying on top of me on the couch, one elbow on either side of my chest. He kissed me slowly, deeply, and extremely thoroughly. I snuggled down into the pillows and put my arms around his neck, settling in for the duration. After a few minutes, a strange beeping noise started to go off somewhere nearby. At first we both ignored it. Then he nibbled on my ear lobe and whispered, "Your dinner awaits!"

I pulled back my head and demanded, "What is that annoying noise?"

"My alarm watch," he said, turning it off and sitting up. "Come on, then!"

He stood up and reached down for me, giving me a hand up. We went into the kitchen, where he had set the little table by the window. A single red rose in a bud vase stood between two white votive candles, already lit. I sat at the table while he served me chicken and wild mushrooms in a light tomato sauce, over whole wheat *fettucine*, with hot garlic bread and a

Caesar salad with toasted *pignoli* nuts. Everything was spectacular, and I told him so in no uncertain terms.

Tree came in the window, back from a jaunt around the yard. He sat on the windowsill next to the rosemary plant and watched us eat, obviously fascinated.

"Don't worry old boy," Tony said, scratching him behind the ear. "You'll get some soon."

"I don't feed him scraps," I said.

"Never? That is so cold, Emily." Tony shivered dramatically.

"Oh, all right. But it just encourages him to beg."

"That is very true. When you give a man a taste of something delicious, he will undoubtedly be encouraged to beg for more."

"And a woman might feel the same way, for that matter," I countered, pushing my empty plate away.

"Oh really?"

"Shall I beg now, or later?" I asked. "And I'm not talking about food!"

His face flushed, and he took my hand to kiss it one finger at a time.

"Did I ever tell you," he asked, "That you are the most adorable, sweet, funny, wonderful, beautiful woman in the world?"

"No," I said, "You must have forgotten to mention it."

"Well then, I'm telling you now."

"Tony?"

"Yes, darling?"

"You'd better watch out, or I'm going to start believing all this nonsense."

"I hope so, Em. I want you to believe it."

"You do? Really?"

"Yes, I very sincerely do. If we both believe in it, then it will be real, won't it?"

"Tony, I have to tell you, I'm not interested in casual sex. I just can't handle it," I said bluntly. "I'd rather be alone and concentrate on working all the time."

"Believe me, I understand," he said solemnly. "I'm not trying to seduce you, Emily. Not the way you think."

He looked at me with an inscrutable expression for a minute, then stood up from the table. He smoothed his hair back with his hand, nervously.

"I think I'd better be going now," he said in a gruff voice. "I think...I hope you have a safe trip, and the funeral isn't too difficult."

He put down his napkin and turned to leave the kitchen as I stood up and ran after him, grabbing his arm.

"Wait!" I cried. "Don't just leave like that! Did I say the wrong thing?"

He stopped and turned back to put his arms around me again.

"Silly girl," he mumbled into my hair. "You always say exactly the right thing. "

"Then why are you leaving?"

He stepped back and composed himself, taking his jacket off the coat rack next to the door and putting it on. I stood and watched him, wondering if I had somehow ruined everything. Just when we had finally started to talk openly with each other.

"Because I make it a point never to fall in love on the third date, Emily," he said, with a sardonic smile. "It's just too impetuous. I always wait until, oh, at least the fourth time I have dinner with someone."

So, we were back to the safe banter. When in doubt, rely on humor. Well, two could play at that game.

"So, we'll wait 'til next time for that, right?" I said, trying to be funny, but it fell a little bit flat.

He nodded and bowed, looking uncomfortable. His eyes

were anxious, appraising my reaction. I decided to let him off the hook, for now.

"Here," I said, taking the spare key to my apartment off the rack on the kitchen wall. I handed it to him. "Now you have the key to my apartment. Watch out, people may talk!" I grinned at him playfully, but he did not respond in kind.

"I'll take good care of Tree," he said. "And, Henry too."

"I know you will. Thank you."

"You need to call me. You need to call and tell me when you're coming home, as soon as you know," he said intensely, insistently. He leaned forward and kissed me on the lips one more time, carefully avoiding contact with the rest of my body. Then he tucked my key into his wallet and put it in his back pocket, opening the door to step out onto the landing. He stood there for a moment, just outside the threshold, looking at me with a fierce, wary expression. Then he pulled the door shut and was gone.

When I lay in bed that night under the swelling moon that sailed in a sea of stars above my skylight, I reflected on how much things had changed since the night before. Lexi and I had transformed from enemies to friends. Lexi's poor sister had transitioned from life into death. Tony and I had progressed from a promising flirtation to...what? Something that might be much more serious, I thought.

It was probably a good thing I was going to be out of town for a few days, to give us both a chance to cool down. Because *cool* was not exactly how I had been feeling around the man. In fact, I thought, restlessly tossing and turning in bed, I would have gladly gone way too far with him right there on the couch if his damned watch had not gone off. Oh my god, yes. I drifted off to sleep, a little smile on my lips.

The yellow moon was smudged by a thin streak of glowing clouds overhead, and I floated beneath it on my soft bed, rocking along on the gentle waves off the coast, and then rising up in the air to hover above a dark mysterious island. Not a single light was on in any of the houses and no cars were driving on the roads. The place looked deserted, or asleep. It looked wild and magical.

I floated toward the center of the island, where a pillar of white smoke was rising up into the dark sky. As I neared it, I heard drums and singing, tambourines and bells. My flying bed settled down on the ground next to a bonfire on a broad hilltop. The fire was surrounded by a circle of amazing creatures of many kinds, dancing and frolicking. There were fawns, centaurs, sylphs and dryads, little fairies with semi-transparent sparkling wings, and even a unicorn. They were beautiful and rare, amazing.

I ran to join the circle, and glimpsed others dancing whom I had not seen at first. Siri was there with her husband and her children, as were Bella and her family, plus Laurie and John. Both of my parents were there as well, and Henry and Margaret, young and spry, dancing with the others as we all joined hands. I turned to my left and saw I held the paw of a large white cat in my hand. I looked to the right and saw that Tony had appeared and taken my hand in his. We all started to dance in a clockwise direction, circling round and round the bonfire, which roared into the sky. We chanted and sang. It was an exhilarating romp, but finally I began to tire.

"Please," I begged, panting, "I need to stop. I have to drive Lexi. I can't be late!"

But the circle spun round and round, spiraling off as I finally broke loose and was flung far out into space, eventually catching my foot on the moon and tripping to fall down, down, down. When I woke up very early in the morning, the sheets had twisted around me tightly and sweat was dripping from my body.

I showered and dressed, watering my plants and making sure to leave the apartment spotless. Then I headed off to learn how the very rich deal with it when one of their own dies so young, so tragically.

Chapter 14

Temperance

SYNTHESIS, MODERATION

Description: A woman pours something from one chalice into another. She is blending two fluids, two extremes.
Meaning: Synthesis or moderation. A tempering of opposites. Softening the extremes through either collaboration or compromise.

Four days later, I dropped Lexi off at her house before heading straight over to work. Lexi and I had caught a flight back to Hyannis in her cousin's private plane very early today. It was raining a little when we hit the Mass. Pike and drove west around six in the morning, and we encountered very little traffic until we got almost to Springfield.

We parked in the driveway in front of the striking four bedroom contemporary home that Lexi owned, set on two landscaped acres in the nicest residential area in town. I got out with her, to help with the luggage. While each of us had started the trip with just one suitcase, we had both somehow acquired numerous bags and bundles along the way. (There were actually *two* shopping trips into the little retail district on the Island, I confess.) I opened the trunk and we divided up the contents. Then I helped carry everything of hers inside. When she finally stood in the foyer, her packages scattered on the floor around her, she turned to face me and delivered her most charming smile.

"I don't know how to thank you enough," Lexi said, very seriously and sincerely. She took both of my hands in hers and kissed me on the cheek affectionately. No more air-kisses, the real thing. "I'm sorry my family is so weird," she added with a grimace.

"Lexi, everybody's family is weird."

"True, very true."

"And your parents were absolutely wonderful to me, and I love your cousins. Anyhow. It was a very interesting field trip. I don't get out of town much, you know," I said lightly as I turned to go.

Lexi stood in the open doorway watching me walk down the path to the parking area. Everything looked clean and refreshed after the rain. The birds were singing, the sun was shining, the flowers were blooming and she was beautiful and blonde and golden all over. She was smiling. All was well in Lexi Land today.

"My work is done, Grasshopper!" I muttered to myself as I got into the car.

"See you at the next DBA meeting!" she called, waving.

Funny how that didn't seem to worry me at all anymore.

"OK, save me a seat if you get there first!" I called, waving back. I turned the car around to go out of the long driveway, admiring a huge bed of pink day lilies. Lexi's world was certainly a lovely place, I had to admit.

The Prius was not in evidence when I parked in the alley behind the store. Letting myself into the back door, I heard feminine voices and laughter coming from the showroom. I realized it was Friday, Pilates day, and the girls were all here for our early morning class. I glanced into the kitchen and saw that scones were cooling on a rack. Our menu board, a giant drawing pad that we displayed by hanging it from a hook on the wall behind the coffee bar, was lying on the table with a couple of magic markers nearby. Reading it upside down, I saw that Siri had made curried chicken salad with almonds today, and we were also offering a dark chocolate fudge cake, which was probably in the fridge. It looked like everything was under control, and we still had over an hour before it would be time to open the shop. I hung my raincoat on one of the hooks by the back door, and turned to follow the sound of my friends' voices.

I stood in the doorway watching for a minute before they noticed me. The lunch tables and chairs had been pushed back against the wall. Six exercise mats were laid out on the floor, five of them facing the one where our teacher, Mindy, demonstrated for us. Everyone was dressed in T-shirts and leggings or sweat pants. The class consisted of Laurie, Siri, Bella and me, plus Mei and my newest friend, Alyssia. She was the mother of Rashid, the boy who had carried my cake upstairs at The Palace, and the happy baby who usually shared the carriage with Siri's daughter. Her low melodious voice rang out now, as she made everyone laugh with a remark about the hamstring stretch they were trying to hold.

"Bellies, bellies, bellies…" Mindy reminded them to pull in their stomachs. "Good!"

Bella groaned and flopped onto the ground. "Holy cow, that one kills me!"

"It's your bad knee, try the modified pose, like this," Mindy suggested, showing her what to do. A petite woman with a mop of curly golden hair and an incredibly strong, limber body, she was a physical therapist friend of Laurie's who taught Pilates classes for extra income. She was teaching us about "the mind-body connection," and we all agreed that the more toned our muscles became, the more focused our minds became as well. It worked in reverse, too. By thinking about moving muscles we hadn't moved in years, we were training them to respond. Mindy had a huge smile, a vibrant voice, and she radiated energy.

Laurie looked up and saw me. "Emily's back! Hooray!!" They all sat up and applauded and cheered. I took a bow. Then everyone started getting up to hug me, as each one welcomed me home. I felt loved and important, basking in their warmth. After Mindy hugged me, she looked at the clock on the wall and suggested this was a good time to stop for the day. We all agreed to meet again next week, and the girls started to tidy up the space. I put the electric kettle on and brewed several pots of Irish Breakfast tea. When all the tables and chairs had been repositioned, we gathered around the coffee bar and drank a cup together.

"So, how was it?" Laurel asked, looking slim and fit in her purple leggings and Green Thumb T-shirt. Today she wore tiny silver moons and stars dangling from her ear lobes.

"Well, first of all, F. Scott Fitzgerald was absolutely right!" I replied.

"'The very rich are different from you and me…'" Alyssia said, recognizing my reference. She taught English at the high school and nodded knowingly. She had slipped a bright blue tunic on over her leggings and sports bra, and was wrapping her head in a colorful turban. Like several of the women, she would be heading straight to work from here.

"You got it," I confirmed.

"Lexi Land is a pretty weird place, eh?" asked Bella, sitting perched on one of the bar stools, a cold pack balanced on her knee. Mindy stood next to her and held it in place while they secured it with Velcro straps.

"Was it all these snobby rich guys with snooty British accents, or what?" perky little Mei wanted to know, piping up in her high girlish voice, and we all laughed.

"Lots of white-haired old geezers wearing black suits, and incredible huge diamonds and pearls on all of the women. At least half of them were over seventy. They all looked so much alike it was impossible to tell them apart. The most interesting characters were Lexi's immediate family, her parents and her two brothers," I said, taking a scone off the plate Siri had brought in from the kitchen. Suddenly I was starved, and remembered I hadn't eaten since last night. Getting off the Island while the opportunity was available had seemed more of a priority this morning.

"Tell us about their house! Is it incredible?" demanded Mindy, taking her teacup and settling down onto the stool next to Bella's.

"Is it obscenely enormous?" Laurie asked.

"Yes! What was it like?" Siri stood behind the coffee bar, cup in hands. She had wrapped one of her wide, long blue-green scarves like a sarong over her low-cut black spandex exercise clothes, and she looked like a voluptuous sea goddess once again.

They all chimed in curiously, and awaited my response with shining, eager eyes.

"It's pretty big," I answered, "I think there are eight bedrooms in the main house, plus there's an addition on the back of the kitchen where the housekeeping couple live. Each bedroom has its own bathroom, and some have a private sitting room too. The house sits up on this big hill overlooking the beach in two directions. And there's also a four-car garage and two other buildings, guest cottages. Two of Lexi's cousins were staying there, they both have young kids. All together, they could probably put up about twenty-five or thirty people, I think, with nobody sleeping on the couches."

"Wow," said Siri. The others nodded agreement. "Where did you stay?"

"Lexi has a suite in the main house, with a second bedroom that opens into her sitting room. I stayed there, with her. The whole place is gorgeous, beautifully decorated, right out of a magazine. Lexi's rooms are all done in Laura Ashley floral prints, very girly and romantic."

"Was she really flipped out?" Bella asked.

"Totally," I confirmed.

"Did you have to scrape her up off the floor, or what?" she persisted.

I nodded.

"Everyone totally lost it at the funeral and they were sobbing and crying," I said, "And then they all got drunk, which kind of made it worse. Some people seemed to brighten up and have a great time, though. I guess it depends on your body chemistry!"

"People can get pretty wild at a funeral," Mindy remarked. "It almost like they need to express an affirmation of life, at a time of death."

"Yes," Laurie nodded. "There is usually a lot of illicit sex going on. Have you ever noticed that?"

I rolled my eyes. "Oh yeah, I noticed!" The girls all giggled.

Siri looked at me with her eyebrows raised. "Emily! Not you!"

"No, no, not me," I replied. "Though it wasn't for a lack of invitations. Lexi's brothers are very competitive, and at some point they decided I was going to be the prize. A bunch of the younger people gathered at one of the guest houses to hang out after the service, and there was a lot of sneaking off happening."

"Does Lexi have a boyfriend? Was he there?" Alyssia asked.

"Actually, yes. He's a *doctor*!"

Everyone said, "Ooooooooooh!" in silly voices, and then we all laughed.

"So how come Mr. Doctor didn't come here to pick her up instead of you having to do it?" Bella asked, sniffing disdainfully.

"Because he was scheduled to perform spinal surgery in Boston, and people were going to be crippled for life if he didn't show up, you know, stupid stuff like that," I said.

"Excuses, excuses!" Bella shook her head.

"He's a very nice guy. Good looking, too. And he really seems to adore Lexi! I guess the only problem is, he works all the time. She's thinking about moving her art business to Boston, so they can see each other more. Her clients will follow her anywhere. "

Everyone nodded, agreeing this would be a wise move on her part. I realized we were all sitting there sympathizing with Lexi, just like she was a real, normal woman like us. I'd been having this unusual sensation quite often over the past few days. It was disconcerting. But it felt, right. Lexi *was* a real, normal woman like us. With the caveat that her point of view was different, so her expectations and definition of "normal" were different.

Being around Lexi was like watching a soap opera happening in 3D all around you, live and in person. She and her fair-haired clan were bigger-than-life, and they all were perfectly dressed and perfectly air-brushed at all times. They all had carefully modulated voices. The women wore tailored suits by Dior or Chanel, and they were lean and beautiful with smooth faces, red lipstick and perfect teeth. They had beautifully styled blonde or silver hair, depending on their ages. Most of them didn't even notice me, but the ones who did at first appeared shocked, then sympathetic in a sort of you-poor-thing way. I guess they didn't think my black linen was appropriate for the occasion, but it worked fine for blending in with the background, which was my chosen vantage point.

The girls started packing up their bags to go home or to work. I told Siri she should take the rest of the day off with my thanks for filling in while I was gone. She looked relieved. I knew it had not been easy for her to spend so much time away from her family.

"Come here," I beckoned as the others went out the door. I pulled a little white paper bag out of my purse and handed it to her.

Siri smiled delightedly and opened the bag. There was a white jewelry box inside. She opened the box and found a small gold Nantucket Basket pendant hanging from a fine gold chain. These charms are a traditional keepsake from the Island, and the design is based on actual historical baskets that have long been made there. Inside the little gold basket with its lid that really opened, was a tiny diamond chip.

"Thank you so much for covering for me, Siri!" I said.

"Oh, you are very welcome!" she said, "Thank you, too! This is beautiful!"

She took the necklace out of the box and put it around her neck. We both admired it on her in the mirror on the wall.

"You know, Bella did a great job of helping out in the shop," Siri said, to my reflection. I looked at her reflected eyes and nodded.

"Well she's a doll, I'm sure the customers liked her!"

"Oh they did," Siri confirmed. "Check the receipts! I think you'll be surprised."

"That good, eh?"

She nodded, smiling, and raised both eyebrows. She started to wave her hands around in that excited manner of hers, and turned to face me directly.

"She starts telling those jokes and people love it! You should hear the way she talks to people on the phone. She creates a very happy atmosphere. Not that you and I are boring," Siri said earnestly, "But we are not stand-up comics."

I knew what she meant. Bella was the one who always made us laugh. That was a very good thing. It was something we could all use a lot more of. Laughter is healing and energizing. It builds trust when shared between friends, and gets things flowing.

The energy always seemed to flow the best when we women merged our motley assortment of characteristics together, balancing and supplementing each other. Each of us was unique, different from all the others in many ways. But we also were very much the same in essential qualities of the heart, the spirit.

For example, we were all women of imagination and creativity. Women who looked ahead, who cared about shaping the future. When we deliberately linked our thoughts and feelings together we created a new being, the group itself, which was *way* stronger than the sum of its individual parts. We gained power from each other and were emboldened by it, daring to try to make a difference in more and more audacious ways. This was one of the most beautiful things, to me, about having these wonderful women as friends.

We usually ended our Pilates sessions with a short group meditation. We all joined hands in a circle, closed our eyes, and envisioned a clean and verdant planet Earth, serenely spinning through space surrounded by a big fat shiny bubble of healthy atmosphere. We pictured frozen polar ice caps, lush rainforests, thriving species of all kinds. And wise politicians all over the globe joining their intelligence and power to enlighten and evolve mankind. We were getting pretty good at holding that mental image, now that we'd been practicing for a while. Sometimes I called the image up in my mind when I had trouble falling asleep at night. I found it comforting.

"I'll talk to Henry about asking Bella to give us some hours on a regular basis," I said, and Siri nodded in agreement. "We've been getting busier, anyhow, and it's a lot easier when there are at least two of us here. We need to be careful not to get burned out from stretching ourselves too thin. Our business is growing!" I took a step back, mentally, and looked at the long-term progress we had made. It was impressive and I was proud.

While Siri prepared to go home, I went upstairs to tell my employer I was back. He was getting ready to go out and seemed to be excited. He greeted me enthusiastically, kissing me on both cheeks. He had never done that before! I immediately wondered what was up. The old boy was very jazzed about something.

"How have things been going while I was gone?" I ventured, watching him alertly.

"Excellent! Swimmingly, in fact! Couldn't be better," he crowed, bustling around the room looking for something. "Of course, we missed you immensely, my dear."

"And how is Tony?"

"What? Tony? Very well, very well. Gave him your message, of course."

I had called the store yesterday and informed Henry of my estimated arrival time, as soon as our travel plans were confirmed. I'd asked him to pass the news on to Tony and Siri.

"Hm," he said, stopping for a moment. "Forgot what I was…oh yes!" He located a straw panama hat on the desk, and put it on his head at a rakish angle. I admired him, nodding in approval.

"Where on earth are you going, Henry Paradis?" I asked suspiciously. He was wearing Teva sandals and carrying a walking stick.

"For a stroll!" he replied, pulling out a pair of sunglasses from the desk drawer. He put them on and struck a pose for me. I chuckled. He swept out the door with a dramatic swoosh.

OK, he obviously was telling me nothing, which was not a new phenomenon around here. My employer was the maestro of mystery, when he chose to be, and he got a tremendous kick out of it. Which was fine with me, cause I loved the old boy and anyhow, *carpe diem*, I had work to do downstairs in my place of business.

I grumbled a little to myself as I went down the stairs. He had already disappeared, as had Siri, and I was alone in the store. I wandered around, looking at everything with fresh eyes. Being away for a while had given me a new perspective. I'd gotten some display ideas from the shops on Nantucket.

I unlocked the front door and put the A-frame sign out on the sidewalk in front of the building. It was a sunny, hot summer day. There was lots of activity up and down the street and across the way I saw John with his straw hat on, pushing a wheelbarrow through the garden in front of the flower shop. He saw me and we waved. I realized how much I loved this neighborhood and the friendly, open, positive attitudes of the people who worked and lived here.

Heading back inside to get to work, I thought about how different they were from the people I had met at the Gladstone funeral. None of my new friends were rich, or dressed in gorgeous clothes, or lived in huge mansions. But they were wealthy beyond the dreams of any reasonable person in terms of happiness and fulfillment. They cared about things that were really important, and if they ever had a spare moment from struggling to pay the bills, they used the time to help someone else.

They were a community, a melding of resources and attitudes, and faiths, and races, and ages, and genders, and sexual orientations, and everything else. Like my circle of women, this community was also *way* stronger than the sum of its individual parts.

I worked on my new display for the antique lace and linens for most of the morning, with very little interruption from either customers or the telephone. It was a quiet day in the neighborhood, and there was no sign of either my wayward employer or my wayward boyfriend. Perhaps they were off being wayward together somewhere, I wouldn't have put it past them. I felt oddly left out and a little jealous. In any case, my day was quiet to the point of nearly being boring, when I heard the back door open and Amy stuck her head into the room.

"Hey!" she greeted me with enthusiasm. She came across the room to talk to me while I was staple-gunning a floral bed sheet onto the free-standing partition I had just made out of the lid of one of the giant wooden crates in the basement.

"What's up?" Amy asked. As an afterthought, she flashed me a peace sign. "You back now? Like, for good and all?"

"Yeah, I am totally back," I said, "Hey, is your Mom OK? How is she doing?"

Amy shuffled back and forth nervously, avoiding eye contact.

"Well, she's better, actually. She might be getting a job soon!" She looked up and I saw she was trying to suppress her hopeful excitement.

"Wow," I said encouragingly, "That is way cool! It's great to hear she's feeling well enough to work!"

"Isn't it?" said Amy. "I thought we were movin' to the hospital at one point." She brushed her ragged bright red and black striped hair out of her face, tearing up. She looked up at me with her heart in her eyes, saying, "I want to thank you for what you did for us, Emily." She looked out from under her long bangs shyly.

"No problem," I said briefly, tearing up a little bit myself. OK, more than a little.

We blinked rapidly at each other for a few minutes, but did not touch. She wasn't ready for that yet, it was clear from the prickly energy that radiated from her body.

"Hey Amy," I said, thinking.

"Yeah?"

"Want to do a couple more things around here every day, and maybe, like, get paid for it?"

She looked stunned. "Like, what?"

"Like, help in the kitchen or clean and dust stuff, pack boxes, that kind of thing."

"I can do that," she said slowly, wonderingly. "I mean, I think I can. Do you really want me to? Like, a job?"

I turned casually and showed her my back for a minute, fussing with the display, giving her a chance to think privately.

"I wouldn't ask you if I didn't think you could do it, Amy," I said.

There was silence behind me. Then, "Sweet! When do I start?"

"How about today?" I said, struggling to hold the sheet and staple it at the same time. "Maybe you could help me with this new display I'm trying to put together!"

"Sure," she said, frowning. "You're going to pin stuff up there? That's like, a background?"

"Yes, exactly."

"Won't that, kind of, make holes in all your stuff?"

"It would, yes, so I need to find a better way to attach them. They used pushpins at the store where I saw this done. They just make a teeny hole."

"You got any ribbons? The nice kind, like from a sewing store?" She had a calculating look in her eye.

"I could easily get some. What's your idea?"

"You could make big loops out of ribbons, maybe with bows if you want, and attach them to the background with staples, then you'd tuck the lace through the loops and it could hang down from them. It would look nice, kind of cascading down…"

It was a dynamite idea, and would look even better than what I'd planned. I was going to put this tall display behind the antique trunk and the shelves where we kept the old textiles. A pile of folded fabrics doesn't look like much, so we needed an artful way to let people know what we were offering.

I went over to the cash register and opened it, taking out several bills. I made a note on a pad inside the drawer, and closed it again.

"Here," I said, handing her the cash. "Take this and go buy the ribbons from the dressmaker down the street. I saw it on her sign, she has notions and thread. If she isn't open, I can drive over to the mall later, or tomorrow."

She received the money solemnly. She folded it up and stuffed it deep into her pants pocket, which I hoped had no holes in it. Her other clothes had them dotted about liberally, probably for deliberate effect.

"Hey, this is awesome, Emily!" she said with a grin, and sped out the back door.

She was back in half an hour with a shopping bag full of grosgrain and patterned fabric ribbons, various colors, to go with the floral sheet which was now firmly attached to its frame. We worked together for an hour or so, and then I stopped and let her finish it. She was obviously more than capable. I decided to give her a shot at the two windows on Crescent Street after we got through the weekend.

By the time Amy had finished our new display looked wonderful and several customers had already commented on it. One elderly lady had actually purchased a lace table runner after stopping to admire the goods. The day slowly crept to an end and I still had not seen Tony, nor had Henry reappeared. Then finally the telephone rang.

"Hello, darling Emily," Tony said, sounding upbeat.

"Hello your darling self," I said, smiling. "There you go again, trying to make me think you like me, or something."

He chuckled, a rich deep sound. "What are you doing right now?"

"Don't you mean, what are you *wearing* right now?" I whispered into the phone wickedly.

"No, but since you mentioned it...?" he whispered back, playing along.

It had gotten hot during the day and I was sweating, fanning myself with a newspaper. I didn't like to use the air conditioning unless it was absolutely necessary.

"More than I would like to be, I assure you," I answered.

"Well!" he said delightedly, "Let me come over there and help you with that!"

"Certainly, you can come over here. You live here, remember?"

"Um, yes. I haven't been there much for the past few days. But, what do you say we meet over at Laurie and John's place for a drink in a few minutes? I'll go straight there."

"Great, I'm starved," I said, realizing it was true.

"You're always starved."

"No I am not, only at meal times, when I'm supposed to be. And, when I haven't had anyone to hug and kiss me for a long time!"

"Well, you poor girl, we will have to satisfy your cravings immediately!"

"Just one thing first," I said, switching to a serious tone, "Have you heard from Henry at all today? He went out for a walk this morning and he never came back!"

There was silence on the phone line for a moment, except for the sound of cars in the background.

"Yes, I did speak to him a little while ago. He was with a friend. I told him we would not be around for dinner. He's fine, don't worry!"

"OK, good," I said, relieved. We said goodbye and hung up.

As I sent Amy off with a large container of leftovers and a satisfied smile on her face, I reflected that people with big money like the Gladstones didn't necessarily have to get so carried away with it. They didn't have to live in huge houses that were empty most of the time, or drive cars that guzzled gas and were killing the environment. They could afford to invest in solar panels instead of buying endless gallons of oil for their heating and cooling systems. They could live responsibly as all inhabitants of planet Earth should, rich or poor. It would be better for us all if everyone practiced moderation.

I went into the little bathroom and brushed my hair, putting on some eye makeup and freshening my lipstick. This cat and mouse game with Tony was making me a little nuts. Whatever was really going on between us, I wanted to bring it right out into the open. Flirting was fun and I loved the verbal repartee, but enough's enough. It was time for some honesty and plain talk, as far as I was concerned. I locked up the building, and set off across the intersection to tell him exactly that.

Chapter 15

The Devil

HEDONISM & OVERINDULGENCE

Description: The horned, clawed, bat-winged Devil stands grinning behind a naked man and woman who are chained to his throne.
Meaning: Hedonism, gluttony and excess. Wild sensual experiences. Sometimes it's healthy to purge these feelings, and sometimes it's dangerous.

The evening sky was streaked with deep rose and magenta, with a few lavender clouds clinging to the western horizon.

Heat radiated up from the black pavement under my sandaled feet. We were hoping for some rain late tonight according to the forecast on the radio, but at the moment it was clear and still, and the air was sultry.

All the outside tables at the Green Thumb were occupied and I didn't see Tony, so I pushed the double doors open and went inside. John and Laurie were both behind the bar, and the place was hopping. A sign near the entrance said, "Please Wait to Be Seated," so I did. Laurie looked up when I came in and saw me, smiling and holding up one finger in a "wait one minute" gesture. I looked around and still didn't see my date, so I walked over to the bar and slid onto an empty stool in front of the beer taps. It was a little early for dinner but I only saw a couple of empty tables. Everyone was out on the town tonight, blowing off steam from the work week and trying to cool down.

"Hi, girlfriend!" Laurie said, putting a cocktail napkin in front of me. "Tony called and we're holding you a spot in the corner," she said, gesturing toward a table for two. "Can I get you a drink while you wait?"

"Yes, definitely. How about a gin and tonic?"

"Lime?"

"Yes, please. Do you have Tanqueray?" I asked, squinting at the forest of liquor bottles behind the bar.

"Absolutely!" she replied, grabbing the green bottle to mix me my favorite summer cocktail. She shook it up in a silver cocktail shaker and poured it onto ice cubes in a tall, frosty glass. She placed the pretty drink on the napkin in front of me. I squeezed my lime wedge into the mixture and took a refreshing sip, enjoying the bubbly bright taste.

Laurie and John were both too busy to talk, so I drank alone while I looked around the room watching the diners enjoy themselves. Nearly everyone was dressed in casual summer weekend clothes, though a few people had obviously come straight from the office and their suit jackets were slung over the backs of their chairs. It was such a hot, humid night that everyone was eager to shed as many garments as possible. Neckties were off, shirts were untucked and collars were opened. A lot of skin was visible in various shades of black, brown and beige, and it all shone with the gleam of sweat, despite the air conditioning and ceiling fans inside the restaurant.

I was still wearing my navy blue cotton sundress, which had successfully gotten me back and forth to the Island. It had little narrow straps and buttoned down the front, or unbuttoned down the front, as I wished. Tonight it was open to the third button and when I crossed my legs the skirt fell open halfway up my thigh.

I had pinned my hair up off my hot neck and shoulders and it was starting to curl, damp from the humidity. A little trickle of perspiration ran down into my cleavage and I shivered.

My eyes must have fluttered because suddenly there he was, standing right in front of me. Once again, I had forgotten how good-looking he was. Or, maybe he actually *was* getting more and more handsome all the time, I don't know, but it definitely seemed that way to me. The nice thing was that he seemed to feel the same way about me.

"Sorry to be late," Tony said, zooming in to kiss me on the cheek. "Welcome home, traveler!"

He stood back a little and stared at me with his dark eyes shining. He wore a vanilla short-sleeved linen shirt and khaki shorts, with brown leather sandals on his feet.

"Don't you look just…adorable!" Tony gloated quietly, his face flushed. He gazed at me admiringly, particularly interested in the third button area. I sat up a little straighter and smiled at him. His eyebrows rose in appreciation.

Laurie came over just then to lead us to our table. It was next to the window in the back on the Crescent Street side, very private and quiet. I thanked her and she grinned at me, taking our drink order and leaving a couple of menus on the table.

While we supposedly studied the menu, we secretly watched each other. I found myself acutely aware of him. I knew exactly how many centimeters away his fingers were from mine on the tabletop. When he raised his eyes and caught me looking at him, he flashed a smile and reached out to capture my hand and raise it to his lips. His full, soft, wonderful lips. My attention was riveted and I forgot all about the serious conversation I'd wanted to have. For just a minute or two. Oh, yes. And then it all came flooding back to me and I remembered.

"What have you been doing since I left town?" I asked casually, trying to get the conversation rolling along so I could steer it in the desired direction.

"Oh, this and that," he answered absently, or perhaps evasively, as he read the menu. He put it down on the table. "I've been working on a new project, an investment actually. I've been on the run."

"Oh?" I said, not very knowledgeable about stocks or investments. Reflexively, I wondered whether he had actually found a new girlfriend, rather than a new financial opportunity. Knowing that I tend to be a little paranoid about such things, I pushed the thought out of my mind.

"To your homecoming," Tony held up his cocktail, and I raised mine. We clinked, and drank. The hum of the busy restaurant buzzed around us.

I glanced out of the window at the view down Crescent Street to the east. The sky was now tinted a dark salmon pink, and right between the buildings at the end of the street, the huge, swollen moon was rising. It looked full and round and enormous, a deep red-gold glowing disk that was just starting to show above the rooftops.

"Look!" I said to Tony. He turned around and we both watched for a minute. People seated outside on the patio were pointing at the sky, and turning their chairs to witness the moon's ascent. Our waiter came over and took our order. Tony chose a bottle of Chardonnay to have with the main courses and I ordered the sautéed oysters appetizer for us to share. He asked for refills on our cocktails, at a nod from me when I polished off my second gin and tonic. I was starting to relax and have a good time, so I figured a little more would be even merrier. It was unfair of me to be so suspicious, I thought. Time to lighten up!

He seemed to be feeling more comfortable too as the conversation started to flow along in an animated fashion, the way it always did when we were discussing one of our common interests. We discussed international politics passionately for a while. By the time I had calmed down, our food and more drinks arrived.

We shared the plate of heavenly oysters, dipping them into some kind of tangy brown sauce. I wondered privately if it was true that they were an aphrodisiac. Squirming a little in my seat, I felt the energy spark between us when our hands bumped or our eyes met. In answer to his questions, I told Tony a little about my experiences on Nantucket. Then the rest of our meal came, and the wine, and everything tasted marvelous. Tony told a few silly jokes and I started to giggle.

I was feeling happy and quite reckless. I even stopped wondering about whether or not to believe what he said, and just reacted to it. I figured that since we had eaten a large meal it would somewhat counteract the alcohol, and I still seemed to be able to navigate between the tables in the restaurant without hitting anything.

When I went to the ladies' room I saw myself in the mirror: eyes glowing, cheeks flushed and a few little tendrils of curling hair escaping from the loose pile pinned up on the crown of my head. I looked like I was ready for trouble, or ready to make some!

When Laurie came over with the check she gave me a funny look.

"Are you OK?" she whispered to me behind her hand.

"What do you mean?" I asked, my eyes wide.

"Emily! You're smashed!"

"I'm not!"

"Yes you are!"

"OK, I am, a little. But it's OK. I'm not driving."

"Don't worry, Laurel, I'm going to take her for a nice walk now. I'll take care of her," Tony said, signing the credit card slip.

"You are?" I said, delighted. "Where?"

"I thought we should enjoy the moonlight and go to visit your favorite mediation spot," Tony said, taking my arm and steering me toward the double doors.

"Good night! Have a fun evening!" Laurie grinned and shook her finger at me warningly.

By now the moon had turned a rosy yellow and risen up above the buildings. Their black shadows leaned out into the streets toward the west. It was very bright outside, and the world was covered by a thin veil of dark golden light.

There were people all over the place. On the sidewalks, in the open windows of the buildings, on the steps and porches and even on the rooftops. They were talking, laughing, fighting, playing checkers, jiggling babies, strumming guitars, walking along with dazed eyes and their arms entwined around one another, kissing. Cars passed and honked, stopped, let people out or picked people up, and proceeded again. People dodged between the cars to cross the streets, not using the crosswalks or waiting for the lights to change. I could hear three or four different kinds of music playing, coming from all directions.

It was still very hot and humid. Many of the men were bare-chested or wearing sleeveless T-shirts. The women wore loose cotton dresses and the girls wore little teeny tiny tube tops or camisoles and cut-off jeans. Their breasts showed clearly beneath the skimpy tops and their flat young midriffs featured pierced navels with shiny gold rings or jewels. The sheen of sweat was on everyone. We reflected the golden moonlight on our exposed bodies and our wet hot skin as the sound of African drums came floating down the street and a car drove by with open windows, playing loud Latin music on the radio.

Tony and I crossed Market to the far corner by the medical building and walked down the sidewalk toward the park. It was quieter over here, mostly professional offices that were closed at night. The park itself was surrounded by more townhouses like the ones on Crescent, and some cute Victorian and Federal era houses.

We walked in companionable silence with our fingers linked, swinging our arms between us. I was definitely a little drunk, probably more than a little, and I was practically skipping along full of energy. The moon made dark splotchy shadows under the trees that lined the sidewalk as we neared the gates, always open, and entered the park. We walked a little way down the pebbled path and there it was, the fountain with the giant carp.

"Oh mighty Poseidon!" Tony intoned, dropping my hand to approach the statue with both of his raised to the sky. "We come here to honor you tonight! And to thank you for revealing this beautiful goddess to me right here in your holy temple!" he said, gesturing as though to draw me to the attention of the fish, to whom he bowed.

"Well, your turn!" he said in a stage whisper, beckoning.

"Oh mighty god of the sea, father of Aphrodite the goddess of love, who was born on the crest of a wave from the foam of your jism," I called out in ringing tones, showing off my considerable mythology expertise, "We honor you!" I bowed to the carp as well, with a very deep curtsy.

"*Jism?*" Tony said, one eyebrow raised. "I never heard that one!"

"Yes, of course, " I said. "He masturbated, and the goddess of love was born from the foam that resulted. You know, full-grown and naked on the half-shell like in the painting. She didn't have an actual mother, she was born from magical semen."

"Really!" he exclaimed, taking my hands to help me rise from my curtsy, which had placed me in dangerously close proximity to the ground. I staggered and clutched at him to steady myself. He put his arm behind me to help, then scooped me up tightly for one of his long, thorough kisses.

A minute or a month later, I couldn't have told you which, we were gaily strolling through the deserted park again, heading further off down the path past the fountain. I felt giddy and daring. The little park was beautiful in the moonlight, secret and private. I breathed in the moist air, scented by some sweet night-blooming flower, and felt a sweeping rush of pure happiness. The playgound and tennis courts were over this way. I found a swing and sat on it, swaying back and forth, enjoying the breeze.

Tony picked up some tennis balls and started to juggle them, throwing first one then the next up in the air, catching them carefully when they fell. He was slow, but really pretty good at it. Just another in the series of surprises for me about this man, who had turned out to be so different from my first impression. It was a lesson in the danger of jumping to conclusions. I might have missed all this, had I gone with my first instincts.

He seemed as happy as I was, maybe not quite as inebriated but enjoying himself immensely. There was a big grin on his face as he concentrated on the tennis balls, showing off for me.

"Where did you learn how to do that?" I demanded to know.

"I taught myself," he answered, dodging to the left.

"Just one of your many natural talents?"

"Exactly!" he said, dodging to the right. "I keep telling you how wonderful I am, Emily! When are you finally going to believe me?" He threw one of the balls over his shoulder and caught it behind his back. I applauded, to his obvious delight.

"And how many of these amazing natural talents do you have?" I asked.

"Oh, quite a lot of them!" Tony said, catching all the balls in his hands, one at a time. He tossed them back into the empty tennis court and came over to me where I sat on the swing.

"Shall I show you a few more?" he asked, pulling me up from my seat. Not to kiss me again as I expected, but to steer me further down the path.

I started to wonder what he was doing, and where he was taking me. Down the garden path, it seemed, in more ways than one. But the moonlight was gorgeous and I was full of excitement, so he propelled me along.

On the other side of the tennis courts there was a fragrant rose garden, but he marched me right through it and out the gate onto the sidewalk of the street that ran along the back edge of the park. This was where some old single-family homes had been lovingly restored and painted interesting historically accurate colors. They had beautiful gardens and little yards in the back, some with front porches featuring swinging benches and rocking chairs. I had driven past here several times and adored this street.

"Come on," he said, pulling me along, "I want to show you something."

We walked briskly down the sidewalk arm in arm, past gracious homes whose lighted windows showed cozy, comfortable rooms where people were visible living their lives. One such scene showed us an older man playing backgammon with a teenaged girl, another revealed a mother with a pile of sewing in her lap, watching television with a group of children tussling on the floor in front of her. As we approached a pretty plum-colored Victorian I waited to see what would be spotlighted in this family's windows. The draperies were drawn shut, but I noticed that a cat had slipped underneath them and was sitting in the front window looking out. It looked sweet, homey. There was a For Sale sign on the lawn and I wondered where the cute kitty would be moving to when his owners sold their home. A new-looking silver car was parked in the driveway. It was a Prius, in fact. Ahoy there, I thought, another ecologically aware fellow traveler! I glimpsed the license plate number and was astonished to discover that I recognized it.

"Isn't that your car?" I asked, frowning, as he silently steered me up the front steps of the house. The front door opened when he turned the knob.

"And, isn't that my cat?" I demanded, as Tree jumped down off the windowsill and came rushing over to me, purring frantically. He rubbed himself madly back and forth against me as I squatted to pat him. Tony closed the door behind us and stood watching with his arms crossed and a satisfied smirk on his face.

The house was nearly empty, with just a few pieces of furniture sitting on the gleaming wood floors. There was a large room to the left with a fireplace, in front of which a dark brown leather sofa and two lamp tables had been positioned. Tree suddenly abandoned my stroking hands and stalked away toward the back of the house in that "follow me!" way of his, tail held high, turning to see if I was coming and saying, "Mmrrr?" He wanted to be fed.

I laughed. "Well, I guess he knows his way around, huh? What have you been up to, Tony Novak?" I asked, shaking my finger at him. "Breaking and entering?"

"It's not breaking and entering if you have a key, it's just entering," he answered.

"And, how did you get this key?" I demanded, starting to wander through the rooms and look around, vaguely following my cat. My voice echoed in the empty space.

"My realtor gave it to me," he replied innocently, walking past me and going into the kitchen, where the large greenish-gray granite island in the center of the room showcased an impressive six-burner gas range. Tree was crunching dry cat food in the corner on the floor, where two small bowls sat on a newspaper. Tony opened the stainless steel refrigerator door and pulled out a bottle of our favorite champagne. An ice bucket and two tall, narrow glasses stood on the granite counter next to the fridge. I slipped out of my sandals and stood barefoot on the cool tile floor.

"Your realtor?" I asked.

"Yes, Emily," he said, popping the cork and pouring two glasses of the bubbly elixir. "Welcome to my new home!" he announced, handing me my glass. "You are the first guest. Well, except for Henry of course. He's been helping me move in."

"Mr. Paradis? He was here today?"

"I told you he was with a friend."

"How on earth could you find this place and complete the purchase so quickly?"

"I'm renting until we can have the closing," he said, "What do you think of it?"

"I love it!" I said, and meant it.

The big kitchen was fabulous, with its cherry cabinets and stainless steel fixtures. There was a double sink with a graceful, curving faucet, and a spacious nook surrounded by windows was in the far corner, where the kitchen table would eventually stand. The island had room for four bar stools on the side opposite the stove. The walls were painted an appetizing *café au lait* color. I liked it very much and it would be very convenient to cook in, the way it was laid out.

"Want to see the rest?" Tony invited, hooking his arm

through mine. We brought our champagne and wandered through the empty downstairs rooms. Everything was spotless and the woodwork was beautiful.

"My furniture is coming from England in two weeks," Tony said as we stood and looked out the window at the backyard, bathed in moonlight. "I already bought a few new things though, just what I'll need until then."

He took the empty champagne glass out of my hand and put it next to his on the windowsill.

"Come upstairs," he said quietly, and led me up the winding staircase.

At the top of the stairs he turned toward the back of the house where the master suite looked out over the garden. A dim light flickered from inside the bedroom as we approached the door and entered. A circular brass table covered with lighted votive candles occupied the center of a plush dark red Oriental rug, and a ceiling fan spun lazily above. In the back of the room near the bamboo-shaded windows was a very large brass bed swathed in white linens, with big white pillows and a fluffy throw of white synthetic fur.

"Very inviting!" I walked across the rug, enjoying the feel of it between my bare toes. I knew he had done all this for me and I was getting the message loud and clear, but I wanted to tease him a little bit more. "You didn't leave those candles lit over here all evening, did you?" I demanded sternly.

"Don't be silly, do you think I want to burn my house down before I even own it?" He spoke impatiently. "Henry lit them a little while ago, right before he went home."

"Oh, so he is in on this too, eh? I'm not sure how I feel about that, it might be illegal you know, with the labor laws and all!"

"Emily, don't be ridiculous. Henry is a *romantic*, you know that."

I walked over to the bed, inspecting the elegant pattern of

the brass head and footboards, with its knobs and curlicues.

"So Henry approves of you getting me drunk and seducing me here tonight, is that what you're saying?" I smiled at him in a friendly way, as he followed me, looking worried. I wandered to the side of the bed and suddenly hopped on, flopping down backwards and sinking deeply into the clean crisp white cotton duvet. "*Mmmmmm...Very* comfortable!" I patted the bed next to me invitingly. "Come and see!"

He flopped himself down too, and then his warm, dark eyes were looking into mine as he lay next to me, propped up on one elbow.

"I'm glad you like it," Tony said. "And now, I am going to say something to you and you want to hear it, so stop wiggling around and torturing me!"

"Yes, Master!" I couldn't stop smiling, enjoying every minute of this. I already knew what he was going to say, and he was right, I wanted very much to hear it.

"Emily, I want you to know that when I make love to you tonight, that's exactly what it will be, do you understand?" He leaned over and kissed me firmly, finally capturing my full attention. "I'm not interested in an affair, either. I'm interested in you." He kissed me again, and looked deep into my eyes.

"Last time you said you were 'obsessed,'" I said. "And now you're just 'interested?' What's the matter, don't you like me any more?"

I started to unbutton his shirt, slowly, deliberately, one button at a time. First his chest, and then his neck, and then his face flushed a deep red. He put his mouth over mine for a longer kiss, filling me with his soft tongue and its spicy-sweet taste. He covered me with his body and pressed me into the mattress, our hips fitting together like they were made to be joined, my breasts crushed against his strong chest. My arms twined around his neck and I answered his questing tongue with mine, my head spinning as I lost myself in the moment.

We kissed, and kissed, and kissed. The layers of protective reserve dissolved and fell away. My heart floated right up to the surface, its brittle shell opening like a flower in the sun. I was ready to be vulnerable now, ready to let him in. The past was behind me and my fear of being hurt again had no place in this new world.

When we came up for air I pulled his shirt off his shoulders, slipping it down his arms to drop it on the floor. His skin was hot and silky smooth, and his curved muscular chest was softly furred. He kissed the tops of my breasts where they swelled above my sundress and used one hand to open the buttons, peeling the fabric back with the other. All I had on underneath was white lace bikinis and by the time he had revealed them I was panting.

My back arched as he took my breast into his mouth and sucked it, nibbling the tip. My nipples were on fire and I reach down myself to pull my panties off, impatient to be naked and to feel his body against mine. He grinned as I rolled him over onto his back and straddled him, unbuttoning his khaki shorts and pulling down the zipper as he watched me approvingly, arms crossed behind his head.

I stepped off the edge of the bed for a moment to slide his shorts down his thighs, snagging the elastic waistband of his underwear with my fingers and quickly stripping him. I lay beside him and ran my hand down his body from the hollow below his neck to where he swelled against my palm with a warm pulse.

His breathing hesitated for a moment and we both smiled, our eyes locked. Then I reached my mouth up to kiss him, lightly running my tongue across his lips, and he responded like a man in the desert who finally finds water, ravenously devouring me, and we were swept away on tingling waves of soft smooth stroking and erotic glimpses of pink and reddish-purple swellings.

Our movements flowed together like a graceful dance. He tasted every part of my body with his lips and tongue before he finally slipped between my legs to push inside me, looking into my soul as I gasped and wrapped my legs around him tight.

Tony closed his eyes and moaned. His handsome face filled my view, inches from mine, dark with suffused color. He opened his eyes and we reconnected, more than naked now. We had stripped right down to beyond the bone, and our spirits touched while our bodies moved together, the ultimate yin and yang.

The coiled spring tightening inside me started to quiver. Then I kissed him hard with my tongue and he immediately reacted, pushing into me and shifting in a subtle way that created intense dizzying sensation. We gasped for air and I saw his eyes flutter   and I let go completely and surrendered to the pulsing shudders that swept over us both, perfectly synchronized, perfectly matched.

A rush of blissful gratitude washed over me, and tears spontaneously ran out of my eyes. All my stress, my fear, my pain and my anger were released. He lay beside me and held me encircled in his arms, perfectly at peace. It felt like home to me, the place where I was supposed to be.

When our lovemaking finally came to an end, or should I say a pause, I had a raging thirst. Naked, I went into the bathroom and drank right from the tap. Tony's shaving gel, razor and toothbrush were on the back of the sink. I noticed there was a huge double Jacuzzi tub next to the big double shower. A container of lavender bath salts sat on the edge of the tub near the faucets, and four fluffy white towels hung from the racks. More candles were lit nearby.

This man had thought of everything! Or, was it Henry? Had he once bought lavender bath salts for her, for Margaret? Did he hope for the same happiness for us that they had found together? It was very endearing. This must be why Henry had been so excited this morning, and why he had behaved so affectionately. He wanted Tony and me to be together. He had hinted as much, several times.

Tony was eagerly waiting for me in bed. Very eagerly! We were starved for each other, seemingly insatiable. I had not made love like this with a man for many years, not since my early college days when I met a boy named Tristan, my first lover, who eventually dumped me. At four in the morning when we were sitting next to each other in the Jacuzzi, soaking in lavender bath salts and feasting on low fat yoghurt and *Veuve Cliquot*, we talked about Tristan.

"He was a fool!" Tony said comfortingly, raising my hand out of the water to kiss it.

"Thank you, but actually he was a genius," I said. "He studied social psychology with Jean Piaget in Switzerland during his junior year abroad, and then he kept going back there every few months for the next couple of years to finish some project they were working on together."

"And he kept leaving you behind?" Tony asked, satisfyingly indignant.

I nodded, still feeling vulnerable when I thought about it.

"He carried my photo in his wallet and told everyone I was his girlfriend, but he only wrote me one letter in three years and when he was home he'd say that while he loved me, he wasn't 'in love' with me. We'd have wild sex constantly for days, and then he'd go away again." I took a sip of champagne and stared into space. "He accused me a being a 'physicalist.' He seemed to think it was a bad thing. I tried to talk to him about it, but he wasn't really interested in listening to what anyone else had to say."

"What is a 'physicalist?'"

I shrugged my shoulders. "He wouldn't say. I guessed he meant I liked having sex too much."

"No, that can't be right!" Tony looked at me doubtfully.

"It's impossible!"

"What's impossible? Having too much sex?"

"No, *liking* it too much is impossible."

"What about people who are addicted to sex?"

"That's different. If they are addicted to it, they aren't really enjoying it any more. It has become a negative thing."

"I might get addicted to having sex with you, would that be a negative thing?" I ran my big toe up his leg and slipping my foot between his knees.

"Emily!" He gasped happily. "You are a very naughty girl!"

"I am?"

"Yes," he said firmly, "Come over here immediately!" He pulled me up over his wet, slippery body, sliding me across his chest.

"Let me show you what I do with sex addicts!" he said in a low growl. He slapped me on the rump and whispered in my ear, "It's time for your spanking now…"

The demonstration lasted for quite some time.

We watched the sun rising from the kitchen windows while we waited for the coffee to brew. I was wrapped in a rumpled bed sheet, and Tony was wandering around the house stark naked. He came up behind me, reaching to unwrap the sheet and put it around both of us, our bodies pressed together underneath. We watched the sky change color as the sun rose.

I felt a little sore and even bruised, but totally balanced and serene. I actually thought I might know now what that boy had been talking about, the difference between "loving" and being "in love." Because there was no doubt about it, I was in love with Tony. Absolutely head over heels, madly, utterly.

We drank coffee and Tony went upstairs to get dressed in his gym clothes, taking my car keys with him to jog through the park and fetch my car from where it was parked in the alley behind the store. My luggage from the trip was still in the trunk. While he was gone, I wandered through the house in my sheet toga, imagining what it would look like furnished.

When he came back very soon he had bagels and cream cheese in a paper bag for our breakfast. We ate them sitting side by side on the back patio while we watched the local bird population fight over the water in the birdbath at the edge of the yard. Apparently it had rained last night, as there were puddles here and there. I hadn't noticed a thing, and Tony laughed and admitted he hadn't either.

He brought my suitcase upstairs and left me there to shower and dress. When I came down the stairs, he was sitting on the brown leather couch reading a newspaper.

"I'd better go to work now," I announced to the room. His eyes lit up to see me standing there, and the color began to rise into his face again. I recognized that look by now.

"Oh no," I said, taking a step backwards and waving my hand, "I mean, I really have to go now!"

He laughed at me, and got up to kiss me goodbye.

"But, you'll be back?" he asked, hopefully.

"Try and stop me."

"I'll never do that!"

"Wise man," I said, and went out the door.

That day I was such a total zombie at work that Siri and Bella were concerned about me, and finally they asked if I was ill.

"No, just a little, um, hung over, I guess," I admitted, rubbing my sore temples.

They looked at each other, then back at me, expectantly.

"OK, so I got loaded last night and slept with Tony! Though sleeping isn't exactly what we were doing..." I caved in and confessed.

"How was it?" Bella demanded.

"Let me tell you after I've had a nap," I replied, and we all giggled.

"That good, eh?" Bella wisecracked, winking.

"He's a very remarkable man," I said, holding my head in my hand. "Did I tell you he's got a house over behind the park?"

They exchanged glances again, and then looked back at me. I told them about the Victorian, the walk through the park, the cat in the window being Tree. They loved it.

"Wow," said Siri, rolling her eyes. "What a romantic story!"

She looked down at the simple gold wedding band on her left hand.

"I still remember the first time I made love with Tom," she said. "I knew immediately that we would be together forever."

"Yeah?" said Bella, "Well I didn't. I thought I was just going to have a fun little summer fling, and be on my way to college in the fall. Then look what happened!"

I broke into a huge yawn and both my ears crackled.

"Wow," I said, "I am wasted."

Bella looked at me sympathetically.

"Why don't you go grab a few winks and I'll stay for the rest of the day," she suggested. "I still remember what it was like, though things have calmed down with us a lot by now, especially since the baby came!"

"Oh yes," Siri said, her eyes big and serious, "It makes a huge difference."

I was having trouble focusing and felt my consciousness begin to slide downhill. I thanked Bella and snuck out to my car, kind of glad not to run into Henry today. I would have felt a trifle embarrassed. I went back to my apartment and let myself in, missing Tree at first and then remembering he was still over at Tony's house. With my luggage, it turned out, and my shampoo and my toothpaste, and everything else that I used on a daily basis. Too exhausted to care, I kicked my shoes off across the room and flung myself down on the bed, falling into a deep sleep immediately.

I awoke at dusk to the sound of my telephone ringing.

"Hello?"

"Hello! Have you been taking a sick day?" asked Tony's voice.

"No, I've been taking a dead-to-the-world day. How about you?"

"I've been happy, happy, joy, joy. Just like the cartoon beagle."

"You mean, Snoopy?"

"Yes, I've been dancing for joy, like Snoopy."

I smiled fondly at the image. He was just too cute for words.

"Aren't you coming back home soon, Emily? I've been waiting all day!"

"I am home, Tony."

"No, you are not!"

"OK, all my stuff is over there anyhow."

"I have your dinner here for you, too," he said. I heard a soprano tone in the background. "And, your cat. This is a hostage situation!"

"I'll be right over," I yawned, and after I showered and changed, I was.

When I walked in the front door, he was dressed comfortably in sweats and a white T-shirt, lying on the couch with Tree curled up on his lap and reading the *National Geographic* from my coffee table, back at my apartment. I could smell something wonderful cooking in the kitchen and there was some quiet, classical music playing.

"My cat, my magazine, what's next?" I demanded.

"Pardon me?" he inquired politely, looking up from his reading and flashing me a brilliant smile. There he was again, so damned good-looking that it swept me right off my feet.

"Nothing. Keep the cat, who cares?" I smiled, as he got up off the couch and came over to kiss me hello. And kiss me again.

And then, to pull me down onto the brown leather couch to kiss me yet again, with that extreme thoroughness that I had recently come to know and love, oh so well.

A few minutes later we rolled onto the floor, and then a while after that, I was sitting on the edge of the granite island in the kitchen wearing Tony's white T-shirt and nothing else, chewing on a chicken drumstick.

"So what did you do today?" I asked.

He was wearing boxer shorts, and nothing else. And it looked very good on him, I must say. Tony is very fit, without being muscle-bound, with a naturally long and lean body type. He continued to attack the roast chicken, which had shown considerable resistance, with a carving knife.

"Oh, I installed the new stereo system and took a nap, then I went shopping and cooked dinner for you and your scruffy little cat," he answered, carefully slicing the breast meat. "I mean," he said with a frown, "Your very handsome, brave, ferocious cat!" He fed a piece of chicken skin to Tree, who was sitting on the island beside me paying close attention to the proceedings.

"And then what happened?"

"And then the most beautiful girl in the world walked into my house," he said, serving the sliced chicken onto two plates.

This sounded good! "And then what?" I persisted.

"And, then the most beautiful girl in the world took off all of her clothes, and I ravished her," he said, carefully spooning freshly shelled peas and chopped carrots onto the plates.

"Really?" I said, crossing one long, bare leg over the other. He glanced at me once, and then glanced again. "You've had an awfully good day, haven't you?" I asked, gazing at him from under my lashes.

Tony abandoned the food and slid his hands up under the white T-shirt along my thighs, my hips, my waist. Soon I was lying naked on the cool granite, smooth and hard against

my skin, spinning off into space as he took me on another
quick tour of the galaxy. This time, when I came back to full
rational awareness, we were sitting on the kitchen floor next to
each other in the dark, leaning back against the island and surrounded by an arc of flickering votive candles. We were eating
dinner, our plates in our laps.

"More wine?" he asked, offering to pour.

"No, thank you," I replied absently, putting my empty
plate on the floor next to me and sighing.

"What's the matter?" he said, concerned.

"I'm just tired, aren't you?" I asked, suddenly exhausted.

Without a word, he put our dishes in the sink and took me
by the hand, leading me up the stairs. He tucked me into bed
and disappeared for a few minutes to turn things off downstairs, where I heard him moving around the house. When it
was dark and quiet inside, he came back to the bed and slipped
in between the cool sheets with me. A thump and a "Mmrrr?"
told me someone else had joined us, too.

Tony pulled me back against his chest and snuggled me. As
I started to drift off to sleep, I realized it felt now just exactly
like it had in my dream, when I'd hovered over him and lay
down next to him on the bed.

Had my dream actually created this moment, made it
happen? According to the theories described by Henry in our
recent conversation, this could be true. Henry had said that
Tony believed he could control his future with his thoughts.
Henry called it being a "visionary." Maybe I was a visionary,
too. Maybe I shaped the future with my dreams, instead of my
waking thoughts. I smiled into the darkness of the big empty
room where we lay nested together in perfect alignment, curled
blissfully in a loving embrace.

I dreamed that Tony and I were in Paris. There was a lot
of traffic and little cars zipping around, and lots of tourists in
the streets. We wanted to go to the Eiffel Tower, but though we

could see it easily in the distance, we couldn't figure out how to get there. Every cab or bus we took brought us back to where we had originally started.

Then suddenly we arrived at the tower, and I was looking up at it. The sky had filled with dark clouds and it seemed like it was going to rain. A jagged fork of lightning came out of the clouds and struck the tower, breaking it in some way. People screamed, and dangerous things started to fall down from the sky. It was terrible!

I woke up shaking in the darkness, with Tony still sleeping peacefully beside me. A summer storm had blown up outside and it was raining hard. I got up and drank some water in the bathroom, then I went back to bed and slept dreamlessly until morning.

Those first few days after Tony and I got together were what we always referred to later as The Lost Weekend. We dropped off the face of the world for a while. He wasn't kidding about it being a hostage situation, but Tree and I were willing prisoners.

We holed up at Tony's house, going out only to get provisions and clean clothes for me. And there was one short trip to the Mall where Tony bought a big flat screen TV with a DVD player, and a bunch of movies. His taste ran to classic films from the forties and fifties, and contemporary action thrillers. We both loved the old mysteries, like the Sherlock Holmes series starring Basil Rathbone, and the Charlie Chan movies.

Tony installed the TV in the built-in shelves in the master bedroom, and I made real popcorn like we do in Iowa, which is an entirely different food from the tough yellow stuff they sell at movie theaters. We turned on the ceiling fan and spent two whole days in bed watching movies, having lots of great sex and talking.

When Tuesday morning finally rolled around I was totally satiated and felt as relaxed as though I had been at some fabulous resort for a month.

Sometimes it's like that when you let out all the stops. It might be overindulgent, it might even be dangerous, but it's also very satisfying to express your desires, passions and obsessions. It completely diffused the tension between Tony and me and cemented our relationship.

That weekend was like an intensive crash course on each other, we talked about so many different things, openly and trustingly, and touched each other's most secret places. I had wanted things out in the open between us, and now they were. My entire world had changed in a critically important way, and the path I saw ahead now was shimmering and beautiful, leading us into the future side by side.

Chapter 16

The Lightning-Struck Tower

VIOLENT UPHEAVAL, DISASTER

Description: A castle tower is struck by lighting coming from dark clouds, flames shooting out of the windows and raining down from the sky. People fall toward the ground, which cracks open beneath them.
Meaning: Violent upheaval, disaster and crisis.

The telephone call from Sarah Bennet came early Tuesday morning while I was still in the kitchen baking scones. She wanted me to come to a special meeting with the Main Street merchants that afternoon to discuss merging our forces for the upcoming promotion. The key players in town had already been approached, and everyone was in favor of the collaboration. Plans were moving forward, and we needed to confirm the budget.

Sarah offered to organize a team of volunteers to work the event, with herself as the head of the stage crew. She had a lot of experience with lighting and sound systems for open air events, having organized several arts festivals and fundraising concerts. I was relieved to have access to her skills and good advice. She took a big burden off my shoulders, and now I could concentrate on hiring the performers and getting the merchants to agree on our cooperative marketing campaign.

When Henry came downstairs for his breakfast, he poked his head around the corner for a quick peek before entering the room. I caught him doing it. When he saw that I was smiling at him, he ventured hesitantly across the threshold.

"Good morning, Emily! Did you have, um, a good weekend?" he inquired timidly.

I nodded, a huge smile on my face. He brightened up and smiled back at me.

"Really?" he asked eagerly. "How marvelous!" He chuckled in a satisfied way, and looked very pleased.

"Thank you, Henry," I said earnestly.

He blushed and looked bashful, lowering his head and muttering, "Hmph! Don't know what you mean!"

"Tony told me that you helped to set up the house, lit the candles for me, all that."

"Did it work?" he asked, looking up with a glint of mischief in his eye.

"I loved it! And I felt very appreciated, by both of you."

"You are, my dear, you are! " he said emphatically.

"Well, I appreciate you too, Henry," I said, turning to put

a warm scone on a plate for him, placing it on the kitchen table. "And after this weekend, I appreciate Tony in ways I never would have dreamed of!"

We both chuckled. Henry sat down and settled in for a chat. I poured a cup of coffee and served it to him. He watched me chop celery for a minute or two while he ate and drank.

"So, things are going well between you two, I gather?" he inquired curiously.

"Yes, Henry, you were right."

"I was? Most gratifying. What was I right about this time?"

"About the path ahead. I shouldn't have been so afraid. I've seen it too, now."

He considered this rather seriously for a moment.

"And what does Tony say?" he asked.

"He says…exactly what I want to hear, whenever I want to hear it. And the rest of the time, he listens. He is the perfect man! He even cooks."

Henry laughed wheezily, slapping his knee.

"Oh Emily," he panted, wiping his eyes, "That was a good one!"

"I'm not joking, Henry," I protested. "He is the perfect man, for me, anyhow. I waited a long time to finally meet him. I can't believe how lucky I was the day I knocked on your door!"

"We were the lucky ones, Emily."

"We all are, Henry."

We smiled at each other with mutual affection. Giving me a pat on the shoulder, he went back upstairs to check on his eBay auctions.

Life floated along like a dream for me over the days and nights that followed. I was surrounded by a pink bubble of happiness, and my creativity was spinning along full tilt. All the merchants were buying ads in the special newspaper insert that was planned to cover the downtown promotion. This was now going to feature an illustrated map of downtown in the centerfold, plus a schedule of the entertainment events. Several of the stores, including mine, were being spotlighted in short written profiles, each with a photo.

I networked with the local arts organizations to find performers, and it looked like our grant money would be coming through. We were keeping it simple, with just six performances under the tent between Friday evening and Sunday afternoon. One was a story-telling session for kids early on Saturday morning, and the rest were various types of live music.

I booked street performers to work the weekend as well, organized in shifts to cover both the Main Street and Market Street shopping areas. I hired several clowns, a juggler on stilts, a woman who made animals out of balloons, folk singers, guitar players, a drummer, an accordion player, three magicians, and a man with a pair of trained dogs who did acrobatic tricks. It was shaping up to be a fun, lighthearted, family event.

Now the only thing I really had to worry about was the weather, which is always a huge gamble with an outdoor festival. I sent positive, sunny thoughts out into the universe, picturing crowds of happy shoppers enjoying perfect summer weather with a slight breeze, not too hot, under clear skies.

I went over to Sorrentino's to talk to Josie about the plans. Rocco was already there, sitting at the table in her kitchen.

"We're gonna set up a freezer chest outside and sell *gelato*, Italian ice cream in little cups," she said. "I was thinkin' about cold drinks too, people are going to be hot and thirsty, I bet!"

"I'm sure you're right," I agreed. "But they'll be hungry, too."

"Yeah," Rocco said, "We can sell pizza by the slice on the sidewalk, too. I got it covered."

He was leaning back against the wall with his feet stretched out, his fingers laced across his stomach.

"How about you?" he asked me, "What are you guys planning?"

"Henry has a bunch of books picked out to sell for just a dollar," I said, "And we're digging through all this great stuff down in the basement to see what we can mark way down. It has to be a real bargain to get people excited, according to what they said at the last DBA meeting. That won't be a problem, though. You should see what I've been finding down there!"

"Like what?" Josie wanted to know.

"Like, a big stack of that blue and white Chinese porcelain, rice bowls, I think they are. They're beautiful, but Henry said they were incredibly cheap when he bought them twenty years ago, so it's a perfect sale item. I'm only halfway done unpacking the shipping crate, there may be something else good in there too."

Bella had been down in the basement with me when I finally opened the crate under the stairs. Frankly, I was a little nervous about doing it by myself. I was tempted to tell her about our resident spirit, but there were no more signs of a ghostly presence and I didn't want to spook her so I kept it to myself.

"We're going to have two tables, one for books and one for the other stuff," I told Josie and Rocco.

"You're a good girl, Emily." Josie patted my hand where it lay on the table. "You do a good job for that old man. He's lucky he found you. You know, when his wife died, we thought he was never comin' out that door again." She shook her head dramatically.

"Yeah," said Rocco, "It was pretty sad. But Henry sure seems to be taking an interest in things again now!"

"I knew her, you know," said Josie. "We used to have coffee every morning."

"You and Margaret were girlfriends?" I asked, realizing they would have been close to the same age.

She nodded sadly. "Yeah, sure we were. She used to help

me take care of the boys when they were little," she said. "God never gave her any babies of her own, you know. But she sure did love kids."

Rocco excused himself and said he had to get back next door to stir the sauce. That left me alone with Josie in the kitchen.

"So?" she said, with a knowing look.

"Huh?" I answered warily.

"I hear you've been going around with that guy, the one who used to have the fancy car!" she confronted me, her hand on her hip.

"You mean, Tony Novak?"

"That's his name? What kinda name is that?" she asked curiously.

"It's Tony Novak's name," I shrugged.

"Yeah?"

"He's originally Czechoslovakian, actually."

"Ohhhh, yeah?" she considered this as though it were a very bizarre fact. "I never met anybody from that place before. He speaks English and everything?"

"Yes, Josie. He speaks like six or seven languages, including Italian! His parents live in Italy, he was raised there."

Her face lit up. "Ohhh! Yeah? That's great! You gotta bring him over sometime!"

"I will. He'd love it."

"I bet he hasn't had a nice red sauce like they make back home for a long time," she said, getting up. "I'll make somethin' special for him. Here," she said, bustling happily around the stove to pack some stuffed shells with extra red sauce into a plastic container. "You take this home tonight and heat it up. He's gonna be a happy man!"

"Thank you, Josie," I said, touched by her excitement.

"You like this guy, Emily?"

"Very much," I nodded.

She smiled at me and reached up to pinch my cheek affectionately.

"You're a good girl, Emily," she said again. "You tell him that. Make sure he appreciates you!"

"I will, Josie. And, I think maybe he does appreciate me. That's one of the things I like about him!"

She nodded in approval.

"He got a good job, Emily?" she considered.

"Well, not at the moment. He's, um, self-employed. But he did interview for a teaching position at the University a couple of weeks ago."

"Oh, that's good!" she said, raising her eyebrows. "That's a real good place to work. They got good benefits there. You tell him to take that job! Then you marry this guy and make some babies, Emily. You'll be a great mama!"

The timer went off on the stove and she turned to open the oven door and peer inside. I thanked her for her sage advice and the food for Tony, and left her to her cooking.

I served the stuffed shells for dinner that night at his house, adding hot garlic bread and a green salad. Tony's furniture had just arrived from London, and we ate sitting at a real table for a change. And what a table! His dining set, with seating for eight, was authentic Chippendale. I understood now why he had gone to the trouble and expense to ship his things. There were some wonderful antiques, many of an age that one only finds in Europe, where "old" means something very different from what it does here. And there were signs of his travels in Asia, beautiful rugs and wall hangings, brass tables and lamps and big heavy candlesticks, silk draperies and a carved teak screen inlaid with ivory. While the pasta warmed in the oven, we moved things around and argued over what should go where.

"I want to use the screen upstairs," Tony insisted, folding it up to carry it to the master bedroom. "It can cover the electronics when we're not using them. It spoils the mood to see all that technology when I'm trying to meditate!"

He had already placed a small Buddha statue in the center of the round brass table, and we each had a favorite floor pillow nearby. We hadn't sat down to meditate together yet, but I was looking forward to it. I was curious to see what it would be like to try to communicate while "traveling the inner planes," as it was called in the books that Tony had loaned me.

Tony and I had not spent a night apart since that first weekend. I tried to take my cat and go home to my apartment, but a couple of hours later he followed me over there. When he knocked on my door, he claimed to be having an attack of withdrawal pangs from his sex addiction. I took pity on him and let him come inside.

I was starting to understand what Henry had meant by saying "a man like Tony." Tony was an amazingly intuitive person, I learned. He believed that when the universe gives us a sign, an intuition, we should spring into action. I had actually seen him do this now, several times. Successfully, I might add. His intuitions were right on the money. I was trying to learn to have confidence in mine as well. It was hard to ignore the negative voice in my head that told me I was being silly, but when I managed to drown it out, the results seemed to justify the leap of faith.

Take my intuitions about Amy, for example. The attractive displays she had designed for our store windows were pulling in more and more new customers every day. The manager of a women's clothing store down the street had noticed, and called to ask me who had done the windows for us. I told her it was a brilliant young art student who was my summer intern, possibly available for some freelance work if the price was right. Amy got her courage up and went over to show them some of her sketches, and they hired her on the spot. She was totally thrilled, and so was I.

Meanwhile, the girls and I had started taking turns every

week hosting Ladies' Night. We met early, right after work, had a nice chat and a quick drink, and then everyone hurried home for dinner with our loved ones. Everyone brought her own beverage of choice, plus any snacks we had kicking around in the fridge.

I invited them all to come over to my apartment, when it was my turn. Tony had left his "Latin Lounge" CD on the stereo, so I turned it on, loud. The first number is a dramatic tango. Bella came over and raised her eyebrow at me, snapping out her hand in time with the music, palm up. I slapped my hand down into hers, we pointed our arms toward the far wall and tangoed across the floor together, giggling all the way. Laurie and Alyssia joined in, and then everyone else, and soon we were all dancing crazily around the room.

"What else do you have?" Siri wanted to know, flipping through my CDs.

"Oooh! Look, play this one!" said Mei, holding up my Aimee Mann album. We put it on and everyone sang as we danced.

I poured some wine for Laurie.

"How's it going with your sweetie?" she wanted to know. "He sure is one handsome man!"

"Oh yeah," said Bella, dancing suggestively. "He can have a three-way any time he wants!"

"You're offering your services?" I asked, pinching her on the butt as she wiggled past.

Somebody put on Sly and the Family Stone, "Dance to the Music." We all jumped up and flung ourselves into it, each in her own way. Siri moved elegantly, swaying and spinning in circles. Bella whipped her body around, moving her arms in wide, expressive motions. She was a fabulous dancer, coordinated and athletic. Laurie was graceful and controlled, with obvious ballet training. Alyssia rocked her hips back and forth to the beat, using her hands and facial expressions descriptively. Mei moved in delicate, flowing motions that matched her spry, petite body, but she sang as loudly as the rest of us, a big voice in a little package. Mindy had great rhythm and that bendable, flexible body. She stepped into sync with Bella, copying her moves. They laughed and flung back their heads, matching their steps as we all sang the chorus together, repeating the words. "Dance to the music," we all sang, jumping up and down in unison. The floor shook.

I started to worry a little about my downstairs neighbor. I wondered if he was home. If so, we might be hearing from him quite soon. I turned the volume down a tad and went into the kitchen to get some crackers and cheese. Laurie had brought guacamole and pita chips, too. I carried everything into the main room and put it on the coffee table. We settled down on the couch and the floor, clustering around to dip our chips into the heavenly green mush.

"Oh Emily, I forgot to tell you," Siri said, "My father has some news about Amy and her mother. He thinks he's found out where they've been living!"

"Really? Where?" I asked.

Alyssia nodded and said, "Yes, Rashid told me about this. Some of the kids were helping out at the church, painting down in the basement, where they have the Sunday School rooms."

"There is a small storage room in the back of the building that is usually locked," Siri said. "But this time it was not, and the boys went inside. It looked like someone had been sleeping there. Two pallets were laid out on the floor and there was a bundle of clothes and personal items."

"Is it possible for someone to stay there without anyone knowing?" I asked, doubtfully. "Wouldn't the minister or the deacons or someone find out about it?"

"Yes, you would think so. It's a mystery," Siri said.

"Do any of you know the people who run the church?" I asked, but they all shook their heads. "What denomination is it, anyhow?"

"I think it's Unitarian, whatever that means," said Bella.

"Rashid knows the minister, who is a woman," Alyssia told us. "She does a lot of work with the neighborhood kids. That's why he was helping with the painting. They're turning one of the rooms in the basement into a gathering place for teens, somewhere for them to hang out and listen to music, so they won't get into trouble on the street."

"That's a great idea," Laurie said. "There really isn't any-where for them to go, at the moment. I see them sitting on the sidewalk smoking cigarettes all the time."

"I hope my son is not smoking cigarettes!" Alyssia said, alarmed.

"No, not Rashid," Laurie calmed her. "He's a good boy, don't worry."

"So, the boys didn't actually see anyone in this room, right?" I asked.

"No," said Siri. "I don't think so. But they told my father they'll be keeping an eye on the place. It's just a matter of time before someone sees who it is."

We moved on to other topics as we polished off the last of the snacks and drained our glasses. The girls got up to find their shoes and bags, helping me bring the dishes to the kitchen and put them into the dishwasher. Just as they were about to leave, there was a knock on the door. Bella was the closest, so she opened it. Tony was standing in the hallway with a Sorrentino's Pizza box in his hand.

"Am I too early?" he asked, looking a bit overwhelmed by the mass of femininity gathered right inside the door.

"Oh no, baby," said Bella, pulling him in the door and shooting me one of her raised-eyebrow grins, "You're right on time!"

He went into the kitchen to put the pizza down on the countertop, and as soon as his back was turned she rolled her eyes and mouthed silently, "SO cute!" pretending to swoon and collapsing into Laurie's arms. Tony turned around to see what was so funny, a little suspicious frown on his face.

"OK ladies," I said protectively, shooing them out the door. "I'll see you all on Friday morning, if not sooner!"

We hugged and kissed each other goodbye and they trooped down the stairs. I went back into the kitchen, where Tony had put the pizza and two plates on the table. He was rummaging in the fridge, and pulled out a bag of tossed salad.

"Did you have fun with your girlfriends?" he asked.

"Sure," I answered, "I always have fun with them. They are really a great group of women."

"I hope I didn't interrupt anything," he said, uneasily.

"No, don't worry. Bella just wants to jump your bones, that's all!"

"She what?"

"She thinks you're cute," I said, putting my arms around him. "It's a compliment. We all think you're cute. Especially me."

He perked up and smiled, wrapping his arms around me too. We kissed, slowly and deliciously.

"I'm glad your girlfriends approve," he said. "I hate to think what would happen if they didn't like me. I'm sure you would break up with me immediately."

"Probably so," I teased, "But only after I had my way with you."

"Emily, are you terribly hungry right now?" he asked thoughtfully.

"Not frantically, we had hors d'oeuvres."

"Good!" he said, pulling my T-shirt up over my head and dropping it on the floor. Unzipped in a second, my skirt fell to the floor as well. Soon, we were using the kitchen counter for a purpose I was fairly certain it had not originally been designed to serve. It was all over with very quickly, but we smiled at each other afterwards in complete accord.

"Can you concentrate on your dinner now?" I asked play-fully, picking up the trail of clothing scattered across the kitchen floor. He was standing at the sink in his boxers, peeling carrots under the running water.

"I'll try," he said, turning his head to wink at me. I kissed him on the back of the shoulder, heading to the bathroom for a minute. When I came back wearing my bathrobe, he moved all the food to the coffee table. We sat on the sofa and ate pizza and salad, watching the local news on TV.

"Look!" Tony said, pointing, "It's about your festival!"

They were doing a live report about the upcoming Sidewalk Sales, talking about the "dog days" of summer and all the fun things there would be for families to enjoy next weekend. Sarah Bennet was on camera, being interviewed in front of the Gladstone Gallery. She was composed and eloquent, an experienced hand at this kind of publicity. Lexi's windows looked great behind her, filled with some colorful new abstract landscapes that I hadn't seen before. They talked about the entertainment events, mentioning the names of the performers who would be playing under the tent. When the reporter signed off, I jumped off the couch and ran for the phone, dialing Laurie's cell.

"Did you see it?" she answered, not bothering to say hello.

"Yes!"

"Omigosh, wasn't it GREAT!" she shouted excitedly.

"Can you believe it? Free advertising! The best kind!"

"Did you know this was happening?"

"No, they must have called Sarah at the last minute, she would have told me," I said.

"Emily, if they're already covering it and it isn't even happening for almost a week, we're going to be mobbed!"

"I certainly hope so," I said. "But I forgot to watch the weather forecast, I got so excited and ran to call you."

"Fair skies for this week, chance of scattered showers after that," Tony interjected, watching the broadcast. I repeated this to Laurie.

"OK, so it might rain a little, and it might not. Just like always," she said. "We have to concentrate on good weather, and that what we'll get."

"Right," I agreed. We hung up and I went back to the couch.

Tony put his arm around my shoulders and gave me a squeeze.

"Congratulations," he said, "You must be happy."

"Things are going well, let's just hope it continues," I said, crossing my fingers.

"You need to picture it working the way you want it to," Tony said, seriously.

I nodded. "OK, will you help me?"

He looked flattered, and smiled at me questioningly. "Sure, do you mean it? Or are you joking again?"

"I'm serious!" I said, taking his hand in mine. "I want to learn how to do it, you know, the way you make things happen."

"OK," he said. "Eat your dinner, then we'll meditate together and I'll show you."

I cleared my plate and we turned off the TV, settling down to sit cross-legged on the floor, facing each other. Following Tony's instructions, I closed my eyes, slowing my breathing down and centering my consciousness within my body. I went deeply into my mind, losing awareness of the room around me as I floated up into my thought body. I deliberately pictured the goal we had agreed on, trying to see it in my mind's eye.

As in a vivid dream, I saw Market Street on a clear, sunny day. It was from the same perspective as if I were standing in the doorway of the shop, looking out. I turned my dream eyes to the left toward a bright glow and past it I saw the big tent, the intersection roped off with stanchions, people milling about.

Families were walking up and down the sidewalks, kids with floating balloons and babies in strollers. Everyone was happy, including me! I held the image and the feeling for as long as I could, finally coming out of it when I noticed that my left leg had gone totally to sleep.

Tony was still sitting opposite me, his eyes open and watching me calmly.

"Welcome back," he said, reaching out for my hand.

"Thank you," I replied, dazed.

"That was an amazing experience, Emily," he said very seriously. He looked at me with piercing eyes, questioningly.

"It was?" I said vaguely, feeling fuzzy. I straightened out my stiff legs and rubbed the tingling.

"You didn't see me, did you?" he asked, apparently disappointed.

"See you where?"

"Standing next to you, in the doorway of the shop."

"Just now?"

"Yes, " he said excitedly, "I went into my mind to picture what we discussed, the sunny day, all that, and there you were, standing right next to me!"

"Which side?" I asked, remembering what I had envisioned.

"You were on my right," he replied firmly. "I saw you looking out at the intersection. You were smiling."

There had been that bright glow to my left, it had blinded me a little when I looked past it toward the intersection. I thought it was sunlight, but I guess it was actually Tony. I told him what I had experienced.

"Maybe if we practice, I'll be able to see you too," I said, very intrigued.

"Do you want to?" he asked, kissing my hand with a smile.

"Yes, of course."

"Then I'm sure you will," he said, definitively.

*　　*　　*

On the Friday that the Sidewalk Sales were scheduled to begin, the day dawned clear and hazy. Tree and I had stayed at Tony's house and the night before we had meditated on the weather again, as we had done several times during the week. The forecast for the weekend hadn't changed much, predicting clear skies for Friday and Saturday, with a possibility of showers for late Saturday night and Sunday. Most of the important musical events were happening on Saturday, when the largest crowds of shoppers traditionally appear to scour the streets for bargains. Our headliner performers were going on stage Saturday night, when we had all agreed to stay open until nine.

We had been getting great advance publicity all week, thanks to a lack of terrorist activity and natural disasters. Slow news is good news, when you're hoping for free advertising. Sarah Bennet reported to me that the phone at her office was ringing off the hook, with people calling from around the region for more information.

At this point the ads were placed, the die was cast, and the merchants were concentrating on their individual presentations. We wanted to impress people who were new to our area, and develop relationships with new long-term customers. It was a good chance to clear out any old merchandise that was hanging around, for sure, but nobody really expected to make a killing financially. We all thought of this as a sales promotion event, with bargains as the bait to draw people into town, so that we could charm them into returning over and over again.

The girls came over for our early morning Pilates class as usual and after we finished, they helped carry the heavy folding banquet tables I had borrowed from Laurie out to the sidewalk in front of the building. Yesterday we had gone over the shop with a fine-tooth comb, dusting and polishing, tweaking the displays. It was an "all hands on deck" situation, since we needed to station salespeople both outside and inside to keep an eye on things. Bella and Siri were both working full-time for the weekend, plus Henry and me of course, and Amy, too.

She had been earning a nice, steady little paycheck every week, to her great excitement and pride. When she'd completed the hiring papers with her social security number and personal information I was hoping for new clues as to the whereabouts of her mother, but Amy entered a post office box instead of a street address. Her last name turned out to be Horowitz. I looked in the telephone book, but nobody was listed under this name in our neighborhood. It seemed to confirm the possibility that they might currently be staying in the church basement.

Siri and I had been piling merchandise in Henry's sitting room all week in preparation for today, and now we lugged the boxes outside to set up. Bella ran home for a few minutes to shower and change, then she came back to take over while we did the same.

Henry came downstairs dressed in khaki shorts, Birkenstock sandals and a purple tie-died Jimi Hendricks T-shirt with his straw hat and sunglasses. He set up a large red and white striped beach umbrella outside to provide us with some shade, lashing it to the railing at the bottom of the stairs with a bungee cord. Opening a comfortable folding lawn chair, he settled down next to a cooler of bottled water to oversee the cash box.

We had covered the two tables with brightly colored tablecloths and organized the items simply into four price groups, labeled with little signs I had inscribed with Henry's calligraphy pens. By noon we were ready to go, and I left Henry in charge while I went over to see what was going on under the big white tent that had been erected in the intersection.

They had been working on it since before I arrived that morning. It looked marvelous, like a fairytale tent with pointed peaks that were flying triangular colored flags. The police had already closed the intersection to driving traffic, letting an occasional vehicle go through to deliver essential items to the crew of workers who were hooking up the electricity and the sound system. A seating area that would accommodate about a hundred people had been planned, and when I ducked under the awning and went inside I saw Rocco Sorrentino and John Laroche setting up the chairs, with a couple of strong young men wearing Green Thumb T-shirts unloading the delivery truck.

"How's it going?" Rocco called when he saw me. He was sweating profusely, which was not surprising. The day was already cranking up to be very hot.

"Good!" I answered, offering him and John a cold bottle of water from the six-pack I had brought with me. "We're all set. How about you? Do your parents need any help?"

"I think Pop has it all together, but thanks for offering," Rocco replied, chugging down a whole bottle of water in a couple of seconds. John followed suit more slowly.

I peered under the side of the tent and saw Laurie setting up a sign on the patio in front of the restaurant. They had decided to open early today and serve lunch, expecting enough hungry passers-by to make it worth staffing the dining room. The Potting Shed doors were standing open, and an old wagon loaded with flowering plants and shrubs had been rolled up in front. A smaller cart with a lime green umbrella shading it displayed pretty bouquets standing in big buckets of water. It looked like Laurie was ready for action, too. It was exciting! All up and down the street, people were bustling about cheerfully, calling out to one another in various languages and setting up tables and chairs on the sidewalk, dragging boxes out of their shops, hanging up banners and signs.

Sarah Bennet appeared, walking across the stage with a clipboard under her arm, conferring with the young man who was testing the sound system. I waved, and she smiled broadly, waving back.

"Testing, testing, one two three," the young man said into a microphone, signaling to his co-worker, who was sitting in front of a big control panel at the back of the tent.

Sarah leaned over and spoke into the microphone.

"Is everybody ready?" she asked, looking at the three of us.

Rocco gave her the thumbs up sign.

"The parking garage is packed!" she said happily. "And they're heading this way!"

I looked down the street and saw that she was right, as a parade of people pushing baby carriages, teens on bikes and skateboards, men and women, and senior citizens carrying shopping bags slowly approached. A juggler on stilts was leading the way. A television news crew pulled up in their live broadcasting van and the police let them in past the stanchions, parking them next to the tent.

"Yikes!" I said, pointing the crowd out to Rocco and John.

"Holy cow," Rocco said, "I better go slice up some pizzas!"

"See you later!" said John, slipping away with a wave.

I went back over to where Siri and Henry were waiting, comfortably settled at our encampment. She had covered Henry's big umbrella with a colorful Indian print bedspread, and more bright textiles were displayed on a quilt rack that propped the shop door open. It looked like something out of the Arabian Nights, and Siri looked like the storyteller with a hundred and one tales, dressed in a cool aqua sari that fluttered around her bare brown legs when she moved.

Amy and Bella were sitting on the front steps, so I went over to join them. I looked at my watch. It was twelve fifteen. The first little trickle of shoppers came around the corner onto Market Street, beginning to spread out down the sidewalk in front of Sorrentino's. I saw Josie standing out front, immediately engaged in conversation with a young woman who was carrying a baby in a hot-pink backpack. Josie reached up and tickled the baby under the chin. I saw the baby smile and crow, pushing up on her feet and waving her arms around excitedly. Then the first wave of shoppers hit our side of the street, and we all stood up to get to work.

Most of the day sped by in a blur of conversation and activity. The next time I looked at my watch it was after six. We had been very busy, inside and outside. There had even been two new rare book collectors up in the library with Henry, a fact that totally thrilled him. I sent Amy down to the basement repeatedly for more crystal vases and wine goblets, and we sold all of the African animals. I brought out a dozen sets of carved wooden salad tongs, and only one pair was left. Salt and pepper shakers and candlesticks had been snapped up like popcorn. Business inside the store had been brisk as well, and we'd given out a lot of brochures and business cards.

The mood of the crowd was upbeat and friendly. I enjoyed talking to the new customers who were curious about the shop and its eclectic mix of merchandise. A lot of people had come from out of town. Many had never been on Market Street before. Every time someone told me that, I gave myself a little pat on the back, mentally. It was great to know that my plan was working!

Two folk-singing sisters were performing under the tent when I checked the time and stopped for a breather. Traffic on the sidewalk had slowed down quite a bit as soon as the music started, and everyone was gathered around the stage to watch. Tony had showed up a little while ago with pizza for all of us, from Rocco's brick oven. He was sitting next to Henry under the umbrella, hearing all about the new collectors who had appeared earlier. He looked over at me and smiled, then turned back to his friend.

"That was nice of him, getting the pizza," said Amy, trying to catch a long strand of mozzarella that was dangling from her slice. She said it wonderingly, like she was puzzled. She looked out at me from under her brows, with a little frown. "I guess he didn't have to, right?"

"Right," I said. "I think he wanted to be nice, that was the point."

"Yeah. Well, I guess he's OK then. You know. If he has to be around here all the time," she said dismissively. She finished eating the pizza and stood up. "OK, man, I gotta go. See you guys tomorrow," she waved at Henry and Tony, and sped off down the sidewalk.

We went home to Tony's house that night and I slept like the dead, then I got up early Saturday morning and went back to the store to do it all again. We had carried everything inside before locking up, but it was sitting right inside the doorway ready to go back outside. The good weather continued to hold, and by ten o'clock the sidewalks were filled with shoppers, clowns and minstrels.

Siri's family came by to say hello. Tom was pushing their daughter in the stroller, while their son ran alongside and her father brought up the rear, carrying a string bag containing several packages. Siri brought Tom and the kids inside to use the bathroom, while Gupta took a seat next to me under the umbrella. Amy came outside carrying two teapots, which she had just washed. She put them on the sale table, and I introduced her to the elderly Indian gentleman.

They shook hands solemnly, his eyes twinkling and hers curious.

"Very nice to meet you, Miss Amy," Gupta said earnestly.

"Yeah," she said, "Same here. So. You're Siri's dad, right?"

"Correct," Gupta replied, looking her over carefully. I wondered what he thought of her pierced eyebrow and the green stripes in her hair.

Amy smiled at him and folded her arms, hanging around like she had something to say. "Um," she said, "So. Siri tells me you're a teacher, right?"

Gupta nodded. "Yes, I worked twenty years as a tutor."

"I was thinking about, um, trying to pass the GED exam," Amy said. "You know anything about that?"

"The Graduate Equivalency Exam? Yes, I most certainly do. You wish to be finished with high school early?" he said, looking at her with renewed interest.

Amy grinned and cocked one eyebrow, the pierced one.

"Are you kidding? I can't wait to get out of that place," she said. "I want to go to art school. My advisor said I might be able to get a scholarship."

Gupta considered this statement for a moment.

"You have a portfolio of your work?" he asked.

"Well, sort of," Amy said, "I have notebooks. Of my drawings, I mean."

"Amy has been doing window displays this summer," I interrupted, "We have her sketches, and some photos of the finished projects. But, isn't she too young?"

"Not if she can pass the exam," Gupta replied. "And get accepted to an art college. It's a tall order, but not impossible."

"I was checking it out before school vacation started," Amy said, warming to him. "The test didn't really look that bad. Except for the math part. I suck at math."

Gupta laughed and threw back his head.

"A common complaint among artists!" he said. "I have heard that many times before!"

"So," Amy said, "I was thinking maybe…if someone would help me study, maybe I could learn enough to take the exam.

What do you think?" She looked at him expectantly, in a casual yet studied way, her stillness the only sign that this was of prime importance to her.

Gupta shot me a glance of suppressed excitement.

"I think, you should come to see me when I am at home," he said, "And we will discuss it further. I want to see your transcript, and I would like to telephone your advisor. But we can certainly work something out!"

"I don't have any money, you know," Amy said frankly.

Gupta smiled at her, his eyes twinkling again.

"Money is not important! Relationships are important. And you have collected quite a few of great value," he said enthusiastically. "You come and see me on Monday morning at ten. We'll talk about the details then." He looked at me and we exchanged nods of approval. He seemed excited about the prospect of teaching again, and the chance to study Amy while she studied mathematics. I felt she was a talented designer, and would do wonderfully in art school. I was very curious to see these "notebooks."

That afternoon the heat outside became more and more intense, as the bright sun bounced off the pavement and made even the plastic arms of our lawn chairs too warm for comfort. I had reluctantly turned on the air conditioning in the shop so we would all have a haven for retreat, and Bella and I sent Henry inside to preside over the cash register in comfort. He was looking a little peaked, and was grateful for the respite. The foot traffic on the sidewalk continued unabated, and the performances under the tent were very well attended. Everyone in the area had come to town, from the looks of it. Across the street, the Sorrentinos were doing a brisk trade in cold drinks and frozen treats. Josie had her grandchildren helping her outside, and I saw Rocco re-stocking their coolers several times.

We heard from people passing by that the heat was supposedly going to break late in the afternoon, when a cool front of

Canadian air was due to enter our region. My sunglasses kept sliding off my nose, slick with sweat, and I guzzled bottled water. The girls were getting a little grouchy, and we were all tired. We took turns going inside to cool off. One of the street magicians came by and asked if she could keep her sweet little white rabbit in his cage at our shop until the end of the day, as it was too hot for him to survive either in her pocket or in her car. We put his hutch in the kitchen on the cool linoleum floor, with plenty of fresh water, and she went back to work.

The kitchen phone rang and it was Sarah Bennet, on her cell phone. There was a lot of noise in the background.

"Hey!" she greeted me.

"Hey, where are you?" I asked.

"Main Street, right in the middle," she shouted.

"How is it?"

"It's a mob scene! How is it there?"

"Great! Tons of people."

"Emily, they want to do a live interview for the six o'clock news!"

"Wow! That's wonderful!"

"Will you do it with me?"

"What? You want me?"

"Yeah, they want to interview me and one of the merchants. I thought it should be you."

"OK, sure." I said reluctantly. The thought of being on TV made me nervous.

"We're doing it at the tent right when the last concert starts. They're going to show it in the background. They've been shooting around town all day, so there's an edited piece back at the studio that they're going to show, too. It's a major story!" Sarah sounded terribly excited.

"Cool! Outrageous! What time do you want me there?" I grinned, swept up by her enthusiasm. She told me and we made plans to rendezvous.

I went into the little powder room under the stairs and looked at my wilted, shiny, sweaty face in the mirror. My frizzy hair was stuffed up into a clip on the back of my head, and there was black dirt in the creases of my neck. My nose was sunburned a rosy red.

I stared at myself and started to laugh out loud. Some TV star! Then I washed my face and neck, brushed and rearranged my hair, put on a little lipstick and mascara, and found some sunscreen for my nose and shoulders. I headed back out to work. When I told the girls and Henry what was happening they were very excited. Tony showed up about then, and helped Henry move the little TV from the sitting room out onto the counter in the shop, so he could watch the news show.

"You'll be beautiful on television," Tony said, "It's your fifteen minutes of fame, like Andy Warhol said. We should record it!" Henry nodded, and hustled up the stairs to set the DVR on his bedroom television to capture the show.

When the time came, I took one last look in the mirror and then I walked over to the tent, looking up at the spires with their festive red and orange flags fluttering a little in the breeze that had finally arrived. My hair lifted a bit off my brow, and I felt cooler, like I could breathe for the first time all day. Maybe I wouldn't be dripping with sweat on television after all! I perked up and started to look forward to the adventure.

I ducked under the tent and went around behind the stage, where the news crew had parked their van. It had a long metal arm attached to the roof that pointed the broadcasting antenna toward the sky. The back doors of the van were open and two men were inside looking at a small monitor, surrounded by piles of electrical equipment.

"Hi," I said, "I'm Emily Ross. I'm here for the interview?"

A dashing young man with blonde hair got out of the front of the van, dressed in crisply creased slacks and a short-sleeved shirt. He came over and put his hand out to shake mine.

"Steve Mason, Channel 40 News, good to meet you!" he said, smiling to reveal a set of perfect white teeth.

We chatted about how well things were going, how much fun everyone was having, how happy the merchants were with the turnout. Then Sarah showed up, calm and poised, and took over the conversation, to my relief. She had estimated counts for the crowds and the number of cars in and out of the parking garage at her mental fingertips. She had sound-bite quips ready to utter. She was a real pro, and I was glad she was there. All I had to do was smile and look friendly, nod my head and agree with her. We went through all of the reporter's questions fairly quickly and he showed us where he wanted us to stand for the interview, right outside the entrance to the tent so that the stage and performers could be seen in the background. The cameraman positioned himself out in the middle of Market Street, to get some of the tent in the shot too. We were all waiting for the signal that it was time to begin.

The cool breeze had picked up quite nicely over the past few minutes, and the little flags fluttered gaily in the sunlight. I squinted up at the sky, and noticed some distant clouds to the north. They looked bluish gray. As I watched, they came closer, obviously moving along at a considerable clip.

"We'd better do this soon," I said to Sarah, pointing at the sky. She looked at it and frowned.

"It's the cold front they predicted," said the cameraman, turning around to shoot the rapidly approaching weather.

"Get back here!" yelled Steve Mason, "We're ready to go live!"

The camera swung back around, focusing on him. He spoke into the microphone, smiling broadly and introducing Sarah and me. The band played in the background, just wrapping up a tune. A bunch of people had gathered to watch the interview, including Rocco and Laurie. We did our interview as rehearsed, and I felt relatively relaxed about it. I didn't say anything stupid, at least. Then they cut back to the station and my part was over. The reporter thanked me, and said the station had asked him to do a live wrap-up at the end of the news show in a few minutes. Sarah and I stepped aside so they could get a good shot of the clowns and jugglers on the sidewalk in front of Sorrentino's.

In the quiet between songs on stage, I heard a deep rumble to the north. Sarah heard it too, and we both turned to look.

Dark, billowing charcoal gray clouds were rolling towards us out of the northern sky. They stretched wide across the entire horizon. A flicker of jagged light shot across them, and in a minute we heard the thunder again. It was definitely heading this way. The wind started whipping along, and up and down the street tablecloths and signs were fluttering and flapping. A handful of paper napkins flew off Rocco's pizza table and soared down the sidewalk.

Everyone started to scramble, pulling things inside and trying to secure lightweight objects under heavier ones. I saw Siri and Bella make a dash up the steps of the shop, their arms laden with sale items. Tony was spreading a plastic tablecloth over the used books, strapping it down with duct tape. I noticed Lexi and her boyfriend standing inside the door to the shop, watching the activity. She waved at me and they ran down the steps to help, while Amy quickly packed things into empty cartons. The sound of the wind was almost as loud as the band playing under the tent, as the news crew went live again to wrap up their broadcast.

The juggler behind Steve Mason was having a hard time, as the wind snatched the balls out of his hands and flung them away. Luckily the spot was short, and the reporter was able to sign off without mishap. Then a big flash of lightning tore across the bruised sky and the thunder growled again, nearly on top of us now. We could see the rain approaching as it moved towards us, coming down in streaming sheets of water, hissing when it hit the hot pavement and sending up clouds of wet steam. Then the air turned greenish gray and the storm swept right over us, soaking me to the skin within seconds.

Lightning split the sky again, right overhead, and thunder cracked with a deafening boom. Behind me, people shouted and I turned around to see someone pointing up at the peaked tent roof, where the big electrical cable emerged and looped to connect to a utility pole on the far corner by the medical offices. I looked up just in time to see a bright ball of bluish light shoot out of the dark sky and run along the cable, sparks arcing into the air. Thunder boomed again, very loud, and someone yelled, "Watch out!" Lighting struck the tent pole again and the big cable was suddenly loose, flapping in the gusty wind and sending showers of sparks cascading down the canvas roof. People screamed, and the cable whipped around like a snake. Parents grabbed their children and ran for their lives.

"Are you getting this?" the news reporter yelled at the cameraman, who was pointing his lens at the tent to capture the chaos. A siren sounded in the distance, then another, and another, as the fire department and police raced to the scene.

Sarah and I stood shivering on the sidewalk in front of Sorrentino's. Josie came outside wearing a plastic shopping bag tied over her curly white hair. She pulled us back under the awning and the three of us watched as the fire department pulled up and took control of the situation. The storm had started to move past, but the street was filled with puddles of water, a potential danger with downed electrical wires on the ground. They finally got the power disconnected and the loose cable stopped spitting sparks. The people who were sheltering in doorways nearby cheered and applauded.

Nobody appeared to have been injured, but we were definitely shut down for the day. The band started to pack up their instruments to go home. The sun came out again, lower and redder in the sky now as it moved toward twilight. Awnings and trees dripped, while birds soared down from the rooftops to splash in the puddles.

Sarah and I looked at each other in dumb amazement.

"It could have been worse," she said reassuringly, starting to regain her composure.

"Yeah, somebody could have been electrocuted, right?"

"Or, we could have been live on TV when it happened," she pointed out.

I looked around for the cameraman, who was shooting the men who were working on the utility pole. Steve Mason walked back over to where we were standing.

"That was great!" he crowed, very excited. "We just did a breaking news segment, and we'll have really good footage for the eleven o'clock news!"

"We're so happy for you," I said glumly. "But that pretty much does it for us today, wouldn't you say?"

He looked startled, then a bit abashed.

"Yeah, well, sorry about that," he said. "But you'll be up and running again by tomorrow, right? For the last day of the sales?"

Sarah nodded confidently. Hooking her arm through his, she led him over to watch the men working behind the tent, talking in his ear nonstop all the way. An ambulance had appeared along with the other emergency services vehicles, and now it let out a little hoot from its siren and pulled slowly out of the intersection, swinging back into the alley behind our building to turn around. I said goodbye to Josie and dragged myself back across the street, in dire need of a towel and some dry clothes.

Our sale tables were standing unattended, dripping onto the sidewalk. I climbed the stairs and went inside. The shop was empty, and I wondered where everyone was. Then I heard voices from the back hallway, and went through the showroom to see what was going on. Tony was standing on the back porch, and Siri, Bella and Amy were outside, watching the ambulance pull out of the alley. They all looked upset.

"What's up?" I asked, coming up behind Tony.

He turned and put his arms around me.

"It's Henry," he said, very tense. "He collapsed. Lexi's friend said it looked like a heart attack. They just took him to the emergency room! I'm going now. Will you come?"

I nodded, shocked and a little dazed, and I looked at Siri.

"You go, Emily, we'll take care of things here," she said quietly, and Bella nodded.

"Just a second," I said, and ran inside to grab my purse and a couple of kitchen towels. When I got back outside, Tony had pulled his car out of the parking space and was waiting for me to get in, the engine running. I spread out one towel and sat on it, using the other one to dry my arms and legs, and rubbing my wet hair. I shivered and looked over at Tony's face, tense and concerned. I had a feeling it was going to be a long, hard night.

I quite simply could not picture my world without Henry Paradis in it. I couldn't, and I didn't want to, so I wouldn't. I deliberately turned my thoughts to a world with Henry looming large within it, calling up his vivid presence in my mind. I held the image there like the seed of a dream as we drove to the hospital in silence, afraid to discover what would happen next.

Chapter 17

The Star

HOPE, OPTIMISM

Description: A woman kneels next to a pool, with one foot in the water and the other on shore. She is perfectly balanced between the conscious and the subconscious worlds.
Meaning: Hope, optimism. Firm belief in the inherently positive nature of life, the glass half-full.

When we walked into the emergency room entrance, Lexi was waiting for us at the door. Her doctor boyfriend, Michael Sheehan, was nowhere in sight. I hoped that the neurosurgeon

from Boston had been able to cut through the hospital proto-
col and would help us find out what was going on.

"I'm so glad you and Michael were there when it happened!"
I said, accepting a warm hug from Lexi. Now the tables had
turned, and she was actually comforting me! It was strange.

Tony went straight over to the window where a nurse sat
behind a desk, and spoke to her. I asked Lexi what she knew.
She said Michael had been allowed to go inside when they
wheeled Henry into the triage area, but she hadn't seen him
since. She'd been sitting in the waiting room, where about half
of the chairs were occupied by people with glazed eyes, who
had apparently been there for quite some time.

"They're asking for insurance information," Tony called to
me, with an irritated, impatient tone. "Do you know anything
about that?"

"It must be Health New England, the same kind as mine.
We work together," I told the nurse. "I don't know what his
number is though. I can get any information you need from
the files at the office, tomorrow." She thanked me, saying she
would give the insurance company a call. Tony went inside the
little office to help her fill out the papers.

We sat down and we waited. And waited. A hell of a long
time. It was the worst kind of soul deadening, physically ex-
cruciating, completely maddening emotional torture I had
ever experienced. The waiting room was surrounded on three
sides by big plate glass windows that held back the matte black
night, and the fishbowl space inside was lit by greenish yellow
fluorescent lights. One of the bulbs flickered slightly in a subtle, nauseating staccato rhythm. We sat in hard orange molded
plastic chairs on a gray linoleum floor, slippery and unyielding.
A TV chattered on and on and on from the corner of the ceiling, where it was mounted on a metal bracket. Presumably this
was to put it out of the reach of any crazed detainees like me
who might want to turn it off, or smash it with something, or

rip it down from the wall and throw it out the window.

I fantasized killing the TV as I slid around in my uncomfortable seat, my damp skirt squeaking a little. I reached up and touched my hair, surprised to find that it was still wet too. I looked down at my bare legs and sandaled feet. There was black grit from the puddles on Market Street between my toes. It seemed poetic. I felt a tiny bit better. But then the air conditioning came on again with a huge gust of frigid antiseptic-scented air, and I started to shiver uncontrollably.

Lexi looked at me with concern.

"You're soaking wet! You must be freezing in here!"

I nodded, my teeth chattering. Tony put his warm arm around my shoulders and hugged me, rubbing my upper arms briskly. "I've got a jacket in the trunk of my car, I'll go and get it," he said, glad to have a mission. He stepped out of the fishbowl door and disappeared into the opaque blackness. Lexi went over and spoke to the nurse, pointing at me. The irritating flutter of that bad fluorescent bulb was giving me a migraine. A needle of pain suddenly shot from the back of my left eye through my left temple and down my neck into my left shoulder. My vision blurred on the edges for a moment. Lexi came back with a clean white hospital towel, which she put around my shoulders, and I clutched it with both hands.

Reaching up to unfasten my hair clip, Lexi looked at my unfocussed expression with alarm, and said sharply, "Emily! Are you going to pass out on me? What's going on, Emily?" She waved her hand in front of my eyes and grabbed my shoulder.

"It's just a migraine. I'm OK."

"You sure? No passing out?"

"Thank you, Lexi," I said, as she sat closer to me and used the towel to dry my hair. I could have done it myself, but I let her do it. I think she needed to help.

Tony came back with his workout jacket and I put it on, gratefully. Lexi loaned me a comb and I got it through my hair with some difficulty, making a quick trip to the ladies' room to clean up the rest of me, as well as I could. Meanwhile, my left eye pulsed painfully with every step I took, every motion I made. I felt disconnected, like I was floating. When I walked back to the waiting room, my feet stepped very carefully across the cold, slick floor, somehow doing this all by themselves. I sat down again between Tony and Lexi, my two pillars of support. They held me sitting upright with their warm adjacent shoulders, between which I drooped, listening now only to the drum-throb-hurt-burn-dizzy-nausea sound of my heart and head, beating together in unison.

Henry, I was so worried about Henry. Henry, Henry. His image flashed before me. His face pulsed along with my blood, on-off, on-off. I saw him the way he looked the first time we met, when he opened the door to my knock. I saw him sitting under the umbrella at the sidewalk sale, in his wild outfit and sunglasses. A deep well of pain swelled up from my tense anxious belly and burned its way up the left side of my back, into my left shoulder, and on up to my temple where it met the answering throb of my left eye socket. I swayed a little in my seat when it blossomed into burning sparkles and took my breath away, closing my eyes and leaning against Tony. He reached over and took my hand, holding it loosely. I zoned out again, riding the next wave of pain down a dark tunnel into a very, very deep place in my mind, a still and quiet place. This was my mental air raid shelter, a place where I could ride out nearly anything. I was surprised to see Henry standing there. He looked confused.

"Not feeling well?" he asked by thinking it at me. "You look terrible!"

I nodded my head in confirmation. The pain seemed duller and more distant now.

"How about you?" I asked mentally, unable to move or speak. We floated in a sort of gray misty place, where we both flickered in and out.

"I'm not sure," he thought back at me. "Did something happen?"

"Yes," I nodded mentally. "You need to come back, Henry. You need to stay with us."

He looked confused again. "Really?" he thought doubt-fully, frowning and stroking his mustache.

I nodded very earnestly, thinking it at him hard, but the imaginary motion set off another big wave of pain and nausea, and I swayed again and felt Tony squeezing my hand. I opened my eyes and he kissed me on the cheek.

The swinging doors that led into the hospital opened, and Lexi's boyfriend Michael strode through them energetically. He spotted us and headed our way. We all stood up to meet him.

"They're taking him up to Intensive Care right now," Michael said, professional and sharp. "He definitely had a heart attack. He's going to be fine. We got him here in very good time, and he's being medicated. They're doing several tests. This will mean some changes in his lifestyle from now on."

He looked at Tony and me appraisingly.

"Does he have any family?" he asked us.

We looked at each other and I shrugged, not really know-ing the answer.

"I think he may still have a brother alive somewhere," Tony said, "But aside from that, we're his family."

"Does he live alone?"

"He lives over the store," I said. "We're there nearly every day, but not at night."

"He may have to spend some time in rehab then. He won't be able to handle stairs for a while. And he's going to need follow-up health care. Someone will have to be there with him. He's in pretty good shape for his age, but he may not bounce right back." He spoke frankly, seriously.

"We'll take care of him," Tony said, determined. "He'll

bounce back faster in his own home. We can work it out." He looked at me confidently and I smiled in agreement, still feeling woozy and sick, but extremely relieved.

Lexi told Michael I was having a migraine and he spoke to the nurse behind the window for a moment, scribbling something on a pad of paper. She came out in a few minutes with a pink tablet in a foil wrapper, and I swallowed it with some water from the drinking fountain. Michael said that Tony and I had permission to see Henry for just a second, but cautioned us that he was extremely groggy and might be asleep. Lexi stayed in the waiting room while Michael led us inside the swinging doors.

We passed through a series of long, shiny, brightly-lit hallways, catching little glimpses of the dramas going on inside the rooms along the way, like the cells on a strip of film. There was a rhythm to the placement of the doorways to my left and my right, and it matched the pounding inside my head as I walked along. I slipped my arm through Tony's and held on for dear life. As we moved deeper into the huge breathing, buzzing, hive of a building, it got darker and quieter. The scenes in the rooms we passed became sadder and more dramatic. The walls turned from green, to blue, to pink. The hallway seemed to close in as though we were entering a smaller space through a funnel, approaching the *sanctum sanctorum*, the very heart of the hive.

The Intensive Care unit was a solemn place. Against a backdrop of high tech equipment, which was everywhere, people wearing scrubs moved silently about their work. A doctor wearing a white jacket and stethoscope over his weekend golfing clothes was talking quietly to someone's family members outside one of the five curtained patient areas. Nurses with sweet, soft faces looked at us with kindness in their eyes. Michael looked inquiringly at the nurse standing behind the station counter, who seemed to be expecting us. She nodded at him and smiled. He led us to the last cubicle and pulled back the curtain, motioning for us to enter and closing the curtain behind us.

The space inside the tiny room was packed with stainless steel equipment, miles of wires and cables, and various monitors with glowing LED lights and dials. It looked like the place where Dr. Frankenstein gave life to his monster. And lying on the bed, if you could call that grasshopper-shaped machine a bed, was my poor Henry. There were wires and tubes attached to him in several places, and his skin looked gray. He was wearing a hospital gown with his limbs exposed, long and skinny. He looked a million years old and extremely frail, like I could easily have picked him up. His eyes were closed and he did not move, but then I saw his chest rise and fall very slightly.

I went to the side of the bed and reached for his hand, but I flinched when I saw that an IV needle was attached to his forearm. I didn't want to disturb it, so I put my hand lightly over his instead. He felt alive, warm. Tony came up behind me and stood close, putting his hand on top of mine and Henry's. We gazed at him in silence. He looked very ill. I teared up and felt like crying but held it back, realizing that my headache had started to abate and I had regained a little bit of self control. Tony's hand felt very warm on top of mine. I tried to conduct his energy through to Henry's hand, below mine. The three of us communed while we watched Henry breathe in, and out.

In a minute Michael opened the curtain again and smiled at us, motioning with his head for us to go. I looked back at Henry from the doorway. He did look very peaceful, and the expression on his face was relaxed, serene. I felt that he was out of danger, that he was going to be OK. I was incredibly glad that we had been allowed to see him tonight. Somehow, it allayed my worst fears and allowed me to move on.

On the way home I called Siri on Tony's cell phone, even though it was three o'clock in the morning. She answered after the first ring.

"How is he?" she asked in a hushed voice. I heard a child mutter sleepily in the background.

"He's going to be OK, but he did have a heart attack," I answered.

"How bad?"

"I don't think they know yet."

"So he will be in the hospital for a while?"

"Yes, we'll find out more tomorrow. They're doing tests."

"It's very late, Emily, don't worry about the store tomorrow morning. Bella and Amy and I can handle it until you get in."

"Thank you, Siri. See you tomorrow," I said, glad to know it was true. We would all see each other tomorrow, thank goodness.

We drove home to Tony's house and went straight to bed, holding each other close as we lay thinking in the dark, too tired to sleep. I drifted off around dawn, finally giving in to relaxation and trying to center my scattered thoughts on a positive outcome.

*   *   *

Two weeks later, Henry was back home and we had settled uneasily into a routine. He was installed in his domain on the second floor, and we were bringing his meals up to him. He was on a very strict diet, so Siri and I were cooking for him several times each day. The doctors were concerned about building up his strength, and they said he was underweight. They told us this was a common problem with older people who lived alone, since cooking for only one person seemed like too much trouble. Tony had bought a little mini-fridge for the study, and we kept it stocked with beverages. I had set up a tea-making station on the corner of Henry's desk, bringing up the old electric kettle from downstairs, where we replaced it with a new one.

I had never been in Henry's bedroom before, but now I was getting to be quite familiar with it. Furnished with old dark walnut furniture, with floral wallpaper and white lace curtains, it still showed many signs of Margaret's presence. Her portrait, in a black oval frame with a simple ivory mat, stood on the tall dresser where Henry kept his clothes. The matching chest of drawers and vanity table had been hers, and her perfume bottles and knickknacks still sat on the lace-covered tops. Her mirror, comb and hairbrush were made of silver inlaid with mother-of-pearl birds and flowers. A beautiful carved teak box from India held her jewelry. Inside the large closet, her clothes occupied the deepest recesses, pushed to the back but not removed, nearly gone but never forgotten.

Tony had temporarily moved back into the rooms on the third floor of Henry's building, and he was living in two places at the moment. Three if you counted my apartment, where we spent some time as well. He laughed and said this was nothing new to him. But it was putting a strain on our relationship, and we missed each other at night too often, especially after how close we had been before.

I felt funny about being with Tony right upstairs over Henry's head, so we had taken to sneaking off to his place or mine during the days, snatching random opportunities to be alone together, to snuggle and make love. It was fun in a way, we turned it into a game. We pretended to be international spies meeting for a top-secret affair. But we usually slept alone at night, and that was very sad, for me. I was a total sucker for this man. It was like an addiction to some chemical substance, and the chemical was his pheromones. He smelled so absolutely wonderful to me that a sniff of his neck would make me high, make me spin away with fireworks and flashing stars going off in my head. He smelled like fresh-baked cookies to me, and it made my mouth water.

Henry's insurance covered the cost of a visiting nurse and

physical therapist, both of whom came by on a regular basis. They gave us instructions for his care that we followed religiously. I wasn't sure how much longer the benefits would last, but he was recovering well, and there were a lot of us nearby to help. The whole neighborhood had pitched in, one way or another. It was very heartening. Henry was a bit embarrassed by it all. Whenever Josie came over with something special for him and labored up the long stairs to deliver it personally, his cheeks turned pink and his blue eyes twinkled. She sat in the visitor's chair we had placed next to the bed and watched him eat, talking constantly. He loved it and was perky for hours. Josie nourished him in more ways than one. I hovered in the hallway and listened in for a while one time. She was talking to him about Margaret.

"Remember the time we all went up to that lake, at night, and Margaret says, let's go swimming, and you and T go in the water buck naked?" Josie asked, and they both burst into laughter. "You two was so funny lookin', you're all skinny and white, with your little white butts shining like the moon! Her and me, we couldn't stop laughing," she said, wiping her eyes with the back of her hand.

Henry ate another bite of the special low-fat turkey lasagne she had cooked for him.

"Those were the days, my friend," he said regretfully. "Life was a lot of fun then."

"It still could be, you old fool," she said, shaking her finger at him sternly. "You just gotta get up out of that bed and come see the world! Life is good, Henry. You need to remind yourself of that."

There was a moment of silence in the room. I tiptoed away, back to the study where I'd been boxing up a shipment of books to be sent out. I had taken over the Internet business, which turned out to be quite substantial. Siri and Bella were in charge downstairs now, with Amy's help, but we all found reasons to be passing Henry's open door on the second floor whenever possible, to look in and see if he was awake and might feel like a chat.

Bella and Siri and I snuck up the stairs to the third floor one morning while Tony was out jogging. They had never seen it before. It had obviously been a fully functioning apartment at some time in the past. At present it was partially furnished and needed some updating. Where downstairs the space was divided into a few rather large rooms, up here the same footprint had been arranged very differently. There were three bedrooms, a study, a livingroom, a dining room, a kitchen big enough to hold a table and chairs, a pantry, and a very nice full bath containing both a stall shower and a claw foot bathtub. The girls looked at the spacious layout enviously, especially Siri, whose family of five was packed into a four-room apartment. Tony's little suitcase was in the master bedroom, where we had made up the big bed with clean sheets. A couple of his shirts were hanging in the closet and a razor and toothbrush were in the bathroom, but otherwise there were no signs that he was in residence. He wasn't spending much time up here.

Tony had heard back from the University and was going for a second interview next week. It was a good thing he didn't have other commitments at the moment, because he was really bearing the brunt of Henry's needs. While the rest of us worked to keep Henry's business healthy, Tony worked on the man himself. Up early every day to go running while the visiting nurse was with the old man, Tony made breakfast for two and carried it upstairs on a tray. Tony sat in the visitor's chair and they ate together. They were often still up there talking and laughing when I came in at eight. I usually went up first thing to check on everyone, taking away the dirty dishes when I went down the back stairs to start the day's baking.

Tony helped Henry with his personal needs, for which we all were extremely grateful. I was glad we women didn't have to intrude on his privacy in order to take care of him. My job was to cook and keep the money coming in. During the days, everyone took a turn checking on our good-natured patient, and someone was up there sitting with him for much of the time when he was awake. Henry joked that he had never had such a charismatic personality before the heart attack, so it had obviously made him more attractive in some way.

We had brought one of the little lunch tables up from the shop and set it up in Henry's study, so that as soon as he could get up and walk around a bit, the three of us could sit there together for dinner. Afterwards, Henry usually watched TV in his bedroom for a little while before falling asleep. This was a chance for Tony and me to play spy vs. spy in the kitchen, while we did the dishes. Sometimes this involved shutting ourselves into the pantry to make out in the dark, which was amazingly tantalizing. It was hard for me to go home alone after that. I really, really missed Tony when I lay under the skylight alone at night looking up at the stars, feeling the memory of our kisses still tingling on my lips.

Henry was improving every day, and that was the most important thing. He got up out of bed and started to walk up and down the hallway. He got out of his bathrobe and into his regular clothes and came into the study, at first to sit and watch me at the computer, telling me what to do about this and that, and then eventually to sit in front of the monitor himself again.

When I first checked his email to reply to any urgent matters I had discovered that Henry had an extensive ongoing correspondence with many people from around the globe. I sent a note to all of them saying he would be offline for a while due to illness. Many of these people were very concerned to hear it, sending back cheerful messages in various languages, which I dutifully printed and delivered to him. I learned that while Henry didn't have any actual relatives that we knew of, his family of friends stretched far and wide. His influence was felt strongly by many of us. Little by little his strength began to return, and the melodious sound of his "Farewell!" as he hung up the phone was soon echoing through the halls, just as it used to.

*   *   *

One quiet afternoon Laurie came over for an espresso and a chat. Siri and Bella joined us and we gathered at the coffee bar. Laurie seemed excited and her eyes sparkled, her cheeks glowing with color. She pulled a computer printout out of her bag and waved it at us.

"Guess who's going to be here next week!" she demanded with a big smile.

We all shook our heads and shrugged.

"Why don't you just tell us, honey?" said Bella, patting Laurie on the back.

"Starhawk!" Laurie announced what she obviously found to be an astounding and wonderful fact, looking thrilled. We greeted her announcement with attentive silence.

"OK...um, who?" Bella asked. Siri and I didn't know either.

"You have never heard of Starhawk?" Laurie asked us in amazement.

"Nope," said Bella succinctly. She walked behind Laurie and made a crazy face, indicating with her finger that Laurie was loco.

"Who is Starhawk, Laurie?" I asked. "And where is he or she coming to, exactly?"

"She's a very famous feminist author and activist. She's written, like, a dozen books. She's also a witch!"

"Riiiiiiight!" said Bella, rolling her eyes.

Everyone laughed, Laurie too.

"No, really, her books are wonderful and she's incredibly smart. Now she's into this thing called 'permaculture' which is very interesting to John and me. It's a kind of totally organic farming that sustains the planet. Starhawk is an eco-activist."

"Wow," said Bella, "She sounds pretty cool."

"I would very much like to hear her speak," said Siri.

"Me too," I said. "When is it happening? Let's all go!"

Laurie showed us the email printout. She had heard about it from one of her organic produce suppliers, whose name appeared in the "from" header. We all agreed it would be fun to go out at night together, and made plans to attend.

When the night arrived we piled into Laurie's Green Thumb van and drove over to the college chapel, where the event was taking place. It was interesting to me that a Pagan priestess was going to speak at the same podium where a Christian minister would normally stand. Laurie told us that the chapel was non-denominational, and was used by many different groups and faiths for meetings and services.

We found a parking place and walked up to the door. Several women stood outside handing out pamphlets about closing down Yankee Rowe, our local nuke, and other hot political topics. Inside the doors there were long tables on both sides of the foyer, with tickets being sold on the left. A young woman with very long blonde hair, wearing an old fashioned gown made of calico print, sold us our tickets. She had dazzling cornflower blue eyes and was gorgeous without a speck of makeup. Next to her was a dark-haired boy about twenty, pierced and tattooed with chains hanging from various parts of his body. He looked intense, too, in a different way. The lobby was crammed full of people, mostly women of young to middle age, milling around and talking excitedly. Books were being sold at the table on the other side of the doors. We moved past and entered the church itself, making our way down the center aisle to find seats. The chapel was nearly full.

I looked around at the other people, fascinated. The crowd was mainly female. Some of the women had short-cropped hair and mannish clothes, obviously Lesbians. Other women were blatantly girly, dressed in ruffled silks or flowered prints and wearing their hair long and flowing. Some of them had put sparkling glitter on their faces and in their hair, and many displayed colorful tattoos. A group of considerably older women with white hair and conservative clothing were sitting in the front couple of rows. A few apparently gay men and college professors were sprinkled throughout the crowd. And then there were the three theatrically dressed long-haired wizards who stood brooding on the periphery like Rasputin, sending their dark electric gazes around to scan the room for...what? An innocent young victim? A bed partner for the night? A talented new magical apprentice? My imagination went wild.

"What's with that, anyhow?" whispered Bella, who was sitting next to me. She nodded her head toward the nearest wizard, who wore a dark purple velvet beret over his shoulder-length curling locks, and sported a neat little Zorro-style mustache and goatee. A large silver pentacle medallion hung on his chest. We couldn't see what it said from where we were sitting, but it looked ancient and mysterious. He caught us looking at him and scowled. Bella nearly exploded from withheld laughter, making a helpless little snorting noise. I started to catch it from her, but then a woman got up from the front row and approached the podium to speak. The crowd settled down and was quiet. The woman said she was a representative from the group who was sponsoring the event, the Men's Education Center. I found that ironic, but wonderfully so. Then she introduced Starhawk, who stood up and took the stage.

She was a nondescript heavyset middle-aged woman with chin-length dark frizzy hair shot with quite a lot of gray. She looked either Jewish or Mediterranean in origin, with an olive complexion. She was dressed simply in a purple top and black pants, with no jewelry or makeup. I felt a little disappointed. This was the famous witch? And then she started to talk, and smile, and look around making eye contact with us all, and I realized in a flash that she was one of the most beautiful women I had ever seen. She drew herself up and suddenly looked much taller, majestic. She transformed herself and radiated power. A little charge went through me, and I shivered with excitement.

All eyes were riveted on her as she told us about her experiences in New Orleans, where she had gone with a group of fellow activists to help with the recovery effort immediately after Hurricane Katrina. She was funny and clever, and her voice throbbed with a slow, sweet energy. As I watched her, something blurry wavered in front of my eyes for a moment, then disappeared, then shimmered in the air again. I rubbed my right eye, blinking to clear it. But the fuzzy glow was still there, when I looked at Starhawk. The rest of the room looked normal. The glow was coming from her, I realized. She was radiating some kind of aura. It shone around her in a thick band about a foot wide.

"Can you see that too?" I whispered to Laurie, who sat on my other side.

"What? See what?"

"That light around her!"

Laurie gave me a huge smile and squeezed my hand, nodding. I noticed that tonight her earrings were little silver pentacles hanging from silver chains. I remembered my intuitive vision of her at a Wiccan ritual, and wondered what she would think of my encounters with the spirit who seemed to inhabit Henry's house, or the information I sometimes got when I touched certain people. I had never mentioned it to her, being so used to keeping my odd experiences private. Most people weren't very comfortable hearing about this kind of thing, and the teasing I received as a child had taught me to stay silent.

Maybe Laurie would feel differently about it, perhaps she had even had some similar experiences. Mr. Paradis had certainly accepted it calmly, as a matter-of-fact thing. And Tony thought he could change the future with his mind. Maybe I was not so odd after all!

Starhawk told us that she had learned in New Orleans that the best person to know when all services and systems break down is not the Harvard PhD, but the person who knows how to make a composting toilet. We all laughed. Then she went on to talk about how in our society we over-value intellectual skills, rather than practical ones. What it really takes for the world to work right is both, in collaboration, she said, and they are equally valuable to society.

Then she spoke about permaculture, telling us about the California community she was a part of, where they were experimenting with the idea. She explained it as the art of designing beneficial relationships between elements like people, plants, animals, air, water and the soil to create a balanced, coherent natural system that can sustain itself permanently. She said, "the world is a web of dynamic relationships, and everything exists in communities." I certainly agreed with that. She said that we needed to turn our minds to managing the planet in a new way. We needed to think of it as a closed system, where every action that benefits one part will impact many others, some in good ways and some negatively.

When the lecture was over she took questions from the audience for over an hour. On the way home in the van I sat up front next to Laurie as she drove. Bella and Siri were giggling about something in the back seat.

"Laurie, how did you first hear of Starhawk?" I asked.

"I read her book *The Spiral Dance* when I was in college," Laurie answered. The little pentacles hanging from her earlobe swung back and forth as she shifted, glinting in the light. "It's one of the most famous books on modern witchcraft and the feminist spirituality movement. She was one of those wild, San Francisco activist hippies of the '60s. They used to put on huge public rituals, where hundreds of people would gather for fire circles on the beach. Her coven is called Reclaiming. They have thousands of members now, all over the world."

"Well, you're right, she did seem very smart. What is the witch thing about?" I asked.

Laurie laughed at me. "The witch thing?"

"Yeah, what's up with that? I don't know much about it."

"Modern witchcraft is a form of religion, Emily. It's usually a kind of nature worship. That's why she is so into taking care of the Earth."

"But, what about spells and all that?"

"Witches believe that it is possible to manipulate the world with their willpower, to make things happen with magic," she said, very seriously. "The word 'wicca' means 'to bend,' as in, to bend or shape reality. And the main rule is that you can do whatever you want to, as long as it doesn't harm anyone else."

That surprised me. I had always thought of witches as the ones handing out poison apples to unwary princesses. And it sounded a lot like what Tony had been teaching me, the power of positive visualization.

"Do you think those women inside there tonight were witches?" I asked her, readjusting my mental image of the term.

"Some of them, definitely. You'd be surprised how normal most witches look. Like Starhawk, for example. But then there are also the flaming charismatics like that guy you and Bella were flirting with," she teased me, grinning.

"I did not!" Bella's protest came ringing out from the back seat.

"I saw you looking at him!" Laurie said.

"Yeah, well, he was like…trying to hypnotize everybody!"

"He didn't like it when you laughed at him, you better

watch out!" I teased.

"Oh-oh, the evil eye! It's gonna get me!" Bella pretended to hide behind her hands, giggling.

"He was just trolling for some new disciples," Laurie said.

"Well he must have a raging ego if he thinks he can get much action with that hair do," Bella sniffed disdainfully. "My beautiful Latino husband is much better looking!"

I was thinking about permaculture again, and the idea that the earth was literally a holy thing to someone like Starhawk, according to what Laurie said.

"It's cool to know that people are out there working so hard on the health of the planet," I said.

"Yes," Laurie answered. "It makes me want to help, too."

"But you do, Laurie, you help a lot! Much more than most people."

"I know, but I can do more. We all can. It's really our only hope, you know."

The mood had turned serious, and we were all quiet as we rode through the dark streets toward home. I looked up and saw a very bright star, all alone in the sky. It was huge. I thought it might be the planet Venus. I thought about that star being part of the same community of which I was a member, way down here on the Earth. That seemed pretty remote and hard to grasp. The star was so far away that I couldn't picture how any action of mine could possibly impact it. So I reeled in my mind and confined my imaginary frame of reference to the Earth itself, spinning along inside its filmy little balloon of atmosphere. That was different. I could easily imagine how gases emitted by my car could float up into that frail envelope and change it, damage it. I could picture how the waste products of all the technology-addicted people in our world could poison the soil and the water.

But I could also picture how things might change. If people lived more consciously, if we paid attention to how the different parts of our eco-community interact and kept the right goals in mind, we could gradually start to do things differently. We could stop the degradation of the system and start to build our resources back up again. Our inner resources as well as our natural ones. People had been focusing on greed, competition and fear for eons, but maybe now was the time for human attitudes to change, before it was too late.

Starhawk had told us that scientists predicted we might have only ten or twenty more years before the global warming caused by the overuse of technology started to dramatically raise the level of the oceans, flooding major cities in all parts of the world. If we were truly all part of one giant web, along with the air and the water and the soil and the bacteria and bugs and fish and birds and animals, what would happen if large numbers of human beings suddenly became aware and started to dream a new vision of the future? Wouldn't it inevitably spark a chain reaction through every filament of the web? It seemed to me that we could start to heal the Earth community by first healing our own spirits, by thinking positively and refusing to be discouraged. All was not lost unless we made it so, by giving in to the seductive pull of entropy. Instead, we should direct our thinking toward nurturing our fellow community members, rejuvenating and restoring them. It seemed like the brightest hope for the future.

Chapter 18

The Moon

INTUITION, ILLUSION

*Description: A full moon shines down from the
sky. Two wild dogs or wolves howl at it. A crayfish
or lobster (the sign of Cancer, the emotions) climbs
out of a pool of water, waving its arms.*
*Meaning: Intuition vs. illusion. Psychic power,
divination and the danger of misinterpreting the
signs, which may be vague or misleading.*

A weird thing happened one cool, rainy, fall morning a few
weeks later. The summer heat had finally broken, the college

students were back in town and the kids had gone back to school. Henry had recovered well enough to be more independent, so Tony decided it was time to deal with his languishing business concerns, which had been neglected due to recent events. He packed his bag, kissed me goodbye, and drove off to New York City for a few days to visit the exclusive galleries that purchased the unique pieces he brought into the country. I still didn't want to leave Henry alone all night, so Tree and I were planning to stay upstairs at Henry's house until Tony returned. I had already moved some of my things there, and I was over at Tony's house picking up my cat when the phone rang, and the answering machine in the kitchen took the call.

"Hello, Tony," a woman's attractive alto voice said, with a slight European accent, "*C'est moi, cheri!* I just confirmed that I can get away, after all. I'd love to see you in New York, so watch for me at the hotel and I will arrive very soon! OK, sweetheart, *ciao.*" The woman hung up with a click.

I stood in the kitchen staring at the answering machine. Tree jumped up on the counter next to it, trying to divert my attention. I stroked him absently. Then I pushed the play button and listened to the message again. Unfortunately, it still sounded exactly the same.

"Well, that really sucks, doesn't it?" I said to Tree. He blinked at me lovingly. I felt like someone had just punched me in the stomach and thrown me off a cliff.

It just wasn't possible. There had to be some other explanation.

I picked up the cat and put him into his carrier for the ride back to work. I cleaned the litter box and bagged it, packing a grocery bag with some cat food, fresh litter and a few catnip toys. There was another explanation, that's all. She was an old friend, maybe a relative. She was an old customer. She was an old…lover? Maybe, not so old. She sounded sexy, sophisticated, and probably gorgeous.

I drove back over to Market Street and brought Tree upstairs. When I was passing through the second floor hallway, Henry heard me and came to the door of the study.

"Is this my new housemate?" he asked, peering into the cat carrier. I brought it into the room and put it down on the floor, unzipping the flap. Tree popped out his head and looked around the room carefully, scanning for danger. Seeing none, he leaped out of the carrier and immediately shot across the room to crouch under Henry's reading chair. He peered out at us cautiously, his tail lashing.

"He'll need a few minutes to check out the new place, but he's usually a good traveler," I said. "He got used to Tony's house fast." I thought again of the message on the answering machine and felt a little sick.

Tree had moved out into the open and was grooming himself now, a good sign. Henry went back to his chair. I saw that he had been reading the *I Ching* again.

"What does the Oracle say today?" I asked, coming over to sit next to him. I had a few questions of my own I wouldn't have minded asking. Tree jumped up into my lap and started to purr loudly. Henry looked over at him and smiled, reaching out to scratch him on the head.

"It says business is good for us, but our foundation is a bit shaky," he said.

"Us? You mean, for all of us? What do you think that means?"

"I suppose it has to do with my health," he mused. "We are warned not to forge ahead full speed at the moment, due to some weak areas in the underlying structure."

"Or, it could mean something else is shaky," I suggested, thinking about Tony, who had suddenly transformed into an unknown quantity in my mind. It's bizarre how such a drastic change can happen within just a few seconds. I needed to be careful not to read too much into this. It was just a phone message, after all. There were several possible explanations. After all, Henry had told me that Tony was an honorable man. I should trust him. He wouldn't lie to me. He wouldn't ruin everything. I started to panic, trying to keep it off my face, smiling blandly.

"Emily," said Henry slowly, thoughtfully, "Do you ever find that the past tends to repeat itself? It changes, and things progress and evolve, but there is still a pattern one can sense underneath. It's like an invisible grid, the warp and woof of life." He looked at me with his mind-reading expression, like my reality was an open book to him.

I nodded my head, trying to appear cool and collected. "Yes, I know what you mean."

"Do you?" Henry said doubtfully. "I wonder."

I looked at him inquiringly, but he did not explain and gazed back at me with a sympathetic expression. He had definitely sensed that I was upset. Tree suddenly stood up and stalked across the coffee table to climb into Henry's lap, turning around in a circle once and then settling down. Tree smiled his curly contented-cat smile, squeezing his eyes nearly shut for a catnap. Henry moved his legs a little to make them both more comfortable.

"Intuition is a tricky thing, Emily," he said. "Sometimes it is truly caused by a psychic flash, and sometimes it's based on an echo of some past experience, set off by a current event that calls up the memory. We react the way we did before, and then a chain of events falls into place, and the pattern repeats. In a way, we make it happen."

Henry leaned over the sleeping cat and looked at me meaningfully.

"It's hard to escape the underlying patterns," he said. "You have to decide to deliberately change the outcome by reacting differently. It takes a leap of faith."

His eyes bored into mine for a moment, and I realized he

was saying something about me personally, not just anyone in general. I wondered what the Oracle had been telling him about me, about my future. I wondered whether he was talking about Tony and me.

"Henry," I protested, shaking my head, "You can't just have faith that things will go the way you want them to. It doesn't work that way! Other people are involved, and you can't control them, or what choices they make."

He smiled at me fondly and stroked Tree, who had totally relaxed now, all four legs outstretched and lolling off the edge of Henry's lap.

"You can't control other people, that is true," he said gently. "But you can try to make sure that what you are feeling and doing is because of what's really happening right now, not because of something that happened in the past."

I sat there and gazed at him, my face crumpling as my eyes overflowed with tears.

"I try not to think about it," I said, wiping my eyes with the back of my hand and sniffling. How did he know these things about me? I hadn't told any of my new friends about my past relationships, not even Siri. It was something I wanted to leave behind me.

"But, it's so hard to forget when something happens, when you're vulnerable to someone and they hurt you," I said, my voice shaking.

I looked at him with my soul exposed and cringing, the young woman again whose heart had been worn on her sleeve, wide open and innocent, in love with love and living in a romantic fantasy.

Henry's eyes were sad as he looked at me with affection, but he did not reach out to touch me. Instead he continued to stroke the cat, who stretched and yawned in ecstasy.

"The drama may be similar, Emily, but believe me, the players have changed," he said, almost sternly. I gulped and nodded, not really convinced.

Just then the phone rang and a minute later Siri called up the stairs that it was for Henry, who picked up the extension. I took advantage of his distraction to end the conversation, which was shaking my usually cool demeanor and delving a little too close to my private emotional secrets.

I took Tree from the old man's lap and brought him upstairs to show him where I was putting the litter box. I set up his food and water dishes on the floor in the third floor kitchen, and then I went into the bathroom to splash cold water on my face and pull myself together. Tony's razor and shaving gel were still sitting on the back of the sink. I started crying again as soon as I saw them. I felt helpless, lost, completely without power. I turned on the water and let it run, staring at the way it swirled around in a spiral to rush down the drain. My mind swirled around with it, rushing into the past, sucked down into a dark slick tube of memories, flashing past like scenes from a movie trailer.

I was madly in love once before. I'd had several other lovers, of course, but only one relationship that was really serious. About ten years earlier, after I had finished school and was off living on my own, I had met a man. I thought he was The Man. He was perfect. Smart, romantic, handsome and funny. He was a writer, with a fabulous imagination, and he spoke in poetic phrases like a character in a book. I was completely charmed by him. He adored me, or so I thought. He called me beautiful, made love to me with great passion, listened avidly to everything I had to say, and he left a single yellow rose on the seat of my car every day, so I found it there when I left work at night. He was also married, something I learned after a few weeks.

He told me the marriage had been breaking up for a long time, not because of me but because it was over. He hadn't told me right away because he didn't want me to get the wrong idea. He said, he was truly free and at this point it was really just a legal matter. He had moved out of his wife's house and into a spare bedroom at a friend's bachelor apartment. We spent some good times together there, but things started to change and I began to feel that he was distracted or depressed. My lover denied it. But his friend told me that after he talked to me on the phone at night, he would cry. His friend asked me why, but I didn't know the answer.

Then my lover told me that he wasn't sure about us anymore, that he wasn't sure I really loved him. If I had, he said, he would have instantly whisked us both away to another town where we could start a new life together. He said, it would happen so fast it would make my heart spin. He said I seemed ambivalent about him.

I searched my soul and found that indeed, I was still worried about the fact that he hadn't told me the whole story when we first got together. I wanted to trust him as much as I loved him, but I just couldn't do it. A voice in the back of my mind kept telling me that something was wrong, that something didn't add up. I admitted to him that he was right, I was uncertain, though I longed to be convinced. I hoped he would take it as a challenge to show me that he really loved me, but instead, he abruptly broke it off.

He twisted things around so it was me breaking it off with him, it was my fault and I had toyed with his affections. The last time I ever saw him, he was leaving for the airport to fly away with another woman, who it turned out had been his lover right before me, the girl who was really responsible for breaking up his marriage, the girl he had really been in love with, all along. I wondered what color her favorite roses were. He said goodbye to me cheerfully, full of excitement about his new life adventure.

I felt stupid, inconsequential, and I was utterly devastated. I kept thinking that he would change his mind, he would come back. I hallucinated seeing him for years afterwards, in a crowd, in the grocery store, passing in a car on the highway. But he never returned, and I never found out what happened to him. It was a long time before I opened up to anyone again.

Until now, until Tony. Somehow, Henry seemed to know about this. Maybe he didn't know the details, he didn't know the man's name, but he knew how it had affected me and he was warning me not to jump to conclusions about Tony because of it. However, that was definitely going to be a whole lot easier said, than done.

*   *   *

I hugged my painful secret close to my chest all day, trying to act as if nothing unusual had happened that morning. Siri looked at me long and thoughtfully, with those warm sensitive liquid brown eyes, but she didn't confront me with a question about what was the matter. I know my eyes were puffy when I came back downstairs from crying. She brought me tea and a kiss, then quietly went about her work, finding an excuse to touch me briefly, every so often throughout the day.

Tony called at about four o'clock. The store was loud and busy when I answered the phone and perched on the stool behind the jewelry counter for a minute to talk to him. The two adorable bird-watching sisters were back again, and we had been having *cappuccino* and brownies together. Several other customers were in the store as well.

"Hello, this is Paradise!" I said, our usual shop phone greeting.

"Hello yourself, I am missing you already, " he said in a low, intimate voice.

I cringed, then my uncontrollable hopeful heart opened reflexively, like the eyes of a deer caught in the headlights of an oncoming truck.

"Me too," I said, smiling. It was noisy in the background where he was too. I heard people talking and horns honking. I guessed he was walking down the sidewalk between appointments.

"How is everything going? How is Henry? How is my cat?" he said.

"They're fine. Tree is up there sitting on Henry's lap, right now."

"Perfect! And how are you?"

"I'm OK. It's pretty busy today."

"Things are going well here too." Tires squealed in the background, and I heard someone yelling, then horns blared again. "I'll call you later then, OK?" He sounded distracted, busy.

"OK."

"Bye-bye, sweetheart."

And he hung up. He used her word, "sweetheart." Had he ever called me that before? Not that I could recall. I wanted to shout disgusting curses across the room. I wanted to rip the telephone out of the wall and throw it out the door. But then I noticed the two perky sets of eyes observing me avidly from across the room. I went back over to the table where the sisters awaited.

"Everything all right, dear?" said Irene.

"Yes, was it bad news, dear?" echoed Rose, in her wavering voice.

Today they were dressed for a fall day, in wool suits and sturdy brogues for walking. They had stopped in after getting their hair done at the beauty parlor down the street. Their heads were adorned with matching caps of perfectly arranged bluish-gray curls. Their hair did not move when they turned their heads, and looked like it was molded out of plastic. Siri and I had complimented them immediately when we saw them come in the door. They blushed and lowered their eyes, glad of the attention.

"No, of course not!" I said, sitting down and taking up my cup. "Just my boyfriend, saying hello."

They exchanged glances and looked back at me curiously.

"Tell us about your boyfriend, dear," suggested Irene. She nibbled delicately on a piece of brownie, which she had cut up with her knife and was eating with a fork.

"Yes, tell us about him!" said Rose. "Have you known him long?"

They both looked at me eagerly, like children waiting for a bedtime story.

"We met at the grand opening of the store," I told them. They both made O's of their lips and nodded their heads, their eyes wide.

"Oh, and, that was just last spring, wasn't it dear?" inquired Irene.

I nodded too, and said, "Yes. Then, over the summer he moved here."

This set off another round of nodding and exchanged glances.

"Oh, well, that sounds lovely, dear!" said Rose. "Is he living nearby?"

"Just the other side of the park, yes."

"And what does he do for a living, dear?" asked Irene.

"He trades in unusual art, furniture, rare books, that kind of thing. He used to work for Coca Cola in China. He's an international businessman."

The sisters sipped their coffee and thought about that for a minute.

"How exciting, dear!" Rose said, and Irene nodded in agreement.

"So, he travels frequently?" asked Irene.

"Yes, I guess so," I said in a depressed tone, picturing end-less months of wondering what Tony was really up to on the other side of the globe. "Not so much recently. He and Mr. Paradis are great friends. Tony's been a huge help, taking care of him." Which was true, I reminded myself. Tony had a heart of pure gold. Of course, other parts of his anatomy might not be quite so inclined to nobility.

"Oh, he sounds lovely, dear!" said Rose.

"Yes, a member of the Jet Set!" said Irene. "Just like Roman Warchovsky, do you remember, dear?" she asked her sister, who nodded in agreement knowingly.

"He was a world traveler as well, dear," Irene continued, putting down her cup to gesticulate more easily with her frail, translucent hands. "First in the navy, then as a foreign war correspondent."

"Yes," quavered Rose, "He was always on the go!"

"Until he met our cousin Margery, that is!" said Irene, and the two sisters smiled and nodded at each other, then at me.

"They married and raised five children," Rose declared, her eyes twinkling.

"Yes, and one cannot do that while flying around the world, constantly putting oneself in harm's way," Irene observed wisely.

"So, he gave up his career?" I asked, curious.

"Well, not really," Irene answered. "Not entirely. He took a job near home at the *New York Times* and eventually won a prestigious award for his writing. Which one was it, dear?" she asked her sister.

"The Pulitzer, I believe, dear. Wasn't it?" said Rose, frowning as she tried to remember.

"Perhaps you're right," Irene said, "It involved quite a lot of money, I do remember that."

"Yes, and just when the eldest daughter was going off to college. What a blessing!" said Rose. Her cup and plate were empty now, and she blotted her thin lips fastidiously with her napkin.

"So, don't you worry, dear!" said Irene, patting my hand. "Falling in love can change a man, even one who is used to a rather unusual lifestyle," she observed, reaching into her black patent leather pocketbook to remove a pink lipstick. She applied it without looking in a mirror, doing a remarkable job, and smacking her lips together a few times. Then she handed it to Rose, who did the same. They smiled identical pink smiles at me from across the table.

"I'll keep it in mind," I said, "Thank you for telling me."

They beamed in pink approval, and eventually tottered out the front door and off over the crosswalk, chattering amicably all the way.

*　*　*

That evening, Gupta was scheduled to stop by and play chess with Henry, so Laurie invited me to come over the Green Thumb for dinner. The two elderly men had formed a strong bond in the past couple of weeks, and Gupta had taken to stopping by frequently to sit and talk with Henry upstairs while they drank tea. Henry had traveled to India years ago and was familiar with many of the places where Gupta spent his youth. They enjoyed reminiscing, seemed to have a lot in common, and played backgammon or chess together for hours. Siri and I were happy that the friendship had formed, figuring it was very good for both of them.

Laurie said tonight was our chance to catch up, as we had both been so busy lately and hadn't had much chance to be alone together. I had been looking forward to it, and wanted to ask her some rather pointed questions. I'd been thinking about everything she told me the night we went to see Starhawk, and I wanted to discuss it without all the other girls around.

I was feeling melancholic when I crossed the intersection

after work to meet Laurie at the Green Thumb. The pump-kin-gold sun was just sliding down behind the buildings to the west, turning the sky blood red and making the air itself seem ruddy, like blush wine. The earlier rain had moved off to the east, and the world looked clean and crisp. There were a few early fallen leaves on the sidewalks, and three crows cawed loudly from the branches of a tall oak tree that grew out of the sidewalk in front of the patio. It was a stark and lonely sound, and it echoed through the quiet streets. One of the huge black birds looked at me with a red glint in its eye, cocked its head, and threw something down on the umbrella of the table below. An acorn rolled off and dropped to the pavement, bouncing across my path. A man with two dogs on leashes walked by, a big German shepherd and a fluffy little white toy poodle. They pranced along contentedly, very much the odd couple, total opposites unified by a common direction and purpose.

I reached into the pocket of my denim jacket and took out my cell phone, stopping for a minute on the patio, where only two of the outside tables were occupied tonight. Looking down at the phone for a minute, I deliberately turned it off, putting it into my purse. Pushing open the double doors, I went into the bar, which was bright and steamy and humming with life. It was a relatively slow night, only about half of the tables in here were taken. Laurie was waiting for me, straight ahead sitting on a barstool, and she turned to welcome me when I entered the room.

"Hey, girlfriend!" she smiled warmly, giving me a hug.

"Hey yourself! How are you? You look gorgeous!" I returned. Laurel looked beautiful tonight in a long flowing skirt, with her wavy, auburn hair and her leaf green eyes. A silver crescent moon hung at her throat, the profile of a face visible on it when she turned. "What's for dinner?" I demanded, starving as usual.

"Follow me!" she said mysteriously and beckoned, leading

me toward the swinging door into the kitchen. John was behind the bar, and he waved at us with a shooing gesture as we passed by, chasing us along.

Inside the kitchen was a loud world of seeming chaos and heated activity. We walked past the sauté line, where flames roared and shot up toward the ceiling as three cooks rushed around like mad, yelling at each other as they shook handles and flipped things, tossing hot food up into the air. Huge dripping pots steamed and fizzed, and the grill sizzled, smoking. We threaded our way through past the busy dishwashing station and the walk-in cooler, and eventually out a back door onto the private patio that ran across the back of the building.

This was where Laurie and John had their organic vegetable and herb gardens. It was a quiet, peaceful enclosed space, an oasis, complete with a trickling water garden. Willow fencing and fragrant boxwood hedges lined the periphery, and a stone pathway led through the grass to the raised vegetable beds. An arbor at the far end of the yard supported a huge climbing rose bush, where a few last red blossoms still clung to the yellowing foliage. A table for two had been set up on the patio, and two comfortable chairs were pulled up nearby. An ice bucket was on the table, with a bottle of wine cooling in it. The noise from the kitchen was muted here, with only an occasional crash or clink penetrating the quiet. I immediately relaxed and felt relieved.

"This is great!" I said, as she picked up the wine and cut the seal. It was a French Chablis, and looked expensive. I started to cheer up.

"I love it back here, too," she said, smiling. "But we don't have a chance to enjoy it as much as I'd like to!" She skillfully pulled out the cork and poured us each a glass. "We got a great deal on some live lobsters today, you're not allergic are you?"

"No way! I'd love it," I said.

"Good, they're already steaming," she said, and after a few

minutes she went inside and came back with a rolling cart, which contained our feast. The cook had already broken out the lobsters and drained the water, so they were easy to take apart. We both ate like pigs, the melted butter dripping down our chins. There were baked potatoes with sour cream, too. I was in high-cholesterol heaven! While we ate, the round white moon slowly crept up over the rooftops and trees until it peeked down into the garden, gilding the lush foliage with silver light. After dinner we put all the debris onto the cart and rolled it away, wiping off the table and ourselves with wet rags and clean towels from the kitchen. We pulled our chairs out into the lawn and settled down with our wine glasses, to watch the moon and talk.

"Laurie, how do you know when it's safe to trust an intuition? How do you know when it's real?" I asked.

"I usually ask the Tarot, if I'm nervous. But most of the time I just go for it," she said, sipping her wine, one arm tucked behind her head.

"You're so brave!" I said.

"Not really, not extraordinarily," she protested, looking at me curiously. "What is this about, Emily?"

"It's about Tony. I don't know what to think."

"What to think about what?" she asked.

"About whether or not to trust him."

"Oh. What makes you think you shouldn't?" she said, paying closer attention now.

"It's not just that, it's really more than that."

"More than what?"

"I don't know whether I can trust any man. I think I'm just emotionally crippled, or something," I burst out, jumping up to pace back and forth on the grass. She sat and watched me, like someone at a tennis match.

"You'd think I'd be able to give the guy a break, but no, just the least little thing like a stupid phone call from some glamorous freaking mystery woman and what do I do? Do I extend the benefit of the doubt like a normal, non-paranoid person? Or do I immediately jump to the worst possible conclusion and turn off my cell phone so he couldn't even call me if he wanted to? I mean, maybe they're not having dinner at some intimate little Greenwich Village bistro right now, playing footsie under the table! Oh my god, Laurie, what am I going to do?"

I flung myself back into my chair and clutched her arm, desperately.

"I see," Laurie said. "You're really in deep with this guy, aren't you?"

"I guess so," I said with a pathetic little sob, as a giant crocodile tear welled up in one eye and rolled slowly down my cheek.

"Shall I get the cards?" she offered gently, standing up.

I sniffed and nodded, and she went inside for a minute, returning with her shoulder bag. She spread out a large square scarf on the grass, then we sat across from each other and she took the cards from their velvet bag. The light from the kitchen windows slanted across the moonlit lawn, revealing the brightly colored pictures as she spread out the cards.

"First of all," I stopped her as she began to look through them, "How do you know this works?"

"It just does," she said. "People have been reading the Tarot for thousands of years. It works the way any kind of divination works. The images in the cards are archetypes that help us to access our latent psychic abilities, they open up the third eye so we can see down the road ahead."

She pulled out the King of Pentacles, and put it in the center of the scarf.

"Now that," she pointed, "Is Tony. Doesn't it look like him?"

The card showed a dark handsome man with a star inside a red disk on his chest, and a bull standing behind his right shoulder. She pointed at the pentacle.

"This stands for money, business. When is his birthday?"

"In May, I think. Why?"

She tapped the card. "Taurus, the bull."

"OK, so that is Tony. What are we going to do with him?"

"He is at the center of the reading, we are asking about his life, what's really going on with him right now. Isn't that what you want to know?"

"Oh," I said, "I guess so. Yes, I do want to know. I want to know the truth."

"Now we shuffle the question into the cards," she said, beginning to mix the cards, closing her eyes.

She stopped after a minute and tapped them together neatly, then blew a long, deep breath into them, as I had seen her do before. She shuffled a few more times, and then handed the deck to me.

"Now you do it," she said, her moon pendant swaying in the silver moonlight.

I shuffled solemnly, trying to picture Tony's face. It wasn't hard. His eyes popped right into my mind, hovering a few inches from mine, in my imagination. I thought of the way he looked at me when we made love, how his eyes narrowed and flickered when he moaned. I shuffled it all into the cards, stopping when the vision faded to cut the deck into three piles, as Laurel instructed. She picked them up in reverse, the last third now on top. She laid the cards out slowly, one by one, in a different pattern than I had seen her use before. This time she dealt just three cards, and laid them out in a row from left to right underneath the card that stood for Tony.

"Past, present and future," she said, tapping the three cards.

The first was the Queen of Pentacles, an attractive brunette wearing a stylish white fur hat and cloak. She held a pentacle identical to the one in Tony's card.

"There she is," I yelled excitedly, pointing. "She speaks French, she's rich, and look at those clothes! How can I compete with that?"

"You are here too, Emily, this is you," Laurie said, pointing at the second card. "She is in the past, but you are in the present."

The middle card was the Queen of Wands, a woman with long braided light brown hair who held a flowering rod, like a walking staff, with a giant sunflower behind her.

"How do you know that's me?" I asked, squinting at the card. "She looks like the country cousin, the Daisy Mae type. Well, I guess it is me."

Laurie laughed and then sobered, tapping the last card. It was the ten of pentacles, and showed a couple with a small child standing before an archway, looking through it at a beautiful castle on a hill.

"The future," she said. "It means family, home, prosperity."

"Ohmigod," I said, "He's going to marry her! She's pregnant! Look at that!"

We both stared at the cards. My heart sank.

"Well, it is another pentacle card, which is not very good since that seems to be a quality they share," Laurie said, "But it doesn't necessarily..."

"Yes it does," I said flatly, "Look at that! I am right between them and their home, their family. I'm the only thing standing between them and happiness!"

Laurie shook her head and pursed her lips thoughtfully.

"Is that what you really think, Em? Is that what your intuition tells you?"

"The hell with my intuition, what about the cards?" I demanded, pointing at them.

"The hell with the cards, what about your intuition?" she said, grinning at me. "That's what the Tarot is all about, Emily, intuition! I know you've got it. Use it!"

I stopped ranting for a moment to think.

"I love Tony, Laurie," I said quietly. "I fell in love with him because of who he is, not because of how he looks, or how many pentacles he has in the bank. He's the only man I've met in a long time who cares about the same things that are important to me."

She nodded encouragingly. "And, how about loyalty? Does he care about that?"

"I thought so," I said. "Henry told me so. And he's known Tony for a long time."

"Well," she said, "It seems fairly likely that you are both right about him."

"OK," I said, looking up at the moon and rubbing the top of my head, which was tingling. "I guess I'll just have to wait and see."

She nodded and began to collect her cards.

"And, turn your cell phone back on, Emily," she said.

"OK," I said, looking for my purse, which was still on the patio. I crawled over to it on my hands and knees and reached inside, finding the phone and hitting the ON button with my thumb. A tone rang out, indicating I had a message waiting. I hit the voicemail button and waited. It was Tony, naturally.

"Hello, darling Emily! Where are you, I wonder? I was thinking about coming home tonight…but, it's late, and anyhow I'll be back tomorrow, with a surprise for you! See you then, about four o'clock I think. Call me when you get this, if you can, I won't be sleeping."

I played it again for Laurie to hear. When the recording finished, she pushed the END button and handed me back my phone.

"I don't know, Emily, he sounds like a man in love," she smiled at me.

"Yes, but which queen does he really want?" I asked.

For that was truly the heart of the question, after all. That night, under the full moon in the garden of life, with the most magical person I knew, I sent out a call into the universe. I called myself. I called my future self, I told her to stop, turn around for a moment, to tell me the answer. Just think it at me, I said, and I'll know.

I closed my eyes and joined hands with Laurie, feeling her energy surge through me, in one hand and out the other, in a spinning circle. I tried to open some kind of receiver inside my head, but I wasn't sure where to look for it. Then I remembered the third eye, and focused my awareness on the spot behind the middle of my forehead.

Immediately I was swept away into a crystal clear vision. Tony was walking down the sidewalk on Market Street with a tall, slender woman with short stylishly cut dark-brown hair. He had his arm casually draped around her neck. They were smiling, laughing. And when I saw her face, it looked familiar to me. She was very pretty, dark and gamine. Actually, she looked a lot like Tony. When they both smiled, it was the same expression, the same features. Like, family members… like brother and sister. I abruptly dropped Laurie's hands and crashed back into reality.

"Ohmigosh, it's his sister from Montreal!" I cried, grabbing my head, which felt like it was about to fly off.

"It is?"

"Of course it is! That's the surprise, he's bringing her here tomorrow! What an asshole I am!"

Laurie burst into laughter, and I joined her. It felt great. We lay back on the grass and looked up at the sky for a few minutes.

"What do you think your customers would say if they looked back here and saw their proprietor lying on the ground staring at the moon?" I asked.

She stared at the sky and raised her hands, framing the

moon in a square between her fingers. "They'd say, what's she dreaming up for us to eat tomorrow?"

"What are you dreaming up, Laurie?"

"Roast pork with apples, and happily-ever-after pie," she said, making a star of her fingers and squinting.

"That sounds good, what is it?"

"Oh, bees' dreams and hummingbird kisses, babies' laughter and sweet, sweet love," she said, rolling over to look at me. "You want a piece of that?"

"Reserve me a whole pie, please."

"You've got it, sweetie!" she said, and put out her hand. I clasped it in mine and we shook, sealing the bargain. "I'll be sure to put your name right on top."

"Thanks, Laurie," I said.

The next day around lunch time one of the boys who worked for Laurie and John came into the shop with a pastry box in his hands. I took it from him and opened it. Inside was a fresh peach pie with EMILY spelled out in rolled piecrust across the top. I put it on the counter at the back of the store, impressed by the amount of effort she had invested.

*   *   *

Toward the end of the afternoon, it happened just like I knew it would. I was standing in the doorway looking out into the street, where a little breeze had picked up the fallen leaves and was spinning them around in circles. Mr. Sorrentino was sweeping out in front of his store and I had just been over there chatting with him. I turned to look down the street past the medical building and there they were, Tony and the woman, walking toward me down the sidewalk. I smiled and waved. Tony saw me and he raised his arm from around the woman's shoulders and waved back, smiling broadly. She smiled too, saying something to him. They crossed Crescent Street and strode up to the bottom of the steps, where I stood waiting. Tony grabbed me and kissed me, twice. Then he introduced us.

"Emily, here is your surprise from New York! My sister, Marika," he said.

"Hello, it's so good to meet you!" she said in that attractive alto voice.

She smiled and we shook hands, then she pulled me in for a little kiss on each cheek. She was very charming, warm and friendly. And she did look just like him, in a more delicate, boyish sort of way.

"I want to thank you for taking such good care of my little brother," she said, hooking her arm through mine as we all walked up the steps. "He has been transformed into a happy man! He used to be so grumpy."

"Really?" I said.

"Oh no, no, no," Tony protested. "Not me!"

"But not any more. Oh my, what a wonderful shop!" she said as we came through the doorway, stopping to look around.

I headed for the coffee bar, where I had laid out some things in preparation.

"Would you like some tea, or a coffee, espresso?" I asked Marika, who was studying a collection of jade dragons in one of the cases.

She was very lithe, flexible, and she bent over gracefully to examine the pieces on the bottom shelf.

"Oh yes, thank you! Espresso sounds great. It's my low energy time of the day," she called to me, moving on to the Russian amber display, "Oh, wow! Tony, do you know what this is?"

"What?" he said, coming over to look.

She pointed. "It's amber from the same part of Russia where our grandmother came from. This piece looks a lot like that big amber egg she used to wear around her neck on a chain, remember?"

He peered into the case. "Yes, I used to hold it when I sat in her lap. I remember."

Marika walked toward me across the room, making her way between the tea tables. She smiled and slid onto the bar stool next to where I stood, tall enough to do so easily.

"What's this?" she asked, looking down at my EMILY pie, which I had taken out of the box.

"It's my magic, happily-ever-after pie," I said with a smile. "A friend made it for me. Would you like some?"

"It looks delicious!" she said, "Come and see it, Tony!"

He walked over and stood between us to look at the pie, putting one arm around each of us.

"It's beautiful, just like both of you," he said.

Marika and I looked at each other and smiled.

"But, do I have to cut it myself?" Tony demanded.

"I'll do it," his sister said, "I'm starved, as usual!"

I looked at her with approval, and passed her the knife. I could tell already that we were going to be great friends, and the three of us would enjoy many good times together. Somehow, I had an intuition about it.

Chapter 19

The Sun

ENERGY, REVITALIZATION

Description: A sun with a smiling face shines down on a laughing naked child riding a white horse.
Meaning: Energy, revitalization. A return of happiness and child-like joy. Contentment, good fortune, safety, family.

Tony's sister stayed for dinner, which we cooked together in the kitchen at Henry's house. The four of us sat down together at the table up in the study. Tree observed our activities from under the reading chair, where he sulked and twitched his tail, unhappy because he had been forced to move from Henry's lap. The two of them had definitely bonded, and at one point I caught Henry slipping him a morsel of chicken under the table.

"I don't feed him scraps, Henry! Do we, Tony?" I scolded.

"No," Tony said, "Never!" He leaned over and offered the cat a piece of chicken skin off his plate. Tree sat up politely on his hind legs and snagged it with his outstretched paw. He ran back under the chair to examine his prize in safety.

"You are incorrigible!" I said sternly, looking at Tony.

He raised his wine glass and toasted me with a devilish grin.

"Oh, just wait and see!" Marika warned. "He's actually much worse than you think. Ever since he was a small child, he's been the family rebel."

"Really?" I said, thinking that the story Henry had told me made him sound like a very responsible, dutiful son, not a rebel.

"Oh yes, just ask my parents about the time Tony ran off exploring and got lost inside one of the Pyramids, in Egypt! " she said. "He was four or five, I think. I remember because my mother and I had to wait under an umbrella in the hot sun for hours, while my father and some men searched. When they finally found him, he had fallen asleep. He was totally unconcerned. He said, 'Mama, what's for lunch?'" Marika laughed and looked at her brother affectionately.

Tony shrugged his shoulders and said, "I was hungry!"

"He was always running off and getting into scrapes," his sister said, "It was very annoying! My parents were relieved when he finally went away to school, so they could relax."

"Weren't you scared, lost in the dark like that?" I asked Tony.

"Not really," he said casually, "I knew Father would find me eventually. He always did! I was looking for the golden sarcophagus. For some reason, I had the idea there was one hidden inside the pyramid somewhere."

"Just the first of many treasure hunts to come, eh?" said Henry with a wink.

"I remember being dazzled by the Egyptian relics at the National Museum in London," Tony said, "I suppose someone must have told me they'd been found in a pyramid."

"Remember when we ran away from the hotel in the middle of the night to find a candy machine?" Marika asked him, and they both chuckled.

"That was your idea, sister, not mine!"

"I had a craving for chocolate one night, when we were all staying at Brown's Hotel in London, and the concierge told me there were vending machines in the Tube station just around the corner," Marika said. "I was afraid to go by myself, so I made Tony come with me. It was quite an adventure!"

"I can't believe the staff would let you leave without calling your parents!" I said, aghast.

Tony and Marika exchanged a sly glance.

"Well, they didn't exactly let us leave," Marika said. "Tony caused a diversion to distract them, and we ran for it."

"I'd been watching American television and was inspired by my heroes, James West and Artemis Gordon," Tony admitted. "Remember how they used to blow things up all the time?"

"Oh, no!" I said, laughing. "What did you do, you bad boy?"

"It was just a small fire, in a trash can in the lobby. There was hardly any smoke at all!" he protested.

Marika poked her brother and said, "I wonder how much Father had to pay to get you out of trouble that time?"

"Well, I believe I paid for it too," he said, "I seem to remember scraping and painting the dock that summer, by myself. And may I remind you, I am not the one with the sweet tooth!"

"That's true, you did it all for me, didn't you, my darling brother?" Marika said. "I only hope that some day, I can repay you!"

Marika was a commercial photographer. She told us about a recent fashion shoot in a Canadian nature preserve, where the models were posed with a herd of live elk in the background. It sounded very challenging to pull off, but a beautiful visual image to capture. She had put a lot on the line to bring the whole crew out there, with all their equipment, and then hope that nature would cooperate. But she won the gamble, it worked. We congratulated her, and Henry insisted she email him the photos so we could see them. He shuffled over to the desk and back, to get his business card for her.

After dinner, Tony drove her to the train station. Marika had to be back at work the next day. I went outside with them to say goodbye. They were walking back to Tony's house, where the Prius was parked. Marika put both her arms around me in a warm hug, and we stood that way for a moment. I kissed her on the cheek and we said "*au revoir*," promising to spend time together soon. Tony said he wanted to make a trip up there some weekend, to show me Montreal. Marika said her guest room was waiting for our arrival. They went off together down the sidewalk looking like two peas in a pod, even wearing similar black leather jackets and jeans, with the same walk and the same cute rear ends.

Henry was exhausted and went right to bed. I did the dishes and cleaned up the kitchen, checking the fridge, making lists and planning ahead for tomorrow's cooking. Then I went up to the third floor and took a shower, turning out all the lights and slipping between the clean white sheets. I was awakened an hour or so later when Tony showed up, back from the train station, and began to kiss me. I helped him slide his jacket off, and he discovered with his hands that I was naked.

"Emily! I'm so glad to see you! My god, " he said, delighted, "I missed you." He lowered his head and buried his face in my hair, inhaling deeply.

"I missed you too," I said, smiling into the dark.

"That's it," he said quietly into my ear, "I'm just not going to travel any more."

"What?" I whispered in amazement.

"Not unless you want to come with me."

"You can't be serious, you're a constant traveler!"

"No, I'm a homing pigeon. And you are my home."

"You said that once before."

"I meant it."

"I know you did," I said, helping to pull his T-shirt off, over his head. Then we both went to work on his pants. "But, aren't you afraid you might miss something, if you aren't out there having adventures?"

"No, I'm afraid I would miss something if I don't stay here with you," he said, getting under the sheet with me. He lay pressed up against me tightly. "I've had all the lonely adventures I need, Emily. Now I want what Laurie put in that pie."

"Oh, you recognized her recipe, did you?"

"I know magic when I taste it," he said, kissing me.

"Tony?" I interrupted.

"Yes, yes, I'll be very quiet, I know. I promise I won't scream, even if I want to."

"OK," I said, giggling. "And, don't pound the headboard into the wall."

"What kind of an oaf do you think I am?" he asked indignantly.

"My favorite kind," I said, kissing him, and that shut him up for the rest of the night.

*   *   *

Henry was off on a research mission, and had accumulated piles of printouts off the Internet regarding alternative energy. He and Tony had both decided to go with solar panels. They said it was an investment in the planet. The big flat roof of the building on Market Street, and the long south-facing roof of Tony's house, were both suitable for this particular system. They checked out all the options, and made a list of local vendors of various products. The old desk in the study was covered with information.

The two of them got together and worked on it every day. They discussed, argued, insisted, and then they compromised and drank green tea, having a marvelous time. They each took assignments and vowed to report back the next day with results. They were very well organized, and Gupta complimented them on their energetic manner of attacking the project.

Gupta had been tutoring Amy at the Rodgers family's apartment several days a week, after school. The first day she was supposed to appear there, he found her at the door accompanied by a pale woman in her early forties. It was Amy's elusive mother, recovered from her illness and come to thank him personally for helping her daughter with her studies. When Gupta told me this, his eyes were on fire with excitement.

He crowed, "Who would have ever believed that she would just walk right into my front door! The object of many months of investigation! I am better than Sherlock Holmes, ha-ha!"

Gupta was able to discreetly question Amy's mother, whose name was Wanda. She admitted that the minister at the church had been secretly letting them sleep in the basement room, and told him that she had been ill for several months with a bad cough, sleeping most of the time.

"It was dark, but dry and safe in there, with little barred windows up near the ceiling. Amy took good care of me," she had told him, hugging her daughter affectionately. "She brought me medicine and food."

Amy had looked embarrassed. "Um, Ma? Don't you have to be somewhere?" she'd asked, looking pointedly at the door.

Gupta said that Wanda told him she had an appointment down the street, at a restaurant. She said a very nice man named Mr. Sun had offered her a full-time job working there. There was an apartment upstairs that might be available too. She said that one of the family's children was apparently moving out.

When I heard this, I immediately called Mei's cell phone number, which was programmed into mine. I told her what Gupta had said. She confirmed that he had hired a new waitress, and that she had told her parents she was moving out of their building. What she hadn't told them yet, was that she was planning to move in with Rocco across the street.

"When are you going to tell them?" I asked.

"I don't know, it better be soon. I just can't get up the nerve."

"What does Rocco say about it?"

"He says, why not just elope and get it over with!" she said, and we both laughed.

I wished her luck and said I would see her at Mindy's Pilates class on Friday. When the exercise class was over and we women all gathered around the coffee bar, I told everyone what had happened with Gupta and Amy's mother.

Laurie looked at me knowingly and said, "See! I told you so! The Tarot works." Silver crescent moon earrings glinted in her tousled hair, partially stuffed up on top of her head with a scrunchy, the rest of it falling down in reddish-brown tendrils.

"Yes," said Siri, frowning, "I had forgotten the reading we did about Amy's mother!"

"The woman sick in bed, with swords or bars around her, remember? And the final outcome card...wasn't it The Sun?" Laurie reminded us.

"Mr. Sun, Mei's father! Of course! You said, they would find safety and happiness," I recalled, impressed.

"Yeah, and all the sushi they can eat, right?" said Bella, and we all laughed.

"Perfect!" I said, "I'm sure it's a very healthy diet, right Mei?"

Mei said, "They say that fish oil makes you happy, but it doesn't seem to be working on my father. He is very pissed off at me right now." She shook her head sadly. She was dressed all in black today, and looked as tiny and trim as a teenaged girl.

"Why is that, honey?" asked Alyssia, rubbing her back comfortingly. A fall of a dozen little silver bracelets decorated her arm, shining in contrast with her glowing dark brown skin. She wore a long purple sweater over her black leggings, and her hair was beautifully done in a million tiny braids.

"Oh, my boyfriend and I told him we want to get married!" Mei told us. "My parents went crazy, you should have seen it. My mother was crying, and sobbing, and my father—he nearly went through the roof!"

"But, why don't they want you to get married?" asked Mindy quietly, her expressive face showing sympathy and concern.

"Wait a minute," said Bella, "I didn't know you were even seeing anybody, you sneak!" She poked Mei in the ribs playfully. Mei smiled and gave us a sly look.

"Who is it?" asked Laurel, guessing. She looked at me. "Emily knows! Don't you?"

I just shrugged my shoulders, smiling enigmatically, or so I hoped.

"Yes, she caught us once, at the movies. OK, it's Rocco Sorrentino," Mei confessed.

"Oooh!" or "Ahhh!" they all said, nodding their heads in unanimous approval.

"That is one sexy man, you are a lucky girl!" Bella complimented her.

"But, why do they object to him?" Alyssia asked. "He has a very good business, doesn't he? And he's not married, right?"

"My parents are very old-fashioned," said Mei sadly, "They don't approve of mixed marriages."

Alyssia threw back her head and laughed, a hearty musical sound. "Honey," she said, "This is the 21st century! They'd better get with the program!"

"Yes," said Siri, "My father had some concern when I wanted to marry Tom, but he got over it quickly. He knew that Tom is a good man, and would be a good husband."

"Well I wish he could convince my parents to lighten up," sighed Mei. "I'm afraid they'll kick me out of the partnership we formed to start the restaurant."

"What do your brothers and your sister think about it?" I asked.

"They are more modern, they grew up here. And they like Rocco. But still, my oldest brother is very mad at me for making this trouble in the family. They prefer a nice smooth road! And I can't blame them," Mei said with a guilty expression on her delicate face.

"So, what are you going to do?" asked Mindy.

"I guess we are going ahead with it. He wants to tell his parents tonight! I hope they don't react the same way!"

"Somehow, I doubt it," I said. "Especially if you tell Josie you want to make babies as soon as possible!"

"Yes," said Siri earnestly, "There is nothing like having a child on the way to pull people together." She smoothed her oversized T-shirt down over her belly unconsciously, with a little smile. Laurie and I saw her do it, and exchanged glances.

"Something you want to tell us, sweetie?" Laurie asked her, putting her arm around Siri's shoulders and giving her a squeeze.

Siri patted her belly and smiled again, nodding. We all

cheered and danced. Siri laughed and joined hands with Bella, who swept her around in circles.

"When are you due?" asked Alyssia, kissing her warmly on the cheek and giving her a hug.

"In the spring, early April we think."

"Holy cow," said Bella, "You people are gonna be crammed into that apartment like sardines!"

"Yes, it is a concern," Siri said, not looking concerned at all. "We are going to need to look for another place. I hope we don't have to move too far away!"

I had a brilliant brainstorm.

"How about, right here?" I asked. They all turned to stare at me. "You can move in upstairs, and then we won't have to worry about leaving Henry by himself any more!"

It was obviously the perfect solution for everyone. The apartment on the third floor was nearly twice the size of the rooms the Rodgers family now occupied, and with the addition of a stove and refrigerator, it would be instantly habitable. And then, Tony and I could sleep where we wanted to! I loved this idea.

"Oh, I don't know Emily, do you think Henry would want us underfoot?" Siri asked hopefully. "The children can be very noisy! And the baby will cry."

"Yes, but think of the advantages. You can feed him, Tom could help with the upkeep on the building, and Gupta would be handy for a game of chess whenever Henry gets bored," I said confidently.

"Yeah," said Bella with a wink, "And, you'd never have to worry about being late for work again, right? We can just get Henry some nice comfy ear plugs."

"Leave it to me, Siri. I'll speak to him about it," I said.

And so I did, as soon as everyone packed up their things and went off to work or home. Henry was at the computer, but he came over and sat down with me when I asked for his attention. Tree was curled up in the reading chair, and let out a sleepy "Mmrrr?" when I picked him up. After Henry sat down, I put the cat on his lap. Tree immediately tucked his nose under his tail and went right back to sleep. I told Henry that Siri was expecting another baby in the spring.

"Splendid!" he exclaimed enthusiastically. "I hope that doesn't mean we're going to lose her?"

"Well, I was thinking the opposite, actually," I stalled, trying to put this the right way. "She wants to keep working, but some things would have to change."

"Very good! Hours and such...?"

"I suppose, but Bella and I can work around that. I was thinking about their apartment."

"Hm, yes? What about it? Never been there."

"It's just a two bedroom, Henry."

"Oh. Ah ha. A bit on the small side, right? I see your line of thought," he frowned, thinking swiftly. "Yes, well, don't suppose they'd like to...hm..." He looked at me expectantly, and said, "You're thinking of upstairs?"

I nodded. He looked startled.

"There are two small children and a baby on the way," I said firmly. "It would not be quiet here anymore, you need to know that."

The old man stared into space for a few minutes, apparently thinking it over. Then his eyes softened.

"Emily, do you know what this means to me?"

"What, Henry?"

"To have children living here, after all these years, all the years of hoping? It's been quiet far too long, my dear!" the old man said, wiping away a tear. "And, a baby, Emily! Can you believe it? What luck!"

"So, I take it you are OK with the idea? Can I tell Siri?" I asked, smiling a bit tearfully myself.

"Oh yes, please do. I should probably meet with her, and

her husband, don't you think? To make them the offer? What do you think about rent? I'd just as soon make it a trade for housekeeping and building maintenance, you know," he said thoughtfully. "I really could use the help. And now that we're going to make our own power, we'll have plenty of heat and hot water for the whole building!" He looked very excited and beamed at me happily. "Send Siri up to see me when you get a chance, would you? No time like the present!"

"*Carpe diem*?"

"Absolutely! Wouldn't Margaret be pleased, Emily? A baby in the house, at last." He looked starry-eyed, stroking the cat absentmindedly.

I left him daydreaming and went down to tell Siri. She laughed and hugged me, very excited. Then she grabbed the store phone and called Tom at work.

"He'll be over at lunch time!" she said, hanging up the phone. "Let's go up there for a minute before we have to open, I want to see it again."

We snuck up the back stairs and slipped into the doorway that led to the third floor. Upstairs, she walked slowly through the space, looking carefully and calculating where her furniture might fit. There would be a bedroom for Siri and Tom, another for her son, and another for the two younger children, plus a separate room for Gupta, who could have the study. There was a big livingroom with a fireplace, and a separate dining room. The kitchen was grubby, but could easily be painted and given a new floor. Only one bathroom for this number of people was a drawback, but we reminded ourselves that there were three other bathrooms in the building, one of which was right downstairs.

We joined hands in the middle of the bare, hardwood, livingroom floor and spun around, laughing. "I love it!" Siri said, "Thank you so much Emily."

"I didn't do anything."

"Yes, you did."

"Well, it will be good for all of us, don't you think?"

She nodded and asked me quietly, "Did you know all of this was coming, the first day we met, on the street?"

"Huh?"

"You offered me your friendship, then you offered me a job, and now, a home," she said, somewhat shyly. "You have completely transformed my life, Emily."

"And you mine, Siri. You brought me to Bella, and the others. We have all transformed each other, haven't we?"

"Yes," she said, "It's true. And my father is like a new man. He takes such an interest in things now, now that he has his friend Henry to discuss it with."

"Friendship is just as important as sex, don't you think?" I asked as we went back down the stairs to the second floor landing.

"Absolutely!" she agreed.

"Men are wonderful, but they're only good at certain things," I said as we stood in the hallway.

"I heard that!" Henry's voice rang out from the study.

"Of course," I said loudly, "They are essential for their wisdom and generosity!"

"Send her in!" came the voice again. "And be warned, I brook no sycophants!"

"Yes, Henry," I said, winking at Siri, who swayed gracefully as she walked down the hall to beard our noble old lion in his cozy den.

✶   ✶   ✶

Tony approved heartily of the new arrangement when I told him about it that night. He had been over to the University for a second interview at the School of Management. They hadn't offered him the job yet, but things looked promising. He had met several of the faculty members, and had observed a couple of classes. He was thinking about it. It would mean a big change in his lifestyle, after having been self-employed for over a decade.

"I'm not used to reporting to anyone else," he said, worried. "I'm not sure I could stand all the paperwork. It's been a long time since I was part of the corporate world, working for a big organization."

"Well then, don't do it," I said. We were lying nested like spoons on the big brown leather couch in front of a sweet crackling apple-wood fire in the fireplace, thanks to a limb that had fallen in the little orchard at the back of the yard.

"Is it that simple?" he said.

"Yes, you don't need to do it for some reason, do you?"

"Only intellectually, not financially."

"You need it intellectually?" I asked, surprised.

"I suppose so. I have always been very attracted to the 'life of the mind,'" he mused.

I remembered what Henry had said about Tony being a natural scholar.

"Well then, maybe you should do it," I said, spontaneously flipping my argument.

"You don't care?" he asked.

"Me?"

"Yes."

"What have I got to do with it?" I demanded.

"Quite a lot, actually. If you wanted to."

"Oh! Well, I think you should do whatever makes you happy, Tony."

"You don't care if your husband has a nice, steady job with good benefits?"

"My what?"

He was silent for a beat.

"Your husband?" he said.

I was silent for a beat.

"My husband," I said, stressing the word, "Had better know that I want him to do something he is passionate about, not just something with good benefits."

I twisted around on the couch to discuss this interesting topic face to face. He was smiling at me fondly.

"I suppose there are good benefits to being passionate, as well?" he said, kissing me.

"Absolutely," I said, kissing him back.

"Emily?"

"Yes?"

"I think we ought to get rid of your apartment," he said. "It's very wasteful for two people and a cat to take up so much space, don't you think?"

"You have a point."

"Are you ready to sacrifice your independence?"

"Yes, I think so. Are you?" I asked.

"Sweetheart," he said, "I gave that up the day I saw you sitting on the bench in the park with your eyes closed, basking in the sun like a beautiful lioness."

"You did? And all this time, I've been trying to entrap you!"

"No, that's just what you thought. In fact, it was I who was trapping you."

We smiled at each other, both of us caught at last, all defenses defeated and finally safe together in blissful mutual captivity. I felt liberated and empowered in a way I had never felt before. I could totally be myself. So this was what it felt like to surrender to trust, to give up fear of betrayal! It was like walking out into the sunlight after living in the shadows for as long as I could remember. I basked in it, like the beautiful lioness I had somehow become, thanks to his vision and its power to manifest in me.

Chapter 20

Judgment

SPIRITUAL AWAKENING

Description: Men, women and children rise from their graves, awakened by the horn of the angel Gabriel, who calls them home to Paradise.
Meaning: Spiritual awakening. Answering the call to a higher level of wisdom. Release from prison or the bonds of materialistic thinking.

In the course of living happily ever after, which is exactly what Tony and I proceeded to do next, my fresh new positive attitude and a constant feeling of exhilaration led me to a host of interesting realizations. I was fearless and balanced inside, so I was looking at the world with more confidence, and I think I was even less distracted, paying more attention. It was an awakening. The lioness was alive and well, poised to pounce, and I threw myself enthusiastically into various soul-enriching projects.

Siri and I both moved, late that fall, and we were all settling into our new homes and getting comfortable with the space. Siri's belly was starting to pop out, and she happily indulged her nesting instinct as she painted and decorated the rooms on the third floor. Tom and the kids left their shoes at the bottom of the back stairs, and tried not to stomp on the floor, but there were lots of cute little giggles everywhere. Gupta was upstairs and down, offering help wherever it was needed. He liked to polish the brass and silver, and the store never looked better. He protested that he was doing Siri's lamps anyhow, so it was no trouble, but I knew that wasn't entirely true and I was grateful to him. He was extremely helpful, and we all told him so.

When I was moving the last of my things over to the house by the park, I stood in my empty apartment and looked up through the skylight, remembering all the nights, all the moons and all the dreams. Just as I was about to unplug it, the phone rang. It was Mom.

"Hi honey, how is the move going?"

"Pretty well, I'm almost done. How are you?"

"Great! I got in nine holes of golf this morning, it's gorgeous down here!"

"That's good, Mom."

"So, you're still sure about this, Emily?"

"Yes, very sure."

"OK, honey, I trust your judgment."

"Thank you for saying so, I appreciate that."

"I can't wait to meet him," she said confidingly, "The girls at the club were all swooning over his picture, he's a real Dream Boat!"

I grinned at that, and made a mental note to tell Tony what she'd said.

"Mom, I was just about to turn off this phone, so you should call me at the new number or on my cell from now on, OK?"

"Sure thing, honey. Just checking in. I'll let you go now, love you!"

"Love you too, Mom."

Tony and I had invited Mom, plus Marika and his parents, to come for Christmas. My brother and sister sent their love, but would spend the holiday together with all their kids in the Mid-West this year. I was excited about hosting the holiday here. We had two good-sized guest rooms that shared a bath, where Mom and Tony's sister could stay, and we could put his parents up at the comfortable hotel on Main Street, a beautiful historic place only a few blocks away.

Tony's parents had never been to New England before. They were flying into Boston and staying there for a few days first, then driving their rental car out to see us. We hadn't said anything to our relatives yet about the idea of getting married. We barely had talked about it ourselves. For now, I was concentrating on getting relocated and readjusted.

It was very different, living with another person all of the time. As I put my things away in the spacious master bathroom, where two sinks and two medicine cabinets gave each of us our own space, I looked at our two toothbrushes sitting together in a single cup in the middle of the counter, where they had been since that first weekend we spent together. They leaned together intimately. That cup was a tiny realm where his territory and my territory overlapped.

This was how I wanted to feel about the whole house, but it still didn't really seem like mine. Integrating my furniture with Tony's helped, but I didn't have much to bring to the situation. I wanted to buy some things and furnish the rest of the upstairs, which had not yet been set up. I could make my mark on the house there. But I wasn't really sure how the money was going to work, either. This was all new to me, and I felt funny about asking Tony about it. He automatically paid for everything whenever we were together, and never appeared to consider this an issue. But I wanted to pay rent, or buy the groceries, or something. I was used to supporting myself, and I had taken some pride in being able to do so. There were a few unresolved issues, like this, hanging between us at that point, but we were gradually sorting things out.

Henry was enjoying his new domestic arrangement, too. He started working on a stamp collection with Siri's son, Thomas. They steamed the stamps off Henry's global correspondence by using the electric teakettle in the study. Henry could keep "the lad," as he called Thomas, busy for hours while they looked at the stamps and talked about the faraway lands from which they came. They had formed a strong friendship. And I saw the way Siri's attitude toward Henry subtly changed, as she took over more and more responsibility for his care and feeding. He gazed at her appreciatively, like the goddess she was, and she treated him with gentle, supportive attention. Henry and Tom worked on the building together most weekends, fixing up the kitchen upstairs and putting in a new stall shower in the Rodgers family's bathroom. Tom did most of the actual work, but Henry printed out instructions off the Internet and supervised.

Things rolled along smoothly that fall, for all of us except Mei. The trouble with her parents had escalated, and when she moved out of their building she ended up getting her own place, rather than moving in with Rocco.

"We decided to get officially engaged first, " she told me. "Living separately is more proper, and we're hoping our families will have a chance to get used to the whole idea of us as a couple."

"That makes sense," I said, "I'm sure they'll come around."

It was still early days, but the plan seemed like it might be working. Rocco hired the private dining room at the Green Thumb for a family dinner on neutral ground, inviting both sets of parents and all available siblings. Everyone except Mr. Sun showed up. But his wife did appear and was quite friendly to the Sorrentinos. Mei thought that all in all, things had gone well.

She laughed and said, "Buddha says, what is real is what you think. I think there is nothing to worry about, if we let everyone else get used to this for a little while longer. My father loves me! He'll change his mind."

Gupta and Amy studied hard nearly every day, and she planned to take the GED test in the spring. She was already looking at art schools for next fall, proceeding confidently with her plan to graduate early. She designed some new Winter Wonderland window displays for the store, and all of our customers commented on them. Her mother, Wanda, was working at Mr. Sun's restaurant and she and Amy had moved into the apartment upstairs in that building. Things had stabilized in Amy's life, and she seemed happier. Her clothing and hair color blossomed with creativity, as she sported lots of tie-die instead of black, and her hair was streaked with hot pink.

One day Amy showed up at the back door with a teenaged boy. She introduced him as Ralph. He was dressed all in black, with chopped hair and multiple piercings similar to hers. She told us Ralph was interested in old books and wanted to meet Henry. She took Ralph upstairs and the two were gone for an hour or so. When they finally departed, I went up to find out what had happened. I thought perhaps the boy had wanted to see the occult books, possibly something on Satanism, or exorcism instructions.

"Not at all," said Henry. "He was looking for old poetry

books, Coleridge, Wordsworth, etcetera. He actually bought an edition of *Romeo and Juliet*!"

I remarked that appearances could be deceiving, and Henry gave me a pitying look. Sometimes I got the feeling he still regarded me as a neophyte, though I felt I was coming along nicely. I guessed there were still a few things I had left to learn.

We had Thanksgiving at Henry's house, lining up three long tables to seat everyone. When we all joined hands to bless the food, a thrilling tingle went through me and I felt a strong connection with them all, my community, my every-day family. I looked around me and saw white, golden, tan, brown and black skin. I saw blonde, red, brown, white, gray and black hair, curly and straight, long and short, coarse and wiry, and feathered in fine little wisps. I saw blue, green, hazel and brown eyes looking back at me. We were like a beautiful rainbow, and when we joined hands and sent our energy around the circle, we merged and became all colors, all races, all humanity. We prayed together for the planet Earth, thankful for our home and for each other's love.

By the time Mom and Tony's family came for Christmas, I had settled in and started to think of his house as our house. Mom and I stuffed and roasted a goose, and Tony's mother made the *buche noel*, a gorgeous chocolate cake that resembles a Yule log. Mom and Tony's mother, Karina, got along famously. Tony's parents were living at the house on Lake Como full time now, and they had seen various American movie stars visiting there, such as George Clooney. Mom, who never missed *Inside Edition* on TV and was an avid reader of *People Magazine*, was completely thrilled. Karina invited her to visit them in the summertime, when the spot was most popular. Mom was so excited she nearly dropped her eggnog!

Tony's father was dark and handsome, a very well preserved older version of his son. Marika looked like him too, while their mother was petite, blue-eyed and fair, now with silver hair. She and Marika both shared an elegant style, very European and so-phisticated. Mom and I talked about it in the kitchen late one night. Even when they were just wearing jeans and pullovers, they looked like they had just stepped out of an *avant garde* fashion magazine. We felt a little dowdy around them. Mom and I looked more like that country cousin in the Tarot deck, and when my jeans got holes in the knees it was just shabby, not shabby-chic. But they were both lovely women, and we liked them very much. Tony's dad spent most of his time with his son and Henry, so we didn't have much chance to get to know him better. His name was Adrian, and he seemed kind of restrained, more formal than the women of the family.

On Christmas Day, Tony gave me an engagement ring. I didn't know about it ahead of time, but I wasn't really surprised either. He'd been humming around the house lately with a mis-chievous look in his eye, so I knew something was up. He had it in his bathrobe pocket when he brought me coffee in bed that morning.

"Good morning, Emily, Happy Holidays!" He kissed me, put the hot coffee mug into my hand and immediately let it go, which very effectively awakened me.

"Happy Holidays?" I said groggily, grabbing the mug to stop it from spilling, and sitting up in bed.

"Well, I don't want to offend you in case you are not a Christian, do I?" He got into bed next to me and leaned against the pillows, enigmatically watching me sip my coffee, which was excellent and brisk. I started to rise into full consciousness. It was a bright, sunny morning and the bedroom was filled with light. My beloved was smiling at me, waiting to be teased.

"And what religion do you think I am? Do you think I'm Jewish? Do you think I'm a Zen Buddhist? How about a Wiccan?" I challenged him, as the caffeine started to kick in. He grinned and rolled his eyes, enjoying getting a rise out of me.

"I think you might be a Druid at heart, darling, or some variety of nature worshipper," he said, reaching over to very gently and carefully pull the strap of my nightgown back up onto my shoulder. I hadn't realized it had fallen off. No wonder he had been staring at me, with that Cheshire-cat smile.

"Well, that's different," I said, smiling back at him. "You're usually taking my clothes off! Are you feeling OK today, baby?"

"I just want you to be properly dressed for the occasion," he said.

"Ho ho ho, for the occasion of…what, my love? Do I get my Happy Holidays present now?" I said, putting my empty mug down on the bedside table so that I could pounce on him. I laid him flat in seconds, easily overpowering him by lying on top of him, and kissing him repeatedly. "So, what is it, let's see?" I demanded, and he raised his hand and put the little red velvet box on his chest right in front of my face. That's when I knew for sure what it was.

This was originally his grandmother's diamond, he told me, and he had it put into a setting designed by our favorite local jeweler. The sparkling stone was at the center of a golden spiral, set into a wide platinum band. Inside the ring was engraving that said: *"AB ~ ER Carpe Diem."* I cried a little when I read it. The ring fit me perfectly, and I was absolutely crazy about it.

"So, I suppose this means if I want to keep the jewelry," I said, admiring my left hand, "I have to keep you too?"

"You could look at it that way," he said thoughtfully, then he flashed me a smile. "But you're stuck with me even if you'd rather have something else. Do you really like it?"

"It's perfect, " I said, "It's us! I love it." Then I kissed him most earnestly, and made an inspired effort to impress him with my sincere enthusiasm for the next half an hour, or so.

At breakfast in the kitchen with the family, we popped open

some *Veuve Cliquot* and celebrated with everyone, toasting the future. Mom and I got a little maudlin about Daddy's not being there, but we swore he was looking down on us with approval from the astral plane, or Heaven, or wherever he was. Then Mom called my sister on the phone and we all three squealed and screamed at each other in excitement. Tony and his father chose that moment to escape to the backyard for a quick stroll, looking at us with a slightly bewildered air.

"Antonin, are they upset?" Tony's dad asked him on their way outside.

"No, I think they're happy," Tony replied uncertainly.

"Oh!" Adrian said, obviously mystified.

"You know women, Father, they always cry when they're happy!"

"Yes, I suppose so. Thank god I'm not a woman."

"I thank god for that too, sweetheart, every day of my life!" called his wife from across the room, and everyone laughed.

For the next few days, the two men snuck off while the women got together and started to plan the wedding, which was tentatively scheduled for next fall. Mom and Karina went to work making lists of things to do. Both mothers-in-law-to-be obviously felt it was high time that Tony and I had decided to settle down. They conspired happily, while Marika and I enjoyed long walks through town, checking out all the shops, and she took lots of pictures, including one of Tony and me on the front steps of our house that still hangs on the wall at the head of the stairs today.

In the picture, he is sitting behind me one step up, with me sitting between his knees and his arms sheltering me, protecting me. I am looking at the camera with a smile that looks happy, but very slightly annoyed, and he is peering around me looking wary. It's a classic shot of us.

*   *   *

In the dark mid-winter, when New England normally freezes solid under several feet of snow, we had a freak warm spell and I personally saw the mercury hit seventy degrees one sunny afternoon in January. People went to the grocery store in shorts. Lots of shoppers who came into the store loved it, and said, "Isn't this weather great? We don't even have to go to Florida this year!" But other citizens were concerned. The polar ice caps were melting even faster than scientists had anticipated, it said on Al Gore's web site. I filled out an email letter to Congress, asking them to take action on the climate crisis immediately, and sent it in at Al's site. He said he was planning to bring all the letters to Congress when he testified, to show how many voters considered this a top priority. I definitely did, and I nagged all my friends and family to make them step up to the keyboard and send a letter, too. I got an email back that started, "Dear Emily," and was signed, "Al Gore." I knew it was a form letter, but it looked so personal, and I was completely thrilled, in a funny way. It made me feel powerful! I knew somebody now, my buddy Al.

One day toward the end of January, Laurie came running over to the store in the late afternoon, saying we needed to turn on the TV in the sitting room. Nobody was in the store at the moment anyhow, so Bella and Siri and I went in there with her. The others sat down while I hovered in the doorway, keeping watch in case a customer appeared and needed help.

Laurie wanted us to watch *Oprah*. She said we had to see it. The guests today were teachers of something called "The Secret," which I had never heard of before. It was out both as a movie on DVD, and in book form, and these people were doing public speaking engagements all over the world to spread the word. It was a runaway, worldwide, self-help smash hit.

Oprah Winfrey introduced the show by saying that in one day, six different people suddenly walked up and asked her if she had heard of it.

When Oprah first came on the air and the cameras showed a head shot of her, Bella started to complain.

"My god," she said, "What is she doing to us? That woman looks way too good today!"

"She does look great with her hair that way, it's so romantic," said Siri.

We all squinted at the screen, examining Oprah thoroughly.

"She looks beautiful in that outfit," I observed.

"Yeah, but she looks too good, I mean, we can't do that, we can't look that good!" Bella exploded, jumping up. "How are real women like us supposed to pull that off? And what is she saying to us, what's the message? That we're slouches if we can't look that good, too?"

"Calm down," said Laurie. "She's a TV star, that's all."

"I know," Bella sniffed unhappily, sitting down again. "I totally LOVE Oprah, I mean, I really do." She looked closer at the screen. "What the hell is that?" she asked, jumping up again and pointing to Oprah's eye.

"What?" Siri said.

"What's that big fat black thing there, on her eye? It looks like a caterpillar!" Bella said suspiciously. "Oprah, what you got on your eye, my girl?"

"I think that's her false eyelashes!" Siri said, amazed, and we all giggled uncontrollably. Then the show started and we were all completely swept away by the power of what was happening on Oprah's stage.

It was all about positive thinking, and the power of visualization. The big "secret" was the fact that, just like Tony had been teaching me, you could make things happen by thinking about them, by imagining them to have already happened.

They were calling it the "Law of Attraction."

I was very excited that something this positive could be so successful with mainstream America. Of course, somebody was also making a lot of money off it, the marketers who had packaged the concept in such an attractive, mysterious way. But that didn't change the fact that people were willing to sit down and listen to this idea, which gave them hope and taught them to be bold and try to change the world. At the first commercial, I used the remote to turn down the sound and told everyone this, saying that Tony had an old book called *The Power of Positive Thinking* by Norman Vincent Peale that outlined the same basic concepts. Laurie mentioned that it also sounded a lot like the principles behind the kind of magic that was used by witches like Starhawk.

When the show was over, Laurie asked us what we thought.

"I think Oprah knows better than any of the rest of them how this secret works," said Bella. "My girl always walks on the sunny side, you know what I mean?"

"Yes, she is a good example for us all in that way," said Siri.

"Even if she looks just a little bit too good, sometimes," Bella compromised.

"You'll forgive her for that?" I asked.

"Yeah, " said Bella, "I guess she's gotta keep up with all the sexy actresses who come on her show. She doesn't want her boyfriend to start sniffing around Jennifer Lopez or anybody, right? I mean, Oprah is beautiful, but she's not a red-hot Latina!"

"Bella, who says a red-hot Latina is any hotter than a red-hot African American?" I demanded.

"The red-hot Latina's husband had better say that, for one thing," she grinned, striking a sexy pose.

"Well, that's what it's really all about, isn't it?" said Laurie.

"What your partner thinks of as sexy?"

"Totally, true, yes," we all agreed, nodding our heads.

"Rolo doesn't even like for me to wear makeup," said Bella coyly. "He likes me straight from the shower, with nothing on at all!"

"Most men say they don't like makeup, but when it's done well, they certainly respond to it," Laurie observed.

"I guess it makes a difference whether you're expecting to be seen close up, or from far away," I mused, remembering stage makeup from my drama club days. "Maybe Oprah wears makeup for the camera, but not when she's at home with her boyfriend."

"I sure hope so," said Bella, "'Cause those black crawly eyelashes look kind of itchy."

"Somehow I doubt that she's afraid to look natural," I said. "Let's give Oprah the benefit of the doubt."

"Yeah, she knew about 'The Secret,' so she must know about this basic girl stuff, right ladies?" said Bella.

We all agreed that Oprah obviously knew a lot of secrets, and a lot of girl stuff, probably more than we did, in fact. Then Laurie headed back across the intersection, and the rest of us went to close up the shop for another night, and go home to our families.

*   *   *

Henry and I had an interesting conversation one day not long afterwards. We were sitting at the table together upstairs, going over the year-end financial reports, which were due to be filed soon. We were operating very nicely in the black, so Henry had decided to put some money into remodeling the back of the building, where the old porch was sagging and needed repair. Laurie had suggested we tear off the porch, blow out the back wall of the showroom and move the seating area behind the coffee bar, lightening the room with a bank of windows and putting in some nice landscaping outside, maybe even a little patio. I loved the idea, and wanted to add an herb and salad garden, so we could grow some of our own fresh organic ingredients.

"It's better to invest the profits in the building than pay it in income tax," I advised Henry, sounding like I knew what I was talking about. "It will increase the value of your business and your real estate."

"Yes, and I'm already getting a nice tax credit for going solar," Henry said thoughtfully. "But that isn't what really appeals to me about the idea, first and foremost."

"Well, what does then?"

"I think if we are smart, we could add a small gallery space, too."

"An art gallery?" I was very interested.

"What do you think?"

"I think I should call Lexi and get her over here to take a look!"

"Very good!" Henry said, getting excited. "I can see it now! A little passive solar greenhouse! Sculpture in the garden! Wind chimes! Lawn art!"

"It's a wonderful idea," I said, "I'll get on it right away!"

"I'll do some research on the Internet," Henry said contentedly.

Plans proceeded and we had some drawings made of the proposed construction. Lexi came over to look at them with me. We walked around outside behind the building and considered the available space. There was a scraggly little grass lawn on the Crescent Street side of the building that could be turned into a nice patio. Lexi said she had a great connection for stonework. We came inside for an *espresso* and I spread the blueprints out on the coffee bar.

"You know, Emily," Lexi said slowly, "I'm thinking about moving the gallery."

"You mean, to Boston?"

"Yes. I've been looking for a good location."

"Are you selling your house?"

"No, I love my house, and we love it here. We'll come out on weekends," she smiled. "Maybe we'll even move back some day."

"I'll miss you!" I said, surprised to find that it was true.

"Well, I was thinking, Em. I wouldn't mind maintaining a presence out here, especially to continue showing my local artists. What if you and Henry sublet the new space to Gladstone Gallery, and you can staff it for me? I'll pay you a commission on anything you sell."

It was a terrific offer, and I knew it.

"Wow, Lex, I'm flattered that you would suggest it!"

"You need to think about it, I know," she said uneasily, taking in the stunned expression on my face.

"Well, not really, in a way."

"No?"

"No, I just don't think it would work for us," I said.

"Oh," she said coldly, "OK." She was not happy with me, and turned away.

"I mean, Henry already has a whole bunch of ideas of what he wants to do with the space. He's very into it," I said earnestly, grabbing her by the arm. "I know he would never consider subletting. But he does want to show any local artists who you think are interesting. What if we compromise?"

"Well, what do you mean?" she said hopefully, turning back toward me.

"What if you give us just a certain number of pieces to show every month, your choice, and we sell them on commission like you were suggesting? We collaborate on marketing?

Share the cost of any mailings or ads?"

"Done," she said with a broad smile, shaking my hand, and then we hugged.

What a change from the old days, I thought. No temper tantrums, no shouting, no Lexi looking daggers at me and hinting that my intelligence level was below par. She had certainly changed. Or, had she? Maybe it was I who had changed. That was a thought. All the details of my life were certainly different. What about my personality?

I decided that while I hadn't been watching, something must have happened to me. My whole outlook was different, and the way I responded to things. I used to be so on edge with Lexi that I took offense at the least little thing. Now, I felt I could dismiss anything negative she said with ease, and turn her around, make her happy. I felt that I was valuable to her, and it made me more secure. I was more secure in general, actually. And that enabled me to be more generous and outgoing toward the other people in my life. Which made them respond to me in a positive way, which made me more secure still. It was like a self-fulfilling prophecy. It was an endless loop of positive reinforcement, the snake eating its own tail, the phoenix born again from its own ashes to soar and burn again, and then again.

Another example, I thought, of how we write the future with choices we make now, and how everything that happens in our lives really is within our sphere of influence, to some degree. Some people are upset when you suggest they may have written the script of their life stories themselves. They have troubles, and sometimes, terrible things happen, and they don't want to feel responsible for creating them. Or they want it to all be up to God, or Fate, or some other Higher Power. They think mere humans don't have the ability to change things like that. But I could prove it. I had changed myself, and by doing so, I had changed Lexi too, and I had completely changed the future of our relationship. I hadn't realized it at the time, but I could see it clearly now.

When I was lying in bed next to Tony that night, listening to his slow, relaxed breathing, I started to think about all of this again. Would I even be here, with this man tonight, if I hadn't been able to stop something that happened to me ten years ago from continuing to write my story today? I had been headed straight for another crash and burn relationship, that night I had dinner with Laurie in the garden. I was ready to run away again. But I was able to stop my typical scenario from reoccurring. That meant, while the things we do today will definitely affect tomorrow, we do have the power to choose differently and step onto another branch of the path at the crossroads.

We have to come to terms with the past in order to change the direction we are heading. The good times and the bad times both offer us a choice, since we can control how we view them, how we react.

We can be daunted, or we can be challenged. We can be discouraged, or we can be inspired. I could fill myself with the qualities I most admire and celebrate my life, and if I wanted to live happily ever after, I could simply choose that reality and start living it right now.

And so, I did. And the time passed joyfully, with my glass more than half full. In fact, it overflowed with thankfulness and appreciation for the wonderful days and nights we were given, the great gift of this life together on our beautiful, verdant Earth.

Chapter 21

The World

FULFILLMENT, SUCCESS

*Description: A beautiful man/woman dances in-
side a wreath of laurel leaves, the sign of triumph.
Angels or animals symbolic of the four elements of
earth, air, fire and water surround her.
Meaning: Fulfillment, victory, transformation.
The end of one complete cycle. The achievement of
a progressed attitude and an evolved spirit.*

In the tender season, the very early spring when red buds swell
on the tips of branches and flocks of little birds chase clouds

of little flies across the sky, I began to sprout new ideas like the seedlings that erupted from the newly thawed earth that quickened all around us.

It was mud season and the floors were filthy all the time, no matter how often we mopped. The girls agreed that it was best to dress in layers so we could shed them as the day progressed, warming up to sixty-five most afternoons now. There was still some snow around, though, in dirty black-speckled mounds near the parking meters and around the edges of parking lots. The ground hog from Pennsylvania did not see his shadow, and spring was due immediately. Siri was swelling up like a beautiful, sexy balloon and the rest of us were expectant vicariously through her.

Then St. Patrick's Day brought a huge Nor'easter, classic New England style, and we were buried under eighteen inches of snow. I decided to warm things up by having Ladies' Night at our house. Despite the icy roads and piles of snow, both drifted and pushed into mountains by snowplows, all of the girls actually came.

New Englanders are hardy souls, whether we come from here originally or not. In fact, none of us came from here originally except Bella, whose parents still lived in the nearby city of Springfield, where she was born and raised. But now, like the native Yankees, we had all come to calmly accept the winter weather, and in truth we really kind of enjoyed it, the beauty and excitement of it. We forged out bravely on snowy nights under white-out conditions in our four-wheel drive vehicles or stoically on booted foot, and we went where we had to go. We were strong and invincible. Once we got there, we partied our brains out.

Tony went out that night, on my advice. He and Tom set out on foot to enjoy the St. Patty's Day green beer served at all the bars in the center of town. Gupta and Henry got to stay home and babysit, falling asleep in their comfortable chairs soon after the children went to bed. The girls took over the house by the park, and we were all wired for a wild time.

Laurie put some CD's on Tony's pet sound system, which by now had insinuated itself into nearly every room in the house. We started with an energetic freeform dance to some music Alyssia had brought, sort of a cross between synthetic computer music and some kind of ethnic, tribal music. It was fabulous. We spread out all over the downstairs and threw ourselves into it. Then we all gathered around the granite island in the kitchen and drank Tony's *Veuve Cliquot*. Siri drank ice water.

"Love it, love it, love it," said Laurie, pointing at the granite island, the six-burner stove and the stainless steel SubZero refrigerator.

"Yes, this place is great, honey!" said Alyssia. "Now, what did you have to do to deserve all this?" She pretended to look at me suspiciously, one eyebrow raised.

"Just lucky, I guess," I said innocently.

"Are you kidding?" said Bella. "They've probably done it in every room of this house, and all over Henry's place too!"

"Well," I said, "Not quite all over Henry's place. Only on two floors, in fact."

"That's good, honey," Alyssia said, patting my hand. "A little restraint is good for the soul."

"So what's new with you, anyhow?" I asked her.

"My son is being recruited by the military, or so they think."

"Rashid? How old is he?" asked Siri.

"He'll be eighteen this summer, and they're already trying to convince him to sign up for the Army!" Alyssia said sadly, shaking her head in disbelief.

"But, won't they send him to Iraq?" Mindy asked.

"You bet your sweet bippy, they will," said Bella.

"They are wooing him with promises of a free college education," Alyssia said.

"But, at what real cost?" said Siri quietly, unconsciously cradling her hugely swollen belly with one arm. She was due in just a few weeks now.

"Bush is trying to get approval for the money to send a bunch more troops over there, did you hear that?" asked Mei.

"Yeah, he said he didn't need permission from Congress to send them. Can you believe that? How arrogant!" said Laurie.

"So, what do you think of Hillary?" I asked.

"I LOVE Hillary!" said Bella. "That is one smart woman! She didn't just dump her husband and slink off when he screwed around on her, she worked a deal with the Democrats that's gonna land her right back in the White House!"

We all agreed that we admired Hillary, for various reasons. I said I wasn't sure that she could get elected, though. A lot of people seemed to be annoyed by her. In a way, she was too well known. It would be harder to paint her as a noble, innocent crusader, which is what we Americans love to elect. No shop-worn merchandise for us, we like our new presidents bandbox fresh and spanking clean.

Alyssia said, "Who would you choose, ladies? A menopausal white woman or a hot young black man? To run against a middle-aged white man on the GOP side, no doubt?"

"That's a hard decision," said Mei. "But I think maybe the black man would have a better chance."

"Well, Tony's parents think our current president is a megalomaniac," I said. "They said he is very unpopular in Europe."

"It's too bad your buddy Al isn't in the White House," Bella said sadly.

"Yes, things would be so different now, wouldn't they?" said Mindy.

"I doubt we would still be in Iraq," I said, "And we'd be doing a lot more about the climate crisis, that's for sure."

"Did you hear that in Australia, regular incandescent light

bulbs are illegal now?" Mindy asked.

Then we all burst forth and started talking at approximately the same time:

"Yes! The whole country is going to use those funny spiral-shaped ones now!"

"I don't like those, do you?"

"They're weird!"

"Yeah, they make a funny color light."

"Yes, but they use much less energy, so it's worth it."

"Yeah, I guess so."

"We can all make some sacrifices, right?"

"It's a small thing to do, when you think about it."

"You're right."

"Yeah, I'm gonna get some."

"They're really expensive, though."

"You can get a deal on a big package of them!"

"They have them at Costco!"

"So, Emily? What kind of light bulbs do you use?"

"Are you kidding? Tony is obsessed with alternative energy! You think he would allow an incandescent bulb inside this house?"

"When are the solar panels coming?"

"They said in the spring, but I think it needs to stop snowing before they'll schedule it," I said, squinting out the foggy kitchen windows at the blizzard conditions. "Wow, it's really coming down now."

We all gathered in the breakfast nook and looked out at the snow, which was fine and icy. It was pale and otherworldly outside. Across the street from our house in front of the park was a lonely street lamp that barely glowed, a small dim pinkish oblate blur. All the details of the landscape were obscured, disguised by white in the air and white on the ground, flattened by a lack of gradation that erased form and eliminated depth perception. Off in the park, I could almost see the translucent outline of a swing set. Icy little grains of snow suddenly tapped on the kitchen windows in a shower of crystals, swept up against the house by the wind. It was bleak, but absolutely magnificent, and we were all safe and warm inside together, with walls of glass to protect us from the weather.

"Tony says that in Beijing, the Chinese are dumping so much pollution into the atmosphere every day that the sky is always thick with soupy smog," I said. "He said when you go inside at night, your clothes are covered with black, greasy soot."

"Yes, they are adding thirty thousand new cars there every month," said Mei. "People are so excited to finally get this kind of technology, they are going a little crazy."

We silently watched the white, white, pristine snow falling for a moment. Everyone kept her thoughts private, but I had a feeling we were all hoping, praying, each in her own way. Then *Latin Lounge* came on the CD player, and Bella shot me an inquiring look, and an impish grin. Within seconds, we were all tangoing across the kitchen floor toward the long, open corridor that ran from the front door to the rooms at the back of the house. Siri had a little trouble until Alyssia partnered her from behind, so the baby wasn't between them. Bella and I were actually getting pretty good at this. We had learned how to snap around and reverse at the end of the hallway. Then it was over, and everyone headed back to the kitchen to devour the snacks.

When Tony came home a little later, stamping his feet in the portico outside the kitchen door to shake off the snow that coated his pants all the way up past the knee, the girls all gathered their things and put on their gear to brave the blizzard. Laurie had driven Siri and some of the others in her van, and Mindy had her car too. They went off gaily into the night, sisters of the storm, warrior queens undaunted by the perils of nature.

We were happy to see snow in New England, when it very well might be no more than a distant memory here some day soon. We all knew that when the baby in Siri's belly was old enough to vote, she would be calling us to account for her options.

*   *   *

The baby came, right on schedule, and Siri named her Hope, after Tom's grandmother. It seemed like the right choice. She was what we all needed, and everyone started to spoil her from the day she was born. We were all completely nuts about her. Including Henry and Gupta, who brought her into the office with them in her cradle every afternoon while Siri worked in the shop. Occasionally we would hear her hoarse little goat-like cry come echoing down the front stairs, then the sound of two grown men singing "Itsy Bitsy Spider" in sprightly tones. Siri would check her breasts, then run upstairs to nurse the baby, and be back in a few minutes. Gupta said he didn't even mind changing Hope's diaper, so Henry generously allowed his friend to be in charge of that.

Construction plans for the addition to the store were progressing. We planned to close for the month of June while the remodeling was done. And during that time, I was going on a little vacation. To China! The University had offered Tony a position as a guest lecturer to their class on Chinese business practices, and he had accepted. In June, about twenty of the students were going to follow up the classroom experience by visiting several major Chinese cities. Tony had used his contacts to get the students appointments to meet with top executives at a couple of multinational corporations. Except for a trip from El Paso to Juarez one time when I visited my cousin in Texas, I had never been out of the country before, and I was very excited.

The timing was perfect for me, with what was going on at work. I was planning to do some buying for the shop, too, and Henry insisted I take a digital camera and laptop so I could keep in touch with him via the Internet. He wanted me to email him photos of any interesting pieces I came across.

We had just been talking about this on the day I went back down to the basement to unpack the last few pieces of porcelain in the bottom of the shipping carton under the stairs. I was remembering the image of Henry as a young man on the docks in Hong Kong that had once jumped into my head when I'd touched his hand. This time I envisioned the young Chinese man opening the red door when Henry knocked, to shake the young American's hand and welcome him to the pottery, leading him inside.

I unwrapped two beautiful teapots and put them on the tray I had brought downstairs for this purpose, then reached into the crate for the next piece. When I touched it, I smelled a whiff of sandlewood and caught a ripple of distant bells, then heard that soft giggle again.

The ghostly presence was with me, I could sense it. But I wasn't afraid this time, for some reason. It wasn't that the intent of the spirit had changed, for my ghost had never expressed any malevolence. It was that I had changed. I accepted what was happening and didn't fight it, giving myself permission to be in this moment and to have an aptitude for unusual perceptions.

My heartbeat accelerated and I reached for the covered jar under the excelsior. It was tightly wrapped in layers of delicate yellowed paper covered with Chinese characters, written by hand with a calligrapher's brush. Inside the paper was a layer of sapphire silk, wrapped around the piece and sealed on one side, with a wax lozenge stamped with some design. This was nothing like the other porcelain we had found in the crate, and I held it in my hands reverently, knowing I had finally come across the piece my ghostly friend had wanted me to find. I felt a breath on the back of my neck, like a gentle sigh of contentment, and a warm glow spread through me.

I called up the stairs to Siri, who was working in the kitchen, and asked her to tell Henry he was needed. In a few minutes they both came downstairs, curious and eager. I showed them the silk-wrapped parcel. Henry did the honors and broke the seal then the three of us carefully unwound the fabric until he was left holding a large blue and white ginger jar, its lid lovingly sealed shut with wax and silk ribbons. Another design-stamped lozenge dangled from the seal.

"What do you suppose is inside?" Siri's eyes were enormous.

"He wanted us to find this," I said, nodding at Henry. "You should open it, but carefully."

Henry nodded, his eyes sad and solemn. We both already knew what, or rather who, the jar contained. He broke the wax seal and unwound the ribbons to remove the top, revealing the light gray ashes within. We all stared for a moment. A small piece of bone lay on top of the ashes, and if we'd had any doubts as to their origin this would have resolved the question. Putting the top back on the jar, we silently climbed the stairs up to the kitchen, where Henry deposited the urn on the table. Siri made tea and we sat down together, waiting for Henry to speak. He had tears in his eyes and cleared his throat several times.

"My dear friend Walter Chung disappeared around the same time the Communists took Tibet and the Dalai Lama was forced to escape. I always assumed that he went into hiding with the monks, or that he was arrested and hauled off to jail somewhere." Henry's voice shook. "We hoped for the best, of course."

"And all along, he was here with you, Henry." I put my hand over his where it lay on the table.

"A lot of people were murdered or arrested in those days. It was dangerous for their families to inquire. Sometimes it was dangerous to admit you were a relative of someone who was caught spying. Walter's wife and children were all sent to the family's country retreat, to hide there until the situation improved. His father kept the business going all alone, in those times."

"Do you think Walter was wounded somehow, or caught and tortured?" Siri asked. "Perhaps he escaped and died in some secret place, hidden by his father."

Henry and I exchanged glances. "The pottery," I guessed, knowing I was right.

"The large kiln where the porcelain was fired might have helped his father to dispose of the body," Henry nodded. "He could have scattered the ashes anywhere afterwards, without danger of discovery. Or…"

"He wanted to honor Walter," I said with certainty. "To send his ashes to a place where his spirit could be free. Back to America, to his friend Henry Paradis."

"Yes," Henry nodded. "And since Mr. Chung himself died soon afterwards, nobody ever knew what happened."

"Until now."

"Yes, until now."

"When the circle can become complete," said Siri, looking at the two of us.

"When his journey home approaches." Henry agreed, smiling at me.

"His family will be so relieved to find out what happened and to have him back, won't they?" Siri said happily.

"Do you suppose they'll give us any trouble about taking human remains through customs?" I mused.

"If anyone can pull it off, my dear, surely you can!" Henry laughed.

"No fear," I said, "My ghostly friend and I will take care

of what ever comes up. I expect a personal tour of the family pottery from him when we arrive in Hong Kong, too! And his brothers had better give us a very good discount."

"I'm sure they will, my dear, I'm sure they will."

We temporarily put the ginger jar in a place of honor on the mantle above the fireplace in Henry's study. From that day on, even after Tony and I had delivered his ashes to his family in Hong Kong that following summer, we would often catch the sound of ghostly bells when passing by the basement door. It seemed that even with spirits, old habits and old haunts are slow to disappear. Even when they have been laid to rest and we've all progressed to the next turn around the spiral. The patterns, and the energy, linger on forever.

✻   ✻   ✻

Tony was happy about the arrangement he had made with the University. He had a chance to try a little teaching, without making a permanent full-time commitment. He was working from home, and had an office set up in the study on the first floor. He did business by phone, fax and email with his contacts around the world, and soon the Fed Ex truck was stopping at our house every day, just like it did at Henry's. Our basement was filling up with boxes and crates.

Tony took me to New York a couple of times to visit galleries there, and we went to the theater and the museums. I started getting used to my new lifestyle, which was quite comfortable and a lot of fun. My only worries now were things like whether to have wild salmon or free-range chicken for dinner. I was never lonely, or depressed. The only thing I ever got angry about was politics, not anything in my personal life. The little lines between my eyebrows faded, and my doctor told me I was half an inch taller, which I credited to Pilates and an overall feeling of lightness, buoyancy. At night, I dreamed of sunlit sidewalks, happy voices, love and kisses. When I awoke in the morning there was a sweet taste on my lips, like honey. Life was very good, and I knew it.

Then one day, I realized that a whole year had passed since I first knocked on the door of number 33, Market Street. I went up to see Henry and told him it was our anniversary. He was sitting in his reading chair, using his foot to gently rock the cradle where little Hope slept. The *I Ching* lay face down on his lap, and the three brass coins were on the table next to him.

"What did you mean, that first day we met, when you said, 'I knew I was right about you?'" I asked him. "Had you been consulting the Oracle?"

"Of course," Henry said. "And I knew that help was on the way. I guessed when you telephoned that you were the one. And a precious one you've turned out to be, my dear!" he added, with a fond twinkle.

"And, did you know about me and Tony, too?"

"Ah, that was more logic than premonition, Emily."

"It didn't seem logical to me! I didn't like him at all when we first met. He seemed very stuck up and kind of dark, and scary."

"That was because you didn't really know him yet. You misinterpreted the signs."

"I guess that's always a danger, eh?"

"Oh yes," said Henry earnestly, "People carry the past with them. They wear it like a mask, and it colors both how they look at the world, and how the world sees them."

"So, how was it logical that Tony and I would fall in love?" I persisted.

"Emily," said Henry gently, "Life is like a giant spiral, and the same form repeats, recycling over and over again. Each time we turn around, the form expands and it's just a bit different, an echo of the same shape, but not the same exactly. You and

Tony are like Margaret and me, the next time around, the progressed form of us. I saw it instantly, when we met. I emailed him immediately and told him he had to come and meet you, didn't he ever tell you that?"

"No, " I said, "I thought he came to see a special book you had found, or something like that."

Henry smiled at me enigmatically.

"Thank you, Henry," I said.

"And you too, my dear," he said, bowing his head to me.

We looked at each other wondering what would happen on the next turn around the great spiral? What dreams would come true next time? What would we learn? How would we evolve? Whatever was in store for us, and I shivered in anticipation, it would be something that grew from seeds we planted today and the energy we fed them to make them germinate and thrive.

"*Carpe diem*," I thought and pictured the future, seeing a long brilliant flash of the road that stretched ahead into a world filled with love, magic and light.

Afterword

The Fan-Shaped Destiny

One of the most interesting aspects of the Tarot's view of life is the way it reconciles the apparently contradictory ideas of an inescapable pre-destined fate, and freedom of choice or self-determination. Picture the road to the future with periodic crossroads, major decision points, where many different paths stretch out ahead and we have the option to choose which one to take. Sometimes the choice is deliberate, more often it is totally unconscious. Once the first tiny step is taken, a series of events are inevitable, falling into place like a row of dominos, until we arrive at the next crossroads, where a choice will be offered again.

This idea has been called the "fan-shaped destiny." It integrates the concept of karma, where our past and current choices are thought to have a direct effect on future events, and the concept of an inescapable fate, a cosmic master plan that rules the future despite any attempt we might make to alter it.

The Tarot believes that these opposite views about fate are both valid and compatible. It also embraces the idea of synchronicity, which skeptics would define as a random, meaningless coincidence of events or "dumb luck." Random factors may enter the destiny equation at any point, according to Tarot, and not necessarily be significant in terms of influencing the future, though they may appear to establish a startling pattern.

Looking beneath this surface level of flashy anecdotal elements, all the distracting razzle-dazzle of everyday life, reveals the larger truth. A gifted Tarot reader must possess considerable psychic ability to apply the traditional interpretation of each card to the seeker's particular questions. Knowing the meaning of the card or looking it up in a book is not enough to really understand the implications, just like having a French-English dictionary does not make one fluent in either language. A really good reader can intuit at a glance what the cards are saying, usually describing the information as a feeling, or the flash of a visual image, or sometimes a sound or scent. The cards are signposts, but the heart tells the way.

All of this implies the very interesting idea that the future is predictable, and that it can be changed. Therefore, "forewarned is forearmed" is the mantra of Tarot readers, who generally stress that while the final outcome card is an accurate prediction based on current conditions, there are definitely steps we can take to steer our lives in another direction, if we wish.

Sometimes conditions change along the way because of choices we didn't even realize we were making. The Tarot offers us a glimpse ahead down the road, identifies people and events in the past and present that will ultimately have major impact on us, and warns us about important characters who will influence our lives in the future. This information helps us to better understand the past, more fully appreciate the present, and prepare for what lies ahead.

Readers who are curious to learn more about the Tarot are encouraged to make use of the Bibliography included at the end of this book. There are hundreds of different Tarot decks currently in print, with a broad range of visual styles and imagery. You should look carefully at all the cards, touch them, and choose the deck that "speaks" to you. I personally recommend the two beautiful Tarot decks by David Palladini, or the classic Rider-Waite Tarot, which was created in 1909 by A. E Waite, a member of the famous Hermetic Order of the Golden Dawn, illustrated by Pamela Coleman Smith.

The black and white illustrations at the beginning of each chapter are from *The Payen Tarot of Marseille 1713*, one of the oldest surviving decks. (The word "Marseille" refers to a style of card, rather than the place they were created.) This Tarot was drawn by Jean Pierre Payen of Avignon, and the original cards are housed in the collection at the Bibliotheque Nationale de France, in Paris. Photographs of them can be found in Yale University's Beinecke Rare Book & Manuscript Library, in New Haven, CT.

The descriptions included in the chapter headings sometimes contain references to symbols absent from the Payen Tarot, but which are commonly found in the many other decks that have been published since the 1700's as artists and seers through the ages have enriched the visual tradition.

Bibliography

Mastering the Tarot by Eden Gray, a Signet Book from New American Library, 1301 Avenue of the Americas, New York, NY 10019, 1971, p. 96-143.

The New Palladini Tarot by David Palladini, U.S. Games Systems, Inc., Stamford, CT 06902 USA, 2005.

The Witch's Guide to Life by Kala Trobe, Llewellyn Publications, St. Paul, Minnesota 55164-0383, U.S.A., 2003, p. 191-243.

www.tarothermit.com, compiled and edited by Tom Tadfor Little, 2007.

Aeclectic Tarot, "Thirteen's Tarot Card Meanings, http://www.aeclectic.net, 2007.

Uri Raz's Tarot Site, http://www.tarot.org.il, 2007.

CPSIA information can be obtained at www.ICGtesting.com
Printed in the USA
LVOW061745150312

273255LV00005B/7/P